ELEVEN WEEKS

A NOVEL ABOUT THE LAST DAYS

ANNA TIKVAH

2nd Edition (January 2015)

"Behold, I am coming quickly! Hold fast what you have, that no one may take your crown."

Revelation 3:11

This story delves into future events. There are many latter-day Bible prophecies which provide a clear, solid basis of expectation; yet, none of us can be completely sure just how every detail will transpire. Will Israel be "a peaceful people, who dwell safely" before, or after Jesus Christ returns? Will believers see the Northern Confederacy of nations take over the Middle East, or will we have already been called away to meet our Lord? Is the 'Magog' in Ezekiel 38 the territory of Southern Russia and Eastern Ukraine, or does it include Germany and France? Will angels call us away, or will someone resurrected from the dead knock on our door? Will we answer to our Lord Jesus Christ at the Judgement Seat, or to our personal angel? When do we become individually responsible to God? What level of understanding makes us responsible? Will other Christian groups also be judged? Will the rejected die instantly, or live out the rest of their mortal days? How long will it be before angels or immortal saints, call the world to recognize their new King?

Many future prophecies foretelling our Lord's return are subject to speculation and may be controversial. I have footnoted references that I believe are helpful to our understanding. However, the purpose of this story is not to create contention over prophetic matters, or predict the 'day and hour', but simply to challenge and encourage all of us to, *"look up and lift up your heads, because your redemption draws near."* Luke 21:28.

ELEVEN WEEKS

PROLOGUE

A Dream?

Was this reality, or only a dream? She was sure she had
heard a trumpet blast and someone calling her name. Why was she
standing alone in the evening twilight peering down into a dark,
rectangular hole?

Looking up at the overturned gravestone she could see her
name eerily engraved upon it. Was she hallucinating again? So
many times the morphine drip created terrifying nightmares and
strange delusions. Was this another one of the same?

Curiously, she reached over to touch the cold, hard
gravestone. Her fingers traced the deep, sharp curve of the letters –
Verity Jane Lovell. It felt real enough. She shivered in the cool
August breeze. The light summer dress she was wearing was
hardly adequate. It was her favourite dress though, with blue
flowers, high waistline and puffed sleeves.

Reading the verse below her name, Verity remembered
requesting this very passage after she had been told she had only a
short time left to live. "For the Lord Himself will descend from
heaven with a shout, with the voice of an archangel, and with the
trumpet of God. And the dead in Christ will rise first."[1] It
summarized the hope she'd clung to so tightly through her illness –
resurrection! But was she still sick and only dreaming about
resurrection? Or had she truly been brought back to life?

Looking around the graveyard, Verity analyzed her

---

[1] 1 Thessalonians 4:16; John 5:25; 1 Corinthians 15:12-55

1

situation. She knew where she was. The little stone chapel in the Grandville cemetery was exactly the same. But the trees were taller. There also seemed to be many more rows of gravestones lining the gently rolling hills and disappearing into the darkness. Some graves nearby were decorated with fresh flower bouquets, while others, like her own, had only a little green shrub in front. As she scanned the shadowy surroundings, unable to see very far into the distance, hers appeared to be the only gravestone that was overturned. It certainly looked real enough!

If this is for real, Verity considered, *then the resurrection has taken place, which means that Jesus Christ has returned, which means that everything I believed and hoped for has begun!*

Could it be? Was it true? Her heart skipped a beat. Shivering with anticipation, she ran her fingers down her arm. It felt smooth and strong. There were no intravenous attachments or even any scars. If she was only dreaming, surely her hand would strike the needles. Surely she would wake herself up. Walking a few steps back and forth, she tested her legs. They felt sturdy and strong. The weakness and pain from the tumour were gone. In fact, she had no feelings of pain anywhere. Looking down, Verity noticed her abdomen was no longer distended. Touching her face, she was elated to find the swelling had disappeared. She felt whole. Running her fingers through her long, dark hair, hope rose quickly in her heart.

"I think I'm alive again," she whispered, joyfully. "I think I've been brought back to life!"

Looking up to heaven, Verity prayed, "Heavenly Father, thank you for bringing me back from the dead!" she exclaimed. "You've healed me completely. This is such a miracle! And if *I'm alive* this must mean that Your Son has returned! You've given him the power to raise us from the grave. Your Kingdom is about to be established on this earth, just as You promised so long ago."

Her mind began to race. *How long did I lie in that hole?*

Have others been raised like me? What am I to do now? Will an angel appear? Will I be taken away to judgement?

She looked around, wondering what to do next. Aside from an occasional car travelling the nearby road, the cemetery was isolated, tucked away on the outskirts of town. Situated as it was on the daily bus route that had once taken her to Grandville District High School, she had passed it by almost every day. To her right was the small town of Grandville. To her left, was the road that could lead her home.

If I were to walk, she considered, *it would take me only a couple hours. I feel strong enough to walk for days. I'm sure I could do it.*

A smile slid over her face as she imagined knocking on her front door and announcing her resurrection. What a surprise it would be for her mother and brother to see her alive and well. *But... will they still be there?* she asked herself. *How long has it been? Will they be ready for Jesus' return? Have they had time to search out truth and believe? And what about... what about Peter?*

The smile quickly vanished from her face as Verity thought about Peter – Peter Bryant. He had been one of her best friends in high school. They had become very close and then she discovered she had cancer! Sadly, she remembered his anger toward God. She remembered begging him to have faith as he sat beside her during the last, dark days, looking so haggard, so forlorn, and so terribly distressed. *I love Peter! I wanted to help him believe in this day – this very day. This day that I think I am now experiencing! What has happened to Peter... and everyone I love? My brother Thomas only started asking questions about God when he heard I had cancer. Did he continue to seek for truth? And my mom, my lovely mother, who stood strong through a difficult marriage and worked hard to support us; did she ever find time to read the Bible?*

"Heavenly Father, what has happened to them?" Verity

whispered anxiously. "Did they turn to You for help? Did they accept the call of the Gospel to be baptized? If this is truly the time of the resurrection and not just a wonderful dream, then it must now be too late for anyone to change. Jesus Christ is here at last. We're all about to be called away!"

A mosquito bit her on the arm and Verity slapped at it. Mesmerized, she wiped away the blood that splattered on her skin. It was all completely real. A real mosquito, real blood and the slap hadn't altered her state of consciousness. Fully convinced now that this was no hallucination, she kneeled down and prayed even more earnestly, "With all my heart, Lord, I thank you for bringing me back to life! You've kept your promises. I'm so thankful that the fulfillment of all things is here at last. I have longed for this day! Please, dear Lord, show me what I'm to do now. Where do I go? Please help me find the ones I love…"

Before she could say another word, there stood right beside her, as if he had been there all along, a young man in shining, white robes, unnaturally bright against the purple evening sky. He held a trumpet in his hand. Sincerity and love shone from his face.

Instinctively, she bowed to the ground, covering her face. As much as she had expected an angel to appear, it was still a great shock to be so close to the Divine!

"Do not be afraid," the angel reassured her kindly. "Jesus Christ has called you back to life." Reaching out, the angel took her hand. As he pulled her to her feet, Verity trembled; she was completely awestruck. "Come with me," the angel said with compassion. "We must visit your mother and brother and," the angel looked at Verity and smiled, "and Peter Bryant."

"Have they all turned to God?" Verity asked anxiously. "How long have I been dead? Are they ready for Jesus Christ's return?"

"Come and see," was his reply.

4

Eleven weeks earlier:

CHAPTER 1

The Final Performance

It was the last scene of the final performance; the scene which Zach Bryant enjoyed most of all. Tall, well-built and handsome, he had been taking intensive dance lessons for the last couple of months. It had all been for this: the three sold-out performances on the last weekend of May. As his feet followed the rhythm of the music, underneath the bright spotlight, Zach knew he was executing the final scene better than ever. The audience cheered as he came to a striking pose right where he needed to be – right in front of Melissa. Only, she wasn't 'Melissa' in the musical, she was Vanessa VanHeusten and he was Marco Darrinett. She looked gorgeous, dancing on the table in a blue, ruffled, sixties' skirt and white peasant blouse. With her ginger-brown hair in a curly pony-tail, she was looking at him in that rapturous way that always filled him with hope. It wasn't hard to lock eyes with her, just like the drama teacher had instructed. Soon, he was certain that she would ditch Shane Lockwood and be his.

Melissa spun around and jumped. Reaching out his arms, he caught her perfectly in midair. The 'whirly-bird catch,' as she fondly called it, was the most difficult move of all. With one sweeping motion Zach brought her feet to touch the floor and then with arms outstretched they twirled three times in flawless synchronization. The audience cheered again and again as Vanessa VanHeusten and Marco Darrinett performed the dance that had taken months to perfect.

Unfortunately, most of Zach's practices had been on Sunday mornings; because of this, his parents – Andrew and Lisa

5

Bryant – disapproved of his involvement in the musical and had told him so repeatedly. Even Uncle James, an uncle that he highly respected, questioned the change of priorities. "You've missed almost every Sunday School class, Zach," he'd implored, "God needs to come first."

However, the last few months of Zach's grade twelve year had been most enjoyable. Being a lead in the high school musical uncovered his hidden talents. He had always done well in sports, but just the other day, the dance teacher told him that he was a 'natural'. And Ms. Allan, the drama teacher, loved *his voice!*

Zach had never been allowed to attend school dances during the four years he had attended Stirling High. He wondered if his father was surprised by his abilities or upset that he had developed them. In actual fact he was very surprised that his parents had come to watch the final performance. It was a Sunday evening! Grandma, Uncle James and Aunt Sandra were in the audience too! Brett and Jenna were there as well, but that was a given. Brett was always supportive and understanding.

The music slowed and Zach focused his thoughts. As he and Melissa came close together in centre stage, a new song began to play. Breathing heavily, Zach was thankful their voices had been previously recorded and were now playing back over the speakers. All they had to do was lip-synch until they caught their breath.

"I'll be yours," Melissa's smooth, clear voice rang out across the audience, "till the end of time."

Melissa's voice was the only voice Zach ever wanted to hear. When they sang this song, in his mind, she was truly singing to him.

"No one will ever break us apart," he replied in perfect harmony. *Hear that, Shane!* he thought.

Zach loved the way they were so perfectly in step with one another. Melissa knew right where she should be; there was no awkwardness or hesitation. And then, as the lights dimmed and the music faded, came the best part of all. Pulling Melissa close, he bent over and kissed her. Ms. Allan said it had to be a long kiss and Zach was very willing to oblige.

Cheering loudly, the crowd gave them a standing ovation. All the actors poured onto the stage, joined hands and bowed to the audience. The clapping intensified. Melissa looked up at Zach with tears in her eyes. "That was the best ever," she said. "You were amazing!"

He squeezed her hand. "So were you," he said earnestly, "as always!"

All the actors bowed again. The school band struck up a marching song. With Zach and Melissa taking the lead, everyone filed off stage toward the dressing rooms.

They were still holding hands as they walked down the darkened hallway with the rest of the actors. "I'm so sad it's all over," Melissa told him, staying close by his side. "It's been so much fun!"

"It doesn't have to be over," he smiled down meaningfully.

She looked up confused, but then seemed to understand his message, "Zach," she started to say, but the drama teacher was rushing toward them.

"Fantastic!" Ms. Allan raved. "You both outperformed yourselves tonight. You brought the whole musical to life. You made it so real. I'm *so* proud of you! Your parents must be bursting with pride!"

Melissa nodded happily. Her parents had supported her from the very beginning. They paid for professional dance lessons and vocal training at the best music academy in Stirling, Nova Scotia.

Zach grimaced. He wasn't sure what his parents were going to think. He'd had to pay for everything himself. Taking part in the musical was not something his parents had encouraged.

So many people wanted to meet Zach and congratulate him on his wonderful performance that it took a long time to reach the back of the auditorium where his family stood waiting. Somewhere along the way, Melissa parted from him in a different direction and he still didn't know what she wanted to say. That was all right. He could text her later as long as he was sure that she wasn't with Shane.

Brett and Jenna met him before he reached his parents. Brett had been Zach's basketball coach since grade nine. With Brett, Zach shared some memorable victories. "Fantastic!" Brett said, thumping him on the back. "Zach, I had no idea you were such a superstar!"

"You could go into acting," Jenna agreed. "Seriously, you'd be a sensation!"

Zach was flattered. "Thanks," he said. "It was a lot of fun." Looking ahead, he could see that his family was getting restless. "I'd better catch up with my folks. They're waiting to take me home."

"You do that," Brett smiled. "And let us know when you have your next show."

Laughing, Zach reluctantly made his way to the back. Would his parents be impressed?

"You did do amazingly well tonight," his mom conceded, as she gave him a hug.

"Incredible!" exclaimed Esther, his young teen sister, hugging him tight.

"I've been enjoying the celebrity status," his twin brother Jake chuckled. "You wouldn't believe how many people have been congratulating *me*."

Zach smiled. Identical twins, with tousled, sandy-blond hair and hazel-brown eyes, it was hard to tell them apart. Many times in their seventeen years of life they had been mistaken for one another.

"God gave you plenty of talent, son," his dad smiled, clapping him on the back.

His father's compliment was a gentle reminder of several late night conversations. Zach shrugged and began walking toward the exit. Maybe his talents were pulling him away from God but that wasn't what Zach wanted to hear.

As everyone followed him out the door, Zach asked his mom, "Where are Grandma, and Uncle James and Aunt Sandra?"

"They waited for half an hour to talk to you," she replied with a smile, "but they had to get back home. Uncle James has a client coming over tonight. They told me to tell you that they really enjoyed the show."

"Great performance tonight," a grade nine girl called out, glancing shyly in the twins' direction. "You must be so proud of your son, Mr. Bryant!" she exclaimed to Zach's dad. "And... " she paused, passing him a few sheets of paper, "um, here's the essay I was supposed to hand in Friday. I'm sorry."

"Everyone did their best tonight!" Zach's dad replied evasively, taking the essay. Looking briefly at the papers, he smiled, "Unfortunately, I'll still have to take five marks off, Sarah."

"But it's not Monday yet," she pleaded.

"It's also not Friday."

Sarah looked disappointed. "Okay. See everyone tomorrow then."

All the others said polite goodbyes, except Zach. Zach was disappointed by his father's lack of enthusiasm. *Why isn't dad praising me like everyone else?* Being an English teacher at the same high school his kids attended, Zach knew his father would be inundated with many similar compliments in the next week. *Will he keep brushing everyone off so dismissively?*

"What a total surprise!" Ms. Campbell said loudly, coming

down the hallway. "The student who never attends school dances is the best dancer in the school! You really should be there at prom this Friday to show the other kids how to do it."

"I'd love to!" Zach said cheerfully. There was probably no way he could get a ticket at this late date, but should opportunity arise, he would gladly take part.

His younger sister, Esther, looked back at him with surprise.

Jake elbowed him in the ribs as they were exiting the school.

"What?" Zach exclaimed, as they stepped outside.

Limping a little, since spraining his ankle in a recent rugby game, Jake whispered quietly, "Now Dad will have teachers on his case."

Zach shrugged coolly. "Good. Then maybe I'll get to go."

It was a somber group that took their seats in the old family van. As Zach's dad turned the key, the news came on and his mom was instantly captivated. "Another earthquake, Andrew!" she exclaimed soberly, directing everyone's attention to the announcement. Sure enough, a large earthquake had taken place in China and aftershocks were being felt hundreds of kilometres away.

"Earthquakes in various places," Zach's mom said to his father, making reference to the words of Jesus.[2]

Playing music on his phone, Zach stuck one earplug into his ear and gave the other to his twin. He didn't want to hear about *another* earthquake. There had been so many major disasters lately – earthquakes, tsunamis, massive floods, spewing volcanoes and weird, weird weather. At school this was all attributed to 'Global Warming'. However, his parents seemed to feel these were signs

---

[2] Luke 21:11

clearly anticipated by Bible prophecy to herald the return of Jesus Christ to the earth.

A soft bleep alerted Zach to an incoming text. It was a message from Jayden, one of his friends from school.

Awesome, was all it said, but Zach knew Jayden was referring to the musical.

He smiled and texted back:

Thx.

Three more texts came in and Zach quickly responded.

Watching him enviously, Jake wished he had been able to afford to take over his uncle's phone plan when he had left to do missionary work in Jamaica. Instead, he had spent all his money on a new aluminum racing bicycle. Although Zach held a Smartphone in his hand he was only able to listen to music and text, since their father had installed software that blocked the internet. They both could remember their dad exclaiming, "What? Give you unaccountable access to the World Wide Web? Are you crazy? Once that door is open, there is no telling where it will lead."

I have the most conservative father in the world, Jake thought, *but I'd be happy just to text! I must be the only student in grade twelve who still uses a landline to communicate! This summer's earnings will go towards a phone!*

"Another six Russian warships are headed for the Mediterranean!" their mother remarked, still listening to the news report. "Do you realize how significant this is?" she asked with a smile, looking back at the twins. "The King of the North is coming down with many ships."

There had been quite a fleet of Russian ships docking at the new ports they had acquired in the Meditteranean. It was occurring regularly and without incident. *Is it really evidence that Ezekiel thirty-eight and Daniel eleven were being fulfilled?* Zach wondered. Having grown up in a family that read the Bible every day, he was fully aware that his parents had plenty of evidence that

11

Jesus Christ would soon return. But he wasn't ready for that return, not for a few more years at least. *Surely it won't happen for a few more years!*

Totally unaware that the return of Christ was only eleven weeks away, Zach looked over at his brother and rolled his eyes.

Jake didn't respond. He looked away. Zach wasn't baptized but Jake was. Three years ago their friend Noah had been baptized. Even though they had all been young – only fourteen – it wasn't long afterwards that the twins had asked to take classes as well. Jake had been baptized at the early age of fifteen. While Zach had attended all the classes with Uncle Peter, he hadn't followed through with any commitment of his own.

It seemed so easy back then. Life wasn't so busy, Jake pondered. *Maybe I was baptized too young,* he thought to himself. *I know it's all true. I know Jesus will come back someday, but I just don't feel any excitement anymore. It bores me stiff. I know it shouldn't, but it does.*

Living only ten minutes from Stirling High, they were almost home, when Dad spoke again. "Plugs out, guys," he said.

Unwillingly, Zach and Jake cooperated.

"What are you listening to?" their dad questioned.

"Just cool music," Zach replied sullenly. He knew that his dad didn't like it when he and Jake zoned out in their own music world and became disconnected from the rest of their family.

"Look, Zach," his father said, looking up at him in the rear-view mirror. "I know you are a very talented young man. I know that with your involvement in this play you've truly *earned* lots of praise and encouragement from everyone at school. I can appreciate that you find it hard to understand why Mom and I haven't been enthused or supportive of your performance. But I just want you to remember that your parents see things a little differently. We know this world is on the verge of Jesus Christ's return, because we believe the prophecies that are in the Bible.

This isn't the time to be living for the moment and disconnecting from God. *And,"* his father added soberly, "if you're interested in some girl at school, bring her to God. Make sure she's committed to Him before you ask her to commit to you. Don't let her take *you away.*"

Mr. Bryant had a few more comments about the importance of living for God, but Zach just shook his head and looked out the window. He'd heard it all before. *Yeah, yeah, yeah,* he thought. *That's why you wouldn't let us buy tickets for prom and why we've missed out on so much fun!* His mom and dad were so enthused about God's promises for the future. *They've been saying Jesus is going to return **soon** – for most of my life. Someday I'll want to have a part in it – but right now there are so many other things on my mind. There's Melissa, and university to think about, plus I've got to beat Abi on that math exam. And then there's basketball...*

Brett Lawson coached the Stirling Scorpions' basketball team. In March the team had almost made it to the Provincials! Brett wasn't a high school teacher, but with a shortage of those willing to coach, he had become involved with the school teams when Zach and Jake had entered grade nine. Over the last four years, he had led the Scorpions to many victories, winning the District championship every year. With Zach and Jake returning in September for an extra year of high school – dubbed by some a "Super-twelve" year – they were both determined to keep in shape and 'go all the way' next season.

We've got to make it to the Provincials! Zach told himself. *And next season we have such a good chance!* The twins were captains of the team, and just last week they had been told that Brett had generously sponsored them to attend a basketball camp in the summer. *We'll have professional coaches. It's going to be such an awesome week!* Zach thought to himself. *I'll improve so much. It will give us the edge.*

"And don't forget," his father continued, winding up his dissertation about where Zach's mind should be, "God's laws and commands aren't there to ruin our lives. They guide us to make choices that give us true peace of mind and real happiness. Following Christ isn't the path of least resistance but it is the path with the least regrets."[3]

---

[3] Deuteronomy 6:24-25; Isaiah 55:1-3; Proverbs 3

CHAPTER 2

The Exercise Routine

"I've got to go to the prom tonight," Zach told his brother firmly, five days after the last performance. The boys were doing their strength exercises in the basement, having just come home from school. It was part of a new plan, now that the musical was over, to get in shape for basketball season. Unfortunately with Jake's sprained ankle, he had to take it a little easier than Zach. Every day that week after school, they had commenced their workout with strength training and then Zach ran five kilometres, while Jake rode his bike.

"How can you go to prom? You don't have a ticket!" Jake asked between push-ups. He had to admit, he wished he was going as well.

"Ms. Allan gave me a ticket today," Zach replied proudly. "She said there were a couple of cancellations and she thought I deserved to go!"

"Seriously?" Jake puffed, working hard on the floor. He was jealous, even though, due to the economic downturn, funding for the prom had been cut in half. It wasn't going to be nearly as good as in past years. To save money the school council had opted to hold the celebration in the high school cafeteria, with the food and nutrition class catering the event. Still, Jake felt he was missing out 'big time'! Everyone else in grade twelve was going. "So, you figure it's worth being grounded?" he challenged.

"Dad doesn't have to know," Zach grunted, his arms straining to get past thirty push-ups. Having been so involved in the musical, he had given up rugby season for play practices. He knew it would take time to regain his upper arm strength. The musical had been a huge personal investment for Zach and all the others who had committed to the production.

Beating his goal by one, Zach collapsed wearily on the ground. "Dad and Mom are going over to help the McKinleys tonight. If you can get yourself a ticket, we could both use the homework excuse."

"Oh sure!" Jake retorted, getting in position for his next round of push-ups. "For one thing, it's Youth Group tonight, and secondly I highly doubt I'll find a ticket in the next few hours."

"She said there were two cancellations."

Heaving his body up and down, Jake thought it through. If his parents were heading out, both he and Zach might get away with going to the prom. Often when their parents left the house to give counseling or visit the elderly, he and Zach had enjoyed the freedom to do as they pleased. Many times it meant a movie night. Living in a household without a television, no Wi-Fi, and only one computer in the living room, any DVD's that were watched had to meet everyone's approval. However, when mom and dad were out, the twins felt free to make their own choices, or… almost. Esther, their younger sister, was usually in on the action and always promised not to tell as long as they didn't watch anything too bad. That set the bar high. Esther's conscience was easily stirred. She was almost as restrictive as their parents! However, this was all beginning to change with Zach's requisition of a Smartphone. Their parents still didn't know all the stuff that Zach could download at school, to show to his brother when they were home.

"Does Melissa know you're coming?" Jake asked, finishing his second round of push-ups with a loud gasp of "fifty!" Feeling rather hampered with his weak ankle, Jake was determined to beat Zach in upper body strength.

"No, but I'll text her," Zach replied. He leaned back in a sitting position to do his abdominal exercises. "She's confused between Shane and me," he muttered, drawing his knees to his chest and extending his arms. "If I can win her over, then maybe she'll come out to Youth Group and other stuff with me."

"I don't know why you're so crazy about her," Jake shrugged, as they finished the abs workout and walked towards the stairs. Jake hadn't run up and down the stairs for weeks but his ankle was getting stronger and he thought it was worth a try. "I mean, she's a nice girl and everything," he conceded, as he attempted to climb the steps, "but whenever Shane isn't around she flirts with *all* the guys! I've heard a few wild stories about her at parties. And apparently she believes in reincarnation. I don't think she'll be interested in coming out to Youth Group."

"Whatever!" Zach replied defensively. "She just needs some help sorting things out. Melissa is a very friendly person. She's not a flirt!"

Jake shook his head, giving up on the stairs routine; his ankle was still too weak. "Nah, it's flirting!" he said firmly, a little resentful that Melissa never flirted with him unless she mistook him for Zach. Melissa was the most captivating girl at school. Jake wasn't sure why she often walked right past him, but then again, she hadn't really paid attention to Zach either until the musical.

In his heart, Zach knew that Jake was probably right in his assessment, but he hated to admit it. He was drawn to Melissa in a powerful way. *Everything will get sorted, once she's going out with me,* he told himself.

"So will you cover for me tonight, then?" Zach begged.

"But we need you at Youth Group," Jake argued feebly, feeling duty-bound to encourage his disinterested brother. He was, after all, half an hour older than Zach and already baptized. "There are so few of us as it is!"

"Yeah! It's pathetic!" Zach agreed.

Joining his brother again for the next exercise, the twins stood at the top of the stairs, flexing their calf muscles, hoping to improve their jumping ability, Jake empathized with the discouragement in his brother's voice. Growing up, they had been involved with an enthusiastic Youth Group, but unfortunately, many of their friends had moved away, far away, and they weren't planning to come back. It was a sad situation, one that Brett Lawson, their basketball coach, had inadvertently caused.

"Uncle James is giving the class tonight on the signs of Christ's return," Jake told his brother, picking up the twenty-five kilogram dumbbells. "He will be kind of disappointed if no one shows up."

"They should just postpone it," Zach muttered, skipping fast with a rope. He noticed his brother wince as he squatted with the heavy bar and knew Jake's ankle was causing him pain. "No one will be there; they'll all be at prom."

"Allan will be there," Jake reminded him.

"Yeah. Allan, Esther and us. That's about all that ever shows up."

Jake sighed, taking a break from the weights to flex his weak ankle. It was true that Abi, Nathan and Jerry would most certainly be at the prom; they had been talking about it for weeks. David would likely be at home playing video games; it was all he wanted to do anymore.

Pulling on a headband to keep his hair out of his eyes while biking, Jake felt a wave of despair. He wished he knew how to encourage his brother to make the right decision, but he was struggling to know how to even motivate himself. He remembered the days when they couldn't wait to go to Youth Group. Growing up, it had been their favourite night of the week. A second deep sigh escaped him.

Perplexed, Zach looked up at his brother, but Jake headed out the door to get his bike.

Wheeling his prized bike out of the garage where he kept it under lock and key, Jake considered his Friday evening options.

18

Should he ask Zach to text Ms. Allan and see if there was another spare ticket? It would be a lot of fun to join Zach. His own popularity had increased dramatically since his twin had become the heart-throb of Stirling High. He imagined there might be a lineup of girls eager to dance with him if they couldn't have his brother. Mounting the bicycle, he soon left Zach far behind. He had to lap the town three times to equal Zach's five-kilometre run.

But if Mom and Dad are heading out tonight, they'll be expecting us to give Esther a ride to Youth Group, he mused. *We can't both use the homework excuse. Only one of us can get away with sneaking off.* Pondering the matter some more, Jake realized that even if lots of girls wanted to dance with him, they would all be disappointed if he couldn't do the cool moves like his brother. He sighed with regret. *I wish I had decided to be in the musical. I'd love to dance like that. I bet I'd be just as good if I took lessons.*

Suddenly Jake remembered that Uncle James had asked him to find out who needed a ride to Bible Camp. It was only five weeks away and Uncle James would likely ask him about it when he saw him that evening. As one of the Youth Group leaders, Jake was often given the task of encouraging his peers to be involved. Uncle James and Aunt Sandra were willing to take anyone who wanted to come to camp. In the past six years, Jake's whole family had faithfully made the two-day drive to Manitoulin Island every summer in order to attend the Bible Camp. They usually travelled in convoy with Uncle James and Aunt Sandra, camping overnight along the way. It was always a lot of fun and a great family adventure. This year, however, the twins' dad had a course he was taking to upgrade his teaching skills. Disappointed not to be involved, he had offered the family van to Uncle James, in the hope that anyone who wanted a ride would be able to come.

I'd better go to the class tonight and cover for Zach, Jake decided with a heavy sigh. *He needs to work things out with*

Melissa.

Finishing his first lap and catching up with his brother once again, Jake slowed to Zach's running pace. "Hey, Zach," he asked, "have you decided whether you're coming to Bible Camp this summer? Uncle James needs to know numbers tonight."

"Are you kidding?!" Zach replied incredulously. "Brett's paid for both of us to go to Basketball camp that week!"

"It's the same week?!"

"Yep. And we need to be there if we're going to make it to Provincials next season," Zach puffed out, continuing to run hard. "Brett emailed me this morning to say *five* players from the Black Hawks are going. We've got to be there! We're the captains!"

"I didn't know we were going to have to *miss* Bible Camp," Jake moaned, navigating around a sewer grate. Until now he hadn't realized that the two events coincided.

Pedaling off quickly to do his next lap, Jake pondered the dilemma. *What will I do? Zach and I are captains. Five of the Black Hawks are going. They're our main competition. We've got to beat them this year! But I don't want to miss out on Bible Camp. Why does it have to be the same week? This stinks!*

CHAPTER 3

Youth Group

Jake drove his youngest sister, Esther, to Uncle James and Aunt Sandra's place that evening, feeling glum. It was seven o'clock. Almost all the other grade twelve students would be enjoying a roast-beef dinner. He would likely be the only one not attending. Plugging his dad's iPod into the family van receptacle, Jake found a song he liked and turned it up.

"This is my favourite song," he told his sister.

"I know," she said, braiding her straight brown hair.

"How do you know?"

"Because you play it *all* the time."

Conceding that this was probably true, Jake hit the arrow key to take the song back to the start so he could listen without interruption. He loved the music, and the message gave him hope. It was about God's love; how God always takes us back and never stops loving us, no matter what we do. *"Heavenly Father, please keep on loving me,"* he prayed silently, *"even though my heart isn't with You right now. Please help me to get my life turned around. I don't know what's wrong with me, but I just don't feel the excitement that I should. Please help me to care about what Your Son did for us and the Kingdom that You've promised to send."*

Jake's life had been so busy in the last few weeks that he hadn't taken time to pray for anything more than his daily food. Occasionally he managed to have a few thoughts in God's direction, but for some reason he seemed to be caring less and less about it all. He wanted to care more, he truly did, but he wasn't

21

quite sure how to make it happen.

"So are you going to go to Jamaica?" Esther asked.

"How did you hear about that?"

"I heard Dad talking to you. He wasn't whispering."

"Nah, I don't think so. Brett is counting on me and Zach to help him win the Provincials next year. Plus, I need to take Calculus again and upgrade my marks if I want to get into Dalhousie University."

"But it would be so cool to help Uncle Peter do missionary work!" Esther exclaimed. "Imagine a whole year in Jamaica. What an amazing experience! If I was done grade twelve, I'd go."

"I don't think I'd be very good at running a kids' vacation Bible Camp," Jake spoke candidly. "You would though."

"You'd be fine, Jake! You and Zach used to do all those funny skits for Sunday School. And you organize our Youth Group…"

"I don't do a very good job," Jake replied, flipping his straight, sandy-brown hair out of his eyes. "I spent an hour on the phone tonight trying to convince Abi, David, Nathan and Jerry to come to camp this summer – *and class tonight*. And not one of them was interested."

"Are they working this summer?"

"Nathan is. He needs money to go to college in September. Jerry is playing soccer and doesn't want to miss even one game. Abi doesn't think she could leave her boyfriend for a whole week and David doesn't think camp is any fun."

"Well, I want to come," Esther smiled, her blue eyes twinkling, "and I'm sure Allan will as well."

"Yeah, there might be three of us," Jake grimaced uncertainly. He still wasn't entirely sure about his own choice.

Driving down Uncle James' long, winding, tree-lined driveway, Esther exclaimed, "Bible Camp is my *favourite* week of the year! How could anyone not enjoy it?"

Jake parked near the garage, under the pines. They both took a long, deep breath as they stepped out of the van. The pungent sea air along the coast always brought back wonderful, childhood memories. Jake would never forget the two amazing years his family spent living in this place. Uncle James had invited them to stay there, while their dad was in teachers' college and money was tight. The log home sprawled out across a neatly manicured ridge that overlooked the ocean. Aunt Sandra had given it the name, "Oceanview Lodge." Deep purple trim highlighted the large, living room windows, contrasting well with the aging grey exterior. Heavy, dark green pines swayed silently in the background, screening from view all other houses in the vicinity. It was a private and beautiful residence.

Grandma Bryant stood at the purple front door smiling; her short, white hair gleaming in the golden, evening sun. Soft blue eyes shone cheerfully in a face adorned with fine lines and creases. During the two years that Jake's family had stayed at Oceanview Lodge, both Grandma *and* Grandpa Bryant had lived in the in-law suite beside them. Sadly, Grandpa Bryant had passed away eighteen months ago. Now Grandma lived alone in the 'granny flat' next to Uncle James and Aunt Sandra.

"Hi Grandma," Jake and Esther called out.

"So good to see you, Darlings," she smiled, giving Esther a hug. "Why I think you're taller than me now."

Esther smiled proudly. More like her mother than any of the other children, Esther was tall, with a sturdy build. Zach had talked her into playing rugby and often boasted to his friends that she could take down any girl with one arm. "I'm five-foot-eight!" Esther told her grandma. "Dad measured me last week."

"Goodness! You're definitely taller than I ever was! And you Jake – you're looking more like your Uncle Peter every day. Sometimes I have to do a double-take."

Jake grinned and gave her a hug. Grandma had told him he

looked like Uncle Peter so many times that he had lost count, but he was always happy to hear it. In Jake's opinion, Uncle Peter Bryant was the best-looking in the family.

"Where's Zach?" she asked.

Jake shrugged. "He had something else on."

"Something more important?"

"No – just… something else."

Grandma nodded thoughtfully. "Well, come on in. Allan's already here and Uncle James is just getting his presentation set up."

Entering the door, Jake took a whiff of a delicious aroma. "Aunt Sandra's been baking?" he remarked hopefully.

"Oh yes, cookies, and pizza, and frozen yogurt – enough for *twenty,* I'd say."

Jake laughed. Aunt Sandra loved to bake and they always had a feast when they came to her house.

Following Esther into the large, airy sitting room with the high, cedar ceiling, Jake took a seat beside Allan. Aunt Sandra came over from the kitchen area, greeting everyone warmly and bringing homemade lemonade. Jake stood back up to take the tray from her hands. Aunt Sandra was on the shorter side, with straight, dark hair that didn't quite reach her shoulders. She had the prettiest blue eyes that twinkled merrily behind her glasses. Since being married, Uncle James often called her *Beauts* – short for Beautiful. When Esther had been younger, she had mistakenly called her *Aunt Beauts,* thinking that was her aunt's name!

Tall and lean, with dark, speckled-grey hair, Uncle James looked up from the laptop he was fiddling with. "Hey, good to see you all!" He looked around more carefully; his kind brown eyes searching the room. "No Zach tonight?"

"Nope," Jake replied, wondering how long he could remain evasive. He took the tray of drinks over to Allan. Almost finished university and in his early twenties, Allan Symons was

24

six-foot-two, dark-haired, and – as per usual – in the early stages of growing a beard. Rumour had it that he hated shaving, which was true, but Allan wasn't crazy about growing a full beard either. Allan had hired Jake and Zach as occasional workers to help him maintain their uncle's landscaping business for the summer. Uncle Peter and Aunt Jessica – who was Allan's sister – were on long-term missionary work in Jamaica.

Leaning over to take one of the cold lemonades off the tray, Allan thanked Jake for the drink and then said, "Look, if you and Zach are free to help us out tomorrow, that would be great. I know you both have morning jobs, and school work, but I can't believe how fast the grass is growing. Derrick and I have twelve lawns to cut this weekend!"

"I'm sure we can help," Jake smiled. Saturday mornings he had committed to help Brett with his lawns and Zach always did Oceanview Lodge, but they were both eager for more hours – school assignments or not. Their bank accounts had dwindled fast over the winter.

It seemed that Uncle James was having some difficulty getting his laptop to communicate with the projector. As everyone chatted about their week and summer plans, Uncle James tried various combinations of keys to get his presentation up and running.

After serving everyone a drink, Jake sat back down. Aunt Sandra took a seat close beside Esther. Aunt Sandra was giving Esther cooking lessons whenever they could fit them in. The two of them shared a special camaraderie. The twins were just as appreciative of the lessons since Esther always brought home her delicious creations! Having married late in life and without any children of their own, Uncle James and Aunt Sandra were especially welcoming to their growing number of nephews and nieces. Everyone loved coming to their house.

Sitting back comfortably on the couch, Jake's eyes were

drawn to the large wedding picture that hung in the center of the long cedar wall. He would never forget his uncle and aunt's snowy, winter wedding held in this very house, or their baptism in the cold lake water a few months before. In a jet-black tuxedo, Uncle James was holding Aunt Sandra in his arms. Snowflakes lay in their dark hair and sparkled on her bouquet of pink roses. The white velvet gown that his aunt was wearing blended into the background snow weighing down the dark pines. In the almost completely black and white picture, Aunt Sandra's eyes shone like blue jewels and the roses seemed to be painted in pink. Both of them were laughing and it seemed to Jake that they had been laughing ever since.

Standing up, Uncle James looked around at all the empty chairs. His presentation was finally showing up on the screen. "Just three of you tonight?" he queried thoughtfully. "I was under the impression that everyone voted for this topic when we made the program last year."

Jake squirmed uneasily. He hoped Uncle James would never find out where everyone else was. He wished he could spare his uncle the hurt.

When no explanation was forthcoming, Uncle James shrugged. "Oh well," he remarked, more to himself, than to the others, "I'm sure everyone has a good reason to be someplace else."

Suddenly remembering another question he had for Jake, Uncle James asked, "Did you find out who's coming with us to Bible Camp?"

"Those you see here," Jake replied, not wanting to explain his own dilemma at such a time, "and maybe Zach."

Looking up with surprise, Uncle James questioned, "No one else wants to come to camp? That's surprising." He looked over at Aunt Sandra, "And I thought we wouldn't have enough seats in the van."

"Actually, I won't be able to come to Family Camp this year either," Allan spoke up. "Someone has to look after the grass and gardens while you're all away. But, God Willing, I plan to make it out for Youth Conference in August." He added with a smile in Jake's direction, "And I'll have extra room in the car if anyone wants to join me!"

It wasn't the first time that Allan had encouraged Jake and Zach to join him for conference, but neither twin was keen to do the required "one-hundred page" Bible study workbook ahead of time.

"Did you remind everyone that Family Camp is held at a 'first-rate' facility?" Uncle James asked Jake in a half-teasing way. "Did you remind them about their good friends and all the fun times we have every year?"

"Sort of," Jake smiled. *Manitoulin Bible Camp is a great place to go,* he reflected, *but I'm not sure I would call it a 'first-rate facility'. It doesn't have anything extravagant – unlike the basketball camp. There are plenty of trees and a sports field, but the beach is small and the lake is shallow.*

"I did remind them about the beach volleyball."

Aunt Sandra smiled dreamily. "I can't wait to hear the loons over the water and the whippoorwills calling out when the sun is setting on the lake. And I love sitting around the campfire at night, singing hymns of praise to God. I feel so close to God when we're all together singing like that!"

"*And* you wouldn't miss teaching the juniors for anything!" Uncle James added, with an affectionate smile in his wife's direction. "You've been working on those classes for weeks. We'll need Andrew's van just for all the project materials!"

"That's true. I am looking forward to having fun with all the kids," Aunt Sandra agreed cheerfully. A Grade One teacher at a little private school, Aunt Sandra loved working with children. She was always researching new crafts and activities. Uncle James had even customized a special room upstairs in the house for her to keep all her supplies organized.

"I love the campfire sing-a-longs, too," Esther chimed in. "And I love seeing my friends! It's so much fun to talk for *hours* in the tent at night."

"Don't forget the ice-cream socials and all the great classes," Allan added.

"Ah yes," Aunt Sandra agreed. "I heard that Brother George is speaking on the theme, 'In the Last Days Perilous Times Will Come.' That sounds very thought-provoking."

Jake squirmed. It was thought-provoking all right; he felt uneasy just hearing the title!

"Since this is our last class before summer vacation," Uncle James said, changing the subject, "I thought I'd show you a few slides of the fun you've all had together over the years."

Jake watched the screen as Uncle James showed pictures of Sunday School picnics and Youth Group outings from the past. There had been so many children. A sad smile came over Jake's face as he saw pictures of himself, Noah, Brennan and David in their ten-year-old innocence. Brennan and he had always tried to be on the same team. Noah had always sided with Zach. If he'd ever had a best friend, besides his brother, it would have been Brennan. Now they saw each other only at camp. Both Noah's and Brennan's families had moved to Ontario. Jake's older sisters had moved, as well, to attend the University of Toronto.

"Look at David in this picture," Uncle James pointed out with a chuckle. It was a shot of the candy toss at the Sunday School picnic. Uncle Peter – Jake's dad's youngest brother – had run around with lollipops stuck to his clothes, tossing out candies for the children and trying to keep out of reach of their grasping hands. In the midst of the chaotic picture was David offering some of his candy to the toddlers who were unable to keep up. David had always been so generous and kind-hearted. Now David spent so much time playing computer games that he didn't want to do anything else or even hang out with his friends. His life revolved around the characters in his fantasy world. His bedroom walls were plastered with posters of fictitious, virtual people.

"I hoped Abi would see this one," Uncle James laughed. Jake looked up to see Abi on the screen with *six* first-place ribbons! Her curly auburn hair was up in pigtails and her face was covered with freckles. "She won the Bible quizzes, the sack race, the obstacle course and the wheelbarrow race! Remember that, Jake?"

Jake groaned. "I helped her win the wheelbarrow race!" he retorted. Abi had always been tough competition for him and Zach. She was small and wiry and the strongest girl he'd ever known. He and Zach could outdo her physically now, but Abi still outshone them with her recall of detail. At high school, Zach was vying with her for top marks in math. Lately, she had hooked up with Brian, the high school hockey hero, who often boasted that he could hold more drinks than anyone else on the team. Since then, they had been seeing less and less of Abi at Youth Group.

"I thought Nathan and Jerry would love this one," Uncle James said with a chuckle. Jake and Allan looked at one other and laughed. The picture was of the four of them, standing in their pajama pants on a small island, wondering what they should do. Mist hung heavy over the lake and a large loon was floating past on the water. Jake could well remember the weekend canoe trip three years ago. Allan had talked all the younger guys into setting up camp on that same small island just off the shore. While they were sleeping in late on the Saturday morning, the girls, who had camped on the mainland, quietly paddled over and stole their canoes. Had it been summertime, it would have been no big deal to swim the one hundred metres back to shore, where a hot breakfast was being served. However, in early October, the lake was frigid and the morning air temperature was only seven degrees Celsius!

Allan and Jerry had changed into their swim-shorts and saved the day. Plunging into the icy-cold water, they brought back a rescue canoe!

"Do you have a picture of our revenge?" Allan chuckled.

With a grin, Uncle James flashed to his next slide. An overturned canoe bobbed in the lake, with four grumpy, half-drowned girls clinging on to it. Being merciful, the boys had delayed the revenge attack until the afternoon air temperature was in the balmy mid-teens. However, there hadn't been a word of thanks for their compassion!

Jake took a long look at the picture. Hannah, Noah's younger sister was in the forefront. Even at eleven years old and half-drowned, she was attractive. Last year at Bible Camp she had followed him around in a rather obvious way. With three years between them, Jake had kept his distance. It was a little embarrassing for a sixteen-year-old to be hanging out with someone who had just entered her teens. *Will it be the same this year?* he asked himself. *Will I feel any different?*

"Never, never take on the guys, "Allan jokingly remarked to Esther, "unless you're prepared to face the consequences."

"It's Abi who does all the scheming!" Esther smiled. "I just follow orders."

There were only a few more slides, and Jake wished the others had been there to see them. Last year the canoe trip had been quiet and uneventful. The fewer that came, the less fun it was, and the less invigorating it was in a spiritual way. Slowly, gradually, other activities with friends from school had become more compelling. Was there any way to reinvigorate the group?

It's almost impossible, Jake thought with dismay. *Especially, when I don't feel motivated to even change myself!*

CHAPTER 4

Reasons to Believe

"Well, let's begin our class," Uncle James said, after Allan had given an opening prayer. "Let's talk about the important prophecies that have been fulfilled which indicate we are on the verge of Christ's return."

Uncle James was a good speaker and everyone else was listening attentively but Jake felt himself fading away. He had heard all this so many times. Little did he know that Uncle James was absolutely right – they were on the verge! Jesus Christ's return was only ten weeks away!

Unaware of the urgency, Jake's eyes glazed over as Uncle James went through the usual evidence beginning with the nation of Israel. In his mind, Jake began comparing his camp options. Manitoulin *was* a great place to go. He wasn't so sure about the challenging talks on 'perilous times' but he did want to see his friends. There were plenty of sports and they always had fun in the lake, even if it was shallow. On the other hand, the basketball camp was truly a 'first-rate' facility! The camp was in a scenic part of Nova Scotia, on a lake. There were kayaks, jet skis, and sailboats available for use in the afternoons. He had read in the brochure that there was a zip-line and a ropes course in the trees. It would be a full day of exercise and fun. At Bible Camp, classes occupied the mornings and evenings, leaving only afternoons free. *I can go to Manitoulin every year,* he told himself, *but the basketball camp is likely a once-in-a-lifetime opportunity... and Brett is willing to pay for it all!*

Jake's attention was captured momentarily when Uncle

James began his visual presentation using old film clips and black and white pictures. He was impressed that his uncle had gone to so much trouble to make his talk interesting. Using shaky old black and white film clips, Uncle James showed them pictorial evidence of the Zionist movement from the late 1800s and onwards. Turning to the prophecy of Ezekiel in the Bible, Uncle James excitedly pointed out the marvelous way God had predicted thousands of years before that this would occur. The valley of dry-bones in Ezekiel thirty-seven foretells the future revival of the Jewish people in the 'last days'. The following chapter goes on to foretell that the Jews would once again become a prosperous nation in the land of Israel. Ezekiel thirty-eight describes the Northern Confederacy which comes against the newly established nation of Israel when they are dwelling safely, without walls, to 'take a spoil'. Chapter thirty-nine prophesies of God's direct intervention to stop the marauding armies from completely destroying everything in their path.

Uncle James also read a couple of paragraphs from a few ancient books while he displayed pictures of the authors on the screen. Jake agreed it was remarkable that way back in the seventeenth and eighteenth centuries, students of the Bible had clearly understood certain Old Testament prophecies foretold the Jews would be gathered and established in their homeland before the return of Jesus Christ to the earth.[4]

For instance, there were the words of Sir Isaac Newton, famous for discovering the law of gravity, yet not so well known for his prolific writings on religious matters. Sir Isaac Newton had said, ``God's covenant with Abraham when he promised that his seed should inherit the land of Canaan for ever... on this covenant was founded the Jewish religion as on that is founded the

---

[4] Jeremiah 30:3,10-11; 31:10; Ezekiel 37:21-22; Joel 3:1-2,16-17;

Christian; and therefore this point is of so great moment that it ought to be considered and understood by all men who pretend to the name of Christians… the restoration of the Jewish nation so much spoken of by the old Prophets reflects not the few Jews who were converted in the Apostles days, but the dispersed nation of the unbelieving Jews to be converted in the end when the fulness of the Gentiles shall enter, it is when the Gospel (upon the fall of Babylon) shall begin to be preached to all Nations."[5]

There was also the quote that Jake knew well from John Thomas, writing in the mid-1800s which said, "There is, then, a partial and primary restoration of the Jews before the manifestation [of Jesus], which is to serve as the nucleus, or basis, of future operations in the restoration of the rest of the tribes after he has appeared in the kingdom. The pre-adventual colonization of Palestine will be on purely political principles; and the Jewish colonists will return in unbelief of the Messiahship of Jesus, and of the truth as it is in him. They will emigrate thither as agriculturalists and traders, in the hope of ultimately establishing their commonwealth… under the efficient protection of the British power… some other power friendly to Israel must then have become paramount over the land, which is able to guarantee protection to them, and to put the surrounding tribes in fear."[6]

Jake's mind drifted back to the prom. It was almost time for the dance to begin. He could well imagine all the fun that Zach must be having. While Uncle James talked about how miraculous it was for a few hundred thousand Jews in 1948 to survive the birth of their new nation, being attacked by millions of hostile Arab enemies, Jake heard only bits and blurbs. He did take notice,

---

[5] Newton, Isaac. *The Mystery of this Restitution of all Things: Isaac Newton on the Return of the Jews.* Retrieved June 5, 2013 from **http://www.isaac-newton.org/snobelen.pdf** pg.6,10.
[6] Thomas, John, Elpis Israel (*The Christadelphian*, 1849, rev.1973),pp. 441-442

however, when his uncle began talking about the future. Ezekiel thirty-eight, verse eight, spoke of the invasion of the Northern Confederacy advancing upon the 'mountains of Israel'. War was an exciting topic to Jake and he did think it would be quite interesting to see it all happen.

"'The mountains of Israel' are in what we call the 'West Bank' area," Uncle James continued, showing a topographical map on the screen. "The world has put a great deal of pressure on the Jewish people to give the West Bank to the Palestinians. However, we know the Jews must keep this land because the Bible tells us that Israel will be dwelling safely in this very area, when they are overrun by the Northern invasion."[7]

Then there's still time, Jake mused. *The Jews aren't exactly dwelling safely yet, so there's still more that has to happen. It could easily be years before Jesus returns!*

"Lately," Uncle James went on to say, "we've seen report after report of the gas finds in Israel. Israel has not only found enough natural gas and oil deposits to be self-sufficient for many, many years, but they will also be able to export. They have found a great treasure and other nations are eyeing it greedily. There has been much speculation in the past about what 'great spoil'[8] will entice the Northern Confederacy to come down into the Middle East. While we won't know for sure until after the event occurs, it is possible these gas finds could be the enticement, especially considering Russia's ambition to dominate in the exportation of fossil fuel."

"So you think Russia will be the leader of the Northern Confederacy?" Esther asked.

"I certainly do," Uncle James replied. "I think there is plenty of evidence from ancient historians, like Josephus, and old

---

[7] See also Ezekiel 36-39; Zechariah 14; Joel 3
[8] Ezekiel 38:12-13

maps to prove that this is so. The land of Magog is subject to speculation. The Greeks called the Magogites 'Scythians'. [9] Some maps show the Scythians migrated to the area of Germany and France, while others show the area of Southern Russia and Eastern Ukraine. What we do know for sure is that the nations which come against Israel will be from the 'uttermost north'. [10]

As Jake's mind wandered between the identification of Magog and his own fanciful thoughts, he randomly drifted off to the novel that he kept hidden under his mattress. There was way too much foul language in the book to leave it lying around where his mom might see it. Plus, there had been some gory violence which she would likely question. But other than that, *Green Diamonds* was full of suspense and great twists in the plot! *Will they catch Rayner?* Jake wondered. *I can't believe he had the nerve to shadow the secret police! I know they're in on the assassination attempt. They've got to be! They were visiting America when the president was gunned down. But this is Rayner's first experience in Siberia. He doesn't even understand the language. I'm sure Irina is not someone he can trust... but he doesn't seem suspicious of her at all. I hope he doesn't tell her the truth when they go out for dinner.*

When Jake tuned in again to the class, Uncle James was speaking about fulfilled prophecy in regards to the European Union. He asked Esther to read from Revelation chapter seventeen, which says, "The ten horns which you saw are ten kings who have received no kingdom as yet, but they receive authority for one hour as kings with the beast. These are of one mind, and they will give their power and authority to the beast. These will make war with the Lamb, and the Lamb will overcome them, for he is Lord of lords and King of kings; and those who are with him are called,

---

[9] Josephus, 'Antiquities of the Jews'. Retrieved April 2014
http://lexundria.com/j_aj/1.122-1.153/wst
[10] Ezekiel 38:6, 15; Daniel 11:40-45;

chosen, and faithful."[11]

Once again Uncle James produced quotations from Bible students, writing far in advance of the fulfillment, that Revelation and Daniel predicted the nations of Europe would one day unite and willingly give their national power and identity to a central authority which would be masterfully orchestrated by the Roman Catholic Church.[12] He had no shortage of news clippings and magazine articles to demonstrate that the Pope was very much behind uniting Europe and taking the reins of influence. In the future, the 'false prophet' of Revelation chapter seventeen, would guide the beast toward a final showdown with the 'Lamb' – the Lord Jesus Christ.

There was one quote from Thomas Newton, writing in 1832, that Jake had never seen before. It said, "Now the power of the Pope, as a horn or temporal prince, it hath been shown, was established in the eighth century; and 1260 years from that time will lead us down to about the year 2000, or about the 6000th year of the world; and there is an old tradition both among Jews and Christians, that at the end of six thousand years the Messiah shall come, and the world shall be renewed, the reign of the wicked one shall cease, and the reign of the saints upon earth shall begin." [13]

"And don't forget," Uncle James told them all, looking directly at Jake, "most likely, while Europe is still in the process of organizing its new empire, Christ will return, raise the dead and judge his household. Most likely, before Europe becomes the beast that will oppose Jesus on his throne, there will be the invasion of Israel by the Northern Confederacy, the destruction of that formidable army upon the mountains of Israel, and the cry going

---

[11] Revelation 17:12-14
[12] Revelation 13 compare with Daniel 7-8, Revelation 17
[13] Newton, Thomas. (1832). *Dissertations on the Prophecies Which Have Been Remarkably Fulfilled and at This Time are Fulfilling in the World. Pg. 489-490.* Retrieved June 5, 2013 from **http://books.google.ca/books**?

out to all the earth to submit to the new King in Jerusalem. We're not sure how much we'll see before we're called away to the Judgement seat of Christ. We could easily be called away tonight."

Hmm, maybe, Jake pondered, pulling his thoughts away from Rayner's dangerous mission to find out who had assassinated the president. *But it could also start ten years from now and just happen really fast!*

Uncle James went on to talk about the looming economic crisis, the increasingly frequent and devastating natural disasters, the prevalence of superbugs, outbreaks of mob behaviour – which are the 'unclean spirits of demons',[14] and signs in the heavens with the sun, moon and stars. He had everyone turn to Luke twenty-one and asked Jake to read some of the verses, which said, "Nation will rise against nation, and kingdom against kingdom. And there will be great earthquakes in various places, and famines and pestilences; and there will be fearful sights and great signs from heaven... And there will be signs in the sun, in the moon, and in the stars; and on the earth distress of nations, with perplexity, the sea and the waves roaring; men's hearts failing them from fear and the expectation of those things which are coming on the earth, for the powers of heaven will be shaken. Then they will see the Son of Man coming in a cloud with power and great glory."[15]

Jake felt he could have recited the section. He had heard it so many times from his parents. No doubt stuff was happening that was pointing forward to Jesus' return, but in his mind that didn't mean the world would end tomorrow! He wondered if Melissa was dancing with Zach. He wondered if he had gone, who might have asked him to dance. *Maybe Kristen? She's pretty. Or perhaps Brianna? It would be fun to dance with either one. And wouldn't it be sweet,* he considered, *if Melissa mistook me for Zach!*

---

[14] Revelation 16:13-16
[15] Luke 21:10-11, 25-27

The prom fantasy ended abruptly when Uncle James closed the class in prayer. Jake was vaguely aware that his uncle had given some sort of last passionate appeal to encourage them all to change their lives and be ready to meet their Lord Jesus Christ, but Jake had missed the appeal entirely.

They all enjoyed Aunt Sandra's delicious frozen yogurt and homemade pizza while they talked about summer plans and activities.

"So you and Zach will be done exams in three weeks?" Allan asked. Allan was Uncle Peter's brother-in-law. Uncle Peter had married Allan's sister, Jessica. He and Derrick – a long-time employee – were overseeing Uncle Peter's landscaping company, EdenTree, while he was away with his family doing missionary work in Jamaica. It was a much scaled-down version of the landscaping company than it had been in the past. For the most part, the crew were only maintaining properties while their boss was away, rather than launching any new projects. Jake and Zach had often worked for their uncle on a part-time basis in years past, so they knew well what was expected.

"That's right," Jake said. "Saturday afternoons are fine and we can start full-time as soon as we're done exams."

"And how many weeks do you need off? Is it just the one, or are you going to decide to join me for Youth Conference?"

"Just the one," Jake nodded, catching Uncle James' glance in his direction. Regardless of which camp he went to, there was only one week he was planning to take off. The intensive Bible study workbook was too high a hurdle for Jake. He just didn't have that kind of time to study – at least not in the summer!

"See you around noon," Allan called out as he headed off home. "And make sure you pick up Zach!"

"Don't worry," Jake smiled. "When there's money involved, Zach will be there. That Smartphone keeps him in the 'poor house'."

CHAPTER 5

At Prom

Working diligently on his homework until his parents had left the house, Zach quickly showered, donned his 'dress-up' clothes and scribbled "Sleeping" on a piece of paper. Taping the paper to his bedroom door, he pulled the door shut behind him with a smile, fairly certain that his mom would be too kind to disturb him if she returned unexpectedly. Prom was supposed to start at six-thirty and it was quarter to eight when Zach headed outside, but he wasn't overly worried if he missed the dinner. *Better late than never!* he thought to himself happily.

It was only a half hour walk to the high school. When he reached the last street, he met another student wearing a dark suit and a bright green tie, heading in the same direction. It was Jayden, one of his basketball teammates, one of the best players on the Scorpion team. They had known each other since Jayden's family had emigrated from Kenya nine years before. Jayden could jump higher than anyone. He could dunk from a stand-still! Best of all, he was a Christian and one of the twins' good friends.

"Snazzy shirt!" Jayden commented, his white teeth flashing brightly in his dark face. "Are you going to the dance?"

"Yeah, thought I'd check it out," Zach replied casually. Instinctively, he smoothed the dress shirt and tucked it into his suit pants. It was rather snazzy! A dark crimson red, the shirt had a subtle shine and changed from black to red depending on the way the light hit it.

"You've never been before, have you?"

"Nah, I wasn't really into dancing before I got involved with the musical."

There was a look of admiration on his friend's face. "Gotta say, Zach – you're a quick learner!"

39

Zach felt smug. He liked the compliment.

Then a frown wrinkled Jayden's forehead. "You're not going to your Youth Group tonight?"

Zach shrugged. "I'm just skipping tonight. Just this once."

"Thought you guys didn't miss Youth Group for anything. Is Jake coming too?"

"Jake's at Youth Group," Zach replied. Changing the subject quickly, he asked, "Why are *you* late?"

Jayden laughed. "I'm not late, really. I just spilt gravy all over my shirt at dinner, so I ran home and changed. What's up with you?"

"My parents needed some help, so I got away late," Zach lied. He felt bad lying to his friend; lies just seemed to slip out before he had a chance to think twice.

Walking into the school with his teammate, Zach showed his ticket at the front door. Loud music was blasting from the cafeteria and he followed the sound. Stirling High wasn't a very large school; there were less than a thousand students enrolled. Built in the fifties, it was rather run-down and dingy, with not much more than the basic essentials for education. However, the student council had done their best to decorate, hanging blue twinkle lights on all the walls and lime-green streamers over every doorway. Looking around for Melissa, Zach instinctively smoothed back his dishevelled, sandy-blond hair. He spotted Abi right away, dancing closely with Brian. "What does she see in that guy?" he wondered. Sure Brian was muscular and playing Triple A hockey, but he ridiculed school and had a poor work ethic. Abi deserved much better. Zach saw Nathan and Jerry over by the refreshment stand, talking to their friends, but he couldn't see Melissa.

It didn't take long for the news to spread that Zach Bryant had arrived. Before he had time to even look for a dancing partner, there were two girls vying for his attention. Before he had time to dance with each one, another girl asked for a turn. It was fun; he enjoyed the attention, but the one he really wanted to dance with was Melissa. Where was she? He dared not text her, assuming she was probably with Shane.

Eventually Zach spotted Melissa and Shane at a table. They weren't even dancing! She looked up and caught his eye. With an impish grin, Zach motioned for her to join him. Smiling, she shook her head and turned away.

The night wore on and while Zach had no shortage of dancing partners, he kept his eye on Melissa hoping he'd get a chance to talk to her alone. When he saw her get up and walk over to the refreshment stand, he made a break for it as well.

"Sorry," he told the blond girl he was dancing with; he couldn't even remember her name. She had told him, but it hadn't registered. "I need a drink."

"Okay," she giggled in a silly way. "But I'll be right here if you want to dance again."

Zach headed toward Melissa. He got to the table ahead of her and picked up a cup. "Want some?" he asked, dipping the ladle into the bowl of punch.

"I'd love a drink," she smiled graciously, "and so would Shane."

"I can't believe you're not dancing!" he remarked, handing her one cup and picking up another.

"We were," she smiled, speaking quietly. She whispered, "Shane hurt his knee. He was, well, trying to do some of the moves you did in the musical and he... sort of fell."

"Poor guy!" Zach remarked, trying to sound more sympathetic than he felt. "Are you allowed to take a turn with me?"

Melissa hesitated and looked back toward Shane. "I'd better not," she said. "He's a little uptight... about... you."

She was about to take the drinks back to her table when

41

someone shouted, "Hey, here's Vanessa VanHeusten and Marco Darrinett! What do you say everyone? Should we ask them to dance?"

Melissa looked up at Zach with a scared expression, but it didn't take long for the crowd to catch on.

"Dance! Dance! Dance!" they cried out, stomping their feet and clapping their hands.

Zach looked over at Shane, who was glaring at him. Such a glare only intensified his eagerness to take up the challenge. "Come on, Melissa," he encouraged. "It's just for fun. They all want us to."

"Zach, I can't," she protested. "Shane will kill you!"

Someone had instructed the disc jockey to play "I'll Be Yours." The soft strains of their song began to fill the room. Everyone stood back to give them the floor. Melissa looked over nervously at Shane.

A hand clutched Zach's shoulder from behind. He turned to see Jayden. "Don't be a fool, man," Jayden said in a very serious tone. "You're gonna get yourself in lots of trouble!"

The crowd called out louder. Zach turned away from his friend and looked down at Melissa. "I'll take the heat," he assured her. "Let's do this."

Taking her hand, Zach led Melissa into the center. Someone brought over a table and Zach helped Melissa climb on to it. The disk jockey started their song again, from the beginning. It had been almost a week since their last performance, but they knew their parts so well that everything flowed just as it had before. Melissa was looking at him once more with that rapturous look that filled him with hope. He locked eyes with her just as they had been told to do in the play. They were a little off-time with the 'whirly-bird catch' but they caught back up to do the third twirl perfectly. *One, two, three,* Zach kept track mentally, as his heart pounded and sweat broke out on his forehead. He didn't try to sing along and neither did Melissa. There was something different in the performance this time. Zach wasn't pretending; this was for real. *Step up, step back, spin forwards, spin back. Lift, hold, twirl, one, two, three, slide her down, balance, turn, face each other, spin away...* They ended their dance as the music faded, face to face, but Zach didn't bend forward to give her a kiss. He knew he was pushing his luck already. The crowds called out for more and Zach would have willingly obliged but he didn't dare. However, he whispered, "I love you," before letting go of her hands.

There was a great deal of applause and lots of calls for an encore, but Zach shook his head. Enough was enough. Now he had to face Shane – not that he was afraid or anything like that. He was in far better shape than Shane, even before Shane had injured his knee, but still – there was no sense adding to the already agitated situation.

Walking past where Shane was sitting, he waved, gave a congenial smile and said, "Hey, no hard feelings, right?"

Glaring back, Shane grunted, "We'll see about that." He added a few more words which were certainly not conciliatory.

Content to have had his time with Melissa, Zach wasn't worried about Shane's threatening demeanor. "Sorry, we had to please the crowd," he shrugged, and then headed off as far from Shane as possible.

For the rest of the evening, Zach kept his distance. He attempted to show several eager girls how to do some of the moves that he and Melissa had performed. Occasionally he looked over at Melissa; frequently he caught her eye. "Poor girl," he thought, "she has to miss out on all this fun to stick by Shane. I hope she soon figures out that she'd rather be with me!"

It was after ten-thirty when Zach left the high school. The moon was only a tiny sliver in the sky and the streetlight in front of the school had burned out long ago. Most of the students had already departed to attend various parties across town. Melissa and

Shane had left before ten and Zach wondered what party they were going to. He had intended to leave earlier himself, in order to get home before his parents arrived, but became entrenched in conversation with a former rugby teammate.

Crossing the road and heading for home, Zach suddenly heard a rustle and footsteps close by. Out of the shadows stepped Shane and a few of his buddies. "Moving in on my girl?" Shane challenged, as he and his four friends drew near – very near.

"I told you, I was just giving in to pressure from the crowd," Zach replied with a nonchalant air, yet feeling apprehensive. He had figured he could take on Shane, but he hadn't counted on four other guys as well. One of them was Trent, a rugby heavyweight and close to one hundred and fifty kilos. He was a great guy to have on the school team, Zach had always thought, but not someone he'd planned to oppose!

"You might think that you're a duo with Vanessa VanHeusten," Shane smirked, "but Melissa Philipson belongs to me. Is that clear?"

All five guys were standing aggressively close. Trent shoved his shoulder against Zach, knocking him somewhat off balance.

"If that's what Melissa wants – then that's fine by me," Zach replied defiantly.

Shane quickly motioned to Trent and before Zach had a chance to put up any self-defense, Trent sucker-punched him. The hits were hard and furious and knocked Zach to the ground. Desperately, he tried to hoist himself back to his feet, but then he saw a massive boot coming toward his face! Instinctively, Zach wrapped his arms around his head. The blow felt like a sledgehammer, smashing into his upper arm and grazing harshly against his skull. He didn't get a chance to block the second kick.

CHAPTER 6

Concussion

Someone was crying. Zach tried to open his eyes. There was a pounding pain in his arm and his head, and his face hurt, too. As he slowly regained consciousness he could feel pain all over his body!

"He's just lying here and blood is gushing out of his head! Please help!" someone was crying. "I don't know what's happened. There's no one else around."

"I'm okay," Zach murmured. It hurt to talk. As he lifted his head, dizziness engulfed him. Through a haze of spinning stars he vaguely thought he saw Abi crouched over him, talking to someone on her phone. Then he blacked out again.

A voice was pleading with him. "Zach, please say something!" the voice cried. "I've called the ambulance. They're on their way! Please tell me if you're okay. Please, Zach! Please say something!"

"No... ambulance," Zach mumbled thickly. "I'm okay... "

Abi was pressing something close to his head. The pain worsened. Zach wondered what she was doing, but was also glad to have her there. "Abi's a good kid, "he thought gratefully, "even if she's going out with a loser. I'm glad she's here."

Zach's right upper arm felt weak and bruised but his other was fine. He tried to get up and assess his degree of injury. However, he only managed to move a few inches before Abi pinned him to the ground.

"You've got to stay still," she pleaded. "I've taken first-aid. The ambulance is on its way!"

Wanting to check things out for himself, Zach tried hard to

roll over, but Abi was insistent. "You were knocked out cold and you're bleeding," she begged. "You need to get medical attention. They'll be here in less than five minutes. Just lie still in case there's something really wrong with you."

"I don't… want to go… to hospital," he groaned helplessly. His lips felt gigantic and he could only move them slowly but he didn't want a big drama. He tried again, more quickly, to get up on his knees. Strong as she was, Abi couldn't hold him down.

"Zach Bryant, you have no idea how bad you look!" Abi cried. "There's blood all over your face and it's pulsing out of your head. You've got to wait!"

With a sudden wave of nausea, Zach threw up, all over the sidewalk.

"I told you to lie still!" she said, sobbing.

"Hey, what's going on?" a familiar, male voice called out anxiously. "Is that Zach?"

"Oh, Jayden," Abi wailed, "thanks for coming back. Look what they did to him!"

In a moment, Jayden was by Zach's side. "Get him away from this mess," he said.

"But what if he's broken something?" Abi pleaded.

"I'm okay," Zach groaned, trying once more to get up.

"He ain't got no broken back," Jayden assured her. "He likely just got a pummeling. Right, Zach?"

"Yeah," Zach moaned.

"He's probably concussed," Jayden added. With strong arms, he helped Abi move Zach to a clean spot on the grass.

"Get me… home," Zach pleaded.

"Sorry, man. I don't have a car," Jayden told him. "Should I call your parents?"

Fumbling in her purse, Abi produced more tissues and tried again to stop the bleeding on his head. "I've already called the ambulance," she said shakily. "He needs to get checked out!"

"Probably should," Jayden agreed, but he asked once more if Zach wanted him to call his parents.

"No-o," Zach groaned. There was going to be an awful lot of explaining to do. He wasn't ready for that yet; he had to think up a good story. Faintly, in the distance, he could hear the ambulance siren.

"What happened, anyway?" Abi asked.

"He got beat up."

"By who? Shane?"

"Likely."

Zach groaned again. It was hard to talk. It hurt. "And four … thugs!" he mumbled.

The ambulance arrived with the siren blasting and bright lights flashing into the darkness. After a thorough examination, the paramedics whisked Zach off to the hospital. There was only room for one other person to go along in the ambulance and Abi wasn't leaving Zach's side.

"You take good care of him," Jayden told her, before the ambulance doors swung shut. "If he's going to be there all night, text me again and I'll get there somehow."

Zach remained conscious once he was on the way to the hospital. In Emergency he was rushed down the hallway to have a CAT scan. While he had a bad concussion and lots of bruising, the scan revealed there wasn't any sign of worrisome bleeding on his brain. A doctor shaved the hair around the gash and put in twenty stitches. Nurses cleaned up the blood and by four o'clock in the morning he was ready to go home.

"Who should I call?" the nurse asked.

Reluctantly, Zach repeated his home phone number; he had already given it to the triage nurse. He knew this wouldn't go over easy. His dad would be furious.

Sitting with Abi in the lobby waiting for one of his parents to arrive, Zach held an icepack to his mouth, while Abi held another one to his head. In a slightly awkward fashion, she was texting her parents with her other free hand to let them know Zach was all right and she was on her way home. Zach sat silently watching the television screen above. He was glad Abi wasn't asking questions. Exhausted, he hoped against hope that his mom would be the one to pick him up. She was a little more understanding than his dad in such situations. He was sure she would take one look at him and feel some sympathy.

However, it was his dad who showed up in the lobby. "You all right, Zach?" he asked tersely.

Zach nodded.

"Thanks for staying with him, Abi," his dad said.

"No problem," she replied.

"Thanks," Zach mumbled painfully. It was hard to look in Abi's direction, since she was still holding the icepack against his head. He hoped she knew he was talking to her.

"You're welcome," she said quietly.

The nurse filled Zach's dad in on all the particulars. His vital signs were good. The scan showed there was no serious injury to his brain, but she strongly recommended that he avoid all contact sports for a month, preferably two. If he had any headaches, dizziness or nausea, he was to come back in.

Two months! Zach thought to himself in dismay. *No way! I can't miss basketball camp!* "Exercise?" he mumbled.

"Moderate strength-training is fine, as long as you take it really easy," she cautioned, "but no heavy-lifting and absolutely nothing strenuous for at least a week. And stop immediately if you feel any symptoms return."

"There's a basketball camp he hopes to go to in a month," Zach's dad told the nurse. "Should he avoid that?"

"Definitely!" she replied. "If he were to have another major blow to the head, it could be serious!" She looked directly at

Zach. "You have to avoid *all* contact sports this summer. If you're feeling better in September *then* you can give it a try – but you have to be very wary of any dizziness, nausea or lack of co-ordination. This is serious, Zach! Concussions can have long-term consequences. They can even be fatal."

Zach's dad nodded in agreement but Zach was distressed. Missing camp would be a tragedy! *There's no way!* he told himself. *I'll be better by then.*

The nurse asked several questions about what had caused the concussion. Zach was in too much pain to reply and he didn't really want to relay any information; he didn't want things to escalate.

"A fight," was all he said.

Leaning on Abi and his dad, Zach managed to walk out to the van. He had never felt so lousy in his life.

"Let's get you comfortable," his dad said, opening the sliding door and reclining the mid-section bucket seat. It was a relief for Zach to lie back against the chair.

It took a while for his dad to get the sliding door closed. Since the inside latch was old and sticky, the door often took a few tries before closing securely. The noisy slams made Zach's headache worsen. When they were all finally settled in the van, Zach's dad turned to him and asked, "Okay, so where were you and what happened?"

Really! thought Zach. *That's the extent of his sympathy. 'Let's get you comfortable' and then whammo, he hits me with interrogation.*

Still feeling disorientated, Zach hadn't had time to think through his explanation. He knew he had to be very careful what he said. With his father being a teacher at Stirling High, not much got past him. He pointed to his swollen mouth. Abi was looking back at him to hear his response. He caught her eye, hoping she wouldn't give the story away. She seemed to understand.

"Hard to... talk," he mumbled.

Zach's dad sighed. "All right," he said. "Let's get you both home."

When they reached Abi's house, just a few blocks away from theirs, Zach caught her eye again as she was getting out. He spoke sincerely, if rather slurred, "Thanks!"

Abi smiled and patted his arm. "See you Sunday. I hope you're feeling better by then." Then she remembered something. "Actually, I guess I won't. We'll be at the cottage."

"Hey, remind your parents that the Alderson family lives up that way." Zach's dad told her. "They'd love to have a memorial meeting with you."

"I'll tell them," Abi replied, "but you know my mom and dad. When they're on vacation – they just want to hang out as a family. We probably won't go anywhere."

With a sigh, Zach's dad nodded. He didn't respond. Zach knew what he was thinking; he had heard it expressed often enough. "Where's everyone's priorities?" his father often said with disappointment. "Everyone's always going on vacation, absolutely loyal to their sports teams, having fun here or there – but what about preaching? What about our commitment to God? What about Bible study and encouraging each other to believe? Especially when we know the return of Jesus Christ is so near."

Andrew, Zach's dad, would always be a profoundly busy man. His dedication to the work of the Lord was absolute and the ecclesial family benefitted greatly. He was a man of high moral standards and ideals who 'walked the talk', yet sometimes his natural family felt neglected and there were those in the Ecclesia who felt he was too judgemental. Sometimes, Zach didn't feel he rated very highly on his father's priority list or measured up to his expectations for a young man of seventeen. He wanted his father's approval, but he often told himself that he didn't care; it was too hard to get, or so it seemed.

CHAPTER 7

Consequences

In the morning, Zach's mouth was even more swollen and painful. His parents had faithfully checked on him every other hour to make sure he wasn't sliding into a coma. Picking up his phone, he texted Melissa before he got out of bed:

Hey, doing anything?

He hoped maybe she'd drop by and see him. She lived only a short walk away.

Putting his phone in his pocket, Zach slowly made his way downstairs, with one hand on the railing. He felt rather unsteady. Jake had left early to work for Brett. Zach had texted his uncle to say that he couldn't help with the gardens, and then fallen back to sleep. He was feeling a lot of pain. "Hi mom," he managed to say, glancing over in her direction.

His mom didn't hear him at first. She was listening to the morning news and intently following the report. "Due to continued instability, civil war and economic collapse," the reporter was saying, "Iran and Syria have formed a new alliance with Russia. Negotiations are also being held with Turkey and Iraq. Will they also become part of this new Northern Confederacy? Time will tell, but the balance of power in the Middle East is dramatically tipping toward the Russians. "

Zach groaned and his mom turned from the eggs she was frying, compassionately. "Oh, Honey, you look so sore! You probably can't even eat these eggs."

With plenty of sympathy, his mom made him a fruit milkshake and gave him an icepack to put on his face. Zach sat down at the kitchen table. His dad brought over a pad of paper and a pen and set it down in front of him.

"Looks to me like your hands are fine," his dad remarked with a wry smile, "so I'm sure you'll have no trouble writing out an explanation of what happened last night. I want to know why you left a 'sleeping' sign on your door when you were not even in the house – and just *where* exactly you were. Plus, maybe you could add a line or two about why you suspect you received that beating... or if this is a case of some random thugs on the loose that we should tell the police about. "

"Andrew," his mom interrupted gently, bringing over the milkshake, "he's not feeling well."

"Don't worry, I'm not asking him to talk," Zach's dad replied. The sarcastic tone in his voice only exasperated the growing rift between father and son. Andrew was frustrated with his son's defiant, dishonest attitude, while Zach was resentful of his father's negativity, which he perceived as a lack of love.

The Smartphone vibrated and Zach took it out of his pocket, laying it down in front of him. He could see that the message was from Melissa. He took the pen and paper grudgingly. He didn't have a good story but he wrote: "I was so tired of sitting still and doing homework that I had to go for a walk. I didn't want you to worry about me, so I put the 'sleeping' sign on my door. I got beat up by a guy that I know from school. Don't worry about it – he's just jealous. We don't need to call the police."

As he read Zach's story, his father frowned. Zach could tell he wasn't convinced.

Zach took a moment to review the incoming message on his phone. It said:

Zach, I'm so sorry about last night. I hope you're okay. Shane needs some time to cool down – please understand.

Whatever! Zach thought to himself with disgust. *Shane is an idiot! Why can't she see that?*

"What's he jealous of?" prompted his dad suspiciously.

Taking back the notepad, Zach hastily scribbled, "That I was in the musical and he wasn't."

"Hmm," his dad pondered. "You do realize, Zach, that on Monday when we both go back to school, there may be rumours going around about this incident and I will have to determine which stories are true and which are not."

Zach didn't look up.

Passing the notepad back to him, his father added firmly, "Also, being a teacher at your school, I am fully aware that most of the grade twelve students were at prom last night. That might explain why you were wearing your best dress shirt on your little walk around town."

With chagrin, Zach realized his dad was right. Rumours would be all over the school by Monday. Everyone would know that Zach Bryant had attended prom and done his waltz with Melissa. It was even possible that when he showed up with bruises all over his face, Shane might not be able to resist bragging about his part in the whole incident.

Ripping off the first piece of paper and crumbling it up, Zach laid out the truth. It took at least five minutes to write out the whole story.

When his dad had finished reading the story, he looked at Zach soberly. "This is what I suspected," he said with deep disappointment in his eyes. "Tell me, was it worth it?"

With a shrug, Zach wasn't sure how to answer. The dance had been fun. Being swarmed by girls was flattering. The chanting crowd and the waltz with Melissa had been an adrenaline rush. Sure, it wasn't all that pleasant to get beat up – and he certainly didn't want to miss out on the basketball camp, but in all honesty, he felt it had been worth it. He would certainly choose to do it again; he would just be better prepared for the outcome. The disappointment in his father's eyes restrained his cockiness. With another shrug, he looked down at the floor and muttered, "I don't know."

"Well, Zach," his dad said resignedly, "you've been dishonest with us, so there will have to be consequences. I've thought it through and decided you're going to have to miss the basketball party."

Zach wrote furiously on his pad of paper: "But Brett is counting on Jake and me being there. He's put so much into this! He wants to play a game and five players have already backed out on him. We can't play a proper game if I'm not there."

"How many backed out on Uncle James last night, after all the work he did on that talk?"

"That's different," Zach wrote. "Uncle James didn't need *me* to be there to do his talk."

"He was very disappointed you weren't there," his dad replied meaningfully. "And what about Aunt Sandra? She always makes so much food for you guys – don't you appreciate her efforts?"

Zach shrugged angrily. He didn't want to think about any disappointment he may have caused. Picking up his pen he wrote, "Dad, please think of some other consequence. I don't want to let Brett down. He's put so much of his own time and effort into helping us to be the best team around."

Looking over her husband's shoulder, Zach's mom read the responses he was giving. "Didn't the nurse say that you weren't to play sports this summer, anyway?" she asked.

"She said at least a month. The party's at the end of June!" Zach wrote furiously. "That's four weeks away. I'll be better by then. I heal fast! I'll be careful!"

His dad picked up Zach's phone and thought through the matter carefully. "All right then," he said, "I'll give you two choices. No party at Brett's or the loss of phone privileges for the rest of the summer."

Not my phone! Zach thought desperately. His two-year

contract cost a lot every month and how would he ever keep in touch with Melissa?

"Which one?"

"I'm not five!" he mumbled angrily, as best as he could. It hurt so much to move his lips! "I'm paying for that phone. You can't take it away!"

"What's your decision, Zach?"

Zach was angry. He couldn't miss the basketball party! It was the last chance the Scorpions would have to hang out together before summer holiday plans led them in different directions. He and Jake were the team captains; they had to be there! He would have to find another way to talk to Melissa. Slamming the table with his good arm jarred his head painfully. Feeling even angrier, he tried his best to storm off to his room, but nearly lost his balance as he clomped up the stairs.

"He's still in rough shape, Andrew," Zach heard his mom say, sympathetically.

"Pride comes before a fall," was his dad's uncompassionate response. *He* didn't sound sympathetic at all.

The response made Zach even angrier; but he was in too much pain to do anything except crawl back into bed.

CHAPTER 8

As Time Goes By

Rumours *were* flying around on Monday when Jake and Zach went to school. The swelling had gone down a little. Zach could move his lips again and he didn't feel dizzy, but his face was black and blue. His mom had given him a super short brush-cut to blend in with the shaved patch and he had a large bandage under his hat. As much as Zach treasured his old 'messy look', as Esther called it, and hardly recognized himself in the mirror – the messy look just did not look cool with a large section missing!

Everyone at school wanted to know what had happened and Zach got tired of repeating in words and texts, "I got beat up by some crazy thugs."

It wasn't long before people were guessing who the 'thugs' might be and then the whole story got out of hand! Zach had to explain that no, there weren't any guns, and no, the police hadn't been called in and no, no one had been arrested.

Shane and his buddies avoided Zach completely and even Melissa hardly said a word to him all day. It seemed she was trying to avoid him as well and Zach couldn't text her to ask why. However, on the way home from school, as Zach passed Jayden's house, it occurred to him that his friend would likely lend him his phone for a minute.

Jayden and his younger brother were practicing free-throws in their driveway. Often Zach would stop and shoot a few with them. Jayden's brother, Isaiah, was in grade nine this year and had a great shot, but he would never make the basketball team. For as long as Zach could remember, Isaiah had been confined to a wheelchair, due to a rare disease that had crippled his legs. Always smiling and cheerful, Isaiah had become the Scorpions' mascot, cheering loudly from the sidelines and waving banners he made himself. Sometimes he did a half-time show. It was amazing to watch Isaiah shoot three-pointers and retrieve the ball so quickly in his wheelchair. He was definitely a crowd pleaser.

"Hi there, Isaiah," Zach called out. "What's your percentage today?"

Jayden and Isaiah always had a running average on how many shots they could make in a fifteen-minute span.

"Only eighty-five today," Isaiah smiled. "I went to a youth retreat for the weekend. I'm out of practice!"

"A youth retreat?" Zach did his best to smile, but it still hurt to stretch his lips. "Good for you, Isaiah." Zach had known for years that his friends were Christian. Often he had considered asking questions about what they believed to try to get a discussion going, but most of the time they were all too busy having fun. Serious discussions seemed out of place.

"You look rough, man," Jayden said solemnly, shaking his head. "Although I gotta say – I like the brush cut." Gently clapping his friend on the shoulder, Jayden added, "I sure wish I'd stayed with you Friday night. I had a feeling you were in *big* trouble!"

"Thanks," Zach nodded. "If you had been with me, they wouldn't have dared to take us on!"

Flexing his muscles in a show of bravado, Jayden laughed. "Yeah! You and me – a formidable force!"

Isaiah threw Zach the ball. "Let's see what your score is today," he encouraged.

With other matters on his mind and a painfully bruised right arm, Zach couldn't get above thirty percent. He quit after ten shots.

"You've only got a few months to get back in top form!" Jayden teased.

"I need to talk to Melissa," Zach confessed, throwing the ball back to Isaiah. "I lost my phone privileges. Any chance I could borrow yours for a sec?"

"Sure thing. Anytime," Jayden replied, taking it out of his back pocket and handing it over. "That's tough, man!" he added sympathetically. "I couldn't live without my phone!"

Hitting the keys as quickly as he could, Zach texted the familiar number he often contacted more than fifty times a day!

Hey, Melissa, this is Zach. My dad took my phone, so I'm using Jayden's. You hardly spoke to me, today. What's up?

Melissa texted in reply:

Zach, I'm so sorry. No more dancing.

How about no more Shane?

I'm too scared to break up with him and I'm staying away from you, so you don't get hurt.

So, that's it, Zach mused. *She's just scared! Well, school's over in a couple of weeks. Shane's working at the Kejimkujik National Park for the summer, and then he's heading off to university. The park is hours away. He won't be coming home very often. Maybe she'll get kind of lonely.*

Gotta go, he texted in reply. But we have to find some way to meet up. I miss you!

I don't want you to get hurt, but I miss you too.

Saying goodbye to his friends, Zach made his way home. For the next few weeks he and Jake had all they could do to keep up with the daily routine. June was always a busy month with end of semester projects, final exams and fast-growing lawns. There was plenty going on at their hall too with the usual Youth Groups, Bible classes and Sunday School picnic. Zach was now expected to be at everything!

In the last semester, Zach's marks had slipped due to his involvement in the musical. He knew he would be lucky to get Honours this year, but there was one subject in which he hoped to do really well. Last year Abi had claimed the math award, beating him by only two percent! He and Abi had been competing all semester. The fact that she had skipped so many classes this year to be with Brian was definitely in his favour, but weeks of neglected homework didn't help his cause. Zach was surprised though, that in losing his phone, his study sessions at home became so much more productive!

Jake was just as intent on doing well, but he was aiming for a Science award. Zach had almost failed chemistry in first semester but Jake was at the top of his class. Calculus gave Jake grief, but not chemistry. Both twins hoped to get into engineering, and high math and science marks would certainly help when applying to universities in December. Jake's top choice only accepted two hundred students out of over a thousand applicants!

However, even with all the intense study, mountains of homework, and calls from Allan and Brett, Jake still managed to finish off the thriller he'd been reading. He tried to talk Zach into starting it. "It's so cool!" he told his brother. "You'll like Rayner! But be prepared to get really 'creeped-out'! Especially when he gets tortured by the secret police! That's so scary! You'll love it!"

"Tortured?" Zach echoed.

"I won't spoil it for you," Jake smiled. "But you'd better keep it hidden. Mom would probably say it's 'unwholesome'."

Zach tucked the book away in a drawer. It sounded like a great summer read!

Finally exams were over. The weeks had flown by. Summer holidays had begun. Most ecclesial activities came to a halt. In the last few years the Stirling Ecclesia had decided that since so many were away at Bible Camps or on vacation, all Bible classes and Youth group activities would take a hiatus. Only Sunday morning meetings remained on the schedule for July and August. As the twins walked home from their last exam they were both relieved that school and a jammed-packed scheduled life was over until September.

"Did you beat Abi?" Jake asked. The math marks had been posted on the wall.

"No," Zach sighed. "She beat me by one percent, and Sarah beat us both. I should have kept up with my homework. It would have been nice to win that math award... it's a two hundred dollar prize. But, the musical did me in."

"Too bad," Jake replied sympathetically. "And what did the guidance counselor have to say?"

Zach had met with the guidance counselor during lunch break. "She says my average is high enough to get into most colleges and universities, but if I want to do electrical engineering, I'll have to upgrade some of my marks." With a shrug, Zach added, "But that's okay. I was planning to come back anyway. It will give me something to aim for. What about you?"

"I did okay," Jake replied modestly. As far as he knew, he had the top marks. There was a good chance he would win the science award; and that was a five hundred dollar scholarship! "But, I'll probably need to retake calculus if I want to get into nanotechnology."

Zach nodded. September was far away. With school out for the summer, all that mattered to Zach now was basketball, the exercise routine and... Melissa, of course.

"So are you going to try jogging today?" Zach asked his brother. Jake's weak ankle seemed much better.

"Yeah, I think I will." He ran a few steps forward to try it out. "It feels fine," he announced.

Zach was pleased that the exercise routine was getting back on track for both of them. For the last week, he had resumed all his former activities without any significant pain or dizziness. He was not pleased, however, that aside from brief glances in his direction, Melissa was still ignoring him. In frustration, Zach paid no attention to her either. He told himself that there had to be something wrong with a girl who would find Shane appealing!

"Hey, Zach," Jake said abruptly. "I have an idea that might be good for both of us. Dad has your phone and no one is using it, but it's still under a contract that you have to pay for. Why don't I ask Dad if I can have it for the summer and I'll pay the monthly fee? Then if you get any important texts I can pass them on to you."

"Fabulous idea!" Zach exclaimed. *If Jake has the phone,* he surmised quickly, *I'll still be able to message Melissa when we're at work, or at night, if it's in our room...* "Do you really think Dad will go for it?"

"It's worth a try."

To the twin's surprise, their father agreed to the plan. But there was a hitch – they both had to promise that Zach wouldn't touch the phone and Jake had to show his father the records each month of where all the texts were going.

It's still better than nothing, Zach thought. *Jake can read the texts to me and I'll tell him what to say in response.* The promise was made and Jake took over the payments.

The first text that came in was from Brett reminding them about the basketball party Saturday afternoon. Excited and happy to be on summer vacation, nine warm, sun-filled weeks stretched out gloriously ahead of them... or so they thought. In reality there were only *seven.*

Had anyone known what little time was left, it would have changed everything!

CHAPTER 9

Brett's Party

Zach and Jake woke up early Saturday morning. They drove out to do their landscaping work for Brett and Uncle James and were back by eleven. Quickly showering and grabbing a sandwich for lunch, they were tying up their shoes when their mom walked into the kitchen.

"Amazing! It's the weekend and you two are done work before lunch!" she exclaimed. "You must really be looking forward to this party."

"Brett and Jenna know how to throw a party!" Jake smiled.

Glancing down at Zach's running shoes, she remarked anxiously, "I hope you're planning to stay on the sidelines today, Zach. You can cheer everyone on but it would be rather risky to get another hit."

"Mom, I'm completely recovered," Zach told her firmly. "It's been over four weeks! Jake and I did a *full* workout yesterday and I didn't feel any dizziness at all. I'll be fine."

With a sigh, their mom reached into the fridge for the orange juice. "Zach, have you googled 'concussions'? Do you realize how serious this is? You shouldn't be going to that basketball camp with Brett, either."

"Mom, you do realize that Brett paid over a thousand dollars for both of us to go," Zach reminded her. "He didn't ask you or dad for a cent. If we don't go, he'll have wasted all that money!"

Their dad appeared in the doorway. "It would have been better if Brett had asked our permission before he registered *either* of you for that camp. And I find it really hard to understand why you would want to go to a basketball camp over Manitoulin!"

"But this is our last chance to make it to the Provincials," Jake explained. "If we'd done a little more training last year... well, we could have gone all the way then."

"And the Black Hawks are coming to this camp!" Zach chimed in. "In fact, half their team is getting this training. Brett's counting on Jake and me to do this for the Scorpions."

"I know," his dad reminded him gently. "I know there are five of you returning for a 'super-twelve' year in September and you have a really good chance to win it all, but Bible Camp happens only *once* a year. This is something special that we've always done. Manitoulin is where your friends are."

"Your friends too," Zach reminded him, feeling he could get some mileage out his father's summer plans. "You and mom are staying home so you can do your teacher's course."

"If I had a choice in the matter, I'd be going to the Bible Camp," his dad said abruptly. "You know that, Zach."

"Well, we don't really have a choice either," quipped Zach. "Our coach has paid for us and told us we'd better be there!"

A knock on the door ended the conversation. Brett was standing on the porch, poised, confident and cheerful as always. Reflective blue sunglasses were perched on his blond wavy hair. His new, emerald-green Mustang was parked in the driveway.

"Good to see you, Andrew," Brett called out, giving the twin's dad a hearty hug. He greeted Lisa in the same way.

"Wow! Your lawn looks fantastic!" Brett commented, glancing around the grounds. "Someone knows what they're doing."

"That's Jake's good work," Andrew said proudly. "He mows the lawns and Zach looks after the gardens. I've got it pretty good."

"You've done a great job with your kids," Brett nodded.

63

"Thanks for letting me borrow them for the day. They deserve a party."

"Thanks for all your coaching work," Lisa said sincerely. "Please watch Zach carefully though. He's not supposed to be playing any sports this summer. He really should be just cheering today."

"I'll take it easy on him," Brett agreed.

Zach shot his mom a dirty look. "I'm fine!" he insisted. "There's *no way* I'm not playing sports all summer!"

Jake took the backseat and let his brother have the front. Riding in the new Mustang was exciting enough – front or back.

"I like the short hair," Brett said to Zach, as he backed out of the driveway. "I can see your face again."

"I don't," Zach moaned. "I look like a geek."

Brett laughed. "In all seriousness, Zach, now you look like a clean-cut guy that I would trust to cut my lawns even when I'm not home."

"Thanks," Zach replied sarcastically.

"Hey. What about me?" Jake chipped in. "You wouldn't trust me?"

"Hmm, you still have that shady appearance," Brett smiled. "I'd be checking your references."

"Come on," Jake scoffed. But he decided maybe it was time to ask his mom for a haircut.

"I get the feeling that your parents aren't too enthusiastic about this party," Brett remarked as they set off down the street.

"They don't want us to go to the basketball camp either," Zach complained, as Brett headed toward the highway.

"Why's that?"

"It's the same week as the Manitoulin Bible Camp," Jake explained. "Mom and Dad aren't going this year, but Uncle James has offered us a ride."

"And how do you guys feel about that?"

"We'll really miss Manitoulin… " Jake answered truthfully, "but the basketball camp sounds amazing! We've got to make it to the Provincials next season – and that will take all the training we can get. Besides you've spent a lot of money and we appreciate what you've done for us."

"That's my boys," Brett grinned, screeching his tires as they hugged the curve of the on-ramp. After merging into traffic he added, "But look guys, I don't want to pressure you into anything. Zach," he said, looking over at him, "if you aren't feeling up to it, don't worry about the money I've spent. I'd rather you were able to play in November – fully recovered, than get injured again and miss the whole season."

"Jake and I were training yesterday and I felt totally fine," Zach replied. "Mom just gets all worked up about stuff like that. Doctors have to be overcautious, so they don't get sued and my mom believes every word they say. Our parents get way too worried about everything. They gave me such a hard time about that school play."

"And you gave such a fantastic performance!" Brett exclaimed.

"Thanks," Zach said. "I wish they could have appreciated it was something I really wanted to do, instead of just counting how many Sundays I missed."

"Your parents certainly are on the more conservative side," Brett agreed with a chuckle, as they sped smoothly along the highway. "They're great people and all, but I know I would have found it hard growing up with so many restrictions!"

"Tell me about it!" Zach nodded, rolling his eyes. "No school dances, no school parties, no Sunday sports… it goes on and on. Everything is a big no. Sometimes it's even a big deal just to watch a PG movie at our house!"

"Come on, Zach," Jake reasoned, feeling, as he often did lately, the need to balance his brother's one-sided remarks. "We don't have it that bad. Dad's always paid for us to do sports. He's even coached us in soccer. And if we want to go to a Young People's gathering, or Bible Camp, or meet up with our friends in the Truth, Mom and Dad have always done all they can to help us out."

"Sure. Anything *they* want us to do – it's a yes," Zach growled.

"Parents make rules to keep you from danger," Brett added, feeling obliged to support Jake. "Like your dad always says, 'Following Christ isn't the path of least resistance but it is the path of least regrets.'"

The twins looked at each other. Zach shook his head and sighed. He had heard that quote often enough! They were nearing Brett's house and Zach could see the cul-de-sac where the basketball net was set up. The other guys were already there. Jayden was shooting baskets while Cory and Tyson were trying to guard him. Isaiah was well-positioned in his wheelchair behind the net, ready to catch stray balls and throw them back into play.

"Well, you guys know that I'm always here for you," Brett told them. "I think you both have a lot of talent, and if I can help you reach your dreams, you know I'll do what I can."

They both thanked him gratefully as they got out of the car. *Brett's such a great guy!* Zach thought. *If only he could have been my father! He is always so understanding and encouraging. He doesn't jump to negative conclusions. He isn't quick to judge or nag me about how I need to change my life.* Both Jake and Zach felt Brett was a friend who cared first and foremost for them – just the way they were.

"Have some fun, guys," Brett called out as the twins ran to join their friends. "I'll bring out some drinks and then maybe we can have a three-on-three game. But, Zach," he cautioned, "take it easy. I trust your judgement on how far to push yourself. But don't feel you're under any pressure to play. We can find a way around the uneven numbers if necessary."

Zach nodded. He felt fine. He couldn't wait to get back into the game. Isaiah threw him the ball and Zach dribbled it in. It was an easy layup and Jayden took the rebound. By the time Brett and his wife Jenna brought out the drinks, sweat was already soaking through everyone's shirts. The iced-tea break was very refreshing. Zach chatted to Jenna about his plans for the summer while he guzzled a tall glass of the cold, sweet mixture. Jenna was a lot friendlier than Brett's first wife, who had been quiet and shy.

Of course, Zach knew that it hadn't been right for Brett to divorce Natalie and marry Jenna. After many intense discussions on the issue he was well familiar with the Bible references involved. He knew that Jesus clearly states in Matthew chapter nineteen, verse four, "He who made them at the beginning 'made them male and female,' and said, 'For this reason a man shall leave his father and mother and be joined to his wife, and the two shall become one flesh'? So then, they are no longer two but one flesh. Therefore what God has joined together, let not man separate. And I say to you, whoever divorces his wife, except for sexual immorality, and marries another, commits adultery." Zach also knew his father felt Brett had not been adequately instructed prior to his baptism in regards to the lifestyle changes Jesus encourages believers to make.[16]

Brett's sudden divorce and remarriage four years prior caught everyone off guard and created a big upset in the Stirling Christadelphian Ecclesia that Zach attended. Many believed that because of Brett's actions the Ecclesia should follow the Scriptural directive given by the Apostle Paul.[17] However, Brett's sincere and heartfelt apology led others to believe the directives were unnecessary, as Brett was already repentant. After months of

---

[16] Mark10:2-12;1Corinthians 7:39; Galatians 5:13-15; Ephesians 4:17-22
[17] 2 Corinthians 6:14-18; 2 Thessalonians 3:6

debate on the matter, the Ecclesia decided to maintain the bond of fellowship they had with Brett.

Controversies can be very stimulating and provide great impetus to dig deep into the Word of God, if they are handled in a loving spirit of meekness, esteeming others above ourselves.[18] Sometimes in order to hold fast to truth, great effort needs to be made to combat error.[19] Jesus warns that "offenses must come" to test our discipleship.[20] Unfortunately, however, in the Stirling Ecclesia, while everyone had learned a great deal about the issue, the overheated debates had disillusioned many of the young and the newly baptized. Even now Zach privately wondered which had been worse – Brett's foolish behaviour, or the hostile over-reactions? Apathy and weariness still weighed heavily on everyone as positive outreach activities struggled to resurface.

Unhappy with the negativity and the final decision, some of the more active members had moved to Ontario, taking their families with them, including many of the twins' friends.

Sadly, Jenna was now not interested in coming out to anything at the hall or even talking about the Bible. Since his re-marriage, Brett hadn't been the most regular attendee either, but Zach felt his coach came as often as he could.

Turning up the music, so they would all have a heavy beat to pump them up and get them moving faster, Brett joined the boys and they chose teams. Then they all went at it, as seriously as if it was a game that counted for the Provincials! Zach felt exhilarated to be back in action; passing the ball to Jayden, going up against Jake for layups, dribbling back to the three-point-line on the road or guarding Cory. He didn't feel as out of shape as he had thought he would. His right arm was back in good form, rarely missing a shot. He felt he had energy to spare. He could play basketball for

---

[18] Philippians 2:3; 2 Timothy 2:24-26; Galatians 5:15; 6:1
[19] 2 Thessalonians 2:10-12,15; 2 Timothy 4:2-4
[20] Matthew 18:6-7; 1 Corinthians 11:18-19

ever. For well over an hour, the games went on. Isaiah cheered from the sidelines and was always there to catch the out-of-bounds shots and passes. Zach's team won the first game. Jake's team took the next two. Then Zach's team won. It came down to a tie-breaker and the intensity increased. It was 'do or die' time.

Cory passed to Jake, but Zach intercepted and stole the ball. He dribbled over the line and came back furiously. He intended to pass to Jayden, but Jake stepped in the way, so Zach changed plans and decided to go in for a layup. Just as he leaped forward to shoot, Tyson jumped to block his shot and Zach rammed full force into his extended elbow. He took the hit directly to his head and... everything went black. The others watched in horror as Zach crumbled to the ground... unconscious!

For five long seconds, everyone stood in shock looking down on their teammate.

"Call 911!" Jayden yelled. "This is serious!"

"Give him a minute," Brett replied, bending down to check Zach's eyes. "Hey, Zach," he said, gently pushing his eyelids up, "can you hear me? Can you see me?"

Voices were calling out to Zach, begging him to open his eyes. He could hear Isaiah above the others. Someone was actually prying his eyes open. Light was spilling in. Grudgingly, Zach complied and came to. His head was reeling.

Brett was crouched over him. "Zach, are you okay?" he begged. "I can't believe we let this happen! I shouldn't have let you play."

Directing everyone else to move back, Brett examined Zach carefully. Brett's father had been a paramedic, so he knew the questions to ask and felt confident he could judge the severity of the situation.

Zach could still see clearly and he remembered getting the hit. Only his head hurt; so Brett and Jake helped him up. Jenna ran to get her lawn chair and soon Zach was settled in a comfortable, partly-reclined position, out of the sun and right next to the barbeque.

Isaiah wheeled over to sit next to him. "You okay?" he kept asking; his dark face lined with worry.

"I'll be fine."

"Do you mind getting some ice?" Brett asked Jake. "You'll find it in the freezer."

Jake took off to get ice, while everyone else decided to take a break and have another drink of the cold iced tea. Jayden brought Zach a drink. Brett and Jenna started the barbeque for lunch. As the sausages sizzled, and the guys took the garden hose to one another in a massive water fight, Jake walked down the long hallway trying to find the kitchen. At last he came to it. He found the ice in the freezer like Brett had said. Grabbing a small hand towel nearby, he wrapped it around the ice cubes.

Somewhat curious, Jake took his time heading back out. The doors to every room were open, so he had a quick peek in each one. Brett had a gigantic computer screen in his study. A leather love seat sat facing it, with many comfortable cushions. A high-fidelity sound system was well-positioned on the wall and the bookshelf was full of DVD's.

Wow! This is awesome! Jake thought enviously. He took a step inside. On the desk lay the movie *Hell Rider*. A guy on a bright red motorcycle was doing a somersault over a large transport truck. Behind him were two cop cars closing in fast. It looked fascinating! *Maybe he'd let us borrow it,* Jake thought. He was about to check the ratings on the back to see if his dad would approve, when he heard the back door open.

Putting the DVD down quickly, Jake stepped back into the hallway. He heard Brett yell, "Hey, Jake, did you find that ice?"

"Coming," Jake called out, walking faster.

Once Zach had the ice on his head, Jake joined in the water fight.

Brett gave Isaiah the tongs and asked him to look after the sausages. Folding his arms together, he turned his attention to Zach. "You realize this means I can't have you go to camp this summer?" Brett said firmly. "Why don't I send another player in your place?"

"I'll be better by then," Zach pleaded. "It's a full week away! And I didn't throw up this time."

"That's true," Brett agreed. "But we can't risk it, Zach. You've got to let yourself heal, or this could end up being a serious risk to your health, short-term and long-term. I'd rather have you in top form when the season starts. Take the week and go to Bible Camp. But remember you can't play sports there, either."

"You can still cheer for everyone!" Isaiah reminded him with a smile.

With an appreciative glance in the younger boy's direction, Zach nodded. He sighed heavily. Zach knew that Brett had a lot to lose by encouraging him to go to Bible Camp. He knew his coach would never talk him out of going to a basketball camp he had personally paid for, unless he truly believed Zach's health was at risk. Inside Zach was crying. On the outside, he tried to keep his composure. *I'm going to miss out on so much!* he thought with despair. *I've never had the chance to have professional coaches before. What secrets will they tell the guys that I may never hear? Will Jake remember everything so he can share it with me?*

"Dad and Uncle James will be happy," he mumbled.

"Yes," Brett agreed. "I'm sure they will."

CHAPTER 10

Choices

Jake was both angry and envious that Zach was unable to go with him to the basketball camp. Now that Zach couldn't go, Jake told himself that he had no choice. They couldn't both let Brett down. Brett was going to send Jayden in Zach's place and was willing to find another player to take Jake's spot if necessary, but subconsciously, Jake was guarding his own position carefully. He knew that as a captain he was expected to learn the skills and come back with all the secret moves and strategy to teach the others. The Black Hawks' captain was going. If another teammate went to the camp instead of him or Zach, they might feel they should be the captain next season.

Jake was truly looking forward to the basketball camp, but he had deep regrets about missing the trip to Manitoulin. The night before Zach and Esther were to leave, Jake lay awake in bed, listening to Zach's quiet, peaceful breathing and thinking about his old friends in Ontario. They never kept in touch with each other, but usually once they were together at Bible Camp, it didn't take long to re-connect. Who would Brennan pick for three-on-three volleyball? Would he be disappointed if only Zach showed up this summer? *But he never emails or calls,* Jake thought. *And last year was kind of strained. They've all moved on to a new level that Zach and I can't seem to reach. They have a great youth group where they live; everyone is enthusiastic about Bible study and being involved. Does Brennan even care about me? He has so many other good friends.*

And then there was Hannah. *I wonder how much she's*

grown up? he thought. *Fourteen is still kind of young. But will she have a crush on me again? Will I care? What if she decides she likes someone else?* Then a new thought occurred to him. *If Hannah and I were to become good friends maybe she would keep in touch… Maybe she would help me stay strong spiritually. I really need a friend like that… Aside from Allan, every one of my friends at youth group is only pulling me down.*

Even with all the rocks in the lake and the nuisance of leeches, Jake loved the Bible Camp surroundings. He had spent two weeks of every summer there since he was ten. Plus, he knew he was very low in a spiritual way. The Bible Camp talks always helped him have a different perspective. He knew he needed it – desperately!

Maybe I can listen to the talks on CD, he thought to himself. *I can even download them after Bible Camp is over. I could even listen to them on Zach's phone while I'm cutting grass! Brett's offered me an amazing opportunity that I may never get again. I don't want to let him down. If I listen to the talks I can get the best of both camps and I'll make sure I get to Manitoulin next summer!*

Content that he was making the best decision, Jake switched on his reading light and pulled out a new book from under the mattress. Abi had lent it to him. She said it was the best book she had ever read, but warned him that his parents wouldn't like it. On the front cover was a bullet-riddled helicopter that was about to crash on a tropical island. Just reading the blurb on the back gave him a sensual, creepy thrill! *Wow!* he thought, *How will these three Americans survive among the savages? How will the two soldiers protect the beautiful nurse they were transporting? Will their wounded comrade on the mainland die? Will they ever be rescued or will they have to rescue themselves?* He could hardly wait to get started.

Zach fell asleep long before Jake, but in the early hours

just before dawn, he woke anxiously from a terrifying nightmare! Shane was trying to kill him! There weren't just four thugs ready to beat him up; the whole rugby team had turned against him! Fists were flying; boots were kicking him in the face, in the ribs, against his legs. He was crying out for them to stop but no one would listen. Waking up with a start, breathing heavily and covered with sweat, Zach was certain he was about to die. It was such a relief to realize he was alone with his brother in his room. Hearing Jake roll over with a heavy sigh was a most reassuring sound!

Lying back against his pillow, Zach relived the dream *and* the actual pummeling he had received. Surprisingly, tears flowed from his eyes as he recalled Trent's boot coming hard toward his face. *What if that concussion had killed me?* he wondered anxiously. *What if I have another blow to my head and it finishes me off? What then?* The questions made him uncomfortable and strangely emotional. *I have no hope of living forever,* he mused. *I haven't obeyed Christ's command to repent and be baptized.* [21]

Rolling over, Zach hit his hand against the bookcase that was his headboard. It wasn't a hard hit but it knocked a large book onto his pillow. Having a bookcase for a headboard was a fantastic idea when he wanted to read at night, but it wasn't great when he thrashed around in his sleep. Reaching over wearily, he picked up the book to shove it back on the shelf. It was his old Picture Bible, tattered, worn and falling apart. When he was eight, it had been his favourite book. He had read it every night. With a sigh, Zach shoved it back onto his shelf.

It took Zach a long time to get back to sleep. It was hard to keep the nightmare from returning. *If I were to die now, there's nothing more,* [22] his anxious thoughts kept repeating. *I know what God has offered. I know Jesus gave his life, so that we can have*

---

[21] Mark 16:15-16
[22] Psalm 49:16-20; Mark 16:15-16; John 3:16,36; 12:48; Acts 16:30-33; Romans 6:1-12; Galatians 3:27-29; 1 Peter 3:21

forgiveness.[23] *I know he wants me to commit my life to Him in baptism.*[24] *I will probably do it someday – maybe even next year,* he assured himself, *but, I'm just not ready to make any big changes yet! I don't have my life in order. And... I just don't feel anything in my heart,* he sighed. *I'd be a hypocrite to pretend otherwise. One day maybe...*

Tossing and turning, Zach imagined what it might be like to stand before Jesus at the judgement seat. "Why didn't you accept my call to salvation?" he could hear Jesus asking him. "I gave you every opportunity. In a world full of darkness, you were one of the few who saw the light! Why did you choose a few short years of pleasure over eternity with me?"

Zach groaned, tormented. He tried to divert his thoughts by replaying his dance with Melissa, but in those lonely, silent hours, he couldn't dismiss his conscience so easily.

Maybe Bible Camp will do me some good, he acknowledged. *Even if I can't play sports and I don't have any fun perhaps it's where I need to be. It might make a difference.*

It was a whirl of activity the next morning when everyone was getting ready to leave. Since there were going to be only four of them travelling to Manitoulin, Uncle James had decided he wanted to take his own vehicle. However, when they tried to pack Zach and Esther's things into the Honda Pilot, it soon became apparent that they weren't going to fit. Even with only four people, there was still a lot of stuff to take: suitcases, sleeping bags, tents, tarps, coolers, a fold-up barbeque, as well as Aunt Sandra's bins of craft materials. Reluctantly, Uncle James began moving things over to his brother's old Astro van.

Jake was trying to pack, as well, for his basketball camp. In the midst of all the activity, just as Jake was zipping up his

---

[23] John 3:13-18; Romans 5:6-10
[24] Mark 16:15-16; Acts 16:30-32; 1 Peter 3:21; Galatians 3:27-29

loaded sports bag, Zach's Smartphone rang.

Jake picked it up. It was Brett.

"Hey, Jake," Brett said. "Look, I've heard that you might rather go to Bible Camp. Now I don't want you to feel... "

Jake interrupted. "No, that's not true. I want to go to the Basketball camp."

"Look, Jake," Brett said patiently. "I don't want you to feel bad about the money I spent. Sure I'd rather you get this training, but I understand how important the Bible Camp is, as well. The money is not a problem. There's another kid on the team that I am sure I can talk into taking your place. I don't want you to worry about offending me. You make your choice based on what you think is best and I'll support you."

For a moment or two Jake was speechless. Everything that he'd carefully considered during the night flashed before his mind. *Brett is giving me one more opportunity to choose. I don't need to feel obligated. I don't have to do this.* He weighed up the options again in his mind. He was very torn. Then he remembered how distant he felt from his friends in Ontario. *No one calls. No one cares.* He thought about the challenging theme for the week, "In the Last Days Perilous Times Will Come." He sighed. The basketball camp had professional coaches. He might be the star player on the team next season after getting this important training. They might win the Provincials. Playing sports all day would be a lot more fun than sitting through hours of talks. Plus, he was finding it hard to concentrate on Bible talks lately; it might end up just being a huge waste of his time.

"I'd rather go to Basketball camp," Jake reaffirmed. "Someone's got to fill Zach in on all the secrets."

"You're sure?"

"I'm sure!"

Ending the call, Jake knew he was now fully committed. The decision had been made and he didn't want any more hassle about it. Shrugging off any niggling doubts, he said a quick goodbye to Esther and Zach who were stuffing their suitcases into the van and took off to the nearby park. Jake didn't want to watch Zach leave. Brett was coming at noon to pick him up and Jake was already packed and ready to go.

    Basketball camp, here I come! he thought. *I can't wait!*

CHAPTER 11

Jake's Song

Twenty-four hours is a long trip in any vehicle, but while the Bryant's family van was old, it was quite roomy and comfortable. Zach could remember previous trips to Manitoulin Island with his whole family on board.

After spending the first couple of hours 'chilling out' with his seat reclined, his earphones in, choosing tunes off the iPod, Zach decided to join in the lively conversation. Uncle James and Aunt Sandra weren't like his parents – on his case for everything – or so he felt. With his aunt and uncle, Zach felt a friendly camaraderie. He liked them a lot.

"I guess this is going to be a rather quiet week for you, Zach," Aunt Sandra was saying with a compassionate smile. "How long has it been since you had that concussion?"

Zach calculated the time. Almost six weeks ago he had been in the final performance. He could well remember the adrenaline-rush on stage with Melissa. Nearly a week later he'd gone to the school dance and been beaten up by Shane's gang of *thugs*.

"It's been about five weeks since I got the concussion," he mumbled, choosing not to tell her about the blow he'd sustained at the basketball party. So far he and Jake had managed to keep the second, small concussion a secret. "The doctor says I have to avoid sports all summer."

"So, what will you do in the afternoons at camp?" Aunt Sandra asked, trying to make conversation.

The question led to a brainstorming session on afternoon

options for Zach. Uncle James suggested canoeing and offered to be his partner if he needed one. Esther suggested he could come with her to choir, which didn't appeal to Zach, even though he loved to sing. *It won't be anything like the musical!* he told himself. Aunt Sandra suggested he try Frisbee-golf or lifeguarding. She also told him about the Agora sessions where people gathered to ask the speakers questions regarding their talks.

Zach thought canoeing sounded the best. *I'll get an upper body workout at least.*

After a while, Uncle James asked, "Hey, Zach, do you have any music on that iPod that you'd like to share?" On the long, straight freeway Uncle James was feeling a little sleepy.

"Sure," Zach said, handing the small device to Aunt Sandra.

Once it was plugged into the dock, everyone was able to enjoy the vast variety of music that had been collected.

"Hey, that's Jake's favourite song!" Esther called out, as an upbeat song began to play.

"Really," Uncle James said, turning the song up a little louder. He listened to it carefully.

Zach liked the song as well. It had a good beat and a nice melody. The message was about God's love, His grace, His willingness to always take His children back, no matter what they had done. It was a song about mercy and forgiveness.

"What do you think of it, Uncle James?" Esther asked when it was over.

Turning the music down low, Uncle James considered his answer carefully. "Without God's grace and mercy, none of us would have *any* hope of salvation," he began. "I do agree with the sentiments, but we have to be careful we don't take God's grace for granted;[25] there is a big *'if'* involved.'[26]

---

[25] Romans 6:1

"What do you mean?" Zach asked.

"God's grace is there not only to forgive us, but also to *bring* us to repentance and to *change* our lives. [27] God is looking for repentance and spiritual growth in us, not stagnation. We are free to serve Christ, not to serve ourselves." [28]

Zach nodded slowly. He wasn't entirely sure what his uncle was driving at.

Aunt Sandra looked back at Zach and smiled. "Uncle James has had a lot of discussion on this topic with one of his Christian friends," she explained.

"I have," Uncle James agreed. "My friend Steve and I don't exactly see eye to eye on this. Steve sees the God of the Old Testament as very different from the God of the New. To him the Law of Moses was an experiment that failed, rather than a 'tutor to bring us to Christ'."[29]

Passing a large transport truck, Uncle James was preoccupied for a moment, but when they were safely in the right lane again, he continued, "I was just saying to Steve the other day, God could have sent his Son into the world immediately after Adam and Eve sinned. God promised them a savior right then,[30] but he waited another *four thousand years*. During those four thousand years, God instituted the Law of Moses which established His standards of behavior [31]and also convicted every human being as a sinner.[32] Regardless of how faithfully anyone tried to keep the Law, failure in one aspect made you guilty of

---

[26] 2 Chronicles. 7:14; Proverbs. 28:13; Matthew. 6:14-15; 1 Corinthians 15:1-2; 1 John 1:7-9; John 15:14

[27] Romans 2:4; 2 Peter 3:9,15

[28] Romans 6:18, 22; 8:2.5-17; 14:7; 1 Corinthians 7:22-23; 1 Peter 2:16

[29] Galatians 3:24-25

[30] Genesis 3:15

[31] Deuteronomy 4:5-8; 26:16-19; 28:1;

[32] Romans 3:9, 19-26; 7:7-16

all.[33] No one could keep it perfectly, or honestly feel that they *deserved* salvation."

"So it was impossible to keep?"

"It was impossible to keep *perfectly* and therefore could not bring salvation in of itself, which is why my friend would say the Law was a failure."

"Wasn't it?"

Looking at his nephew in the rear-view mirror, Uncle James asked, "What is one good reason the Law couldn't be a *mistake?*"

"Well, I suppose because God doesn't make mistakes," Zach reasoned.

"Good answer," Uncle James smiled. "God doesn't make mistakes, as He knows the 'end from the beginning'.[34] So of course the Law had a valuable purpose. It elevated the behavior of everyone who followed the decrees. It taught us the holiness of God – which He asks us to imitate. [35] I also believe that none of us can ever appreciate grace unless we are fully convicted in our hearts that we deserve the opposite. Once God established a healthy, respectful appreciation for His holy standards[36] and a conviction that we are all sinners deserving death, [37]He then brought His Son into the world and revealed more fully the new covenant of grace."[38]

"But wasn't David saved by grace after his sin with Bathsheba?"[39] Aunt Sandra questioned. "I thought there wasn't any sacrifice that could be given for sins of that nature."

"You're right," Uncle James agreed, switching lanes to

---

[33] James 2:10
34 Isaiah 46:10
35 Leviticus 19:2; 20:26; Hebrews 12:14; 1 Peter 1:13-19; 2 Peter 3:10-14
36 Proverbs 1:7
37 Romans 5:6-21; Hebrews 12:18-29
38 Galatians 3:19-24
39 Leviticus 20:10; 24:17; Psalm 51:1-17

allow for merging traffic. "Grace is given throughout the Old Testament, because God is the same God today as He was then. David confessed his sin and recognized he deserved death, and God told him he was forgiven. [40] God is and always will be a God of love and grace, but His mercy is extended to those who are convinced of His majesty and their own inadequacy. He looks to those who are poor and of a contrite spirit, and tremble at His Word."[41]

"So... do you like the song, or not?" Zach asked.

Uncle James chuckled. "I like it. It's good to be reminded that forgiveness is extended on the basis of mercy and grace, not our own good deeds.[42] I'm just saying, don't lose sight of the respect we should have for God and His righteousness.[43] No effective parent-child relationship can function with *unconditional* mercy, like this song portrays. There is a big 'if' involved. God laid a foundation of fear and holiness before sending His Son, for a good reason. I read an article just the other day, which said, 'Any so-called faith in Christ which professes to release men from obedience to God is not faith, but presumption.'"[44]

"What is the big 'if'?" Esther asked.

"The big 'if' is a repentant attitude and a true desire to change our ways to God's,"[45] Uncle James explained.

"Okay," Zach reasoned, still trying to determine how his uncle felt about the music, "I think you're saying that you like the song, but you feel it lacks balance."

"Exactly," Uncle James nodded.

---

40 2 Samuel 12:1-14

41 Isaiah 66:2; 57:15; Psalm 51:17

42 Ephesians 2:8-10

43 Romans 6:1

[44] Ngozi, Fibion, "The Test of Discipleship", *Gospel News*, May-Aug 2013 pg. 25. Print. See also: Jn.14:15,21;15:1-4,10-14; Matt.19:17;1 Jn. 2:4; 5:2,3; Rev.14:12; 22:14

[45] 1 Peter 5:6; Isaiah 58; James 4:1-10

Esther was thinking over everything that her uncle had said. "If good deeds aren't important to God, then why do we try to do good?"

Uncle James looked up at her in the rear-mirror and smiled. "Good deeds are very important, Esther," he told her. "Jesus did good works.[46] God commands us to do good works.[47] If we truly have faith in God and sincerely love Him, good works will flow from us.[48] But faithful believers do good not to earn anything from God or to receive praise from men.[49] They do what is right, when their hearts are right with God; when God's Spirit, as found in His Word, dwells in them.[50]

Aunt Sandra agreed with her husband and added, "The offer of eternal life and the sacrifice that Jesus made for us is too great to be repaid by any good deeds we can do.[51] Salvation is a priceless gift.[52] I like to think that good deeds are our way of saying thank you to God – if that's not too trite a way of explaining it."

"No, that helps," Esther assured her.

"You know," Uncle James added, "I have always liked the analogy William Tyndale used at one of his last defences. He was challenged about whether we are saved by faith alone, or whether we need works. His answer – by the way – *cost him his life!* He said, 'The fruit on a tree does not MAKE the tree good or bad. It simply demonstrates what kind of tree it is.' That quote has always stuck with me. If our lives lack good works, or are filled with *bad*

---

[46] John 10:32-33;
[47] Matthew 5:16; 2 Cor. 9:8; Colossians 1:10; 1 Timothy 5:10; 6:17-19
[48] Luke 6:45; 1 Timothy 1:5
[49] Matthew 6:1-8
[50] John 6:63; Romans 8:1-16; Galatians 5:16-25; Luke 17:7-10
[51] Matthew 18:23-35: Romans 5:6-8; 1 John 4:9-10
[52] Romans 6:23; 5:12-21;

works, we have to question the value of our belief."

Esther and Zach were quiet for a few moments. While Esther was contemplating how good deeds fit into the balance of life, Zach was considering the concept of 'unconditional mercy'. He wondered whether or not he fully appreciated the big 'if', and the right balance between God's mercy and judgement.

Noticing that it was six o'clock, Uncle James turned on the World News. There were a number of big stories. Five super tornadoes had ripped across the United States, causing millions of dollars of damage and over one hundred deaths! Massive dust storms had created extraordinary chaos in Arizona, fires were raging in California and an earthquake had hit Ottawa, causing structural damage to the Parliament buildings. To top it all, Turkey and Iraq had joined the growing alliance with Russia! The news reporter was calling it the 'Eurasian Union'. Britain and America were alarmed by the aggressive, bold moves of the new Union. Even Canada was voicing concern. Russian warships continued to stream into the Mediterranean, troops were massing at borders and weapons were being stockpiled in Syria and Iran. Everyone was asking why there was a need for such a strong military presence.

"Well, we all know what Russia intends to do!" Esther cheered. "Now you'll have some more things to add to your talk, Uncle James."

"He's doing that talk again this week," Aunt Sandra told her quietly, still astonished by the news they had just heard.

"It's all happening so fast, I can hardly keep that talk up to date!" Uncle James exclaimed.

But there's still a lot that has to happen, Zach told himself. *It could easily be another ten years before the Russian Confederacy moves down into Egypt and up into Israel.*[53]

---

[53] Daniel 11:40-45

CHAPTER 12

At Camp

The rest of the trip went smoothly as they did the daily Bible readings together, played a few travelling games and had a fantastic meal at a little French restaurant. They stayed overnight in a small hotel, rose early next morning and spent another long day in the van.

It was close to eight o'clock the next night when they turned onto Cooper Drive. Golden sunlight streamed though the darkening forest as they rumbled down the dirt road that led to the Manitoulin Bible Camp. A calm feeling settled over Zach as he and Esther gazed out the windows watching rays of sunshine flicker through the trees. Aunt Sandra tried to spot a deer.

Zach felt like he was returning home, coming back to another world with different friends and different priorities. *What kind of week will I have?* he wondered. *Will I be envying Jake the whole time or glad to be here?*

"How far is it from the highway to the camp?" Esther asked.

"About two and a half kilometres," Uncle James replied.

"Perfect!" Zach exclaimed. "If I run to the highway and back every morning I'll keep up some training. I don't want Jake to outdo me in everything when we get home!"

"Maybe I'll join you," Uncle James said, much to Zach's delight.

"Really?"

"Your Uncle James is training for the Kids with Cancer marathon again," Aunt Sandra said proudly. "He's running three times a week."

Uncle James' charity marathon had raised thousands of dollars to help kids with cancer. Zach and his family had cheered him on several times.

"Good for you, Uncle James!" Zach exclaimed. "I'd love to run together!"

Pulling in past the open gate, Zach looked up to see Noah and Brennan heading toward them. His old friends recognized the Bryant's van right away. Waving and shouting they followed the van all the way to the campsite where Uncle James always pitched his tent.

Parking under a large maple, Uncle James reached over and squeezed his wife's hand. "We're here, Beauts! Let the good times begin!"

Esther and Zach rushed out of the van to greet their friends. Uncle James and Aunt Sandra were eager to see everyone as well. They all hugged and remarked on the changes they noticed from the year before. Esther was taller than Brennan, and Noah had caught up to Zach.

"Hey, I like your hair!" Noah exclaimed.

Zach smirked and rubbed his hair uneasily. He still wasn't sure he liked his new hairstyle – or lack of one! It wasn't stubble anymore but it was shorter than he'd had it for years. He looked at Noah. A redhead with an athletic, wiry build, Noah had always been on the small side – but not anymore!

"How did you get as tall as me?" Zach chided affectionately, pushing his friend away.

"I'll be taller than you yet!" Noah grinned, pushing back.

"Never!" Zach exclaimed with a laugh. They locked arms and attempted to push each other backwards. It wasn't as easy as it used to be for Zach to win and they ended up on the ground in a laughing heap.

Then Hannah showed up with a group of four other girls.

Jake's shadow! Zach thought, remembering the crush she'd had on his brother ever since Jake had taught her and her friends how to play ping pong. As he picked himself up from the ground and brushed off the dead leaves, he did a double-take. Hannah was up to his shoulder and quite grown-up. *She's pretty,* he thought. *She's changed a lot!*

"Where's Jake?" Brennan queried anxiously.

"He didn't come this year."

Even as he said the words, Zach felt a strange sadness envelop him. The crestfallen looks on his friend's faces, made him feel worse.

"Is he working?" Hannah asked, twisting her long blond hair into a ponytail. Her lovely blue eyes were filled with disappointment.

"No, he's at a basketball camp."

"Ah! That's sad!" Brennan replied.

Zach felt like lashing out that it wasn't sad at all! That Jake was having the opportunity of a life-time! That if he hadn't had two concussions, he'd be right there with him… but as he opened his mouth to speak, suddenly he wasn't so sure. Maybe it was sad.

"I wish I had called him," Brennan mumbled more to himself than anyone else. "I just assumed he'd be coming."

"Hey, do you guys want to help us set up?" Uncle James asked hopefully, pulling two big blue tarps out of the van.

Noah and Brennan were eager to pitch in and Zach was thankful for a change in the conversation. Hannah and her friends left to look after her young nieces at the park. With Uncle James' assistance, the guys strung up the tarps and set up the tents, all the while catching up on the year that had passed. Noah and Brennan had finished grade twelve and were trying to choose between the universities that had accepted them.

"I was accepted at Dalhousie," Noah told Zach. "But at the

moment it's my second choice." He laughed. "Nova Scotia is a long way away!"

"But you could live with us!" Zach exclaimed excitedly. Having Noah back in Nova Scotia would be such a boost to all of them.

"That *would* be fun," Noah reflected.

When all the setting up was done, Zach went with his friends to see the lake. The sun was slipping down toward the horizon as they settled on the large rock by the shore. Delicate pinks and faded orange streaked softly across the sky. The clouds had a golden edging. Without much of a breeze, the water lapped quietly against the rocky shore and mirrored the sunset perfectly.

"I'm glad you're here, Zach," Noah said with warmth in his eyes. "I wish Jake had come too. You guys make camp so much more fun!"

Zach smiled. It was nice to know he was still part of the group. "I don't know how much fun I'll be," he sighed. "I had two concussions last month, so I have to avoid sports for the *whole* summer."

"You're kidding!" Noah and Brennan echoed in surprise.

"No sports? Zach, that's tragic!" Noah exclaimed.

"I know," Zach grimaced. He looked down the beach to the racks of overturned canoes. "I might take up canoeing instead."

"We were hoping you'd join us for three-on-three volleyball again. We've signed you up."

For a moment Zach thought about giving it a try… but quickly changed his mind. He had to be in top form for basketball. He couldn't risk another hit.

"Sorry, guys."

There were heavy sighs from both his friends.

Looking up, Zach saw Hannah and a bunch of her girlfriends walking down the beach. "Hey," they called out. "Ice-breakers are on at the teen classroom!"

"Ice-breakers!" Brennan exclaimed. "We'll be there."

That night as Zach wandered back to his campsite alone, he thought about the basketball camp. Sure, he was glad he had come to Manitoulin in many ways, but he wondered enviously what his brother was doing. Jake would have already had a full day of training, whereas Zach had been sitting lifelessly in a van, travelling for hours on end. Jake would be trying to decide if he wanted to try windsurfing or dragon boat racing, while Zach was stuck with canoes. Jake would be...

"Ouch!" Zach suddenly stubbed his foot on a rock. He had forgotten to grab a flashlight before the sun went down and it was dark on the playing field. "Oh, that hurt!" he said angrily. Then he heard giggling. It sounded quite close by.

"Who's there?" he asked, peering into the darkness. He couldn't see anyone.

"Just us." There were more giggles.

"Who's 'us'?" Zach didn't recognize the voice.

"Don't step on me," his sister's voice called out with alarm. "We're watching the stars."

"Isn't it past curfew?"

"Yes, but Uncle James and Aunt Sandra are coming to watch, too," Esther explained, sitting up. Zach could see his sister now – a dark shape against the trees, and quite close by. "Hannah's sleeping over tonight and Uncle James said he'd show us the constellations."

Two bright flashlights were coming their way. "Sounds cool," Zach said. "Mind if I join you?"

Aunt Sandra brought a large blanket that she spread out for everyone. Lying on his back beside Uncle James, Zach was amazed at the depth of stars he could see. The sky was exceptionally clear.

"It's so nice to get away from light pollution," Uncle James sighed.

Having a good knowledge of the stars and a cool laser beam pointer, Uncle James showed them various celestial wonders. He was in no hurry to rush everyone off to bed. Patiently he explained where the constellation of Orion was and pointed out the bright lights of the planets Mars and Venus. As they lay there, looking up at the marvelous display, Uncle James asked, "Why do you think God created so many stars? Just think – each one is a vast ball of burning gas, just like the sun. Why make so many?"

"Or why did God create so many species of trees?" Aunt Sandra added. "Just one variety might have been sufficient."

"It is amazing," Hannah agreed. "Why are there hundreds of different kinds of butterflies, and thousands of flowers?"

"So, why the overabundance, Zach?" Uncle James asked his nephew specifically.

Zach thought deeply. "Well, I suppose it demonstrates that God's creativity... and power is... profoundly vast!"

Suddenly Hannah called out, "Look, a shooting star!"

Zach caught the tail end. It had streaked right across the sky. "Amazing!" he shouted. For the next fifteen minutes they all watched intently for shooting stars. Aunt Sandra was the first to notice the second bright streak.

There were several minutes of silence as they watched for shooting stars and absorbed the awesome display of power above them.

Speaking quietly, Aunt Sandra quoted a psalm. "'When I consider Your heavens, the work of Your fingers, the moon and the stars, which You have ordained, what is man that You are mindful of him, and the son of man that You visit him?'"[54]

The verse resonated in Zach's mind long after he crawled into his sleeping bag. *God's creation is so magnificent,* he

---

[54] Psalm 8:3-4

considered. *I'm just a tiny speck down here on the earth in His eyes. I have all these huge plans for my life but so do millions of other people. What are my plans compared to God's?*

The answer was simple. *Insignificant!*

CHAPTER 13

Canoeing

Zach headed glumly to the small, sandy beach on Sunday afternoon. Uncle James had been asked to help run the baseball program, so he was unable to go canoeing with his nephew. Still, they had run five kilometers together that morning and Zach was pleasantly surprised how well his uncle kept up! Sure Zach had sprinted the last kilometer by himself, but Uncle James had a good, steady pace. He was in decent shape!

Standing on the beach, Zach wondered if he would be able to steer a canoe alone. *I could always go watch everyone play baseball,* he thought to himself. *Jayden's crippled brother told me I could cheer on the team. Isaiah is amazing,* he considered. *He always makes the best of his situation… and gives what he can to others.* But Zach didn't have the heart to cheer or throw balls back from the sidelines. The temptation to get involved seemed too compelling, so he had decided to stay away.

The beach was crowded with young parents and children. Kids were digging in the sand and wading into the warm, shallow water. It was a hot, sunny afternoon and gentle waves rippled across the small lake. A few young girls stood waiting for a turn in the paddleboats, but there weren't any teenagers around, *at all!* The teens were all playing sports. Zach looked up at the canoes on the racks. *If I paddle alone, will I go round in circles?* He sighed. *Guess I'll figure it out somehow.*

As the lifeguard helped him bring a shiny red canoe down to the water, Zach was surprised to hear someone call his name. Looking up, he saw Noah striding toward him with a tackle box and two fishing poles in his hand.

"Hey, Zach," Noah called out. "Can I join you?"

"For sure!" Zach replied enthusiastically. "You're not playing sports?"

"It's kind of hot out today," Noah shrugged. "Canoeing sounds more exciting."

Zach didn't reply but he smiled appreciatively. He knew it wasn't too hot. Noah would play sports any day regardless of the weather! He was very thankful his friend was choosing to join him.

Pushing out into the water and paddling hard together, they glided quickly across the lake. Noah guided them to a spot where he claimed his dad had caught a fish two days before. There were not many fish in the small, shallow lake – but every now and then someone would come back with a good catch. They took turns casting and rowing. While there was absolutely no action on their lines, they kept trying.

"Have you thought about coming back here for Youth Conference in August?" Noah asked, pulling the line in slowly.

"No. Not really."

"You could stay with us for the next five weeks and fly back when the conference is over."

Zach considered the option briefly. "I've committed to helping out with Uncle Peter's business," he said. After another moment's reflection he added, "and don't you have to do a whole lot of Bible study for Conference – like an entire *one hundred page workbook*?!"

"Not more than you could get done in the next month. And it's been a fascinating study! I've learned so much about the life of Job."

"Have you finished it already?"

"I have one chapter left. I've been working on it since February."

"When do you ever find time to do *Bible study*?" Zach moaned. "Between school, homework and sports I am flat-out until it's time for bed. I mean we read the Bible every night as a family

– but to do extra study on top of that? How do you do it?"

"I always spend an hour on it right after I get home from school."

"Hmmm, that's when Jake and I work out."

"Don't you get enough exercise playing sports at school?"

Zach thought back on intramurals and after-school practices. Often he even had Phys. Ed. He did get a lot of exercise, but, "Jake and I are in training," he explained rather proudly. "Our coach thinks we have a good chance of making it to the Provincials next year. We only missed out by one game last season! So, he's given us a strict exercise program. It's helped a lot."

"You need some time for spiritual training, too," Noah smiled. "Just doing an hour a day has given me a whole new perspective."

"A new perspective on what?" Zach questioned.

Reeling in his taut line for the third time, only to discover another entangled weed, Noah was disappointed. "It's hard to explain," he replied slowly, pulling the weed off his hook. "It's kind of like playing an intense game of basketball where you suddenly come alive and feel a surge of energy. When I get into Bible study, it becomes exciting and I discover things that amaze me. So often, I'll have some problem or issue I'm struggling to figure out – and I'll find *the answer* in the study I'm doing."

Looking up skeptically, Zach reeled in his own line to pull off the weeds. He couldn't imagine Bible study could compare in any way to a basketball game!

"Have you *ever* caught anything in this lake?" he asked his friend.

"No, but my dad caught a sixteen-inch bass the first day we got here!" Noah boasted. "I know they're out there somewhere."

But when another fifteen minutes went past and there hadn't been so much as a nibble, the boys changed plans and decided to see how fast they could skim across the water in the canoe. Action was what Zach loved – fast, intense, heart-racing action. It was even better when it ended with a refreshing spill into the lake. Noah had purposely leaned over too far!

CHAPTER 14

The Last Days

Classes began Monday morning. The study on Moses –
whom Zach had always thought he knew so much about,
challenged him to carefully consider the similarities between
Moses' life in Egypt and his own in Stirling, Nova Scotia. In
Egypt, Moses had grown up with an abundance of everything:
riches, pleasure and fame. Zach was quietly impressed that Moses
had chosen to give it all up, 'choosing rather to suffer affliction
with the people of God than to enjoy the passing pleasures of sin,
esteeming the reproach of Christ greater riches than the treasures
in Egypt; for he looked to the reward.'[55]

*Moses didn't choose to be with God's people because it
was more fun,* Zach reflected. *He gave up the fun to **suffer** with
God's people! Would I have made the same choice?* he asked
himself. *Or would I have chosen to remain a prince in the palace?*
It didn't take long to answer that question. He knew he would have
chosen to stay in the palace. *And what about my life?* he asked
himself. *Am I taking everything this world has to offer and
enjoying the 'passing pleasures of sin'? Have I ever given
anything up for God – anything that is difficult to part with?*

While the talks on Moses captured Zach's imagination, the
second series, 'In the Last Days Perilous Times Will Come'
impacted him to truly re-examine every aspect of his life! It had
been a whole year since Zach had last escaped from all the
distractions of the world and allowed God's Word to take hold of

---

[55] Hebrews 11:24-26

his heart.

Uncle George, as everyone affectionately called him, began his talks Monday morning telling the teens that he was going to take them through a study of the 'Last Days' – the time period right before Christ's return. "We all know this is where we are in history," Uncle George stated, "we are in the *last days*'. Jesus questioned whether or not he would find persistent faith on the earth when he returned.[56] So as we investigate the warnings the Bible gives us about *our* time period in history, we need to be constantly asking ourselves – how does this apply to us? And especially how does it apply on a *very personal* level?"

Growing up in a household that read the Bible every day, Zach was familiar with the passage that Uncle George took them to in Second Timothy chapter three. However, he had never considered it personally.

"Now, as we read through these verses," Uncle George said, "I want everyone to think carefully about whether or not our society fits this description – or whether you think more time is needed for it to become this corrupt." Looking in Zach's direction, Uncle George asked him to read out the verses to the class.

A little skeptical that society could already be as bad as it would get before Christ's return, Zach read the passages slowly. As he read he thought about each characteristic in light of his youth group and his classmates at Stirling High. "'But know this,'" he read, "'that in the last days perilous times will come: For men will be lovers of themselves, lovers of money, boasters, proud, blasphemers, disobedient to parents, unthankful, unholy, unloving, unforgiving, slanderers, without self-control, brutal, despisers of good, traitors, headstrong, haughty, lovers of pleasure rather than lovers of God, having a form of godliness but denying its power.

---

[56] Luke 18:8

And from such people turn away!'"[57]

He looked up at Uncle George in astonishment when he was done. *Everything fits!* he thought.

"Thanks, Zach," Uncle George said, and then he began to go through each characteristic in more detail. Uncle George even had newspaper quotes to prove these characteristics were the prevailing attitude. The scariest part was that Zach began to see himself in the verses! Had he become just like the civilization which was soon to be destroyed? How often had his parents told him that he thought the world revolved around him? *I've been very self-centered recently,* he considered, *disobeying my parents, lying to them, unthankful for what I have and unloving. In the last few months I've acted in a 'headstrong, haughty' manner, determined to live life as I please, regardless of what anyone else thinks. And with the school play I certainly loved pleasure more than God – the musical came before everything! Am I like the people described here as having a 'form of godliness' – calling myself a Christian – but denying God's power to transform my life?* Always before when Zach had compared himself to the other 'renegades' in his youth group, he felt confident that he was leading a fairly good life, even if he hadn't yet chosen to be baptized. After all, he wasn't doing drugs, or obsessed with violent video games. He'd never even had a girlfriend. But now faced with the list of wrong attitudes in Second Timothy three, he felt guilty. He left class that day with his head down, carefully thinking things over.

What if these really are the last days, the last minutes before Christ returns? he pondered. *I know I'm on the wrong side. I need to change!*

---

[57] 2 Timothy 3:1-5

CHAPTER 15

The Boys Cook Dinner

"I feel so out of shape," Zach moaned Wednesday morning at breakfast. "I haven't done anything the past few days." He and Uncle James had made great plans for jogging the camp road every morning, but with evening devotionals, teen choir practice, and card games until midnight, it was difficult to rise early the next day. So far, they had only jogged once.

"In that case, maybe I could challenge you to an arm wrestle," Uncle James grinned. "A whole week without training and you might be on par with me."

"Bring it on!" Zach was eager for the challenge and Uncle James put up a good fight. There were a few tense moments when the challenge looked like it could go either way, but three times in a row Zach flattened his uncle's arm in less than a minute.

Folding his defeated arms together, Uncle James sat back and studied his nephew with amusement. "What do you think, Sandra?" he asked, his brown eyes twinkling. "Would Zach reach my *incredible* level of fitness, if we kept him out of training for a whole month?"

Esther was proud of her brother's strength. "I hate to say it, Uncle James," she exclaimed, "but even if Zach didn't do any training ever, you might need to go back in time a little… hmmm, maybe ten years, to beat him!"

Her uncle chuckled. "What are you saying?" he asked, mockingly indignant. "That I've lost my physique?" He flexed his arm muscles. "There's still a good bulge here!"

Aunt Sandra and Esther laughed as Zach showed off his

biceps; they were considerably bigger.

"Ten years ago, Zach wouldn't have had a chance!" Aunt Sandra chipped in supportively.

"That's my wife!" Uncle James smiled. Then he seemed to think it over more carefully. "Just a second… ten years ago Zach was only seven."

Aunt Sandra tried to explain what she really meant but it ended in laughter.

Turning his attention back to his nephew, Uncle James said, "Well, Zach, you have been paddling every afternoon, getting an upper body workout, so maybe that's not your area of weakness. Perhaps we should try leg lifts."

"How would you do leg lifts around here?" Aunt Sandra laughed affectionately.

Uncle James pondered the matter carefully. "I know," he said with a smile. "Let's see who can do a tree-squat the longest."

"Tree-squat?" Esther queried, but Uncle James was already heading toward the large maple that sheltered his campsite. With a grin, Zach positioned himself in front of a birch, facing his uncle.

"You're timing us, Beauts?" Uncle James called out.

Aunt Sandra moved her arm so she could see her watch and gave the countdown.

Zach and his uncle dropped down to a squat position with their backs against the tree. Time ticked by and Uncle James' legs started to shake. He held on for a bit longer, even though his face was going red, while Zach held his position with ease. Finally, Uncle James admitted defeat.

"One minute and twenty-seven seconds!" Aunt Sandra exclaimed.

Zach held on for another whole minute before pronouncing victory.

"Maybe you're not so out of shape after all," Uncle James

grinned, patting Zach on the back.

Zach laughed.

"Just remember," his uncle added in a more serious tone, "that 'bodily exercise is profitable for a little; but godliness is profitable for all things.'[58]" Rubbing his nephew's short hair affectionately, Uncle James added, "Just because you can't see your brain growing bigger, don't discount what's happening in there this week."

Zach nodded. Maybe things weren't as bad as he thought.

"Why don't you invite your friends over for dinner tonight?" Aunt Sandra suggested suddenly to Zach and Esther. "I have enough chicken for at least four extra people."

"Can I invite Hannah and Elizabeth?" Esther asked.

"I could ask Noah and Brennan," Zach considered.

"Sure!" Aunt Sandra said. Then she remembered something. "Oh, you're giving the talk tonight, aren't you?" she said to Uncle James. "Maybe tonight isn't a good night for company."

"Right – and we have the Agora session until five. That leaves us a little short on time."

"Esther and I could cook the meal," Zach suggested. "Just leave out some instructions for us."

"Really?" Aunt Sandra asked.

Esther nodded fervently. "Mom leaves me instructions all the time."

As Aunt Sandra dubiously considered the matter, Uncle James gave the answer. "They'll have fun with it, Sandra," he said. "Give them a chance."

Then Uncle James looked at his watch. "Hey, it's almost eight-thirty!" he said. "We'd better get over to the pavilion. Time

---

[58] 1 Timothy 4:8

for classes to start."

Once again, that morning, Uncle George's class was thought-provoking and challenging. The day before he had considered 'the scoffers' that would come in the 'last days',[59] looking particularly at the negative effect the theory of evolution and the philosophy of humanism were having on society's worldview.

"Today's class," Uncle George announced at the very beginning, "is about the decline of morality in the world and the effect that licentious living is having on believers.

"Here's an interesting paradox," Uncle George continued, "Today we have gays and lesbians clamouring for the 'right' to be married, while many heterosexual couples are disregarding *"marriage"* and initiating sexual relationships long before making a covenant to one another. Ungodly behaviour is becoming commonplace, even among those who profess to be 'Christian', but we must never lose sight of God's standard of morality. Remember, young people, it is not for the world to define morality for us. [60]As believers we must hold onto the standard that God has set."

Uncle George had the class turn to several passages on the matter. The one that struck Zach the most was First Corinthians six, verse nine. Hannah read the passage from the NIV, "'Do you not know that the wicked will not inherit the kingdom of God? Do not be deceived. Neither the sexually immoral nor idolaters nor adulterers nor male prostitutes nor homosexual offenders nor thieves nor the greedy nor drunkards nor slanderers nor swindlers will inherit the kingdom of God.'"

"Be not deceived," Uncle George repeated firmly. "If God is warning us not to be deceived, that means that we may easily

---

[59] 2 Peter 3:3
[60] 2 Corinthians 10:12-18

find ourselves justifying these actions and behaviours, especially when we see them so prevalent around us. But in God's eyes, sexual relationships outside of a marriage covenant are wrong – regardless of how 'committed' we may feel we are to the relationship! If we choose to engage in sex before marriage and justify our actions, the warning is that we may be rejected at the judgement seat. 'Marriage is honorable among all, and the bed undefiled; but fornicators and adulterers God will judge.'"[61]

"And notice too," Uncle George pointed out from First Corinthians six, "that 'homosexuals' and 'sodomites', are among the 'unrighteous'. Homosexuality is *not* an 'alternative lifestyle' that God recognizes, whether a 'marriage' has taken place or not![62] It is wrong for a man to marry a man, or a woman to marry a woman. Don't let the world convince you otherwise. "The Apostle Paul urges us in First Corinthians, 'Shun immorality. Every other sin which a man commits is outside the body; but the immoral man sins against his own body.' [63] God wants to be Lord of our bodies and dwell in us as His holy temple. [64] All sin comes from our heart, [65] and we are all afflicted with varying weaknesses toward one sin or another. But *every single one of us* can make a choice whether to enflame and follow the base desires of our hearts, or pray for God's help to overcome the flesh, deny ourselves, and seek His righteousness." [66]

"Now in saying all that," Uncle George added in softer tones, "There is forgiveness for those who have sinned but sincerely repent. If you cry to God for help, and don't 'make provision for the flesh' [67] God will help you to overcome. He

---

[61] Hebrews 13:4
[62] Romans 1:24-32; Leviticus 18:22; 20:13; 1 Timothy 1:9-10
[63] 1 Corinthians 6:18 (RSV)
[64] 1 Corinthians 6:13-20
[65] Mark 7:18-23
[66] Matthew 26:41; Luke 22:40-46; 1 Corinthians 10:13
[67] Romans 13:13-14

wants you to overcome! He promises to make a way of escape for every temptation, but we have to choose to take it.[68]

Terry, one of the older teens interjected, "Isn't all sin equal? You just said that everyone struggles with sin in one way or another. So if I have sex before marriage, or break the speed limit, or yell at my parents, or become a homosexual… it's all *just* sin. We're all sinners. We can't help ourselves. All we can do is to trust in God's grace and mercy."

"It's true that 'the wages of sin is death',"[69] Uncle George smiled, "and in that sense, regardless of what we do – we all deserve death. But – the consequences of some sins far outweigh others. I may break the speed limit and face a fine of two hundred dollars. However, if I choose to kill someone when I'm angry, I will likely be in prison for the rest of my life. I will feel great remorse for the pain and loss I have caused others. And don't be deceived, the consequences of *sexual immorality* can play havoc with our future relationships and emotional wellbeing."

Zach couldn't help think of his father's oft-quoted axiom, 'The Christian life isn't the path of least resistance, but it is the path of least regrets.'

Terry was shaking his head.

"There is also a big difference between wilful sin and accidental sin," Uncle George added kindly. "There is no sacrifice to cover *wilful* sin; there wasn't one in the Old Testament and there isn't one under Christ. Hebrews chapter ten, says, "'For if we sin willfully after we have received the knowledge of the truth, there no longer remains a sacrifice for sins, but a certain fearful expectation of judgment… "[70]

"What is 'wilful' sin?" Hannah asked.

"The word means 'willingly, to act with intent and

---

purpose, premeditated',” Uncle George told her. It's a decision to sin, rather than an accidental lapse of weakness.”

“But, we're under grace,” Terry argued. “The Law of Moses failed because humans are too weak to keep God's laws. We just need to believe in God's grace to save us despite our failings. We can't be righteous; God makes us righteous if we have faith in Him.”

Uncle George opened up the discussion for a class debate. For ten minutes many opinions were aired and a few passages were suggested. Hannah found a verse that supported what Uncle George had been saying. She read out First John two, which says, “Now by this we know that we know Him, if we keep His commandments. He who says, ‘I know Him,’ and does not keep His commandments, is a liar, and the truth is not in him. But whoever keeps His word, truly the love of God is perfected in him. By this we know that we are in Him. He who says he abides in Him ought himself also to walk just as He walked.’”

In many ways, Wednesday's class was the most intense appeal Uncle George had given all week. In the canoe, that afternoon, Zach and Noah spent a great deal of time discussing the issues he had raised. Lulled into thinking that because ‘*everyone was doing it,*’ it must be okay, Zach felt the pathway he had once contemplated taking was suddenly barred with a large “Road is closed” sign. For the first time ever, Zach was thankful that Melissa was going out with Shane! *Whoa, if I'm going to live by God's standards, I need to be very careful who I go out with.[71] Melissa would drag me down so quickly!*

Zach came back to his tent early that afternoon, drenched head to toe from another canoe race that ended upside down in the lake. As soon as Noah had changed into dry clothes, he came

---

[71] 1 Corinthians 15:33; Proverbs 13:20

over. Unfortunately, Brennan was unable to join them for dinner as his family had already made other plans.

Noah and Zach were eager to get dinner ready. Esther hadn't returned from the sports field yet, but Aunt Sandra's instructions had been left on the picnic table, stuck under the edge of a large cooking pot.

"Okay," Zach said, scanning the list. "It looks like we're cooking chicken strips, rice, and making a salad. What would you like to do, Noah?"

"I've never made a salad," Noah replied, "but I can probably fry the chicken."

"I'll leave the salad to Esther," Zach said. "I haven't made one of those either." He picked up the box of rice and examined the instructions on the box. "This sounds foolproof. I'll do the rice." Setting the box down, he consulted Aunt Sandra's list once more. "Oh yes!" he exclaimed. "She wants us to make chocolate pudding. Yum! I love chocolate pudding!"

Chocolate pudding wasn't on Brett's healthy eating list. Zach figured that since he was taking the week off from exercise, he was also exempt from the diet. As Noah got the propane stove going and set the grill plate on top of the burners, Zach read the pudding box.

"We're supposed to add two cups of milk to each of these packages," he told Noah. "Only trouble is, I used the last bit of milk on my cereal this morning. Maybe Aunt Sandra picked up some from the camp store."

Checking the cooler, Zach quickly determined they were still out of milk. He took the chicken strips out of the cooler for Noah.

"No milk," he said. "So what do you figure we should do?"

"Maybe we should just leave it," Noah suggested. "Aunt Sandra might have some other dessert tucked away."

"Do you know how long it's been since I've had chocolate pudding?!" Zach asked.

Noah shook his head with a smile and began laying the chicken strips on the pan.

"Too long!" Zach stated, realizing he couldn't even remember .

Then an idea occurred to him. "We could do a little substituting! Isn't that the mark of an experienced chef?"

Noah rolled his eyes.

Zach thought hard. "Milk is only a liquid! Surely we could add another liquid and it would work just as well."

"Maybe you'll come up with a new recipe!" Noah laughed. "Aunt Sandra will be impressed, if it's good. What do you suggest? Juice? Water?"

"Hmm, juice might add the wrong flavour," Zach pondered. "But water should be fine."

So intent were the two of them in mixing up their watery, chocolate concoction that the chicken was totally forgotten until a burnt smell wafted past them.

"Oh no!" Noah exclaimed. "Not the chicken!"

Zach laid down the eggbeater to examine the extent of the catastrophe. The chicken was scorched on one side. "You get a *fail!*" Zach laughed, helping his friend flip the chicken to the other side.

Noah turned the burner down to low. "I'd better try for golden-brown on the other side," he smiled, "or I'll never live down my bad reputation. Girls don't forget things like that."

"I guess we need to get the rice cooking," Zach suddenly remembered. "And where are the girls? We need them to make the salad."

Glancing at his watch, Noah exclaimed, "It's five o'clock! Your uncle and aunt will be back soon."

"Okay," Zach said, trying to get everything in order. "I

don't know why this pudding isn't getting thick. We're only supposed to beat it for two minutes and we did it for ten. But you get the rice cooking and I'll work on the salad."

Zach placed the pudding in the cooler, hoping a little refrigeration might help it to set. The boys worked feverishly for the next ten minutes, expecting the others to show up at any time. The salad was ready and the rice cooking before Esther appeared with her friends, Hannah and Elizabeth. She was carrying *a litre of milk!*

"Sorry we're late," she apologized. "But our volleyball game just finished."

"Sure," Zach complained with a smile. "Leave us to do all the cooking while you girls *play!"*

He caught sight of the milk. "Hey, where did you get that?"

"From the store," she replied. "Aunt Sandra told me I'd need it for the pudding."

Zach and Noah exchanged sheepish glances. "Oops!" Zach said.

"What's wrong?"

"We already made the pudding," Noah replied confidently. "There's no need for milk. Zach's created a new recipe."

"Right. A camping recipe!" Zach announced, folding his arms across his chest. "When you don't have milk – use water." He puffed out his chest and stood tall. "Our recipe has less calories and is far more adaptable to a camp menu."

Hannah and Esther examined the pudding in the cooler. "And you can drink it like tea," Hannah giggled, letting the pudding pour off a spoon back into the bowl.

"I think something's burning," Elizabeth said, looking toward the stove.

"Oh, not again," Noah moaned, turning from the pudding catastrophe back to his chicken. Sure enough, the other side was beginning to scorch.

"Here come Uncle James and Aunt Sandra," Esther called out, seeing them in the distance, walking down the road. Zach looked up to see his aunt and uncle strolling across the sports playing field with three little children in tow. There were almost always children following Aunt Sandra; she had won many little hearts teaching at camp.

"Come on, girls," Esther said, "let's set the table. At least Aunt Sandra will find *one* thing done right!"

"What do you mean?" asked the indignant Zach. "*Everything's* done, thanks to us!"

Aunt Sandra took the young children to their own campsite and then returned to check on the meal. She did her best to be positive over the burned chicken, starchy rice and rather hastily put together salad. "I certainly appreciate the effort," she remarked with a smile, scraping black crumbs off the chicken strips with her knife.

Uncle James asked Noah to give thanks for the meal. Then he helped his nephews serve everything out. The rice didn't want to come off the spoon and the chicken was speckled and dry. "Just remember," Uncle James reminded them in his most fatherly tone, "that we thanked God for this food. If you were orphans living on your own in Kenya you might not have had anything to eat all day, or the day before."

"Yes," Aunt Sandra agreed. "That presentation we had this morning was heart-wrenching. I'd really like to help financially with all the good work that is going on over there, James. Imagine six hundred children in one Sunday School!"

"You'd be in paradise!" Uncle James chuckled.

Elizabeth held up her lettuce for inspection. Not only was it a huge piece but it was also quite wilted and brown around the edges. "Did anyone check the lettuce before they threw it into the bowl?"

Trying to keep a straight face, Zach answered with mock disdain. "We're camping, girls. Our motto is, 'waste not, want not.' I'm sure in the Sahara Desert such lettuce would be worth... maybe ten dollars a leaf!"

"It's more decorative this way," Noah added with a snicker. "The brown adds a little contrast with the green."

"Since when do you throw the whole cucumber into the salad?" Hannah asked, wrestling a huge piece with her fork.

"Hey," Zach remarked in defense, "we like veggies and dip. Who says it has to look like salad?"

"It all tastes the same, anyway," Noah added.

Zach looked up to see Hannah holding the core of a tomato on the tip of her fork. "And how do you explain this away?" she asked with a giggle.

"*Compost* and dip?" Zach suggested and they all began to laugh.

Uncle James and Aunt Sandra laughed with them and the laughter continued as the girls exaggerated their efforts to cut up the huge lettuce leaves and hacksaw their way through the charred chicken.

When everyone was nearly done, Zach went to check on the chocolate pudding. "Oh no!" he groaned, looking into the cooler.

Uncle James and Noah jumped up from the table to see what had happened. Aunt Sandra remained where she was with her face in her hands. Somehow the bowl had shifted and chocolate syrup had run over everything in the cooler. It was an incredible mess! Zach picked up the bowl and instantly jumped back as chocolate sauce dribbled onto the ground in front of him.

"So who wants dessert?" he asked laughing.

There were no takers among the girls.

Noah and Zach decided to try it, but after a few spoonfuls and lots of teasing from the girls, they declared the pudding an official disaster and poured it out in the bushes.

"Did we get at least a C plus?" Zach pleaded with his aunt after dinner, as he helped her clean out the cooler. Noah and the girls had kindly offered to do the dishes.

Aunt Sandra laughed, washing off each chocolate-covered package of food. "It depends," she said with a smile, "as to whether you're referring to the entertainment value, or your culinary expertise!"

CHAPTER 16

The Storm

"I'm sorry, man, I can't join you at the lake today."

Zach looked over at Noah and shrugged. "No worries," he said. "I don't expect you to canoe with me every day."

Noah sighed. "Brennan signed me up for the three-on-three volleyball tournament and he really needs me this afternoon."

"Go have some fun," Zach grinned. "But I'll expect you back on the lake tomorrow!"

Noah laughed and promised to be there. Then he hurried off to his game.

For a moment Zach wondered if he should go watch the tournament. It would be exciting. Brennan, Noah and Simon were up against some stiff competition and he could cheer them on. *But what if someone gets injured and needs a substitute? I'm not sure I could stop myself from jumping in.*

Wandering down toward the water, Zach was deep in thought. He and Uncle James had gone out for a jog that morning and while he hadn't told his uncle, he had felt very light-headed on the way back. *What a pain this concussion-stuff has been! Will it always be a problem for me? And what if I'm accidently hit again? Could it get worse?*

Not only was Zach feeling a little unnerved by the dizziness he had experienced that morning, the talk his uncle had given the evening before had kept him awake for many hours. Uncle James had made a strong case for believing that Jesus could come back at any time. Zach had always thought that he would see Israel dwelling in peace and the sudden Northern invasion before Jesus returned to gather his saints to him. However, Uncle James put forward the view that Jesus may come unknown to the rest of the world, [72]resurrect the dead, [73]judge those who are responsible to him and then spend time, maybe ten years or more, instructing and building a relationship with the saints. Uncle James called this 'the marriage feast of the Lamb'.[74] "The time when Jesus Christ is preparing the saints," Uncle James suggested, "may be when the prophet Elijah will go throughout the land of Israel turning 'the hearts of the fathers to the children, and the hearts of the children to their fathers' as it says in Malachi. [75] Elijah's work in preparing the nation to accept their Messiah may be what precipitates the time of peace and prosperity for Israel, spoken of in Ezekiel thirty-eight.[76] When Israel is feeling safe and secure, that is the cue for the Northern confederacy of nations to storm the Middle East, [77]take Egypt [78]and return to decimate Israel, cutting off two-thirds of the population. [79]It will likely be at this time," Uncle James said, "when all the nations are gathered against Jerusalem, that Jesus and his saints will come to the aid of the Jewish people."[80]

For the last couple of years, Zach had delayed making a commitment to God based on his view that there was still more to happen before Jesus could return. *What if Uncle James' view of prophecy is right?* he pondered. *What if there's nothing left that needs to happen before we are called away to judgement? What if Jesus truly could be here tonight, or tomorrow?* The answers to these questions were disturbing. *I know I'm not ready,* he told himself. *I'm totally not ready!*

---

[72] 1 Thessalonians 5:2-4; Luke 12:35-40; 2 Peter 3:10
[73] Acts 17:30-31; 2 Timothy 4:1; 1 Peter 4:5
[74] Matthew 22:1-14; Revelation 19:5-9; Luke 14:13-24
[75] Malachi 4:5-6; Matthew 17:10-13
[76] Ezekiel 38:7-12
[77] Ezekiel 38; Zechariah 14
[78] Daniel 11:40-45
[79] Zechariah 13:8-9
[80] Zechariah 14:2-5

As Zach neared the beach, he was surprised how intense the wind was down by the shore. White caps topped the waves and foamed up on the sand. A dark cloud lay on the horizon. *Looks like a storm is brewing,* he thought. *Maybe we'll have rain by nightfall. I hope it doesn't hit until we're all in our tents asleep. Rain and camping don't mix well.*

Going against such a wind would make it very difficult to canoe alone. Zach knew he would almost certainly find himself turning in circles. He put on a lifejacket and looked down the shoreline for anyone he could invite to go with him… and then he saw Hannah.

Striding down the beach in a bright pink T-shirt and white shorts, Hannah appeared to be looking for someone. Catching sight of Zach she waved and began walking toward him. "Do you need someone to canoe with?" she asked, hopefully.

"Sure," Zach said with a friendly shrug. Taking a second lifejacket from the clothesline that hung by the shore, Zach handed it to her. Hannah would be welcome company. *Did Noah say something to his sister?* he wondered.

As they were bringing the canoe down to the water, one of the lifeguards warned them to be careful. "I haven't let any of the younger kids go out today," he said. "That wind is awfully strong. Something is blowing in. Don't go too far."

"We'll be all right," Zach assured him. "It might be tough heading out but at least we'll be blown back to shore!"

"Just stay close by."

Zach nodded but he thought the lifeguard was over-reacting. If the wind had been blowing in the opposite direction the warning might have been necessary.

Insisting that he steer, Hannah climbed into the front of the canoe. "I didn't have any sports this afternoon," she said, taking off her sandals. She preferred bare feet whenever possible. "Our team got knocked out of the tournament after our second game!"

114

Privately, Zach pondered that Hannah's team hadn't had a chance. He had seen the names on the sports bulletin; three fourteen-year old girls up against older teen guys – what were they thinking?!

It soon became apparent to him that Hannah wasn't sure how to canoe either.

"You don't need to paddle on both sides; just stick to one," Zach told her.

"Okay."

"Are you comfortable holding the paddle like that?"

"Not really."

"Try moving your hands further apart."

"Okay. I've never done this before," she giggled.

"Really?"

"Are you being sarcastic?" she giggled again.

"Of course not! You look like a pro. I was going to ask you for lessons."

A large splash of water landed on his shorts. Zach smiled. Of course he could have easily drenched her in return but he didn't want to do that. The wind was chilly.

"It'll be an easy trip back," he reminded Hannah. "The wind will blow us in."

She turned around to give him a friendly smile. Sometimes Zach found her smile enchanting. This was one of those times. Hannah's smile was warm and inviting. Whenever he began to compare her to Melissa, though, the enchantment quickly faded.

"I really enjoyed your uncle's talk last night," Hannah said, taking a break from paddling and turning to face him.

Zach nodded thoughtfully. He'd noticed during his uncle's talk that Hannah was diligently taking notes. It looked like a good way to keep focused on the class. He thought he might try it sometime.

"What did you think of the talk?" she asked.

"It was good," Zach admitted half-heartedly, straining at the paddle.

"Just – *'good'?*" she questioned with a puzzled expression. "That talk made me *so* aware of all that is going on in the world! What with Russia becoming a guardian to Turkey, Iraq and Iran, and building up ships at Port Tartus – and many nations condemning Israel and calling for Jerusalem to be an International city – everything is happening just as God said it would. All nations are going to be gathered against Jerusalem very soon.[81] I've decided when I get home I'm going to get baptized."

"Right away?" Zach exclaimed, paddling harder since Hannah had decided she'd rather talk.

"Well, I might need one or two more baptismal classes," she considered. "But my dad has been going over things with me for a year and now I want to speed it up. Jesus could return at any time!"

A shiver went down Zach's spine. "But you're so young," he objected. "Aren't you only fourteen?"

Digging in with her paddle again, Hannah glanced back reproachfully. "I know people who have been baptized at fourteen. It's not *that* young! Besides I'll be fifteen in a month."

"Sorry," Zach apologized, realizing he had upset her. "I guess your brother was baptized at fourteen and Jake was only a year older."

Hannah smiled. It was obvious she remembered that detail well.

"But didn't you feel, after your uncle's talk, that Jesus is going to return any time now?" she questioned earnestly. "It's so close! I want to be ready. Your uncle quoted that verse, 'He who believes and is baptized will be saved.' [82] I know how important it

---

[81] Zechariah 12, 14; Joel 3
[82] Mark 16:16; See also: Acts 2:38, 10:48; Romans 6:3-8; 1 Peter 3:21

116

is to be '*in Christ*' and have our sins forgiven. I want to be a part of the promises." [83]

Zach looked back to shore. They were making very slow progress, especially with only one person doing the work. He didn't really want to discuss this topic. His own thoughts were disturbing enough. Bending his head to the wind, he paddled with all his strength.

"Are you baptized, Zach?" she asked, digging in again with her paddle.

He had hoped she wouldn't ask that question. "No."

"So, don't you feel the urgency?"

"Sometimes."

Seeing how hard Zach was paddling, Hannah put in more effort as well, for a while. She stopped asking deep, penetrating questions. Zach was relieved. His uncle's talk had been unsettling but he still wasn't sure what it meant for him. *People have been preaching about the nearness of Christ's return for years,* he told himself. *It's certainly getting closer every day – but I don't think it's time to panic.*

Eventually, they made it out to the middle of the lake. The wind was getting stronger and the sky was clouding over.

A drop of water landed on Zach's arm. Then a few more landed on his face. He brushed them off, thinking that the wind was spraying the lake water against them.

"It's raining," Hannah called out. "Should we head back?"

Looking up at the sky, Zach realized that the dark cloud which had been on the horizon was now looming above them. "Sure," he agreed, but then it began to pour.

A freak storm had blown in quickly and with the rain came a fierce wind. There were even pellets of hail. As Zach attempted to turn the canoe around, the waves were coming across the lake so

---

[83] Galatians 3:27-29: 2 Corinthians 5:17; 1 Thessalonians 4:16

high that some were splashing over the sides of the canoe. Hannah was trying to say something to him, but Zach couldn't hear; he could barely even see; the rain was so heavy!

They managed to turn the canoe around but were swamped by a wave that was at least two feet high. The canoe began to sink and they scrambled to find a bailing can. As the warm lake water began to pour in around them, Zach looked up to see a look of shock on Hannah's face. Wearing clothes, neither one of them had planned to go swimming.

Overturning into the shallow lake, the canoe floated upside down. Its former occupants floundered in the choppy water, attempting to find their footing in the thick mud below. Not for a moment did Zach feel they were in any danger, especially not with lifejackets on. The water only came up to Hannah's waist, with the occasional wave sweeping past her shoulders.

The noise of the rain and the wind was deafening; talking was nearly impossible. Zach motioned for Hannah to help him right the canoe. Together they tugged and pulled, flipping the canoe back over. Zach was thankful for its buoyant design. The paddles and safety kit had been carried off by the waves. They would have to retrieve them when the storm died down.

Hannah was searching for something in the water. "I've lost my sandals," she called out to him.

"We'll find them later!" Zach hollered back.

Bowing their heads against the driving rain, they pulled the canoe toward the nearby shore. It was private property that was out of bounds to everyone at the camp, but in these exceptional circumstances they needed a safe haven to wait out the storm.

It was about fifty meters to shore and progress was slow, stepping over so many slippery, sharp rocks and tugging on the canoe. They were both relieved to reach the sandy beach and find shelter under the overhanging trees.

"They'll be worried about us," Hannah tried to shout over

the noise, as they settled on a rock under a large tree.

Zach looked toward the camp beach. He could barely see anyone or anything through the downpour and assumed that anyone on the distant shore would be unable to see them. "It'll be over soon," he shouted back.

As they sat crouched under the trees, drenched from head to toe and half-blinded by the pouring rain, Zach could see that Hannah was shivering badly. The wind was intense. Blowing against the wetness of their clothing it felt very cold. Zach contemplated whether or not to put his arm around her. He didn't want to put any ideas in Hannah's young, fourteen-year old head, but he didn't want her to die of hypothermia either.

"You cold?" he called out.

"Freezing!"

Reaching out, Zach drew her close.

"Thanks!" she said; her teeth chattering.

As they sat close together in the pouring rain, Zach imagined himself telling Jake about this very incident. *"Yeah, and Hannah was freezing cold,"* he heard himself telling his brother, *"so I had to put my arm around her to keep her warm – poor thing."* Would Jake care? He smiled to himself. It was kind of funny, in an ironic sort of way.

The wind began to die down and the rain decreased. Looking over at Hannah, Zach caught her amused glance in his direction and they both laughed.

"How did we get *here?*" he chuckled.

"I don't know," she replied. "I thought I was going for a nice little canoe ride – I didn't expect a... a... *shipwreck!"*

"Shipwreck!" Zach threw his head back and laughed. "It wasn't a shipwreck."

"Sure it was," Hannah smiled, her teeth chattering. "Our boat was swamped by the waves and we went down with the ship. It just wasn't a very deep lake... thankfully," she added with a grin.

"But we have our ship back," Zach protested.

"We had to rescue our ship," Hannah argued. "And now look around us," she said, "it's like we're stranded on a deserted island. We can't see any other people."

It was true that through the heavy rain they couldn't see far beyond where they were sitting. Zach could see the beach again but all the people had run for shelter. "But we could walk to them if we wanted to," he argued back.

"And I'll have to go deep-sea diving to find my sandals," she giggled.

"You're a nut," Zach laughed affectionately.

They continued to amuse themselves over whether or not they had been in a shipwreck until Zach noticed that the two lifeguards had reappeared and were anxiously pacing the shore and looking out across the lake.

"We'd better let them know we're safe," he called out. Standing up, he began waving his arms. Hannah did the same. Soon they could tell that they had been spotted. Picking up an extra set of paddles, the lifeguards climbed into a canoe and set off towards them.

Hannah was still shaking badly. "Keep your blood flowing," Zach told her, as he began doing jumping-jacks.

Following his lead, Hannah joined in and they jumped steadily until they warmed up enough to re-enter the water. With a little 'deep-sea diving' the sandals and safety kit were easily found. The paddles had washed up on shore.

CHAPTER 17

The Other Camp

After the very first day, Jake was certain he had made the right decision. Basketball camp was exactly what he needed to develop the skills that could make the difference next season! It was hard work; it was demanding, but he loved every minute.

Everyone woke at seven and did an hour of exercise before breakfast. The camp was in a scenic part of Nova Scotia, on a lake. The trail that Jake, Jayden, and all the others ran on every morning followed the shoreline. In the early morning sunlight, mist rolled across their pathway. Loons and herons busied themselves catching breakfast in the calm, peaceful water. It was a beautiful sight! Jake felt like he could run for hours in such a picturesque setting.

With a weak ankle, Jake didn't start off as the fastest runner. However, he set his sights on moving up the line from day to day. He aimed to at least match the Black Hawks' players. Competitive juices were flowing strong and he yearned to regain all the muscle power he'd lost in the last two months.

Sometimes while he was running on the trails or lifting weights in the training room, Jake thought about what his brother would be doing. He knew he wouldn't be playing in the married-versus-single competitions that Jake loved, or in any three-on-three volleyball games. Instead, he imagined his brother sitting on the hard wooden chairs listening to one boring talk after another as he slowly became more and more out of shape. *I'll be passing him by in every run next week,* Jake thought to himself with a smile.

Even when Jake thought about the old friends that his brother would be hanging out with, he didn't feel more than a twinge of regret. *I don't have to try and pretend to be someone I'm not*, he told himself. *Zach is probably trying to sound like he knows lots about the Bible and has faith in God and stuff like that – I get to be here with people who think I'm great just the way I am.*

Sometimes it bothered Jake to think that Hannah might be following Zach around, but then again, he was getting a good number of texts every day from Melissa, since she couldn't get in touch with his twin. *We can just trade girls,* Jake thought with a dreamy smile. *I wouldn't mind at all.*

After breakfast the coaches worked individually with all the attendees for an hour on developing their foul-shooting abilities. This had always been an area of weakness for Jake but by the third day he had gone from a sixty-percent average to eighty! Jayden was at ninety! *What a difference this will make,* he thought with delight. Playing center position, he was often fouled. Many times Brett had told them that games can be won or lost at the foul-line. In a close game the foul shots are vital.

In the afternoon, the boys were free to go cliff-jumping into the clear, deep water – without any slime or leeches. There were many other water activities to choose from: windsurfing, kayaking and wakeboarding. There was even a jet-ski. They had all signed up for a turn on the jet-ski! In the woods were high-ropes, climbing-walls and fabulous trails. Jake was trying it all and having a marvelous time.

Not everything was perfect. Sometimes the jokes were crude, and Jake was sure from the snickers and looks that a couple of the guys were passing around lewd pictures on their phones. Once or twice Jake had overhead the Black Hawks' captain whispering about the so-called 'insulin' injections that he gave himself after breakfast, which likely explained his 'ripped' physique. Jake was thankful to have Jayden with him, for moral support. Not that Jake was tempted to do drugs of any kind. He had no desire to ruin his body or his life in such a short-sighted way, but he felt stronger in Jayden's company. From what Jake had observed, he and Jayden were the only Christians there, or at least the only ones brave enough to admit it.

For the first few nights, Jake was so tired when they crawled into the thin, hard bunks that he fell instantly to sleep. However, on the fourth night he woke up around midnight. A few of the guys were huddled close together around Trevor – the Black Hawks' captain – laughing rather loudly. They were the same guys that had been passing around the phone pictures. An eerie blue light emanated from the center of the group and their eyes were focused on the source of that light. "Oh! That's so awesome!" one of them whispered, although not quietly enough. "Go back again!"

Whatever it was that they were watching on their laptop, they all seemed awestruck by one particular scene. "What's up?" Jake whispered curiously, sitting up in his bed.

"You gotta see this, man!" Trevor said quietly. "It's great!"

"What are you watching?" Jake asked warily. His good friend was still snoring heavily in the next bunk. Jayden had been proactive, bringing earplugs and an extra pillow to put over his head.

"Hell Rider. He jumps four trucks on his motorcycle!" Trevor whispered. "Check it out."

"Hell Rider!" Jake remembered seeing the movie on Brett's desk. If Brett owned the movie, it had to be okay. It looked so exciting! Eagerly slipping out of bed, he joined the others.

Police cars were chasing the motorcyclist, but he drove up the ramp of an empty car transport truck on the side of the road, picking up enough speed to jump four vehicles that had crashed in a pile-up blocking the highway. One of the officers tried to follow but didn't make it and slammed into the side of an overturned transport. The rest of the police cars came to a screeching halt in front of the blockage, with no choice but to watch Hell Rider speed away. Jake took a seat on the bed with the others. This was great! A movie in the middle of the night and no one to tell them to go to bed! It wasn't hard to become fully absorbed, until suddenly there was a scene with a girl. That was when he began to feel uncomfortable.

What's the rating on this? he wondered. *I can't believe Brett has this movie!* But Jake couldn't drag himself away, even when things got out of hand.

I won't watch this stuff anywhere else, he promised himself. *I'm only here for a week. Dad would ground me for a year if he caught me watching this stuff! But, as Brett says, Dad is rather extreme. Brett must think it's okay.*

Jake was surprised by the effect the movie had on him long after it was over. He didn't feel tired at all. Lying awake in the darkness he could hear Trevor and Kyle whispering across the room. They were comparing conquests they'd had with various girls and strategies on how to get what they wanted. It was not the first time Jake had heard such tales. The boys' change room at school was generally full of 'trash-talk', but this was the first time Jake had listened carefully. The sensual feelings the movie stirred up were way more powerful than anything he'd ever felt before and he relished the tales. Not only that, but the next day as he jogged around the trail and practiced his one-hundred-and-one foul shots, he kept wondering if the guys had any other movies to show... or stories to tell.

They did! After the lights were off, curtains were closed and almost everyone asleep, the laptop came out and the usual crowd gathered around. Jayden was invited but he was too tired to stay up – or so he said. Jake was just as happy his friend decided to go to bed. He had an uneasy feeling that Jayden's conscience might be stronger than his own. The second movie was worse than the first. None of the guys with the laptop were the least embarrassed to watch the graphic scenes that flitted across the screen. They repeated the most tantalizing ones. Jake kept telling himself he'd never do this again when he got home; his conscience burned with shame. Verses ran through his head, He who "shuts his eyes from seeing evil… Your eyes will see the King in His beauty;" "Turn away my eyes from looking at worthless things…"[84]

The salacious images and the crude, wild tales were hard to forget. Jake had always hoped that one day he'd find someone to marry. Up until now, that someone had always been a girl who believed in God and wanted to live by God's morality. Of course, she also had to be pretty, kind, intelligent, and fun to be with… However, marriage seemed an eternity away. *I still have to get through university, find a job and all that, never mind the effort it might take to find the right girl. How can I wait that long? Zach and I are probably the only teens in Stirling High, or even our youth group, who haven't tried things out. Do I have to wait? What if I experimented a little and then confessed my sins and repented? God will always take us back… won't He?*

Jake didn't realize that inside his heart, a monster was arising. Spiritually low, he lacked the godly wisdom to perceive that his thoughts were dangerous.

When it came time for everyone to pack up, Jake and Jayden got into a debate with the Black Hawks' players over who was most likely to win the Provincials. It was a dumb argument that both sides knew better than to engage in, but it delayed the packing up that needed to be done. The Black Hawks' coach stormed in and ended the dispute by demanding his players be in his van in five minutes.

Brett still hadn't arrived, so Jake and Jayden were in no

---

[84] Isaiah 33:15-17: Psalm 119:36-37; Psalm 101:3

hurry. They stuffed their clothes into their bags and shook off the dirt from their running shoes while the other players filed out of the cabin.

A text came in from Melissa:

Hey Jake. I'm seriously thinking of breaking up with Shane. He's never around anyway. Do you think I should? Does Zach still care about me?

It only took Jake a moment to respond.

Sounds like a wise move to me. As far as I know, Zach still cares, but if he ever changes his mind about you, I won't. ☺ Love ya!

With a smile he tucked the phone in his pocket. *My brother will be happy to hear she's going to ditch Shane,* he thought. *Lucky Zach!* With all the fanciful thoughts he'd been indulging lately, Melissa was appearing more and more often in his dreams.

The phone vibrated again. There was a response:

Jake – you're so funny! Please tell Zach I miss him. It's nice to know he has a double – in more ways than one. ☺

You bet!

Looking around the cabin, to make sure he hadn't left anything behind, Jake spotted something black under Trevor's bed. He stooped to investigate and was astonished to see the laptop.

"Trevor left his laptop!" he exclaimed. Jake stooped over and pulled it out.

"The Black Hawks left already," Jayden told him. "How can we get it back to them?"

"I guess I could drop if off at the administration building."

Dark thoughts entered Jake's heart. "Or I could take it home with me and see if I can find his address," he told his friend, all the while thinking, *Then I can enjoy it for a week or so... or... better yet, I could give it back when we meet up for basketball in November. I'll just say I was keeping it for him and I couldn't find his address. Then I can watch all those movies again – as much as*

I want. I'm sure Zach will love them too.

"Are you sure you want to take that trash home?" Jayden asked quietly.

Jake looked up at his friend in surprise. Jayden's eyes were searching; they pricked his heart. *Does Jayden know what's on this laptop?* he wondered. *I thought he was always asleep when we were watching stuff.* Unfortunately, Jake didn't have the courage to ask, or the motivation to talk things through with his friend and seek advice. Jake wanted the laptop; the beast within was crying out for more.

"I'm sure Brett will know how to get in touch with Trevor," he told his friend, avoiding his eyes. "I'll give it to Brett, if I can't find the address myself."

Inserting the laptop into his sports bag, Jake took one last look around the cabin before heading out the door. His bag was much, much heavier now. Inside, was ample sustenance to feed many monsters and spin his thoughts completely out of control.

Seeing it as sensational entertainment, unaware of the poisonous effect it would have on his heart, Jake stifled all pricks of conscience. Uneasy with the decision, but afraid to create a rift in their friendship, Jayden shrugged and silently followed his friend out the door.

CHAPTER 18

In the Heart

Uncle George's last class was on 'covetousness'. Zach had
seen the title in the program book and had an inkling the class
would be on materialism; his dad had often made such a
connection. The session began with the warning Jesus had given in
Luke twenty-one, about the 'last days'.

It was Hannah's turn to read the passage out to the class.
"'But take heed to yourselves, lest your hearts be weighed down
with carousing, drunkenness, and cares of this life, and that Day
come on you unexpectedly. For it will come as a snare on all those
who dwell on the face of the whole earth.'"[85]

"Notice what the world will be like when Jesus returns,"
Uncle George pointed out. "Jesus doesn't tell us we will have to
endure fiery persecution like believers in ages gone by – although
this is an ongoing problem in some countries. He isn't telling us to
pray that we might survive famines and terrible pestilences –
although there are believers today, in some parts of our world, who
struggle to find enough to eat. No, Jesus is telling us that the
majority of believers will be living at a time of plenty, with lots of
wasteful parties and pleasure-filled opportunities consuming their
lives. The pursuit of pleasure may be what will keep us out of the
Kingdom. Jesus says that if we become caught up with our
indulgent, busy society we may miss the signs of his return.[86] We
may not be ready!"

It hit home to Zach. He felt convicted that the indulgent
world by which he had been so mindlessly enveloped was

---

[85] Luke 21:34-35
[86] Luke 17:26-33; 2 Peter 3:8-15; 1 Thessalonians 5:1-7; Luke 8:14

128

suffocating his interest in spiritual matters. He had been willingly oblivious to the signs of Christ's return which Uncle James had listed in his talk the night before. *And I missed that same talk a few weeks ago going to a dance that left me with a concussion! These verses are a warning to me,* he marvelled. *I've been missing the words of Jesus. I'm not heading toward the Kingdom; I'm ignoring the call and running in the opposite direction.*

"Now, I've chosen to talk about covetousness in my last class," Uncle George explained, "because I believe this is one of the most serious issues drawing us away from God in our world today, especially in our Western world. The problem of covetousness affects rich and poor, young and old, and everyone, no matter where we live in the world. However, I do feel that in Western civilization the thorns are much thicker and many more are being choked."

Uncle George started with an interesting passage from Ezekiel chapter fourteen. In that chapter, God clearly told Ezekiel that He wouldn't listen to the men of Judah, because they had *'idols in their hearts'.*

"We know the way Josiah combated idolatry when he was the King of Judah," Uncle George reminded them. "Josiah went out and smashed every idol to powder."

Many of the teens nodded, remembering their study of King Josiah at Kids' Camp the year before.

Uncle George continued, "We talked this week about the advice Jesus gave us to combat a problem when it's taking us away from God. Jesus tells us to cut it off – whether it be an eye or a hand! It needs to be forsaken, blocked, tossed out the living room window and hurled far away![87] But how do we get rid of an idol in the heart? Has anyone ever struggled to combat an *idol in the heart?"*

---

[87] Matthew 5:29-30

The class looked uncertain. Zach wasn't sure what Uncle George meant. What was an idol in the heart?

Uncle George read Colossians three, verse one to five, from the RSV, "'If then you have been raised with Christ, seek the things that are above, where Christ is, seated at the right hand of God. Set your minds on things that are above, not on things that are on earth. For you have died, and your life is hid with Christ in God. When Christ who is our life appears, then you also will appear with him in glory. Put to death therefore what is earthly in you: fornication, impurity, passion, evil desire, *and covetousness, which is idolatry,'"* he empathized. *"'On account of these the wrath of God is coming.'"*

"What is the link to idolatry in those verses?" Uncle George asked.

Zach put up his hand. "It says that covetousness is idolatry – but I'm not sure I understand why."

With his PowerBible computer program on the screen, Uncle George showed them the meaning of 'covetousness'. "Covetousness", he said, "is the Greek word 'pleonexia', which means 'avarice, i.e. (by implication) fraudulency, extortion: covetous(-ness) practices, greediness'."

When Uncle George examined the root word 'pleonektes', they discovered it had the meaning, 'holding (desiring) more, i.e. eager for gain (avaricious, hence a defrauder).'

"In other words," Uncle George said, "covetousness is longing for something more, something you want to possess." Displaying the Ten Commandments on the screen, from Exodus chapter twenty, Uncle George pointed out the last commandment was, 'You shall not covet...'

"God told us not to covet," Uncle George said, "and He listed out various things that we are inclined to covet, just to make sure we get the point. What are we told not to covet?"

Brennan replied, "Your neighbour's mansion, his wife, his

servants or his animals, or anything that belongs to your neighbour."

"Now what might God add if He was giving this commandment today?" Uncle George asked with a smile.

The class had many suggestions – cars, iPods, iPads, Blu-ray players, expensive clothes, expensive pets, luxury cruises in the Mediterranean. The list went on and on.

Uncle George laughed. "I'm glad you're getting the point," he said. "Anything that competes with God and His Son for our hearts, our time and our dedication, is an idol. If we are willing to sin to get it – then it's an idol. So, we need to ask ourselves, what keeps *us* from having time or money to spread the Gospel and help those in need? What excuses are we giving for why we can't take part in the preaching efforts, or make the Bible class, or attend study days? What do we find ourselves thinking about, obsessing over, and crowding out spiritual thoughts?"

Uncle George gave everyone time to consider those questions and ponder them privately. It wasn't hard for Zach to answer the questions for himself. However, he recoiled at the thought of parting from the things he knew he cherished more than God. *Maybe they are okay as long as they don't come before God,* he told himself. *Maybe I just need to revamp my priorities.*

"Now, a further question to consider," Uncle George continued. "Let's say you own a nice sports car, but in order to pay for it you have to take a second job. With two jobs, you don't have time to do much else than work, sleep and drive your fast, flashy car. You may decide it is an idol for you. Can you get rid of it?"

"You can sell it," Noah suggested.

"You can," Uncle George agreed. "You can sell it, give it away, or even smash it, or burn it if you have to. It's a physical thing and it can be physically removed."

"But, what if you don't own a nice sports car, or even have the money to afford one, but you long for one in your heart? What if you wake up in the middle of the night longing for that gorgeous, brand-new Corvette, or that flashy blue Porsche? What if you find yourself consumed by schemes of how you can make enough money to buy that Lamborghini, or worse – find yourself thinking of ways to steal one? What will you do? How will you get rid of an idol *in the heart?*"

No hands went up; everyone just looked at Uncle George with blank expressions. They had no idea.

He nodded thoughtfully. "This is a problem you will face at some point in your life," he told them. "Do you think the problem will go away if you decide to never look at car magazines again and avoid going past dealerships?"

Everyone thought about it.

Brennan spoke up. "That might help, but you may still see one as you're driving on the highway."

"We're supposed to *flee* temptation,"[88] Hannah suggested with a shrug.

"Good point, Hannah," Uncle George praised. "And we often cite the example of Joseph as an example in that regard.[89] But what if you decide to flee from civilization and live in the remote mountains of British Columbia? Will you no longer have the idol in your heart?"

Some of the class thought it would go away; others weren't so sure.

"My guess," Uncle George said, "is that even in total isolation you may still be thinking about how you can get that gorgeous, new Corvette – *if it is truly an idol in your heart*. You can travel half-way around the world and it will still be on your mind. Any other suggestions?"

"Maybe you should just decide to get it," Zach offered

---

[88] 2 Timothy 2:22; 1 Corinthians 6:18; 10:14
[89] Genesis 39:1-13

with a smile. "Once it's yours, then you'll stop thinking about it so much and you can get on with other things."

Uncle George asked the rest of the class whether they agreed with Zach. Some did and some didn't.

"However," Uncle George replied to Zach, "if you have to give *everything* you have to get it – then you might find yourself worrying at night about someone taking it away, or what will happen if you crashed it. Or if you didn't have enough money to buy it in the first place, you might be consumed by working to pay for the lease. You may even feel guilty for spending so much time and money on yourself. Or – worse yet – if you had to steal it, you might find yourself conscience-stricken and worried that you will be discovered and arrested."

Everyone could appreciate the perplexity of the problem. "There *is* a solution," Uncle George smiled.

"Just tell yourself to forget about it," Noah chimed in. "Be satisfied with the old Dodge caravan that your parents don't want anymore. It has more room anyway!"

Noah's closest friends laughed, knowing that he had just 'inherited' an old Dodge caravan.

With a nod, Uncle George acknowledged this was a possibility. "Paul does counsel us to choose contentment," he agreed. "We can read his advice in First Timothy chapter six."

Zach skimmed through verses six to ten as they were read out loud. "Now godliness with contentment is great gain. For we brought nothing into this world, and it is certain we can carry nothing out. And having food and clothing, with these we shall be content. But those who desire to be rich fall into temptation and a snare, and into many foolish and harmful lusts which drown men in destruction and perdition. For the love of money is a root of all kinds of evil, for which some have strayed from the faith in their greediness, and pierced themselves through with many sorrows."

Uncle George pointed out the consequences of falling into

a covetous state and told everyone that contentment was a choice of mind that would help in the situation. "However," he went on to say, "some idols in the heart refuse to go away, regardless of how we might tell ourselves to forget about them. We may frustrate ourselves for years trying to overcome our fleshly desires by simply telling them to go away. We can't fight flesh with the flesh. Often such a focus on what we want to forget only leads to it lodging more firmly at the forefront of our mind."

He paused at looked at the class. "There is an aggressive, effective method to overcome an idol in the heart."

The class waited anxiously to hear the solution.

Beginning with the passage, "Do not be overcome by evil, but overcome evil with good,"[90] Uncle George explained that it is necessary to examine the source of the evil that is gripping our hearts and positively pursue the opposite. He took everyone to Ephesians chapter four and led them through verses twenty-two to the end. There he pointed out that Paul counsels believers to 'put off the old man' by putting on the 'new man' – created in Christ. If someone struggles with telling lies – they are to focus positively on *speaking the truth*. If they are tempted to steal – they are to concentrate on *giving* to others. If they find themselves swearing or speaking rudely, they are to make an earnest effort to *edify* others with wholesome words. Anger and bitterness are to be overcome by a deliberate attempt to be *kind* and *forgiving*. Ephesians chapter four is an aggressive, positively-focused plan to combat evil by doing what is good.[91]

"Now, not all of you will be tempted by the gorgeous, new Corvette you see parked on the street," Uncle George smiled, looking especially at the girls in his class. "But if your idol is a beautiful mansion or a wardrobe of fine clothes or other 'things'–

---

[90] Romans 12:21
[91] http://manitoulinfamilycamp.com/2011/RyanMutter/Ephesians

you have a desire to be wealthy. If this is your idol, then listen to what Jesus told the rich young ruler, 'Sell all that you have and distribute to the poor, and you will have treasure in heaven; and come, follow me.'"[92] Overcome the idol of mammon by *giving* your time and money to a worthy cause in Christ."

"Some of you," he continued, looking across the whole group, "may be filled with desire for your own fame, glory and honour – or pursuing the perfect, physically-fit body."

Zach squirmed.

"Are you bowing to the demands of the world?" Uncle George questioned. "Are you striving for glory and honour now – before the Kingdom? You may gain it for a few, short decades if you're lucky, but Jesus warns that you may gain the whole world and lose your own soul. [93] Choose to be like Moses, who walked away from the seducing opportunity for fame and advancement in Egypt, and suffered affliction with the people of God, instead."

"Perhaps some of you are coveting another person," Uncle George suggested.

Zach sat up straight.

"Are you finding yourself sinfully fantasizing about another person?" Uncle George asked the class. "If you have an imagination that spins out of control in destructive ways, harness your thoughts and efforts to turn that creative energy into something positive and helpful. Be inventive with a new preaching activity that you can throw your creative abilities into. Pray for God's help to edify that person spiritually. Use your imagination to think through ways you might help *them or others* to do what is right and grow in faith and service to God."

It suddenly occurred to Zach how much this all applied to him. He wanted Melissa… and Melissa didn't belong to him. He

---

[92] Luke 18:22
[93] Matthew 16:26

had never woken up in the night thinking how he could get a gorgeous, new Corvette, but he certainly had plenty of dreams about Melissa! Even here at Manitoulin, thousands of kilometres away from Nova Scotia, she was as much in his heart as when he was dancing with her side by side. He began to realize that he was consumed with a number of things in a far more powerful way than he was with God! Was Uncle George offering a solution that would work? *Until now my first goal has been to make Melissa my girlfriend,* he realized. *Perhaps I need to consider how I can help Melissa and Jayden find the Truth… and live forever. Maybe I need to use my imagination for a worthwhile project in service to God.*

Then Zach shook his head and sighed. *Even before that,* he told himself firmly, *I need to concentrate on becoming a 'new man' myself! How can I encourage others to be baptized and commit their life to Christ when I haven't even made that decision? It's time to change.*

CHAPTER 19

Forever Friends

Zach straightened his collar. Looking into the small mirror that Aunt Sandra had hung on a maple tree, he carefully added a little gel to his short stubby hair. It was the last evening of camp and as always, there were musical and dramatic performances from all age groups to close out the week.

One week was far too short. Zach couldn't believe how sad he felt that it was coming to an end so soon. He wished he could spend his whole summer here with Uncle James and Aunt Sandra, listening to the talks that were changing his perspective, hanging out with Noah and Brennan, and even... Hannah.

"That's quite a shirt!" Aunt Sandra commented, coming out of the trailer. She was dressed up to go to the evening performance as well.

Zach looked proudly down at his shiny, crimson shirt. It had come through the pummeling rather well. The rip in the sleeve had been expertly repaired by his mom and since the blood stains had been almost the same colour, there were no traces to be seen. It was still his favourite shirt!

"Trying to catch the ladies' eyes?" Uncle James teased, following his wife out of the trailer. He sniffed the air. "Nice smell!" he exclaimed. "Did you use the whole can of Axe?"

"Just trying to keep them mosquitoes away," Zach grinned.

"Right!" Uncle James nodded, fully unconvinced.

It was with a heavy heart that Zach followed his aunt and uncle to the main pavilion. "One week isn't long enough," he told

137

Uncle James, a little surprised by the wave of emotion he felt. "I've got to get back here for Youth Conference somehow."

Putting his arm around his nephew's shoulders, Uncle James chuckled. "If Allan is driving, I'm sure he'll appreciate your company."

"Yeah," Zach agreed. "He's been trying to talk us into going since January."

Noah was saving a seat for him in the pavilion and Zach took it appreciatively. He looked around for Hannah and saw her a few rows ahead with her friends. Her long blond hair was a mass of ringlets. Zach sighed.

"You okay?" Noah asked.

"I just can't believe this is already the last night," Zach moaned. "I'm not ready to go home."

"Then why not stay?" Noah asked, as if it was the easiest thing in the world to arrange. "My parents would be happy to have you."

"I'd love to!" Zach exclaimed. "But I have to work. Jake and I are helping Allan run Uncle Peter's landscaping business while he's in Jamaica." He paused reflectively. "But I am planning to come back for Youth Conference – somehow or other!"

"Yeah!" Noah cheered. "And see if you can stay for the week after, as well."

"Okay – and you're going to choose Dalhousie? Right?"

"I probably will," Noah nodded, "if I can stay with you." Then he paused thoughtfully and added, "You know, Zach, after all the great talks this week, I've been thinking I might just take this year off and do missionary work someplace. I'm finally out of school and free to make choices. I'd like to give a year of my life completely to God."

Zach nodded in stunned silence. *Noah wants to do missionary work? Noah wants to give a year of his life to God! Really?*

There were many performances that night, beginning with the youngest classes singing Bible songs, and then a play by the intermediates, and finally the teen choir. When eighty teens squeezed on to the platform to sing the songs they had been practicing all week, it was by far the largest age group. Zach found his place in the choir behind Hannah and tweaked one of her long golden ringlets. She turned and gave him one of her fully enchanting smiles. Zach smiled back. Hannah was looking quite spectacular.

The teens practise was more than evident and not one song was boring; in fact, Zach had been surprised by how much he had enjoyed the experience. The title of the final song was, *Here at Last*. It was a glorious piece of music that climaxed with a chorus rejoicing over the return of Jesus to the earth and the change we will undergo when we are granted immortality. [94]

As Zach sang with the others, he felt another wave of emotion. *What's wrong with me?* he wondered. *I'm becoming an emotional basket-case!* All week long he had been practicing the very same songs, but only now did he truly feel the impact of their meaning. "We will all be changed, in a moment grasped in time," he sang with the others, "in the twinkling of an eye, the dead shall all arise, at the trumpet's final call, when God is all in all."[95]

Zach actually felt as though the sentiments in the chorus were his own. Tears were welling up in his eyes. He really wanted to be there when Jesus returns and grants everlasting life to the believers. This meant something to him! It was in his heart! *How did one week change me so drastically?* he asked himself.

The campfire was blazing up into the dark night sky as Zach followed Noah and Hannah. Since the evening program had lasted longer than usual and there had been an ice-cream social

---

[94] 1 Corinthians 15:49-57
[95] Phil Rosser, *"Here At Last",* A Songs of Deliverance Project, 2011. www.theseventhday.com.au

afterward, the teen devotional was late in starting. It was almost eleven o'clock.

"You and Noah should talk your parents into coming out to Nova Scotia this summer," Zach told Hannah. "They haven't been back for years. They must miss everyone and the ocean."

"I'll try," she smiled sweetly. "I know they miss everyone. We all do. Maybe if something big was happening – like a study weekend, or a preaching campaign... or... even *a baptism...* they'd consider making the trip."

Zach looked over. He couldn't miss her meaningful glance. "There just might be a baptism," he said with a smile, "unless of course, the candidate fails the interview."

Hannah looked up excitedly. "You?" she asked.

"One of the Bryant twins."

There was only one Bryant twin that wasn't baptized. Hannah was elated. "We could get baptized on the same day and then *we'll* be twins!" she said eagerly.

With a laugh, Zach tweaked another one of her springy curls. "Maybe," he said. It was an interesting suggestion. He liked the way his friendship with Hannah encouraged him to live for God.

Picnic tables surrounded the campfire and Zach motioned to Hannah to sit beside him. She didn't need any convincing. All the teens crowded in and Noah and Brennan joined them on the table. Uncle Mark, who was Hannah and Noah's father, was giving the devotion that evening and he had brought his guitar. To begin with they all sang their favourite campfire hymns. Zach noticed that Uncle James and Aunt Sandra were across from them, singing along in the shadows. He remembered this was what Aunt Sandra said she loved best about camp. Looking up at the stars, he sang with the others, 'Blessed be the Name of the Lord... '

Zach felt closer to God than he had ever felt in his life. *'I'm ready to commit my life to You, Lord,"* he prayed. *"I thought I*

140

was missing out on all this world had to offer, but now I realise that what I truly want is right here with You. All that I've been chasing after is soon to be taken away, judged, destroyed and Your Son is coming back to set the world right. I want to be there with him. I want to help cleanse this earth and bring this whole world to see and know Your truth. Heavenly Father, please help me to change. Please help me to remember all this when I get back home, and not to set up idols in my heart where You belong.'

Uncle Mark stood up to give the devotion and everyone fell silent. The crackling fire could be heard distinctly. A whippoorwill cry echoed across the nearby lake. Using his flashlight to see his notes, Uncle Mark spoke about discipleship and what it really means to follow Jesus. He impressed on all of them what love Jesus had shown in giving up his life completely for the salvation of others. He reminded everyone of God's love in giving His Son and providing a way for believers to have their sins forgiven and to come 'boldly unto the throne of grace'."[96]

"And remember," he told them earnestly, "that Jesus said, 'If anyone desires to come after me, let him deny himself, and take up his cross daily, and follow me.'"[97]

Uncle Mark then talked about counting the cost and realizing that to follow Christ is to make a decision to give up one's life now to serve God and His Son. "For whoever desires to save his life will lose it, but whoever loses his life for my sake will save it. For what profit is it to a man if he gains the whole world, and is himself destroyed or lost?[98]"

"Serving God is a very serious commitment," Uncle Mark said, "because God wants our whole heart, soul and mind. [99] He's not interested in a half-hearted response."

---

[96] Hebrews 4:14-16
[97] Luke 9:23
[98] Luke 9:24-25
[99] Mark 12:30

"Now, I want you to look around at everyone here tonight," Uncle Mark said to the group, as he came to the conclusion of his thoughts. "You all have good friends back at home, where you'll be heading tomorrow. Some of them may be in the Truth, some may come to the Truth through you, but I want you to value the relationships you've made this week. These are your *forever* friends."

Zach looked around at all the faces in the flickering firelight. *My* forever *friends,* he mused.

"These are the friends you hope to live with eternally in God's Kingdom," Uncle Mark went on to say. "Value them. Help them. Don't lose touch with each other. Don't let them go."

Noah put his arm around Zach. In a sudden outpouring of affection, Zach put his arms around Noah and Hannah. "Forever friends," he whispered.

Hannah looked up with a smile and then she, likewise, put her arms around Zach and the girl sitting next to her. In a matter of seconds, the whole group had embraced each other in a circle; even Uncle James and Aunt Sandra were included.

Uncle Mark smiled and nodded his approval. "Encourage each other throughout this next year," he told them. "Tell your friends to hang on to God's promises. Don't allow each other to be swallowed up by the cares of this life, or 'the pleasures of sin for a season', but stand strong. When Jesus returns we want him to 'find faith on the earth'. We want him to find that *persistent* faith in us – don't give up!"

They all bowed their heads as Uncle Mark gave a prayer to end the evening. Uncle Mark prayed for all the young people. He prayed that God would keep them safe on their return home and strong in faith through the upcoming year. Zach felt tears build up behind his eyelids. He was glad it was dark.

When the prayer was over, many of the young people stood up to leave. The group hug slowly dissolved but Zach didn't want the evening to end. Seeing that it was past midnight and past curfew, most people were retiring to bed.

"Hey, do you have a cell phone?" Noah asked.

"A Smartphone actually – but it's at home," Zach replied, hoping Jake was taking good care of it.

Thankfully, Noah didn't ask why he had left it at home, he just said, "I'll give you my number before you leave tomorrow and then we can text each other."

"That would be good," Zach agreed. He looked over at Hannah.

"You can text me too," she smiled.

"Okay!" Zach said. "So, both of you need to give me your numbers tomorrow and maybe we should do emails, too. That means you both have to be up at seven o'clock to say... good-bye." There was a catch in Zach's voice and for a moment he didn't trust himself to say anything more.

"We'll be there," they assured him. Hannah touched his arm. "Goodnight, Zach," she said reluctantly. Uncle Mark had his flashlight in hand to guide her way back to the campsite.

Zach nodded and swallowed hard but he didn't say anything. He wasn't ready to say goodnight to anyone. *Goodbye* was going to be even harder!

CHAPTER 20

The Decision

Following Uncle James and Aunt Sandra back to their campsite Zach wished he could talk to someone. "Uncle James," he said meekly, "I guess we need to get our sleep tonight for the big trip tomorrow?"

Uncle James looked at him in a puzzled sort of way. "We'll need to be up early, Zach," he began to say and then he looked more closely at his nephew's face. "You okay?"

Zach didn't speak. He just shook his head and shrugged. Uncle James laid his hand on his nephew's shoulder and motioned to his wife to carry on to the campsite. Stopping to give her husband a kiss, Aunt Sandra said goodnight to both of them and made her way down the road with her flashlight in hand.

"What's up?" Uncle James asked, as they walked slowly out to the large playing field. It seemed so long ago that they had watched the stars on that very first night. Just as before, it seemed to Zach that the sky was teeming with millions of tiny, twinkling lights. There was no one else on the field. Around them, in the shelter of the trees, a few lantern lights shone softly, while families got ready for bed.

"Uncle James, this week has changed my life," Zach blurted out emotionally. Unwanted tears began running down his face. "I don't know what's wrong with me," he tried to explain to his uncle, embarrassed. "I have no idea why I'm crying."

"It's okay, Zach," his uncle assured him calmly, rubbing his back. "Concussions can lead to a heightened emotional state. But it's just you and me here, and I understand."

144

Waiting for his nephew to gain control, Uncle James was quiet for a while before he asked, "Why has your life changed, Zach?"

"I came up here wishing I had gone to the basketball camp with Jake," Zach explained with a shrug, "and now I… don't want to go home! I don't want to go back to being the person I was – and I'm worried that I will. Up here, I can see that the return of Jesus could be very soon – maybe before the Provincials, university, or all the other cares of this life that drag me down. I had forgotten how great my friends are here – how much I care about them – how much God's plan of salvation is so much better than anything the world offers. I forget so easily! I always lose touch with my friends here… and I need them, Uncle James. I need them to help me remember what's really important in life! What do I do?!"

Sitting down on one of the large rocks that lined the playing field, Uncle James looked up at Zach thoughtfully. "What do you want to do?"

Zach paced back and forth. "I want to be baptized. I *need* to be baptized! But I'm worried that I'll get back home and be sucked right back into the way I was before."

"Zach!" Uncle James exclaimed with surprise, standing back up to give him a hug. "That's wonderful to hear! You want to be baptized – that's great!"

The hug was warmly appreciated.

"But what if," Zach pondered uneasily when his uncle sat back down. "What if when I get back home I feel differently?"

"What will make you change your mind?" Uncle James asked.

Rubbing his short hair with his hand, Zach contemplated the matter. "Girls… basketball… being too busy," he listed.

"In what way?"

"I just forget about the long term view of it all. I get

wrapped up in the here and now, and before I know it, other things have crowded God out of my life."

"So, what's made the difference this week, Zach? How have you come to this new perspective?"

Zach thought long and hard. "I guess getting away from everything," he replied, "and all the great talks on the Bible." He paused and then added forcefully, "It sure helps a lot to have good friends!"

Uncle James considered the matter. "It's good for all of us to get away from the pull of the world," he agreed. "Up here, whether we've come to listen or not, we're spoon-fed. God's Word is poured into us and in this calm wilderness with no worldly distractions, that Spirit Word can take root in our hearts."

Looking around, Zach had to agree. The camp was a wilderness – rugged, natural, quiet and isolated from many of the tempting sights and sounds that modern civilization brings.

"But, Zach," his uncle continued earnestly, "God's Word isn't restricted to the wilderness or the desert. God can reach you anywhere if you give Him your ear. You've felt His power this week, even though you might have been initially resisting. Imagine what God will do for you, if you *willingly choose* to open your heart to Him."

"True."

"Listening to God is the first important step, Zach," Uncle James encouraged. "Making a commitment to Him is the next. You know then, that you won't be on your own. God will be doing all He can to help you win the battle. But, you may need to adjust your priorities. You know how hard you've been training to win the Provincials. If you want to keep this new perspective and grow in Christ, you'll have to ensure that every day you're getting your *spiritual* food and *spiritual* exercise. That will be vital to grow."

"Like prayer and reading?"

"Praying, reading, studying, and finding ways to live for

Christ. It takes time and commitment and thought. It may mean giving up other things."

Giving up other things? Zach sighed. *What would they be?* He wasn't sure he could give up anything, just yet. Here at Manitoulin, it had all been *taken away* from him – giving things up willingly would be much harder!

"Uncle James, that's what worries me," Zach confessed. "I'm not sure I'll be able to do that when I get home."

Uncle James looked up at him thoughtfully. "Pray about it, Zach," he encouraged. "Let God show you the way. I think you're ready to make this decision. God will be on your side."

The conversation went on much longer. It was late when Zach and his uncle finally headed to the campsite to sleep. Zach crawled into his sleeping bag with a new resolve that he felt confident he could sustain. He had asked Uncle James to make all the necessary arrangements for his baptism, once they got home. Following Uncle James' advice, he had decided he would set aside a time every day to work on the Youth Conference study, and aside from his job with EdenTree, everything else would have to revolve around his new goals. If he met up with Melissa, he planned to share his hope with her – but that was it. He wasn't going to try and date a girl who was pulling him away from God. *I'll invite her to my baptism,* he thought sleepily. *I'll invite her and Shane and Jayden. I'm going to focus on trying to share God's truth with Melissa – not winning her as my girlfriend.* He groaned and rolled over. It was easy enough to set such goals but he still wasn't sure how it would all pan out.

As he lay in the dark listening to the breeze blow wistfully through the trees, the crickets chirp quietly in the bushes and a blood-thirsty mosquito hover outside his tent window, Zach was very thankful for his uncle. Uncle James agreed with his new perspective; he understood that dedication to God was more important than winning any basketball game, or getting the best marks in math. *I think Brett understands that perspective too,* Zach reflected, remembering how considerate Brett had been about the basketball camp. *But 'considerate' isn't the same as 'encouraging',* he decided. *I think Brett struggles just as much as I do to keep godly priorities front and center. He's a fantastic basketball coach but he may not be someone that will give me the best spiritual advice.*

CHAPTER 21

Goodbyes

Zach paced back and forth in front of the washroom block, hoping Noah and Hannah would show up before he had to leave. Uncle James was still showering. The plan was that when he came out they would be leaving. They had twelve hours of driving ahead of them that day which would only take them into Quebec, and that was only halfway home. The van was already loaded up and left running. Having jumpstarted the dead battery once already that morning, Uncle James didn't want to risk losing the charge.

Looking at his watch, Zach saw that it was five to seven. Surely his friends would be coming soon! He wondered if he should go and wake them up.

"Hey, Zach," mumbled a weary voice.

Turning around, Zach saw Noah. He was wearing his pajama pants and a large grey hoodie. Two tired eyes peered out from the under the hood. Flopping against Zach, he gave him a heavy hug. "Goodbye, my friend," he said. "But God willing, in a few short weeks, we'll meet again... either here, *or in Jerusalem!*"

In Jerusalem, Zach pondered, realizing that Noah was hoping Jesus would return very soon! He clapped his friend on the back. "Thanks for everything this week," he said. "You have no idea how much you've helped me!"

Noah looked at him in a puzzled way. "Helped?" he questioned and then he smiled. "Oh yeah, I taught you how to fish... and how to flip a canoe."

"You did! And that 'char-broiled' chicken was amazingly charred!"

They both laughed.

"Zach!" A girl's voice rang out. "I'm so glad you're still here!"

Zach's heart skipped a beat. Only six weeks ago he had thought that Melissa was the only girl in the world for him, now he wasn't so sure. He turned in the direction of the voice as Hannah came running up to hug him. She was dressed in similar attire to Noah, except that her hoodie was purple.

"My alarm didn't go off," she laughed, as they embraced. "I planned to be up an hour ago. I would have been so upset if I had missed you!"

At this point, Uncle James came out of the washroom looking fresh and clean. "Ready to go, Zach?" he called out.

Zach nodded and then turned to his friends. "Okay, contact-details everyone." He passed them his information on slips of paper. Noah took the piece of paper from Zach and handed him a small piece of birch bark with his cell number and email address scrawled across it. It was barely readable.

"Would you like to decipher this for me?" Zach teased.

Noah read it out for him extra carefully.

Hannah handed him a folded note. "Read it later on your trip," she smiled. "And this," she added, placing a white quartz rock into his hand, "is treasure from the shipwreck."

Laughing, Zach clenched his fingers around the rock. There were many white quartz rocks on the beach, but this one was going to be extra special! He looked into her teasing blue eyes. "It was *not*... a shipwreck!"

"It was a *full scale* shipwreck!" she giggled.

Uncle James opened the sliding door of the van. Aunt Sandra and Esther climbed in.

Zach gave Hannah and Noah one more hug each, and with a sad 'goodbye' reluctantly took his seat, next to his sister. Uncle James tried unsuccessfully to get the sliding door shut. After fiddling with the latch and taking directions from Zach about where to find the 'magic spot' that required a hip-check, the door clicked tight.

Zach and Esther waved out the windows until everyone was out of sight. Then they looked at each other sadly.

"It's going to be a whole 'nother *year* till I see everyone again!" Esther said despairingly.

"We have to talk them into coming out to see us!" Zach decided, folding his arms across his chest. "I'll work on that when I'm at Conference."

"Lucky you!" Esther replied. Only fourteen, Esther was too young to attend Conference.

Aunt Sandra liked Zach's idea. "We should plan a special week over the Christmas holidays, James," she suggested with excitement. "Then we could invite all the kids' friends to come stay at our lodge."

"Oh, that would be wonderful!" Esther exclaimed. "We could have Bible talks at our Ecclesial hall, skate on the lake, go cross-country skiing around your house... "

"I'm sure we'd fit forty easily," Uncle James nodded, as they reached the outskirts of Mindemoya. He sped up when they reached the main highway.

From there the idea gathered momentum and kept their minds off the sad fact that, with the exception of Zach, they were heading far away from their friends for a long period of time.

At noon, Uncle James and Aunt Sandra turned on the radio to hear the news. On Manitoulin Island they had enjoyed shutting out the world for a week, but now they wanted to catch up on everything that had happened.

"This just in," the CBC reporter was saying in a sober, incredulous way. "California has been decimated by two major earthquakes overnight. Shortly after midnight the first quake took place along the San Andreas fault-line, only kilometers away from the city of Los Angeles. Measuring 8.5 on the Richter scale, the earthquake decimated the city. Los Angeles has been declared a state of emergency with hundreds of collapsed buildings and many freeways destroyed. Eight hours later a second quake with the magnitude of 6.3 occurred, one hundred kilometers off the coast of San Diego. Tsunami warnings are in effect all along the coastline and evacuations are taking place immediately. There is no word yet on how many people have been killed but estimates are in the thousands… "

"James, this is unreal!" Aunt Sandra exclaimed.

Uncle James looked over anxiously at his wife. "When is your brother getting back?"

"I don't know. I'm sure Laurie was going to be in San Francisco this weekend."

As they cruised along the highway, Zach listened intently to the conversation in the front seats. He had met Aunt Sandra's brother only once, briefly. Laurence Carrington was CEO of the Stirling Bank in Nova Scotia. He was an incredibly busy man, constantly travelling from place to place. From what Zach had gleaned over the years, Aunt Sandra often tried unsuccessfully to include her brother in her life. He remembered hearing her say that if she had a visit with Laurie once a year, she was doing well.

Taking out her phone, Aunt Sandra sent her brother a text. To everyone's relief, he texted back to say his plane had been diverted to Las Vegas and he would soon be on his way home.

"Oh, I'm so thankful!" she told Uncle James.

Nodding, Uncle James smiled and reached over to take his wife's hand. "You're a good sister, Beauts. I just wish you had a more loving brother."

Aunt Sandra smiled appreciatively in her husband's direction. "That's okay," she replied. "God's given me you and your family. I'm perfectly content."

As his aunt and uncle engaged in an endearing conversation, Zach gazed out his window at the ever-changing scenery. He wasn't sure why Aunt Sandra cared so much for a brother who never seemed to have time for anyone outside his business world. While he knew that Uncle James was very supportive of his wife's feelings for her brother, he also knew that his uncle was often frustrated with Laurence Carrington's lack of response.

Choosing to give his aunt and uncle some privacy, and uninterested in listening to CBC's ever-falling stock exchange report, Zach looked over at Esther. She was asleep. He pulled Hannah's note out of his pocket. He wasn't ready to have anyone tease him about Hannah just yet.

Opening it up discreetly, he read:

"Zach, I'm glad we got to know each other better this year at camp. I'm going to miss you! I hope you remember to text me. Love, Hannah."

At the bottom of the note her contact details were written clearly in pink ink.

"Hey, Zach," Uncle James said, as they came to a stop at a major intersection. "Did you hear that?"

"Hear what?" Zach replied.

"Remember that freak storm that blew through camp during the week?"

I'll never forget it! Zach thought to himself, but to his uncle he only said, "Yes."

"They just said on the news that it turned into a massive tornado up north. A trailer park was decimated."

"What unusual weather we've been having!" Aunt Sandra declared, as the light turned green and the old Bryant van lurched forward. "In the last five years we've had violent weather all over the globe."

"What is God trying to tell us all?" Uncle James replied.

Zach didn't say much, but he felt relieved he was making the choice to be baptized. Fluffing up his pillow, he laid his head

153

against it and tucked the note into his pocket along with the special rock. One week at Bible Camp just wasn't long enough. He could hardly wait to come back!

CHAPTER 22

Time to Chat

The next morning, when Zach opened the window-blind of their small motel room in Quebec, he looked out to see a cloudy, grey morning and torrential rain.

"I'll take the luggage out to the van," Uncle James offered as he finished his complimentary breakfast in the small hotel restaurant and turned away from the TV screen. They had been watching the special report on the earthquake in California while eating pancakes and syrup. Tsunamis had reached the coast during the night and caused massive flooding and extensive damage in San Diego and all the way along the coast line. The flooding had halted the rescue attempts in Los Angeles. Video clips of crumbled office buildings and twisted lengths of pavement half-submerged in murky sea water were staggering. Million-dollar houseboats, cars and massive luxury liners were scattered like mangled toys across the flooded scene of destruction. Some people were still being pulled alive from the wreckage, but the death toll had reached two thousand and was climbing steadily.

While Zach's eyes were transfixed on the screen, there was a news flash of an upcoming special report on the FIBA Basketball World Cup to take place in Boston in two weeks' time. *That would be cool to watch!* Zach thought, but Uncle James was already standing up to leave.

"I'll help you," Zach said, standing up.

"Thanks, Zach," Uncle James smiled. "If you don't mind bringing the suitcases down from our rooms, I'll take them out to the van. There's no need for both of us to get wet in this deluge!"

In about ten minutes all their luggage was loaded into the

van. However, when everyone dashed from the motel into the van, they realized that Uncle James was sitting in the driver's seat in very wet clothes!

"James, you really should change," Aunt Sandra pleaded. "Why don't you run in and put on some dry clothes?"

"I'll be all right, Darling," he said, reaching over to squeeze her hand. Driving away from the motel, he explained, "I don't want to get stuff out of my suitcase. Everything's packed in tight. Just turn on the heat and we'll be fine."

"Uh… the heat doesn't work," Esther chimed in as they turned on to the highway. "This van is very old."

"James!" Aunt Sandra begged.

But anxious to get back on the road, Uncle James couldn't be persuaded. As they sped down the highway, the heavy rain created foggy condensation on the windows. It was only a matter of minutes before Uncle James had to turn on the compressor. No one else minded the cool air blowing around, since it was such a warm day. But no one realized how cold the air circulation felt to someone sitting in damp clothes. As the others read and discussed the Bible readings for the day, Zach noticed his uncle shiver. However, they were deep in conversation over a verse in Matthew eighteen, where Jesus said, "And if your eye causes you to sin, pluck it out and cast it from you. It is better for you to enter into life with one eye, rather than having two eyes, to be cast into hell fire."

Uncle James asked Esther and Zach to come up with some practical applications of that verse. After all, it had been an important passage in the Bible talks that week. Zach struggled to think of an example that wouldn't impact his life too deeply. Esther was sitting beside him and might remind him later of what he had said.

Esther, on the other hand, had plenty of examples and was not afraid to share. "Well, for some people like me, novels and magazines are a problem," she admitted. "If the things we are reading are causing us to dwell on sinful thoughts, then maybe we have to get rid of those books. If they are in our home, they will always be there tempting us to read them again."

Aunt Sandra agreed with Esther and encouraged her to fill the void with books that would be helpful and encouraging. She reminded her niece of the passage in Philippians four, verse eight, that says, "whatsoever things are true, whatsoever things are honest, whatsoever things are just, whatsoever things are pure, whatsoever things are lovely, whatsoever things are of good report; if there be any virtue, and if there be any praise, think on these things."

Zach was quite happy when everyone forgot that he still hadn't come up with an example. He shrewdly turned their attention to the next few verses about the lost sheep. Uncle James reminded them that when Luke recorded the 'lost sheep' parable he added Jesus' words, "there is joy in the presence of the angels of God over one sinner who repents."

God doesn't want one little one to be lost, Zach reflected, looking at the passage. *There is joy in heaven when one sinner repents. This could be me. Is there rejoicing in heaven right now because I am making the decision to turn my life around?* It was powerful to consider that his decision could have an impact above. Then he pondered it all a little further. *Are there other little ones that God wants found? Are there other lost sheep?* He knew that there were… right in his own youth group back home. And those lost sheep were his friends.

Suddenly, Esther remarked, "I've got it!"

"Got what?"

"It just all came together for me!" she said excitedly to Aunt Sandra. "Do you remember, on our way to camp, we talked about doing good deeds?"

Everyone nodded.

"And then you just reminded me that if I give up novels I should fill the void with good material… which reminded me of the classes Uncle George gave this week. He told us that to overcome evil, we need to focus on doing good. So, I just thought that, perhaps, if we are filling our lives with doing good things for God – to say thank you to Him for the gift of salvation – it will help us to crowd out the evil that wants to pull us in the other direction!"

Aunt Sandra and Uncle James were happy to see Esther's enthusiasm.

"You're thinking it through all right!" Uncle James smiled.

"I like that," Aunt Sandra agreed, reaching over to squeeze Esther's hand. "When we fill our lives with service to God, we don't have time to get into trouble."

"Just don't think that sin won't find its way in the backdoor somehow," Uncle James cautioned. "However, I believe what you are saying is scriptural. Does it say something like that in Galatians chapter six, Beauts?"

Aunt Sandra found the passage and read it out, "'Do not be deceived; God is not mocked, for whatever a man sows, that he will also reap. For he who sows to his own flesh will from the flesh reap corruption; but he who sows to the Spirit will from the Spirit reap eternal life. And let us not grow weary in well-doing, for in due season we shall reap, if we do not lose heart. So then, as we have opportunity, let us do good to all men, and especially to those who are of the household of faith.'"

"There it is," Uncle James nodded. "Doing good is 'sowing to the Spirit', which reaps eternal benefit in our character development and spiritual growth. Sowing to the flesh leads to corruption."

A couple of hours later, after Uncle James had sneezed several times in a row, Aunt Sandra insisted that he pull over at the next gas station and change. That he did, and they carried on, with

Uncle James in dry clothing. But the sneezing continued.

"So, Zach," Uncle James said, as they drove along a straight stretch of highway, "since you've requested baptism, why don't you and I go over the important teachings of the Gospel message and just see if you're ready? We have a good ten hours ahead of us."

Zach was happy to use the time efficiently and took out his Bible. In between plenty of sniffling and a few sneezing attacks, Uncle James quizzed Zach on all the first-principle teachings in the Bible. They went through everything that Zach would be asked in a baptismal confession of faith.

"What causes us to sin?" Uncle James asked.

"Our lusts," Zach replied.

"Do you have... have...," Uncle James sneezed, "a passage for that?"

Zach thought hard. "There is one in the Epistle of James."

"What does it say?"

Looking it up, Zach found the passage in the very first chapter, verse fourteen. "'But each one is tempted when he is drawn away by his own desires and enticed. Then, when desire has conceived, it gives birth to sin; and sin, when it is full-grown, brings forth death.'"

"That is a really important passage to remember," his uncle nodded, keeping his eyes on the road. "That passage also shows us that temptation itself isn't sin; we sin when we give in to the temptation." Pausing first to blow his nose on a tissue that Aunt Sandra had handed him, Uncle James asked, "Are there any other places where we learn that sin comes from our hearts?"

Esther found a few verses in Matthew fifteen, which said, "But those things which proceed out of the mouth come from the heart, and they defile a man. For out of the heart proceed evil thoughts, murders, adulteries, fornications, thefts, false witness, blasphemies."

Aunt Sandra quoted Jeremiah seventeen, verses nine and ten, "'The heart is deceitful above all things, and desperately wicked; who can know it? I, the LORD, search the heart, I test the mind, even to give every man according to his ways, according to the fruit of his doings.'"[100]

Taking it to the next level, Uncle James asked Zach to read Hebrews chapter two, verse fourteen. He then gave him a challenging question. "How did Jesus, in his death, destroy him who had the power of death, that is, the devil?"

While they sped down the wide, straight highway into Nova Scotia, it took a few references in Romans to work out the answer. The book of Romans deals extensively with the problem of sin and death. Looking at chapters five and six they collected some important points, such as, 'through one man sin entered the world, and death through sin, and thus death spread to all men, because all sinned.'[101] They found a chapter where sin is spoken of as a king that 'reigns' unto death.[102] Zach discovered verses which say we can choose to be 'slaves' of sin and earn the 'wages' of death or servants of righteousness and be given 'the gift' of eternal life in Christ Jesus.'[103]

Trying to summarize the information, Zach said, "It seems that similar analogies are used for both sin and the devil. The devil has the *power* of death; sin *reigns* unto death and *pays wages* of death. They seem to be spoken of interchangeably."

"So how did Jesus destroy the devil in his death?"

"In at least two ways," Zach replied. "He never gave in to sin during his life – therefore he didn't deserve the wages of death. And when he died on the cross, his human nature died also, of course, and never tempted him again. He was made immortal when

---

[100] See also Genesis 6:5; 8:21; Proverbs 6:18; Mark 7:21-23
[101] Romans 5:12
[102] Romans 5:21
[103] Romans 6:16,23

160

he rose from the dead."

"I would agree," Uncle James nodded. "Jesus' human nature was a source of temptation for him, just as it is for us. [104] Because Jesus never sinned the grave could not hold him[105] and now those who are associated with Christ through baptism can have their sins forgiven. God has determined that His Son's faithful sacrifice breaks the hold that sin and death has on believers. Instead of God's creation being destroyed by sin, sin has been destroyed by Christ."

The conversation carried on for hours and Zach wrote down many passages on the back page of his Bible. He asked questions too, clarifying certain matters that were still confusing him. Even Esther joined in the conversation. The time went by quickly and soon they were crossing into Nova Scotia.

---

[104] Hebrews 2:17-18; 4:14-15
[105] Acts 2:24

CHAPTER 23

Repentance

Uncle James' cold worsened as they drove home on the familiar highways. Finally, he asked Aunt Sandra to drive while he took a nap. Esther moved up to the passenger seat to talk to Aunt Sandra, and Uncle James slumped into the seat beside Zach. Propping pillows up against the window, he was soon sound asleep and snoring heavily.

With a few hours' driving left, and his uncle in need of peace and quiet, Zach had plenty of time to think. He knew that the decision he was planning to make would require a lot of changes. His relationships with Melissa and his parents would need to change. He had to pull back in his pursuit of Melissa and he had to change his attitude toward his dad. Lately he and his dad had become increasingly antagonistic and Zach knew that it was partly his fault for the downward spiral. *It's going to be difficult to make changes with Dad,* he felt, resentfully. *It's going to be really hard to admit I've been wrong. I feel like he owes me an apology for treating me like a child and never being around to do anything fun. But… I know Mom and Dad are only trying to keep us safe from evil. And it's not like they are spending all their time on themselves; everyone in the Ecclesia seems to need them. They help a lot of people. I don't like the way they are always suspicious of my motives and whether I'm telling the truth, but I guess I have given them plenty of reasons to doubt.*

Deep down, Zach knew that his rebellion had caused his dad to lose faith in his son's ability to make good decisions. Lies and deceit had often seemed a shortcut to freedom but they had done deep damage to a true open spirit of trust.

It's going to be hard to say sorry, he mused, *but I know it's something I have to do. God says I need to honour my parents.*[106] However, the longer Zach imagined himself asking for forgiveness, the easier it became in his mind. *I hope I can do it as soon as I get home,* he pondered. *I need to start off right, before things have a chance to go wrong.*

It was late when Aunt Sandra drove up to the twins' home in Stirling, Nova Scotia. Zach's dad was still awake and came out to help sort through the luggage and exchange vehicles. Uncle James was very tired, sneezing and coughing intermittently. They said quick goodbyes and then Aunt Sandra drove off to take her sick husband home.

Zach's dad turned to Esther first. "Good to see you back, Honey," he said cheerfully. Giving Esther a big squeeze, he then turned to hug Zach.

As it had been for the last couple of years, the hug seemed distant and forced. Zach felt resentment welling up inside him again. There was no doubt in his mind that his dad loved Esther, and that Jake was his favourite son. It made him angry that his dad didn't seem to care for him as much, even though Zach knew he had pushed his father away many times!

"Hi, Dad," Zach said evenly, returning the distant hug. He swallowed hard. Inside was a strong desire to stay aloof, play it cool and immediately retire to his room for the night.

No, I've got to do this, Zach told himself. *I've got to do it tonight.* "Dad, I need to talk to you," he mumbled.

His father looked surprised. "Right now, Zach? It's one o'clock in the morning!"

"Yeah, I know," Zach sighed. *Maybe,* he argued with himself, *it can wait till tomorrow.*

---

[106] Matthew 19:19; Ephesians 6:2

"Night, Dad," Esther called out, heading up the stairs. "We had a fantastic time! I'll tell you all about it in the morning."

"Night, Esther," Zach's dad said affectionately. "I'm looking forward to a full report!"

I'm sure if Esther wanted to talk now, Dad wouldn't complain, Zach thought unhappily.

"You need to talk to me, Zach?"

"Yes, I do."

His dad motioned toward the living room and they both sat down on the mismatched couches, facing one another. "What's up?" he asked. "Is something wrong?"

"No," Zach replied, "I had a great week at camp." Even such a simple admission was difficult at first; however, it spurred him on. "I guess it was what I needed – a chance to get away from everything and time to think. The talks were great; my friends were great and I wish I could have stayed there for the rest of the summer."

"If you want to go back out, Zach, we'll find a way."

There was no mistaking the loving support his father was willing to give him. Maybe apologizing wouldn't be so hard after all.

"I'd really like to go to the Youth Conference," Zach said. "I know it's a lot of Bible study, but I think it will be good for me. I think I need it."

There was a happy, surprised smile on his father's face. "Zach, I'm pleased to hear that," he said. "Let me know if you need any assistance."

"Thanks," Zach replied gratefully. Now it was time for the tough part. Zach took a deep breath. "Look, Dad," he said. "I… well… I've made a big… no, a *huge* decision to… well… to change my life. I'm really sorry for all the trouble I've caused you lately. I was chasing the world and now… now I want to get baptized – as soon as possible!"

It was rare for Zach's dad to be speechless. For a moment or two, his dad looked at him, his disbelief slowly giving place to joy. "Zach!" he said, standing up and holding out his arms.

Moving forward, Zach gave his father a hug.

"Zach," his father said again with the utmost sincerity, holding his son tight in a warm embrace, "I am overjoyed! Mom and I will do whatever we can to help you. This is wonderful news!"

"Thanks, Dad," Zach mumbled gratefully. "I'm sorry for all the trouble I've caused."

Holding his son at arm's length, he said, "Thank you for your apology. I appreciate it. We have had some tough times – you and I. I'm sorry for all the harsh words I've spoken. Sometimes I've been too quick to react, without knowing the full story."

"That's okay. So have I."

"You know that Mom and I have felt a lot of anxiety about you, because we love you and want you to have a part in God's promises. I'm *so thankful* you went to camp. I wish Jake had gone with you! But then again, I wish we *all* had gone."

There was a deep look of concern in his father's eyes, as he spoke of Jake. Zach was surprised. "Maybe he'll come to Conference with me," he suggested. "He needs to get away as much as I did."

"I hope you can talk him into it," his dad said, in a dubious tone.

What's up with Jake? Zach wondered. Was something wrong?

CHAPTER 24

Catching Up

"Hey, Zach, you getting up for work?"

"Is it that time already?" Zach groaned, rolling over and pulling the pillow off his head. Sunlight was streaming into their disheveled bedroom. Suitcases and camping gear still needed to be sorted out and put away. Squinting, Zach looked up sleepily at his brother.

Jake was looking down at him with impatience in his hazel-brown eyes. He was already dressed in tattered jean shorts and an old red T-shirt.

"We're supposed to meet Allan in half an hour. We've got all the lawns to cut today."

Zach skipped a shower and headed out to the car with his brother, carrying a bowl of cereal.

"So, was it good?" Jake asked, after Zach had given thanks for his morning meal.

"Fan-tas-tic!" he replied, as Jake backed out of the garage.

"Really? What was so great?"

"The talks really made me think – a lot! That was probably the best part. I've decided to get baptized."

"Seriously?!" Jake replied, turning out of the driveway and on to the main road. "Whoa! I sure didn't see that coming. That's amazing!"

Zach nodded, as Jake accelerated quickly. "I know. My life is going to have to change. I told Dad about it last night. I want to get baptized as soon as I can."

"Cool!"

Jake's excitement seemed feigned. Shoveling in a spoonful

166

of soggy cereal, Zach looked over at him with a puzzled expression.

"How's Brennan? And Noah? And all the rest?"

"They were *totally* disappointed you weren't there! Especially, since I couldn't play sports. Noah and Brennan were counting on one of us playing in the volleyball tournament with them."

Jake nodded slowly. "Yeah, that would've been fun."

"Hannah was disappointed, too," Zach added guardedly. He spooned in another mouthful of cereal.

Jake laughed. "Did she follow *you* around all week?"

"Hannah's a really nice girl," Zach replied evenly, looking away.

"Nicer than Melissa?" Jake asked, trying not to sound too hopeful.

"By far!" was his brother's surprising admission.

"By far?" Jake echoed. He suddenly realized he was way over the speed limit and took his foot off the accelerator.

Zach decided he had better not say too much about Hannah. There was only one Hannah and he didn't want to share. "I actually got really close to everyone this year," he said, and then added sadly. "I didn't want to come home. I'm planning to go back out for the Conference. I'll ask Allan about getting a ride today. Jake, we have so many good friends that go to camp – friends that believe the same as we do. You need to come too. You'll love it!"

"What?! We can't take more weeks off work! Who's going to help Derrick run EdenTree when Allan is away?"

Zach shrugged. He hadn't thought about that. "Yeah, maybe you're right," he moaned. But then, suddenly he had an idea. "Maybe Jayden will help!"

The idea was a good one. Jayden was a good worker and he had been unable to get a job for the summer because he had been so busy fundraising for his mission trip to Uganda at the end of July. Jayden was planning to only be gone for a week and the twins knew he would be keen to make some pocket money when he returned.

"Sometimes we're just too busy, Jake. We haven't been taking time for God."

Jake looked at his brother strangely. It had always been his job to admonish his 'younger' brother, not the other way around. After all, he was the older brother not only naturally but spiritually. He knew he should feel happy that his brother had this radical change of heart, but he didn't. He felt resentment and anger. "You don't sound like Zach," he said with a skeptical tone.

"I hope I don't! I want to change." Zach paused to slurp down the remaining milk from the bowl. "So, how was your week?"

"I'm really glad I went!" Jake exclaimed. "There's nothing like training with professional coaches. I learned so much! And now I feel like I'm in better shape than ever. My ankle is completely fine. I'll have to fill you in on some of the new plays. We learned this amazing press break! I'm going to tell Brett all about it after work today. And you should see Jayden shoot foul shots now. He hardly misses – *ever!* And I'm up to an eighty percent average myself!"

Envious feelings were leaching into Zach's heart. He knew it was going to be hard to hear about the basketball camp and all that Jake had experienced. *Heavenly Father, please help me,* he prayed silently. *Don't let me get swallowed back into this again.*

"One night we had a captains' meeting," Jake went on to say. "All the captains were invited. I wish you had been there. I can't remember everything but it was really important stuff about leading a team."

"Like what?"

"Well, we watched some videos of actual NBA games and the coaches pointed out the difference that some of the captains made to the team. Positive captains kept everyone's head in the game even when things were going bad. A bad captain can defeat the morale of the whole group if he lets himself get down. Good leadership can make the difference between winning and losing."

"Yeah, I can see that."

"So, if you and I keep up our confidence next season regardless of how the game is going, we can make the difference in a close game. We can affect the morale of everyone for good!"

"I guess that's true with leadership in any situation."

"Yeah, perhaps," Jake mumbled, wondering where Zach was heading with such a comment. Then it dawned on him and he quickly pushed the thought away. "I have two new things to show you when we do our workout tonight," he added rapidly. "They really help with jumping and making your shots. It's fun. You'll like it."

How am I going to fit in a workout and Bible study? Zach was asking himself. Noah had told him to do it as soon as he got home, but that's when he and Jake always worked out. There was supper and the family Bible readings to fit in as well, and he didn't really want to be jogging around town in the dark.

I can be flexible, he told himself. *I'll do my workouts with Jake as usual and my Bible studies in the evenings.*

"Sounds good!" Zach smiled. "I do feel out of shape. But, since I'm going to the Conference, I have to get the workbook done in the next five weeks. So, every night, I'll be working on it 'til I go to bed."

"Are you *serious?!*" Jake replied. Checking his speed, he slowed the car down again.

"You could do it with me," Zach suggested.

"I'm on summer holidays, Bro," Jake complained. "I don't want to be sitting at a desk, studying all night. I get enough of that in school."

They were both quiet for a few minutes. Zach tossed his

bowl and spoon on the floor in the back of the car and Jake concentrated on making a left hand turn at a busy intersection.

"You might want to leave yourself a spare evening every now and again," Jake said with a mysterious smile. Turning onto a side road, Jake proudly told his brother, "I picked up a *loaded* laptop at the basketball camp! One of the guys forgot it in the cabin and I found it."

"Shouldn't you be trying to contact him and let him know you have it?"

"I don't know his last name, yet," Jake replied in a nonchalant manner. "We'll see them when basketball season starts up again. I'll give it to him then."

"What's it loaded with?"

"Fantastic movies!"

"Movies?"

"Great movies! And make sure you keep it a secret! If I keep the laptop hidden, then you and I can watch it anytime we want in our room. No more waiting till mom and dad are out of the house."

"Amazing!" was Zach's initial response, and then he began to question, *Do I really want to go behind mom and dad's back again? Is it right for us to keep someone else's laptop? How will I ever stick to my resolve, with a 'loaded' laptop in our room?* Zach felt uneasy. The thought of trying to focus on Bible study while Jake was lying in bed watching a cool movie, seemed incredibly daunting.

"Anyway," Zach added, as they reached the first place on the lawn mowing schedule, "I'm going to invite Melissa and Shane, and Jayden to my baptism. Think they'll come?"

"Maybe," Jake replied, parking the car. "Melissa has been texting me a lot since you've been gone. Half the time she's wondering what you're up to. She told me to tell you that she's breaking up with Shane and she misses you a lot."

"Really?" Zach said slowly in a rather stunned way. It wasn't the excited reaction Jake expected. He hoped it meant Zach wasn't interested in Melissa any more.

Jake wanted to put his brother's feelings to the test. Maybe his brother was willing to switch girls? "Melissa wants us to see *Colorado* with her. It's this new movie that just came out. She's heard it's really good!" Looking sideways at his brother, he added, "But I guess you're going to be busy doing *Bible study!*"

Zach swallowed hard as he got out of the car. It was his first day back from camp and already he was facing intense pressure to forget changing and revert to living for the pleasures of the moment. Melissa was breaking up with Shane? She was missing him? This was going to be harder than he thought. Could he handle sitting alone at home while Jake took Melissa to the movies? He lashed out, "What's with you, man! You should be happy that I've changed and try to help me stick to it – not do everything you can to knock me back down."

Jake was surprised by his brother's outburst. "I'm totally happy for you!" he exclaimed angrily, just as Derrick and Allan pulled into the driveway with the garden trailer in tow. "Why would you think I'm not? But you don't have to become a *fanatic,* just because you're getting baptized!"

Allan and Derrick stepped out of the truck, greeting the twins with a hearty hello. They ambled over to help them take the lawn mowers off the trailer.

"I heard you're looking for a ride to Conference," Allan said to Zach. "I've got three spare seats. I'm happy to take you… Jake too, if he wants! I hope you don't mind though, if we stay for the week after Conference as well?"

"That would be amazing!" Zach grinned, feeling encouraged. "I'd love to stay on! Noah invited me to stay at his place."

"Who's going to run EdenTree?" Jake retorted.

"Derrick has a friend who's also doing landscaping this summer," Allan told him. "I said we'd give him a couple weeks off in September if he'll do our customers while we're away."

"But we'll be back in school in September!" Jake protested.

"It might be tricky," Allan agreed, "but I figured for two weeks we can all cram in working three hours every night and all day Saturday. And I have a couple of university friends who will gladly do some extra work if we need them."

"I'm sure Jayden would love some work," Zach added.

"Yeah, Jayden's a good guy," Allan considered. "Don't worry about it. We'll manage somehow."

Jake thought through the options. *One week sure made a big difference for Zach. I'm probably in need of a spiritual boost myself. Maybe this is my second chance.* But then he shook his head. "I'd consider it," he told Allan, "if there wasn't so much Bible study to do first. I'd never get through it in only five weeks!"

"Sure you could," Allan encouraged him. "It took me about fifty hours. If you do about two hours a day from here on in, you'll get through it easy. And you can always finish it off on the twenty-four hour car ride to camp!"

Filling his mower with gas, Jake shook his head again. "I'd have no life for the rest of the summer!"

"What you'd have," Allan persisted, "is a lot of help from God in transforming your mind. I've learned so much from that study!"

"If we did it together, it would be fun," Zach suggested.

As Jake pushed the mower up and down the sloping hills of the estate, he thought about what Allan had said. *Maybe this is what I need,* he thought. *Maybe I'm not feeling anything because I'm not making any effort to seek God.*

But I've got to stay in shape! he argued. *That week at camp was great and I want to keep up my training till the season begins. Plus, Melissa is showing some interest… I don't want to bury my head at home for five weeks, like Zach is planning to do. Plus, I wouldn't have time to watch movies…* It was one last thought, however, that clinched his decision. *If Zach and Allan are going to be away for two whole weeks, they will be missing out on making almost a thousand dollars. That's a lot of money!*

Allan weed-whipped around the trees. Derrick looked after the gardens and Zach mowed the lawn. Zach was thinking hard about his brother's comments. *Am I becoming a fanatic?* he considered. *Yeah, probably announcing that I'm going to be doing Bible study every night sounds that way. But if I want to go to Youth Conference – which I do – I really have no choice! It's the only way I'll get it all done.* He sighed with regret. *Had I started when Allan first told me about it, it wouldn't have been hard at all. I wasted so much time with that musical.*

It was after five when they got home from work. Jake was anxious to show Zach the new workout. They changed quickly, grabbed a banana and a yogurt and headed outside.

"I hope you found something to improve our vertical," Zach said, inhaling the contents of the yogurt container in one gulp.

"Sure did!" Jake exclaimed. "We had a guy at camp who used to play in the NBA, and he coached Canada's National Men's Team too! I asked him for the best jumping exercise."

"Really?" Zach said, impressed by the qualifications. "What did he say?"

"It was profound!" Jake teased. "He said that the best thing to do to strengthen jumping muscles, was to *jump.*"

"Whoa – that's deep."

"Seriously though, I'll show you what he made us do," Jake said, flinging his banana peel into the garbage can. He took up a position on the paved driveway, under the basketball net. "Jump and touch the rim ten times," he said, hurling himself off the ground, "and then we'll run up and down the little hill over there. Then nine jumps and a hill run; then eight, all the way down to one."

The boys eagerly started the drill. By nine jumps their legs were aching. "My legs are killing me! This better work," Zach complained.

"It will," said Jake. "My vertical improved by five centimeters in just one week of camp!"

After the last hill run, the boys collapsed on the grass to catch their breath.

It had been all Zach could do to keep up to his brother. As he lay panting on the grass, he hoped Jake's next drill wouldn't be so intense.

"I've got the best shooting drill you've ever seen," Jake boasted. "It's called 'Thirty-Three'."

Once they had recovered a little more, Jake grabbed a ball and took his position along the baseline facing the net.

"So, you start here," Jake began, jumping in place just beyond the three-point line that they had painted on the driveway, "You shoot and follow through to get your rebound." Making the play, Jake grabbed the ball after it swished through the net and said, "That's three points."

Running back to where he started, Jake faked the shot, took one hard dribble and nailed a two-pointer. "That's another two points," he told Zach. "Get your rebound again and the last shot is a layup." He returned to where he started, up-faked, and then drove hard to the hoop and laid it in. "The layup is only worth one point in this drill," he said as he caught the rebound.

Jake took his next position at a forty-five degree angle from the basket, still beyond the three-point line. "Now we do it all over again from here." Finding the bottom of the net with his three-pointer, he missed his two-pointer and dunked the ball hard on his layup.

"So that's ten points for me so far. The next spot is from straight on, and then you repeat the same thing from the left side."

Jake continued the drill, making most of his shots. Zach razzed him for missing a left-handed layup.

After finishing the baseline drive, Jake was at twenty-four out of thirty possible points.

"So why is the drill called 'Thirty-*Three*'?" Zach asked.

"Because you finish with three foul shots." Standing behind the foul-line, Jake hit all three easily.

"Wow – you've been working on your free-throws, Bro!" Zach marvelled.

"So, I got twenty-seven points," Jake said, "that's three off my best score at camp. Now it's your turn!"

Zach had difficulties on his first turn, trying to remember when to shoot, when to fake and drive, and where the position for each shot was supposed to be. He only scored eighteen points. "That was awful!" he moaned.

"Don't worry; once you get it, you can just shoot away without thinking. That's the key! The camp coaches were always preaching, 'Don't think too much. Just let it flow.'"

The boys played 'Thirty-Three' until their mom gave them the 'ten-minute' warning; it was almost time for dinner. Although they never beat Jake's high score from camp, they enjoyed themselves immensely. Zach felt the drill had good potential.

"Next time we should bring a stopwatch and time ourselves as well as keep score," Zach suggested, as they took positions on the grass for ten minutes of strength training.

"Great idea!" Jake exclaimed, between push ups. "The time can be the tie-breaker in case we get the same number of points."

"Yeah – and let's keep track of how we do each day," Zach puffed, trying to keep up with his brother. *I'm going to make thirty-three one day!* he thought to himself. *This is really good!*

CHAPTER 25

Taken Down

Allan had to make a trip to the plant nursery the next morning to pick up some new trees for a customer. He told the twins to sleep-in and meet him for work at noon. The boys enjoyed the late start and the time to eat a larger breakfast. As they stood around the stove waiting for the bacon to crisp up, Zach asked Jake to send two very important messages to Hannah and Noah. The first message was:

Hey, it's Zach. How's it goin? Got back from camp safe. How about you?

It wasn't long before a message came back from Hannah:

So good to hear from you, Zach! I'm hoping to get baptized in two weeks, God Willing. What about you?

Unsure of what to say, Zach asked Jake to text the second number with a similar message. This time there wasn't an instant response.

Walking into the kitchen, the twins' father turned on the nine o'clock news. The lead story was about the potential collapse of the United States economy. "Trillions of dollars in debt," the reporter was saying, "the economy has reached a breaking point. All non-essential services will be shut down in two weeks' time. Expect long delays at the border, hospitals and any government office. Consider alternative methods of shipping – postal backlogs may get out of hand. For the foreseeable future, military spending has been slashed. The U.S. will defend its own borders only… "

"That fits nicely with Ezekiel thirty-eight," their father commented. "The 'young lions' watch the Northern invasion and

176

are powerless to respond."[107] Perhaps a financial crisis is the way that God intends to tie their hands."

Zach and Jake looked at one another. A financial crisis in the English-speaking world sounded unpleasant; they hoped their father was wrong.

Sitting down at the table with a cup of coffee in his hand, their dad said, "I was talking to your Uncle James last night, Zach. He says that he had long talks with you on the way home, going over all the important teachings of the Bible. He feels you are ready for baptism."

"Can I be baptized this Sunday?"

"It's good to see your enthusiasm," his dad chuckled. "But why don't we give it a month or two, and just make sure this isn't a rash decision. Making a commitment like this to God is something you want to be very sure about."

"Dad, I'm *absolutely* sure!" Zach replied firmly, flipping the bacon. "I've done a lot of thinking about it and I know I'm ready."

"You're ready to give your life, your heart, and your mind to God? You're ready to be a 'new man' in Christ?"

"I am, Dad," Zach nodded. "I know what this commitment means – that's why I've taken so long to make it."

"Following Christ isn't the path of least resistance, you know, but…"

"It's the path of least regrets," Zach finished with a smile.

Not having seen the gradual change in Zach during the week he had been at Bible Camp, Andrew was a little skeptical. However, after questioning him concerning the new way of life for a disciple of Christ, Zach's unwavering responses persuaded his father that his son's change of heart was sincere. They both agreed

---

[107] Ezekiel 38:10-13

to aim toward a baptism in two weeks' time.

"Hannah's hoping to be baptized then as well."

His dad looked puzzled. "Hannah...Vandeburg?"

"Yes," Zach smiled, taking the bacon out of the pan. "Hannah Vandeburg – Noah's sister, Esther's good friend."

"Is that right?!" his dad said with amazement. "Wonderful! Hannah is a really nice girl."

"And, uh, by the way, Dad," Zach added, suddenly remembering, "Noah might be going to Dalhousie in September, if... if he doesn't choose to do missionary work instead. Could he board with us?"

"Of course! That would be really nice for you and Jake."

"Great!" Zach exclaimed with a smile. "Can you let him know?" he asked his brother.

Jake sent another text to the non-responsive friend, as Zach cracked eggs into the frying pan:

My Dad says you can stay here if you go to Dalhousie.

Noah might be coming here? Jake thought to himself. *That will change things.*

After his father had made a few phone calls to arrange for Zach's interview and probable baptism, the boys sat down to eat breakfast. Zach was munching on a perfectly crisp piece of bacon when his mom entered the kitchen.

"How's James?" she questioned her husband quietly.

"No better," his dad remarked with a serious tone. "He couldn't talk long on the phone. It was aggravating his cough. Sandra says he will be off work again today. She's going to take him to see the doctor this afternoon."

"Oh good, he probably needs a dose of antibiotics."

Zach could tell his parents were rather concerned that Uncle James had a cold, and he wondered why. Who worried about a cold in the middle of summer? It would soon be over and gone. With Jake's help he sent a text to Hannah:

Hey, sounds like I might be baptized the same day as you!

We'll be twins! she texted back.

Jake looked up to see the smile on Zach's face. *He really likes this girl,* he thought. *What did I miss out on at camp? Is Hannah really better than Melissa – 'by far'?*

With a laugh, Zach told Jake to type:

Sweet!

It was sweet! It was moral support. The only drawback was that now there was no chance that Hannah and Noah would be coming out to Nova Scotia to see his baptism. *Oh well,* he shrugged, *Allan and I will soon be back in Ontario.*

The next three days passed quickly as Zach diligently followed his new routine: get out of bed in the morning – pray, work for EdenTree till five, come home, do the new workout with Jake, eat dinner, do the Bible readings with his family and then sit down to do the Youth Conference book for two to three hours.

It was a very busy schedule, and Zach's legs ached from the drills Jake was putting him through, but the study on Job was more interesting than he had anticipated. He had always wondered about the satan in the book of Job and now he was finally taking the time to investigate. *It's so strange,* he thought, *because, after the first two chapters, satan disappears from the record. In fact, in the rest of the book, all the calamities that come upon Job are attributed as coming from God.[108] Who is this satan? Did he have any powers of his own? It seems he has to get God's permission to do anything to Job, and God takes responsibility for all the affliction Job suffers.[109]*

He thought it over carefully. *I know that the Hebrew word 'satan' means 'an opponent or an adversary' and sometimes it's*

---

[108] Job 1:21-22; 2:3,10; 42:11
[109] Job 2:3-6

even translated using those words. Maybe I'll find something there. Looking up the Hebrew word 'satan' – Strong's number 7854 – Zach scrolled through all the places 7854 appeared in the Old Testament. The first passage in the listing was one where a Divine angel stood in Balaam's way as 'satan' – or, as it is translated in the New King James – as an *'adversary'* against him to keep Balaam from sinning against God.[110] In the next passage, David was referred to as being a possible *'adversary'* to the Philistines. [111] Several other passages in the listing were clearly *human* adversaries[112] and some were ambiguous.[113]

So satan is someone who opposes or is adversarial to another – for good or for bad, Zach considered. *The angel that stood in Balaam's way was a satan for good as he stopped Balaam from going to Balak without God's permission. But in the New Testament, Jesus calls Peter satan because he was trying to talk Jesus out of giving his life for the world.[114]*

Turning back to the book of Job, Zach considered the various suggestions he'd heard for the identification of Job's satan. *Was satan a Divine angel that wanted God's permission to test Job's faith? There certainly are other incidents where angels are involved in bringing calamity on the earth and testing the faith of believers. [115]Or was satan another human being who was jealous of Job? Was he one of the three 'friends' – or maybe all three of them? After all, it was the words of Job's 'friends' that caused Job to charge God foolishly – not the afflictions.[116] And God rebuked*

---

[110] Numbers 22:22-32
[111] 1 Samuel 29:4
[112] 2 Samuel 19:22; 1 Kings 5:4; 11:14,23,25,
[113] Psalm 109:6; Zechariah 3:1-2
[114] Matthew 16:21-27
[115] Angels of destruction: Exo.12:23- 27 cp. Psa. 78: 48-51; 1 Chron. 21:12-16; Rev. 16. Angels testing believers: Gen. 22:1-2,11-12
[116] Job 1:21-22

only the three friends at the end of the book – not anyone else.[117]*Or maybe,* Zach thought, *the answer lies in identifying the 'sons of God' who were with satan in the opening chapter.*

While he was looking up other places where the phrase 'sons of God'[118] appears in Scripture, his mom came into the kitchen where Zach was studying. She was talking to someone on the phone about an event and began leafing through the calendar.

Zach was distracted. He couldn't help noticing the circled dates of the musical. Seven weeks had passed since the final performance and although he didn't know it, there were only four weeks left until… until life would change *forever!*

Remembering back to the performance, Zach thought to himself, *Everything revolved around the musical back then. Nothing else mattered except putting on a great show and getting Melissa's attention. Jake thinks I'm being fanatical with Bible study, but at least this new routine is helping me to let go of my old life and change things around. If I had as much free time as Jake, I might be fanatical about something else, like I was before with Melissa and the musical. Where did that get me? Beat up and running away from God!* He flipped through the unfinished pages. He had only just begun and there was still a lot left to do, but Zach was determined he would be going back to Manitoulin Island.

For the first week and a half, Zach worked in the kitchen so that the light wouldn't keep his brother from sleeping and his brother wouldn't distract him from studying. However, on Wednesday night, the night just before his baptismal interview, Esther decided to make up for two weeks of missed piano practice – all at once – so Zach picked up his books and went to his room.

Jake was lying on his bed reading a scary-looking novel. A

---

[117] Job 42:1-8. For a consideration of the possibilities: Pople, John. "The Sufferings of a Righteous Man, A Study in Job." Talk 2 – Satan. Retrieved June 5, 2013 from **http://www.bibletalks4u.com/pople-john.htm**
[118] Gen. 6:2-4; Job 38:7; Jn. 1:12; 1 Jn. 3:1-2. Cp. Deut.31:14 & Josh.24:1

pair of evil eyes looked through a keyhole dripping with blood.

"How can you study for so long?" Jake asked his brother after a while. "It's like you're back at school!"

Zach looked up reproachfully. Jake was certainly not supportive, and Zach found his brother's hostile reactions strange. *Where is the brother that used to encourage me to try harder? Jake has always been the 'good' son; the one making the right decisions. Sure he has a few areas of weakness but for the most part he's always led in a good direction. Is he taking a summer break from God?*

"This is way more interesting than school work," Zach told him. "I'm finding all these cool links to the life of Job! Did you know that almost everything that happened to Job was part of the curse that God said He would put on Israel for their disobedience? There are so many links back to Deuteronomy twenty-eight. It's almost like Job is a type of the nation of Israel. Listen to this comment:"

Zach proceeded to read a few lines from the workbook with excitement. "'The book of Job was likely written near the end of Israel's wandering in the wilderness, perhaps around the same time that Moses proclaimed the words of Deuteronomy twenty-eight to the nation. This prophecy stated that Israel would be blessed for righteousness and cursed for disobedience. While this held true nationally, it could be misunderstood on a personal level. [119] With all the allusions back to Deuteronomy twenty-eight, Job's friends seem to have been well aware of the prophecy and made incorrect deductions. They concluded that if someone were struck with calamity it demonstrated that person had sinned. [120] The greater the calamity the greater the sin! In looking at Job's

---

[119] Pople, John. "The Sufferings of a Righteous Man, A Study in Job." Retrieved June 5, 2013 from **http://www.bibletalks4u.com/pople-john.htm**

[120] Job 8:3-20; 18:5-21

182

suffering with this mindset they were convinced that he must have been the worst of sinners.[121] God worked with Job and his friends to demonstrate that this was not a fair assumption to make toward Job or anyone else that suffers. [122]Regardless of the circumstances we might find ourselves in, we must always speak right of God.'" [123]

Jake felt uneasy with his brother's enthusiasm. *How can Zach be so turned on by the Bible?* he wondered. It was one thing to choose to do the right thing because you knew it was expected of you – but Zach seemed strangely excited about it! Jake couldn't imagine ever feeling so excited about the Bible. Since his baptism he had led dutifully, if somewhat grudgingly in spiritual matters – but never with enthusiasm. Instead of being encouraged by his brother's change of heart, Jake only felt guilty and resentful. *Why isn't Zach as passionate about basketball and the championship anymore?* he wondered. *Why isn't he still crazy about Melissa? Why didn't he even ask what my new novel is about? How come he hasn't started reading Green Diamonds? I gave it to him before he went away. How could one week make such a difference? Would I be this excited about the Bible if I had gone to Manitoulin? Maybe I should go to the Conference. Maybe it could change me.* He looked at the thickness of the workbook Zach was writing in. *But it's so much work!* he sighed internally. *This is my vacation. And I'm already hours behind what he has done. I could never catch up unless I took the next two weeks off work. I can't imagine spending two weeks at a desk in the summer!*

"So do you mind if I take Melissa to the movies?" Jake asked in a nonchalant manner. "Like I don't want to move in on your girl or anything, but if you're not interested in her

---

[121] Job 4:7-8;11:5-6; 34:36-37
[122] Job 2:3; 42:7-12; Hebrews 12:5-11
[123] Job 2:9-10; 42:7

anymore…"

"She was never my girl," Zach reminded him uneasily.
"Are you sure she's actually broken up with Shane?"

"No, but she plans to. Shane's been working all summer
and he's heading off to university this fall – all the way to Ottawa.
Besides *she's asking us* to go to the movies with her."

"I don't think she's the kind of girl I should be interested
in – or you either," Zach replied, rather resentful of Jake's interest
in Melissa and feeling a little concerned for his brother's
wellbeing. "Do you really want to get pummeled by Shane?"

"Shane's out of the picture."

"Maybe, and maybe not."

Pulling the phone from his pocket Jake sat up in bed.
While Zach seemed to be disengaging from his pursuit of Melissa,
Jake's plans were revolving around her more intensely every day.
He couldn't stop thinking about her. Had he been at Bible camp
that summer, he might have realized he was setting up an idol in
his heart. He might have considered 'positively pursuing the
opposite'.

Hey Melissa. What's up? he texted.

Not much, was the instant response.

So when's our movie date?

Friday night?

Sounds good!

Is Zach coming?

No, he'll be doing his Bible study instead.

What?!!!

Zach has changed in a major way!

Can you give him a message from me?

Sure!

Jake shared the message that came in for his brother:

Zach – what's with you? I hardly hear from you anymore!
Colorado is a fabulous movie! You can't miss it! Please be there
tomorrow night. Love, Melissa.

Zach tried to read the previous messages but Jake snatched it away.

"What did you tell her?" Zach wanted to know.

"I just made a movie date for Friday night. She wants to know if you are coming."

"And what are you going to tell Dad?" Zach questioned, knowing just as well as Jake did, that their parents would not be impressed with such a date.

"I don't know," Jake fumbled irritably. "Maybe I'll say I'm going to see Jayden for a few hours."

"So, you'll lie?"

Jake looked perplexed. "I'll come up with something, Man! It might not be an outright lie. But why are you worried about lies? You lied about prom, and about... "

"Yeah, but that was before I realized I needed to change my life."

At that moment, Jake heard his mom calling his name. He left to see what it was that she wanted.

Zach sighed and rested his chin on his hand, wondering what he should do. It was very tempting to join his brother for a movie date. *But I'm trying to change my life,* he thought. *A date with Melissa could set me back in a major way. What if she gets all cuddly? And I'd have to lie to mom and dad, which I don't want to do any more.* His eyes focused in on the white rock that sat on his desk – his treasure from the 'shipwreck'. He picked it up and examined it carefully.

Jake returned in a few minutes with a laundry basket of clean clothes.

"Tell Melissa that I'm sorry, but I have other plans for Friday," Zach said. "I really don't think you should be going either," he told his brother earnestly. "Melissa's beautiful; she's charming and she's... *wild.* For guys who want to do what's right she's not going to be helpful at all."

185

Jake was amazed his brother was finally admitting what they both knew well. *I can't believe Zach isn't interested in a date with Melissa!* he thought with astonishment. *He really must not be interested in her anymore.* Sitting down on his bed to text the message that Zach wasn't coming, Jake was elated. *He's giving her up, right when she's showing interest! This might just work in my favour!*

With a smile, Jake lay on his bed, imagining his movie date with Melissa, while Zach quietly filled in a study chart comparing Job's three 'friends'.

Hearing their parents call out goodnight as they headed to bed, Jake pulled out the laptop that he kept carefully hidden away. *Zach's been working for quite a while,* he considered. *I wonder if he'd watch a movie with me now?* In the past, they'd done everything together. Zach had always been a willing 'partner in crime'. This turn-about was driving Jake crazy.

"Think you'd have time to watch a movie with me?" Jake asked.

Zach hesitated. "I was hoping to do another hour on Job," he replied. "And then we need to get some sleep so we can get up for work in the morning."

Jake noticed the hesitation. The monster wanted company. "Okay, well, I'm going to watch one. I'll keep the earplugs in so I don't disturb your study." Picking up the laptop Jake settled himself comfortably against his pillows and turned it on. He looked through the selection of movies, wondering what might interest his brother. He remembered his first introduction to R-rated movies. *If I could get Zach to watch just one with me maybe he'll find them just as addictive. Then maybe he'll be normal again. I feel bad watching this stuff when Zach's sitting there studying his Bible!* He looked at the list carefully. *Perhaps I should show him Hell Rider!*

"Hey, Zach," he called out. "Have you ever heard of 'Hell

Rider"?"

Turning around, Zach asked, "What's it about?"

Jake told him selected parts of the storyline. "It has the best cop chase ever! You gotta see it sometime! The stunts this guy does on his motorbike are unreal! You'll love it!"

Curious and feeling badly for turning his brother down so many times that evening, Zach got out of his chair and came over to steal a peek. Starting the movie, Jake said, "Just watch the first scene. It starts with him practicing his stunts on the track. It's so cool!"

One scene won't take long, Zach assured himself. *It does sound cool and I've already worked an hour on the study. Besides Jake really thinks I'm becoming a fanatic. Maybe if I show a little interest in the movie, he'll stop bugging me so much.* Taking the pillows off his own bed, Zach made himself comfortable beside his brother. He was awestruck by the stunts and mystified by the cop's intense pursuit of Lance – the motorcycle rider. *Why do they want to catch him so badly?* he wondered. *Does Lance hold some deadly secret? Has he been framed by someone else? Are the cops corrupt? Just ten minutes more,* he told himself a couple of times. *This is cool!* Then suddenly, right in the middle of the most exciting chase, the scene flashed to a darkened motel room where a cop was questioning Lance's girlfriend. Zach was astonished when she started taking off her clothes!

"Jake, what's the rating on this?!"

"Don't worry. Brett has it," Jake assured him. "This is the only bad part and you've *got to* hear what they say – it's *so* important! You'll never figure out the plot otherwise."

Zach's eyes were transfixed by the scene but his heart was racing. He heard a noise in the hall and wondered if his mom was up. *What if Mom comes into our room right now and sees what we're watching? She'd be so upset! Dad would never allow stuff like this in the house! They'd be so disappointed, especially after*

I've told them I've changed. But it was so hard to tear his eyes away.

"Jake, we shouldn't be watching this," he complained weakly. "You should skip it."

"You missed it!" Jake said reproachfully, backing up the movie, so the whole, heart-racing scene began from the start. "You've got to listen to what they say."

Inside, Zach's conscience was telling him that this was bad; that he shouldn't be watching such scandalous scenes but another part of him was totally enthralled. He'd never seen anything like this before. The new possibilities being suggested made his heart race!

If Brett owns this DVD, he told himself, *then obviously Brett thinks it's okay. And I'm not baptized yet...* he assured himself. *I haven't really made a commitment to God.*

Zach missed the crucial words for the second time and didn't complain when his brother skipped back to watch the whole heart-racing scene *again.* From that point on Zach lost all willpower to tear himself away from the movie. *I have to find out what happens. I'll do extra study tomorrow night...*

Jake smiled inwardly. *This is more like it! Zach's enjoying this with me.* He was introducing his brother to a new brand of excitement and he was sure his brother would become just as quickly addicted as he had been.

Jake had told Zach that there was only one bad scene but he hadn't been entirely truthful. There were others, and Jake kept repeating, "Oops, I forgot about this."

As Zach allowed himself to watch, he told himself, *I'll never, ever do anything like this again. This is a one-time indulgence. I've just got to see how it ends.*

But Dad always says the best defense is to never give in the first time.

Just this once...

Dad says once you've broken down your first line of defense you're more easily overcome the next time!

The first defense is already broken. I might as well finish this off.

When the movie ended, somewhere near midnight, Zach was just as awake and wired as if it had been the middle of the day. He tossed and turned for some time in bed, feeling ashamed for the direction his thoughts were going. His lusts were ignited by the images now burned into his mind. One part of him yearned to dwell on the scenes, while the other was disgusted to have them in his head. It was such a paradox! *I should have asked Jake what the rating was,* he thought regretfully, *but I never thought he would suggest watching stuff like this. What's with Jake? I'm surprised Brett owns this movie. I should have walked out after the first bad scene... then I wouldn't have so much of this in my head.*

He thought about praying to God for forgiveness but he felt too ashamed to even begin to approach God when so many impure thoughts were swirling around inside. Only three days ago he had asked to be baptized, promising his dad that he was ready to stop serving sin and give his life to God. Now he had just invited sin into his heart through the lust of the eyes and it didn't want to leave. Unable to sleep, Zach finally left his room and went outside for a walk. Jake was sound asleep.

A muggy night, it was peaceful and quiet down near the bay. The moon was a bright half-crescent and the sky was filled with stars. He looked up at the heavens and remembered the beautiful evenings at Manitoulin. With all the light pollution in Stirling, he could see only a small fraction of the heavenly host. *I wish I were back at camp,* he thought, *where there weren't so many distractions and strong pulls in the opposite direction.*

Zach wandered down to the Harbourfront. He didn't feel one bit weary physically, but mentally he was exhausted. Walking along the boardwalk he tried to determine what he should do. He longed to talk to someone about the way he was feeling but didn't know if anyone would understand. *Dad won't have any sympathy!* he decided. *I hate to think what the consequences will be if Dad ever discovers that laptop! Who can I talk to about this? I wonder if Uncle James ever watched such movies? He wasn't always a believer. But Uncle James is still really sick. I can't talk to him.*

Standing beside the ocean, listening to the waves surging against the tall wooden piers, Zach thought about the talks he'd heard at Manitoulin. He remembered Uncle George talking about idols of the heart and how they refuse to go away. "But there is a more aggressive method to overcome idols in the heart," Uncle George had assured them. "Be not overcome by evil, but overcome evil with good... positively pursue the opposite."

Zach looked around. There was no one else in sight. Kneeling down on the wooden planks, he bowed his head and prayed. "Heavenly Father," he began nervously. "I hardly feel I can come before you tonight. Please forgive me for filling my mind with those images. I knew it was wrong. I knew I should have stopped myself, but I didn't. I am struggling to escape from these thoughts. They are raging within me. Please Father, help me to overcome. Help me to be strong against the flesh and to commit my life to You fully in baptism as I have planned to do. And please, Heavenly Father, help me to help my brother. I realize the force of this evil to tear us both away from loving You and Your righteousness. You are holy and You want us to serve You in holiness. What I watched was the opposite of all that You are. Please strengthen both of us to overcome. In Jesus Christ's Name," Zach prayed earnestly, "Amen."

Walking home, Zach felt fortified, even though the tantalizing images still pulled at his heart. "Overcome evil with good," was a verse that kept coming to mind.[124] There was no way

---

[124] Romans 12:21

he would be able to sleep, not yet. Tiptoeing into his room, he looked reproachfully at his brother, sleeping soundly in bed. "Why would you *knowingly* invite me to do wrong?" he whispered.

Picking up his workbook, he was reminded of the way Job's three 'friends' had been even more effective at bringing Job low than all the afflictions heaped upon him from God. *Jake,* he mused, *you've become like a satan to me!*

Walking out of the room, Zach felt his self-righteous indignation had been turned upside down. A panicky feeling washed over him. *I used to give Jake such a hard time about every spiritual choice he made. I used to go on and on about all the fun I was having away from God... Was I a satan to him? Were my actions responsible for where he's at now? I need to help my brother!*

CHAPTER 26

Alone

"Is there a reason you're sleeping at the kitchen table?" Zach's dad remarked in surprise, entering the room still wearing his pajama pants. "Jake's already showering."

Wearily, Zach opened his eyes. His neck felt stiff from sleeping on a Bible. His head pounded. He looked at the clock and grimaced. *It's ten to eight. I've got to be at work by eight-thirty! It's going to be hard to function on only three hours of sleep.*

"I'm pleased with the decisions you've been making lately," his father said proudly, realizing Zach had been working on his workbook. "You're really taking this study seriously. Are you enjoying it?"

If only you knew what decision I made last night, Zach thought with shame. "I'm loving this study!" he said.

"Let me know if you need any help," his father encouraged.

Zach didn't talk much to his brother that Thursday; he wanted to lash out, he wanted to help, and he just didn't know what to say. He needed time to think it over.

After work, he had his baptismal interview with Uncle Craig Symons and another older Brother in the meeting. It was very similar to his talk with Uncle James. However, Uncle Craig brought in many interesting practical connections to each doctrinal point. "Since God is One," Uncle Craig told Zach, "we ought to be united in mind and purpose as well."[125] When they discussed the inspiration of the Scriptures, Uncle Craig said, "Since we know the Bible is the inspired Word of God, we need to read it regularly. It's

---

[125] John 17:11,21-23; 1 Corinthians 12:20,27

the Spirit power that changes our hearts and minds." [126]

There were many questions involving a believer's separation from the world,[127] marriage in the Lord, [128]ecclesial activities and responsibilities,[129] politics,[130] and making wise choices regarding the influence of the media. All who heard his confession of faith were satisfied with his knowledge of the Gospel message and personal commitment to follow the Lord Jesus Christ. Plans were made in earnest for his baptism that Sunday.

On Friday morning as the twins drove into work just after eight, it was already abnormally hot. A heat wave was stretching from Boston all the way up to Nova Scotia, and they knew it was going to be a difficult day out in the sun. Zach still didn't have much to say to his brother. He was still angry that Jake had purposefully talked him into watching *Hell Rider*. Thinking over some of the issues they had discussed at his interview the night before, he remembered one passage in particular.

"Uncle Craig showed me an interesting passage last night," he told his brother.

"Really." Jake didn't look over.

"Yeah, in Romans chapter one, it lists many things that God considers 'wickedness' and then says, "Who knowing the judgment of God, that they which commit such things are worthy of death, not only do the same, but have pleasure in them that do them."[131]

"What about it?"

"Uncle Craig says we shouldn't take pleasure in watching or reading about sin."[132]

---

[126] 2 Timothy 3:15-17; John 6:63; 3:5-8; Luke 4:4/Deut. 8:3; Rom. 10:17
[127] 1 John 2:15-17; 1 Peter 4:1-5; Ephesians 4:17-23
[128] 2 Corinthians 6:14; 1 Corinthians 7:39
[129] Hebrews 10:25; Titus 1-3
[130] Hebrews 11:13-16; Ephesians 2:19; Philippians 3:20
[131] KJV
[132] Ephesians 5:5-12

"Why are you telling me this?"

"Jake, you know why."

Turning the car radio up loudly, Jake made it clear this was not something he wanted to discuss. His own conscience was trouble enough; he didn't want to hear it from his brother.

Zach knew they needed to talk about Jake's new obsession at some point, but he still wasn't sure what he was going to say or do. He could just be a 'rat' and tell his dad about the laptop, but Jake would know who had squealed. He didn't feel he should break the bond of trust that they had always shared in their relationship. *Somehow,* he thought, *the better way is to convince my brother to stop watching bad stuff. How can I do it, if he doesn't even want to talk about it?*

As usual, the twins spent the day mowing and weed-whipping, while Derrick and Allan pruned and tidied the gardens. It was difficult working in the hot sun; they all had to take frequent water breaks.

When Zach and Jake arrived home, they convinced each other to brave the heat and do their new exercise routine. However, after only the second set of rim jumps and treks up the hill, Zach felt sick to his stomach and had to stop.

"Sorry, Jake," he said. "I can't finish today. It's too hot."

Walking into the house, Zach was discouraged that he was taking so long to get back into shape. Jake was way ahead of him in everything. He took two Advil but his head continued to pound. The ice cubes melted quickly in the large glass of water he poured for himself. Their house wasn't air-conditioned.

It was difficult to sit down and study Friday evening, knowing his brother had gone to the movies with Melissa. No lies had been told. Jake didn't have to explain where he was going, since his parents had left after dinner to visit old friends. Esther had gone to stay overnight with another family in the meeting. Zach felt very alone. He was sure the movie theatre was air-conditioned. At home they had only fans. It was rarely so hot in Nova Scotia! *I could still get there in time,* Zach thought. *I wonder what the rating is for Columbia? How close are they sitting?*

It was hard to fight against the strong, magnetic pull to go, to be with Melissa, to see another racy movie. *I can't go,* Zach told himself. *I'm getting baptised this Sunday. I'm making a commitment to leave the world behind.*

Zach emailed Hannah for some moral support, but there was no instant response. The house phone rang and Zach ran to pick it up eagerly, hoping it might be one of his friends. It was Aunt Sandra.

"Hi, Zach," she said anxiously. "May I speak to your mom or dad, please?"

"Sorry, they are out right now. Do you want me to tell them to give you a call?"

"Please!"

There was a little catch in Aunt Sandra's voice that gave Zach concern. "How is Uncle James doing?" he asked. "Is he over that cold yet?"

"No, it just gets worse and worse," she replied despairingly. "I don't know what to do. He's finished the antibiotics and is a little better but he seems so hot tonight. I know it's a hot night but I think he has a fever. Would you know if your mom has a thermometer? I can't find ours."

"I'll check," Zach told her. The first aid kit in the bathroom was well-stocked. He found a thermometer easily.

Without a car, Zach was unable to take the thermometer over, but his aunt came and picked it up. She didn't stay long and her face was lined with worry. She left saying, "If your Uncle James has a fever, I'll be taking him back to the doctor Monday morning."

Sitting down at the kitchen table, Zach tried to focus his thoughts, but he was having difficulty concentrating. Walking around the house in a daze he decided to check his emails on the family computer.

Jayden had sent through an email with an itinerary for his trip to Uganda. Zach looked at it with interest. Building homes for needy widows and orphans in a foreign land sounded like an exciting adventure. He was impressed to read all the ways that Jayden and Isaiah had fundraised for the mission, especially the last one. For a whole week Jayden and Isaiah had run a mini basketball camp for the novice division. Twenty neighborhood kids had participated. *Cool idea, guys!* he thought. *I love your spirit!*

There were also emails from his older sisters congratulating him on his decision to be baptized. The oldest begged for the service to be put on Skype so that she could watch it happen. Then Zach opened an email from Uncle Peter and Aunt Jessica. It read:

Dear Zach,

We are so pleased to hear that you've decided to give your life to Christ! You are making the best decision ever! We are very thankful God has called you to join His family and find salvation in His Son.

Your dad says you plan to go back to school for another year, even though you have all the credits you need to graduate. We know that it's very important for all of us to consider our future plans wisely. One day, if Jesus still hasn't returned, you will need to have a good job that can support a family. But just in case you are open to taking a year off before you delve into the commitment of college or university, Aunt Jessica and I would love to invite you and Jake to spend a year with us in Jamaica. There's so much that could be done here with children and teens. Remember the Bible skits that you and Jake used to put on for us? They were so well done and entertaining! Remember the Kingdom Feast, when you dressed up as the King and your beard kept falling off? You guys are hams! If we had the two of you with us, we could run some vacation Bible Camps throughout the year and even set up a youth program. Please give it your consideration. We could really use your help spreading the Gospel message in this island country.

　　We'll be thinking of you and praying for you next Sunday. God be with you in your new life walking with Him.

　　Love,

　　Uncle Peter and Aunt Jessica, Susanna, Jimmy and Seth

At the end of Uncle Peter's email, was a passage in a blue font, from Luke chapter nine, which said: "If anyone desires to come after me, let him deny himself, and take up his cross daily, and follow me… For what profit is it to a man if he gains the whole world, and is himself destroyed or lost?"

This was the second time Uncle Peter had personally invited him and Jake to help in Jamaica. *Interesting idea,* Zach pondered. But his heart was set on winning the Provincials. To leave school and go to Jamaica for a year would require giving up basketball, his friends, and the opportunity to improve his chemistry mark and get his top university choice. However, Uncle Peter's quote caught his eye, "For what profit is it to a man if he gains the whole world, and is himself destroyed or lost?" He remembered Uncle Mark had closed his devotion at camp with a similar passage.

Zach closed the emails and went back to the kitchen, intending to get on with the workbook. Sitting down, he didn't pick up his pen. Resting his throbbing head in his hands, he wondered, *Could I give up basketball? What if I try to play next season and get another concussion? Will it be a wasted year of my life? I might not get my top university choice with my poor chemistry mark, but surely I'll get into most programs. My math marks are good. How cool it would be to spend a year with Uncle Peter! Imagine having the freedom to give my life totally in service to God… Maybe God is calling me to do this?*

But Jake will really think I'm a fanatic!
Maybe I could talk Jake into coming?
Brett will be devastated!
Is Brett more important than God?

No, he thought with a deep sigh, sitting up straight in his chair. *But I just can't give up next year. I've got to get better grades for university. I've got to think of my future. I'll be missing out on making money working with EdenTree… and Brett is counting on Jake and me to help win the Provincials!*

Dismissing Uncle Peter's appeal, Zach picked up his pen and looked at the workbook. He was on chapter twenty-nine. Job's righteousness was a shining example. *He is blameless and upright,* Zach marvelled as he read through the chapter. *Job cared for the widows, the orphans, the lame and the blind. He gave them what they needed and defended their cause. Have I ever looked after anyone that's needy, when there is no benefit to myself?* Thinking hard for a few minutes, Zach failed to remember any such occurrence. *Is that what missionary work would be like?* he wondered.

Taking a few gulps of water from his tall glass and still feeling slow and sluggish, Zach read through an article his dad had given him on the life of Job. He was interested to read that one of the benefits of Job's suffering was the education of his friends. His friends had misconceptions about God and the way that God worked in the life of a believer. At the end of Job's sufferings, God commanded Job to pray for his friends so that they could have forgiveness for their harsh words and false statements about God. Ironically, the man the friends had condemned in their speeches was the very man God told to pray for their forgiveness! [133]

Job was a type of Christ! Zach marvelled. *He was*

---

[133] Lawson, Jack. "Job", *The Lampstand,* Vol. 18, No. 6. P.370

condemned by the very people he came to save. In the agony of crucifixion, Jesus brought salvation to the world!

Zach sat back, deep in thought. *What is my responsibility to the world – to my friends?* he considered. *Would God ever use my life for the benefit of someone else?* He remembered his decision at camp to help Melissa find truth. He hadn't tried anything since he'd come home. And Melissa wasn't the only friend that needed help; there was Jayden, and David, and Abi, and Jerry... *I'm going to phone them all and invite them to come to my baptism,* he decided.

He phoned everyone, but most of his friends were out and he had to leave messages. The only one who answered his call was Abi and she was eager to come. "I'll be there as long as my parents will give me a ride," she told him.

Abi was with her parents at their cottage on the peninsula, near Sydney, a three-hour drive from Stirling. Generally, she and her family stayed at their cottage all summer long. Zach hoped her parents would choose to make the trip.

Turning back to his study he investigated the references to wisdom in Job chapter twenty-eight. Job had asked, "But where can wisdom be found? And where is the place of understanding?" Job went on to say that wisdom is not found in the land of the living or in the depths of the sea; it can't be bought with even the finest gold. The chapter concludes by stating that only God knows where wisdom is found; "Behold, the *fear of the Lord*, that is wisdom; and to *depart from evil* is understanding."

Following various links to 'wisdom' in the Bible, Zach discovered that true wisdom is an understanding and appreciation that God's laws are vastly superior to our own sense of 'right and wrong'.[134] When he came to Proverbs four, he read the whole chapter. "Hear, my children, the instruction of a father, and give

---

[134] Deut.4:6; Psa. 111:10; Prov. 3:1-24; 9:10; 1 Cor.1:17-29; Rom.1:20-28

attention to know understanding… Let your heart retain my words; keep my commands, and live… Wisdom is the principal thing; therefore get wisdom. And in all your getting, get understanding. Exalt her, and she shall promote thee… She will place on your head an ornament of grace…" *Just like Job before he was afflicted!* Zach marvelled. *Because Job loved God's ways, he became renowned as a man of wisdom! When he spoke, people listened, because he spoke and lived the words of God.* [135]

He read on: 'Take firm hold of instruction, do not let go; Keep her, for she is your life… The way of the wicked is like darkness; they do not know what makes them stumble… My son, give attention to my words; incline your ear to my sayings. Do not let them depart from your eyes; keep them in the midst of your heart; for they are life to those who find them, and health to all their flesh. Keep your heart with all diligence, for out of it spring the issues of life.'

"Keep your heart with all diligence," Zach pondered when he went to bed that night. "For out of it spring the issues of life." *The decisions I make, are made from what is in my heart,* he considered, lying on his bed in the dark. It was a very dark night and a strong wind was blowing. Jake still wasn't home. *I need to guard my heart,*[136] Zach told himself. *I need to keep God's wisdom flowing in. The biggest battle I need to fight – is the one inside of me – the battle in my heart!*

As he lay there thinking over these thoughts, he recalled a point his father had made during the readings one night, "We must be 'born of water and of the spirit,'" [137] he had said. "'God's thoughts are higher than our thoughts. Jesus' words are spirit and

---

[135] Job 29
[136] Luke 6:45; Matthew 15:18-19; Luke 8:15; 1 Timothy 1:5; Hebrews 4:12

[137] John 3:5-8

life [138]. It's by taking in the words of life that 'Christ is formed in us', that a 'new man' [139] is born.

It was shortly after three in the morning when Zach woke up to an intense thunderstorm. He was startled to hear someone fiddling with his bedroom window. Slowly it slid open. Someone was coming through the ground-floor window!

"Sh-h," Jake whispered with a grin as he landed on the carpet, dripping wet. "I don't want mom and dad to know I'm home this late."

Wearily, Zach looked up at his alarm clock. "It's after three, Jake!" he whispered back. "How many movies did you watch?"

"Only one," Jake smiled with a shrug, pulling off his wet clothes. "Melissa wanted to go for a walk. It was great until the rain started! She broke up with Shane, so she's feeling rather lonely." With a quiet chuckle he added, "She asked about you."

With a groan, Zach put his pillow over his head. "I don't want to hear anymore."

Wrapping himself in a blanket, Jake sat down on his brother's bed. He pulled the pillow off his brother. "Zach," he said. "You've got to be honest with me."

Zach rolled over and faced his brother. "About what?!"

"About Melissa. I won't move in on your girl if you still care about her. Seriously!"

"She's not my girl, but of course I care about her," Zach replied passionately. He sat up in bed. "Jake, I'm choosing this Sunday to commit my life to God! I'm not going to date someone who doesn't share that commitment and you shouldn't either. Melissa needs help to find God's truth, but she will drag you down in a dating situation. Come on, Jake," Zach pleaded, "you know

---

[138] John 6:63
[139] Galatians 4:19; Colossians 3:10; Romans 8:9; James 1:18

you would have been telling me the same thing a month ago! Melissa doesn't know that morality matters."

"Probably not," Jake agreed. "But, you've had your fun, while I've been trying to do everything right all these years. I just want to break free for a bit – not in any crazy way. I just want to experience life a little."

"That doesn't sound good, Jake!"

"You had your fun and I covered for you, right?"

"But Jake, I'm *choosing* to leave it all behind… and you're *already* baptized! I can tell you the "fun" wasn't worth it. It didn't do me any good – it almost took me completely away from God."

"I'll probably make the same choice as you… eventually," Jake replied evenly, leaving Zach's bed and climbing into his own. "Just cut me some slack. Let me find my way like you found yours."

Perplexed and unsure how he should respond, Zach didn't say anything more. However, he felt very torn up inside as he wondered, *What does Jake feel he's missing out on? And what's he planning to do? Something's happening to my brother and it's probably Melissa! Will she go out with him?*

Zach thought it all over carefully as Jake drifted off to sleep. He groaned. He knew that compared to Shane and the other guys Melissa had dated, Jake would seem like a perfect gentleman. *If Melissa fell for me, I guess I shouldn't be surprised if she falls for my twin brother. But what's this going to do to him? It can't be good. Maybe I should involve Dad. Or should I just let Jake figure this out on his own?*

CHAPTER 27

Into the Water

Determined to invite all his friends to witness his baptism, Zach made several attempts to contact everyone. His final round of calls included one to Jayden, and this time he was able to leave a message with Jayden's mom.

"A baptism?" she repeated incredulously. "Why are you going to all that trouble, Honey? Just believe in your heart and you will be saved." [140]

Zach had a few passages ready in case anyone asked him that question and Jayden's mom listened politely as he explained why he believed baptism was essential to salvation. [141]

When he called Melissa, he was happy that she answered. Melissa was eager to talk, but rather confused with the concept. While she wasn't in a hurry to end the conversation, Zach found it difficult to explain his decision to someone who didn't even believe God existed.

While Melissa wasn't really sure what she believed about the origins of life or the existence of a 'higher power', she was firmly convinced that such discussions didn't matter!

"I really like you, Zach," she told him, "but I'm not interested in becoming a Christian – there are way too many dumb rules!"

Zach knew well in advance that Melissa wouldn't be coming on Sunday. He hung up the phone feeling even more worried about Jake's budding relationship with her. He soon learned that some of his Youth Group friends wouldn't be there

---

[140] Romans 10:9
[141] Mark 16:15-16; Galatians 3:27-29; Romans 6:3-12; Acts 2:38

either. David's family was away on vacation, and Jerry was in Truro for a soccer tournament.

On Zach's special Sunday morning, Jayden was one of the first to arrive at the small white Christadelphian hall, just outside of Stirling. He was pushing his brother Isaiah in his wheelchair.

"Hey, guys. Thanks for coming today!" Zach greeted them.

"This is a cool thing that you're doing, man!" Jayden exclaimed, flashing a bright smile. "I've never seen a baptism before. Gotta say, I'm rather curious."

"Yeah," Isaiah agreed. "Very curious. Mom would've come too, only she's helping out at the food bank this morning."

Brett filed in behind Jayden and gave Zach an encouraging clap on the back. "I'm so happy to be here today! Glad you're joining the club!" Knowing that Zach would be sitting at the front, with his family filling the row of seats, Brett invited Jayden and his brother to sit with him.

"Joining the club," seemed like an odd statement to Zach. He pondered the phrase as he helped his father set up Skype so that his sisters in Ottawa could watch the service. Once Skype was up and running, he chatted to his sisters while everyone was filing into the hall.

Of all his Sunday School friends, Abi was the only one who showed up. She and her mom walked through the door just after the organ voluntary had begun. "Mom drove me here," she whispered quietly to Zach, as she slipped into the row behind him.

Looking over appreciatively at Abi's mom, Zach said, "Thanks!"

"No problem," she smiled graciously. "Abi really wanted to come."

Sitting at the front of the small meeting hall, with Jake on one side and his parents and sister on the other, Zach reflected on how much his life had changed. *I've changed because of what I've read and heard,* Zach thought. *Look at what God's Word has done to me! I was rebellious and full of myself and God reached out and turned me in the opposite direction. Here I am committing my life to Him. Today, I'm choosing, like Moses, to give up the life in Egypt and all the pleasures this world has to offer. I'm choosing to take up my cross to follow Jesus.*

Zach pulled out a new notebook and pen as Craig Symons rose to give the exhortation that morning. Uncle Craig, as Zach had always affectionately called him, was Uncle Peter's father-in-law and had taught the twins in Sunday School for the last four years. Completely grey and very lean, Uncle Craig's blue eyes sparkled with conviction. He and his wife were still enthusiastically involved in nearly every outreach activity organized by the Ecclesia.

"Good morning, Brothers and Sisters, and a special good morning to Zach," Uncle Craig began. "I'm very pleased that Zach is making this commitment to His Heavenly Father and our Lord Jesus Christ. When I first began teaching the twins in the senior Sunday School class, four years ago, Zach and Jake were keen and capable students. Many times the questions that they asked caused me to go home with more homework than I assigned them!"

There was some muffled laughter.

"We had some great sessions early on. And then," Uncle Craig recalled, "as time went on, those questions gradually ceased. There were Sundays when I wasn't sure that anyone was listening." He paused for a moment. "Zach," he said, looking directly at him, "I'm so thankful to see enthusiasm in your eyes again. Whatever happened this summer has been for your good and I'm very happy God has led you to this decision."

With a smile, Zach nodded. He knew what had happened. He had finally taken time to listen to God's call. He had finally realized he was a sinner in need of forgiveness through Jesus Christ.

Jake fidgeted restlessly with the ribbon in his Bible. He was finding it harder and harder to concentrate on Sunday mornings. With all the movies he was watching, the creepy novels he was reading, and the snapchat photo Melissa had sent him that morning – never mind the intense texting conversations – there were too many enticing fantasies pulling him in other directions. He had started sowing to the flesh,[142] and inevitably, and sadly, he was reaping corruption. Master Sin was adding shackles to his willing slave, one by one.

"I'd like to talk this morning about repentance," Uncle Craig said, "because that's what baptism is all about. We confess our sin, our need for forgiveness in Christ, and our decision to crucify the flesh and walk in the spirit."

"When we do wrong," Craig continued, "we usually feel sorry for what we have done. But, it's interesting to note, that there are two different types of sorry; one leads to life and one leads to death. Let's read from Second Corinthians seven, verses eight to eleven."

Uncle Craig asked everyone to turn to the passage. He explained that the Apostle Paul had been upset with the Corinthians in his first letter, because they were allowing one of their members to continue in a sinful situation, without rebuke. But when a Second letter to the Corinthians was written, the Apostle Paul was able to praise them because they had listened to his warning, were sorry for their wrongdoing, and had changed the situation. Reading from chapter seven, verse ten from the NIV, Uncle Craig read, 'Godly sorrow brings repentance that leads to salvation and leaves no regret, but worldly sorrow brings death.'"

"It's possible to be sorry for what we have done but not to change anything in our hearts," Uncle Craig continued. "We see it

---

[142] Galatians 6:7-8

easily in our children. Little Freddie takes a lollipop from the candy jar without asking. If no one discovers his theft, Little Freddie quite happily enjoys the treat. When he is caught and punished there may be plenty of tears. But are those tears because Freddie is truly ashamed and sorry that he stole? Or is he crying, because he got caught and can't have any treats for the rest of the week?" Uncle Craig smiled, "The test is whether Little Freddie steals again the next time he has a chance, or – chooses to avoid the temptation."

"Think of Judas Iscariot," Uncle Craig elaborated; "he was very sorry that he had betrayed Jesus. So sorry was Judas for his actions that he cast down the money he'd been paid, in the temple, proclaimed that he had betrayed an innocent man, and… *took his own life.* Judas' sorrow is not the kind that will lead us to God's salvation. Godly sorrow leads us to change our hearts and behaviour. Godly sorrow leads us to confess our sins, ask for forgiveness and find help to overcome our weakness. Judas' sorrow was of the *worldly* sort, which only leads to despair and death. The disciple Peter also betrayed Jesus that same night, through his fearful denials, yet Peter's sorrow led to his humbling and a complete change of heart. He became a stronger man, prepared to proclaim Jesus Christ regardless of persecution."

Zach looked over at Jake to share his enthusiasm for the things that were being said, but Jake was staring out the window with a smile on his face. He seemed far away in thought. As Uncle Craig went on to give another example – citing Esau's worldly sorrow over losing his birthright,[143] how he 'sought it carefully with tears', but found no way to change his father's mind – Zach began to wonder what Jake was thinking about. As he did this, he quickly found his own thoughts in places that he didn't want them to be. *How can I be thinking these thoughts?* Zach chided himself.

---

[143] Hebrews 12:16,17

Here I am about to give my life to God, and my mind is in the gutter! Taking notes and harnessing his thoughts to concentrate on the words being spoken made a difference. It helped!

Uncle Craig then talked about Joseph – the joy Joseph must have felt when he saw his brother Judah's heartfelt distress over Benjamin's plight. The joy of knowing that Judah was now more concerned about their father's feelings than his own.[144] He referred to David's sin with Bathsheba and the months that dragged by before David was fully convicted *in his heart* that he had sinned and was unworthy before God.[145]

"Godly sorrow is all about changing hearts," Uncle Craig continued. "In Proverbs chapter four, verse twenty, we are given some good advice. I want to pass this on to you today, Zach." From the NIV, Uncle Craig read, "My son, pay attention to what I say, listen closely to my words. Do not let them out of your sight, keep them within your heart; for they are life to those who find them and health to a man's whole body. Above all else, *guard your heart*, for it is the wellspring of life."

That's the very same passage I was reading just the other night! Zach realised.

"'How can a young man keep his way pure?'"Uncle Craig asked, quoting from Psalm one hundred and nineteen. [146]"'By living according to your word… I have *hidden your word in my heart* that I might not sin against you.' This is the way to change hearts," Uncle Craig continued. "Jesus overcame his temptations because the Word of God was in his heart. [147] God looks in the heart. [148] He is looking for hearts that willingly choose Him and truly love His ways. Let His word live in you, Zach, that He might

---

[144] Genesis 44 & 45
[145] 2 Samuel 11 – 12 :15; Psalm 32:1-5
[146] Psalm 119:9-16 NIV
[147] Luke 4:1-14
[148] 1 Samuel 16:7; 1 Chronicles 28:9; Psalm 147:10-11; Jeremiah 17:10; 29:13; Revelation 2:23

guide your life, just as He has for your brother Jake." Uncle Craig smiled across at Jake as he said this.

Hearing his name, Jake escaped from his daydreams. With a weak smile in return, Jake felt decidedly uneasy at being held up as a good example for Zach to follow. He had been imagining himself driving up to Melissa's house in the bright yellow corvette that he had seen for sale on the side of the road that morning. *Now, what exactly was Uncle Craig saying when he mentioned my name?*

"Today, Zach," Uncle Craig continued, "you've changed your allegiance. You are choosing to no longer willingly serve King Sin. [149]Before everyone here, you are choosing to give your life, your heart, and your mind to Your Father in heaven and serve Him. Today you are thankful that Jesus, your Saviour, absolutely gave his heart, mind and life to His Father, providing all of us with forgiveness and showing us the way to live.[150] There will be days ahead when you will fail; days when you will disappoint yourself and Your Heavenly Father in the decisions that you make, or the things you do – or don't do. Forgiveness is available to you, Zach – don't despair or give up like Judas. [151]Don't deny your sin – as David did for months in utter misery.[152] Don't serve insincerely – like Esau, completely despising the great birthright. [153]And don't neglect a dying love in your heart – nurture it with the Word and prayer – take away the thorns.[154] Confess your sins, repent, and go forward, forsaking the evil way…"

Zach nodded, as he scribbled down the message. He was encouraged. His heart was open to the words. The words might have had an impact on Jake, as well, if his thoughts had not drifted

---

[149] Romans 6:12-23
[150] Romans 6:1-10; Luke 9:23
[151] Matthew 27:3-5; Acts 1:16-18
[152] Psalm 32 & 51
[153] Hebrews 12:16-17
[154] Luke 8:7,14

off again, estimating how much money he was going to make with EdenTree that summer.

After the exhortation, hymns were sung, while Zach changed clothes and headed over with his family to the small lake that was within walking distance of the hall. The others followed soon afterwards, setting the laptop carefully on a nearby stump so that his sisters could watch. His father baptised him, taking him down into the water, to put off 'the old man of the flesh' [155]and bringing him up a new man, dedicated to God. It was a high calling but Zach knew it was the only decision with an eternal promise of life. His family and several others gave him big hugs when he came up out of the water and on Skype, his sisters were cheering.

At the end of the service there was, as usual, a 'Prayer for the Brethren' when special requests were made for any brother or sister in need. Zach's dad gave this prayer and his most earnest request was that God would be with his sick brother James. He asked that he would soon find health and strength to recover and that Aunt Sandra would be strong in faith. The only sadness for Zach on his day of rejoicing was the absence of two of the most important people in his life.

"Texts are pouring in for you," Jake told him after the service was over. He showed his brother the phone. All their old friends in Ontario were sending messages to congratulate Zach on his baptism. All his absent aunts and uncles had sent texts as well.

Jake was reading the messages with his brother. He pointed out the one from Hannah.

It said:

Zach, I'm so happy I've made this decision and that you have too. I now know where I'm going in life. We belong to Christ now and for always. Happy new Birthday – twin! Love, Hannah.

"You've got a new twin," Jake remarked.

---

[155] John 3:3-8; Romans 6:1-6; Ephesians 4:22-24; Colossians 3:10-13

"We've been born again on the same day."

"True."

"I have something for you," Abi said, on her way out of the meeting hall. She smiled and passed Zach a small packet.

Zach looked at her with surprise. Several of the older members of the Ecclesia had given him helpful books to commemorate his baptism, but it was a total surprise to get something from Abi. He took the package appreciatively.

"I hope you'll wear it," she said with a bright smile. "If I ever decide to get baptized, I think I'd wear something like this. Then I could tell everyone about it!"

Peeling back the layers, Zach uncovered a braided leather bracelet. Something was engraved on the rectangular metal plate in the middle. Zach held it up close to see the words. "A new man in Christ," it said.

"Abi, this is amazing!" Zach marvelled. "Yeah, I'll definitely wear it! Thanks so much!"

"You're welcome," she smiled.

Seeing Zach fumble to tie it on, Abi offered to help. It was much easier to fasten with two hands.

"So, when are you going to... be... baptized?" he asked her tentatively, as she tied the cords. The question came out awkwardly; Zach wasn't used to encouraging his friends in a spiritual way.

Looking down, Abi shrugged her shoulders. "I have to clean up my act first," she mumbled.

"I can relate to that," Zach nodded. He paused, but as much as he was unaccustomed to encouraging his friends in spiritual ways, he suddenly felt compelled to try harder. *Abi is a good friend,* he reasoned. *She's been there for me when I needed her. The bracelet was such a kind gift. What have I ever done for her? Nothing, except view her as competition!*

He gave her a hug.

211

"Don't wait too long, Abi," he said earnestly as they parted. "Remember, Uncle Craig said it's not about being perfect – you know; it's about being sorry. "

"Come on, Abi," her mom called out from a distance. "It's a three-hour trip back!"

"Why don't you come with Allan and me to Youth Conference?" Zach said on the spur of the moment. "I had such a great time at Manitoulin! It was so good to see everyone again. I learned so much! It helped me to make this change."

Abi sighed. "Oh, I don't know. I have a lot planned already. I'm supposed to be going to Brian's cottage with his family that week."

In Zach's mind there could hardly have been a worse excuse; a week at Brian's cottage would pull Abi in the opposite direction. "Look, I'll send you the workbook, if you send me your email address. I'll help you with it, over the phone – or however we can. You'll love it, Abi! I know you will!"

"I'll send you my email," she said half-heartedly. Turning away to head out with her mom, Abi gave Zach a parting glance. Her eyes were troubled and Zach felt at a loss to help. He was surprised by how much he had already said. Since when did he pressure people like that?! But he knew that deep down Abi wanted to change. She just couldn't see her way out of the situation she had chosen to enter.

Little did Zach know that he would never see Abi's face again. Neither one of them realized how quickly time was running out. No one did. The door would soon be shut. The opportunity to repent and find forgiveness was coming to an end.[156]

Jayden and Isaiah came over and marvelled at the pile of books Zach had been given. While their church was very actively involved in the community and helping out all over the world,

---

[156] Matthew 25:1-13

Bible study was not emphasized.

"They're expecting you to do lots of reading!" Jayden said picking up a book that caught his attention.

With a laugh, Zach told them, "If you see anything you like, feel free to borrow it. Until Youth Conference is over, I'll be flat-out studying Job every night. So if it's not about Job, I probably won't get to it until the fall."

"Really?" Isaiah looked at the books eagerly; he had a longing to learn more.

Jayden examined the book he had picked up. It was called, *Stormy Wind Fulfilling His Word.*[157] "This one looks interesting. It's about historical battles – which I love to read! Sure you don't mind?"

"No, take more if you like. You've got another month of holidays!"

"I'll be off to Uganda tomorrow," Jayden reminded him quietly. "But I could use some reading material on the flight."

"Right! All the best with that!" Zach exclaimed. "How much did you guys raise for house-building?"

"Ten-thousand dollars!" Isaiah cheered.

"Are you serious?!"

"Didn't you see our picture in the paper last week?" Jayden asked.

Zach shook his head uneasily. "Sorry, guys, I rarely read the paper. But send me a copy if you can. I'd love to see it!"

Sitting down, Jayden examined the rest of the books and showed some to Isaiah. Many of the topics and Bible characters were unfamiliar but, "Hey, look," he said to his brother, "here's one on Jonathan."

"My favourite Bible hero!" Isaiah beamed. "Can I borrow

---

[157] Benson, Tony. *Stormy Wind Fulfilling His Word, The Place of Weather, Volcanoes and Earthquakes in Fulfilling Bible Prophecy.* Christadelphian Scripture Study Service, 2010.

this?"

Zach laughed, "Of course." Looking down at all the books, Zach picked out one that he thought would cover the important teachings of the Bible. "You can borrow this, too," he said to the brothers. "It's about the simple Gospel message. I'll be interested to hear what you think of it."

"Okay," his friend agreed. "I'll read this and then we'll have a discussion! It's about time!"

"Yeah, it probably is," Zach admitted.

That night, after dinner, Jake handed Zach the confiscated Smartphone. "Dad wants to talk to you in the kitchen," he said, looking very upset. "You're getting it back early."

Surprised, Zach took the phone eagerly and headed to the kitchen.

"I know this is being returned to you before summer is over," his father told him. "But I realize the need you have to keep in touch with your friends in Ontario. I just hope that the contacts you make with this device will be as helpful to you in your new walk in Christ, as I hope you will be to them. Use it wisely, Zach. It can be a tool for good, but it can just as easily lead to evil."

"I'll use it wisely," Zach said.

Looking serious for a moment, Zach's dad added, "I had Jake show me a printout of that phone's texting history. There seems to be thousands of messages sent first by you and then Jake to one particular number. I don't know who that particular number belongs to. But I am hoping it isn't responsible for the decline I've witnessed in both my boys while they were contacting it so frequently. Would you have any opinion on the matter?"

"Melissa has been a problem for both of us," Zach admitted freely.

"I thought as much," his dad replied. "Is there any way I can help?"

"Bible Camp helped me," Zach told him. "I realized how

much I needed good friends. Maybe you could take Jake on a long car ride and have a talk to him. He needs your help."

Nodding thoughtfully, Zach's dad agreed this was a good idea. "I'll see what I can do," he said, and he fully intended to follow through with the plan. In the past, fishing trips had been a good option for long, private conversations, or even a hike along the Oceanview trail. However, Andrew didn't comprehend the urgency. Like everyone else, Andrew had no idea how close they were to the last day – the very last day before Christ's return. Too preoccupied with finishing the course he needed for September and handling a multitude of difficult pastoral issues in the Ecclesia, he was only vaguely aware that his son had been hijacked by King Sin. He had no idea that Jake needed to be saved with fear 'pulling [him] out of the fire'. [158] Unfortunately, his son's needs were too far down on his long list of priorities to instigate any deep conversations that week.

As Zach walked back to his room, he checked his text message history. There were very few messages that had come through to him after his friends had realized he'd had his phone confiscated. There wasn't a trace of the 'thousands' that had gone out to the one particular number his father had mentioned. The entire history on that 'thread' had been deleted, but... the ten-second photo flash and some very intimate conversations would remain in one young man's memory for life.

---

[158] Jude 23

CHAPTER 28

Bad News

All week long there were predictions that a major hurricane was heading towards the East coast. Hurricane Kennedy was to reach Nova Scotia sometime by Tuesday. It was classified as a Category Four Storm. Many people, including the Bryants, boarded up their windows. Some tried to be prepared by cutting down dead trees and limbs to prevent them from falling on their houses and cars. Scores of people left the coastal regions and headed further inland.

Tuesday night the hurricane hit. Kennedy was downgraded to a Category Three when it hit land, but even so, the wind and rain were thunderous. Zach and his family barely slept. Garbage cans rattled down the street. Trees groaned and scraped against the house. Every so often loud cracks and booms were heard as branches broke off and fell to the ground. Huddled around their clock radio, the boys listened to coastal storm surge warnings and incoming damage reports until suddenly the electricity cut out.

Zach's phone alarm woke them up the next morning. The power was off and it was still raining heavily. Even though it was seven o'clock in the morning, Zach could barely see through the dark gloominess that enveloped them. Trees close to the house were bent over with the wind and the lawn was covered with water. Broken branches lay everywhere. There would be no gardening work today. As he and Jake headed to the kitchen for breakfast, Zach's cell rang. It was Aunt Sandra. In an anxious tone she asked to speak to his dad.

The boys could only hear one side of the conversation as they set the table for breakfast. From their father's alarmed responses, they gathered that someone was seriously hurt or sick.

"Uncle James is in the hospital," their father said, after ending the phone call. "Aunt Sandra took him in last night before the storm hit. She says he's contracted *pneumonia*, of all things! His oxygen levels have dropped dangerously below normal so they've admitted him and he's on a powerful antibiotic drip."

"How serious is that?" Zach asked with concern. Uncle James was very special to him. "Will he be in for a day, or a week, or what?"

"I wouldn't think more than a couple of days," his father assured him. "They have pretty strong meds to clear up stuff like that."

The rain finally stopped late Wednesday night. Thursday morning the Bryants joined an army of volunteers to clear the main roads. There was a lot of damage all over Stirling.

By Friday the main highways reopened but many side-streets were still a mess of fallen tree branches and flooding. When they contacted Aunt Sandra to check on Uncle James' wellbeing, they found out that while she had finally made it home that Friday morning, so many branches had fallen at Oceanview Lodge she was unable to get up her driveway.

"I'll see if I can head over there today and clean it up," Zach's dad told his mom. "Maybe Esther can help me and you can spend some time with Sandra and my mom. It sounds like they would appreciate your company."

Zach's mom agreed.

After they had helped the neighbours cut up and remove a few large limbs that had fallen on their street, the twins' parents and Esther headed to Oceanview Lodge while the boys headed to work. Almost every EdenTree customer had trees down. The heavy rain had eroded gardens and lawns. Along the coastline rogue waves had wreaked havoc inland. There would be no shortage of work for a while.

When the boys arrived home that evening, tired, wet and muddy, their parents had exciting news. Uncle Peter and Aunt Jessica were flying home from their missionary work in Jamaica to see Uncle James and spend time with their family!

"They've been planning to get back for a visit, anyhow," Zach's mom explained, when Zach's eyes widened with the news. "They've been gone almost a year now, so it will be really good to see them again."

"Is Uncle James going to be okay?" Zach asked, wondering if this sudden visit meant his uncle was in critical condition.

"I would think so," his mom said, reassuringly. But Zach could tell she was uncertain.

Esther was thrilled with the news that little Susanna, Jimmy and Seth were coming home for a couple of weeks. Hearing that they were planning to stay at the Bryant's Oceanview Lodge, she began thinking up fun activities to do with them. Their favourite was always to go to the beach and hunt for shells, crabs and little lobsters.

However, when the twins had gone to their rooms to change and their parents thought everyone was out of hearing range, Zach heard his dad say to his mom, "His heart condition has the doctor's worried. The pneumonia is putting more strain on him than his heart can handle."

Zach heard his mom gasp.

"Thomas and Purity are also coming with Peter and Jess," he heard his father say. "Even Kara is flying in from Ontario. They should all arrive tonight."

"Do we need to pick them up?"

"Craig is looking after it. And the McKinleys have offered their van so that everyone can get around while they are here."

"God bless them," his mother sighed. "We have such wonderful friends!"

Now Zach was alarmed. As fit and healthy as Uncle James looked, he knew his uncle's heart would always be weak after the attack he had suffered years before. It alarmed him that so many friends and family members were coming! "Please, Heavenly Father," Zach pleaded earnestly, "don't let Uncle James die. We need him here!"

Esther overheard her parent's conversation as well. When the twins headed outside to do their exercise routine, she followed. As they did their warm-up stretches, she asked, "Who is Kara? Mom says she's coming in from Ontario. How does she know Uncle James?"

Knowing that his sister knew Uncle Thomas and Aunt Purity, Zach explained that Kara Lovell was Uncle Thomas' mother.

"Likely she's coming here *especially* to see Uncle Thomas and Aunt Purity," Jake surmised, stretching from side to side, "since they've been in Jamaica for a year with Uncle Peter and Aunt Jessica."

"She has some connections to us, too," Zach added proudly, "because her daughter Verity used to be really good friends with Uncle Peter. Until she died, that is."

"Really?" Esther prodded. "Someone died?! I don't think I've heard this story. Who? When? What's this all about?"

Pulling on one hamstring muscle, Jake began the story, "When Uncle Peter lived in Ontario he went to high school with Uncle Thomas, Aunt Purity and Verity. He first became friends with Verity, and I've heard he was really in love with her, but then she died of cancer."

"When she was only sixteen!" Zach added emphatically, following his brother's lead in the warm-up routine. "But she had already found the Truth and was baptized, and that led to Uncle Thomas becoming a believer, and his mom – Aunt Kara Lovell. *"*

"And then Uncle Peter became a believer," Jake said with

a smile, as he jogged on the spot, pulling his knees up extra high. "Uncle Peter told our family all about the true Gospel message. So really, all of us should be thankful for Verity."

"Just think – she was younger *than we are*, while she was searching for truth!" Zach exclaimed.

Esther sat down on the curb; the grass was still too wet from the storm. She was curious. "Okay, so then, how did Uncle Peter end up with Aunt Jessica? Isn't she a lot younger than him?"

Passing a basketball to his brother, Jake replied, "Uncle Peter and Verity used to visit the Symons while they were reading and discussing the Bible, so when Uncle Peter first met Aunt Jess, she was just a little girl in their house."

"After Verity died, Uncle Peter took off to Australia," Zach continued, as he and Jake began passing the basketball back and forth; they were eager to start on their rim-jumping, hill-run routine. "When Uncle Peter came back to Canada ten years later, Uncle James had just had a heart-attack. He was living here in Nova Scotia. Uncle Peter wanted to stay out here and be with his brother. Since the Symons had moved here by then, he lived with them."

"And that's when he really got to know Aunt Jess," Jake smiled, driving a bounce-pass hard at his brother. Zach caught it, faked him out, and gave him a surprise pass behind the back.

Esther was thinking it all through carefully. "So how long has Verity been dead, then?"

Zach wasn't exactly sure. As he and Jake gave each other increasingly difficult passes, he made a rough estimate. "Probably around twenty years."

"That's a long time," she considered sadly. "I really like Uncle Thomas. I wish I'd had the chance to meet his sister."

"Maybe you will at the resurrection!" Zach called out, missing his brother's pass and running to catch the ball before it went on the road.

Jake began his rim-jumps and Zach tossed the ball to Esther and joined him. Esther sat and watched the boys for a while as she thought about all the connections she hadn't realized existed. *Uncle Peter loved someone else before Aunt Jess!* she pondered. *And that girl died young! How sad! She was Uncle Thomas' sister. Because of her, our family became believers...* When the boys began their third hill-run, she went inside to help make dinner.

CHAPTER 29

The Invitation

"Melissa!" Zach called out, as he slammed on his brakes.

He was on his way to Oceanview Lodge Saturday morning when he saw her. There was still a lot of clean up to do from the hurricane. His brother Jake was helping Brett with his yard, and Esther and his parents had gone in early that morning to visit Uncle James.

Zach hadn't seen Melissa for weeks and now she was standing on the street corner waiting for the light to turn so that she could cross the road.

Swerving right quickly, Zach took the closest parking spot on the downtown street. Melissa pranced over in sparkly, high-heeled sandals. With a summer tan and blond highlights in her copper-brown hair, she looked even prettier than he remembered. "Hey, Zach!" she called out with a merry laugh. "I haven't seen you all summer!"

Never a modest dresser, Melissa was at her skimpiest in the heat. Leaning into his open window, she rested her arms on the ledge. He could smell her sweet, enticing scent. A wisp of her silky, hair blew across Zach's face. Giggling, she tucked the stray piece behind her ears. Alluring images flashed across Zach's mind.

"I can't believe it's been over two months since we did the musical!" she giggled again.

Zach nodded. "Has it been over two months?!" he exclaimed. Mentally, he calculated that almost ten weeks had past.

"Think you'd remember how to do the whirly-bird catch?" she teased.

Zach laughed. They had practiced that move more than

any other. He had no trouble remembering the steps but whether or not he could still execute them was questionable. "That was so hard!" he recalled. "I'd probably drop you if we tried it today."

"Just for fun, we should give it a try," she suggested with a cute, whimsical smile. "Why don't you come over tonight? My parents are away and I still have the music."

Zach's heart raced. He would love to dance with Melissa again! She'd be back in his arms... All of a sudden, old feelings rushed back in full force.

"I actually... broke up with Shane," she added. "He's going to Ottawa for college, you know."

"Yeah, Jake was telling me. Ottawa is far away."

"Too far to come home for weekends!"

With hesitation, Zach looked into her smiling eyes. Melissa was finally free... and now he wished that she wasn't!

At that very moment, Zach felt his phone vibrate. He reached into his pocket to check the incoming message and saw it was a text from Hannah:

I heard the terrible news about Uncle James! Mom and Dad want to drive out to see him. Maybe I'll see you next weekend, God Willing! Please tell him he's in our prayers. Love, Hannah

Zach took a deep breath. Hannah's message gave him strength. "I think I'll pass on tonight," he sighed. "I'm working at my Grandma's today to clean up from the storm, and my uncle is really sick. He's in the hospital." Changing the subject quickly, he asked, "What are you up to?"

"Just hanging out with some friends," she replied, rather surprised by his flat turn-down. "Wal-Mart has half-price on beach towels, so we're heading over to get some." Teasingly, she asked. "Do you want one?"

"I already have three."

"That should do you!" she giggled. Reaching over she touched Zach's new leather bracelet. He let her pull his arm closer.

223

"What does it say?" she begged sweetly, trying to read it.

"A new man in Christ," he told her plainly.

"Is that from when you were… bap – tised?" she asked, somewhat unsure of the pronunciation.

"It is."

She nodded uncertainly and then said with reluctance, "Well, I guess I should let you get to your job." With a sudden, inviting smile, she added, "Just text me if you change your mind about tonight."

"Have a good day," he smiled reluctantly. "I should get going."

Impulsively, Melissa leaned in and kissed him on the cheek. "Good bye, Zach," she said softly, stepping back. "I miss you!"

"Yeah, see you," Zach replied, feeling very torn. The kiss was nice. *Is she just flirting with me, or is she serious?* he wondered, putting the car in gear and waving out his window as he drove away. *Did she ditch Shane for me? Is she looking for a long-term relationship, or just a fling? We could be so good together!*

With his hands on the steering wheel, the "New man in Christ" bracelet was easy to see. It was a reminder of the commitment he had made to God. Unfortunately, baptism hadn't taken away any of the old feelings and passions; they were still alive and well.

Since his dad and Esther had worked hard the day before to clear the tree-lined driveway at Oceanview Lodge, Zach was able to drive all the way to the garage without any difficulty. He got out of the car and looked around. This was truly his favourite job site. Not only did he love being by the ocean, but he always felt more at home here, than anywhere else. It was sad to see so many broken trees and fallen limbs on the lawns. The shoreline had changed shape along the cliffs, due to incoming waves, and a lot of seaweed was tangled in the low-lying bushes. *I'll clean it up in time,* he told himself, *but it may take a few days.*

Glancing over at the purple door, he half-expected to see Uncle James saunter out to join him as he so often did on a Saturday morning. Grandma and Aunt Sandra always made sure that he had numerous refreshment breaks and some creative cooking to sample. Since the beginning of summer, Aunt Sandra had started making the best fruit smoothies, and Grandma's cookies were second to none!

This Saturday was quite different, however. Uncle James was in the hospital. Although their car was in the driveway, Zach wasn't sure if Aunt Sandra and Grandma were home or not. And instead of the usual mowing lawns and tending gardens, there was a lot of heavy debris to clean up. As he chain-sawed fallen trees and stacked the wood alone, his mind kept returning to the images he wished he'd never viewed – and a beautiful face peering in his car window. The encounter had brought it all back – every feeling he'd tried to forget. *Melissa was so close. She kissed me! Shane is out of the picture. He's moving to Ottawa. Melissa invited me to dance with her, not to practice for a performance, but to dance for fun. It could be fun. Her parents aren't home. We'll be alone. She wants it that way. I could give it a try and see how things go. She'll always love me more than Jake – I know it. I just have to text and say that I've changed my mind.*

With a deep sigh, Zach knew that to go would be to invite trouble. With the light of God's Word in her life, perhaps one day Melissa would come to understand and appreciate the wisdom of God's ways – but that light wasn't there yet. If he was to have any interactions with Melissa, he knew it needed to be fully accountable, in a public place, with other people around. *But I've been hoping she'd want me to be more than a friend, for so long! And Jake is taking my place. If I go tonight she can be mine – I'm sure of it! Maybe if I go, I could spend some time talking to her about the Bible...*

But I know I won't, he thought with despair, dragging a tarp full of twigs to the compost pile. *Especially not,* he thought, *if she starts kissing me again!"*

All it would take was one text.

"Oh! I hate these thoughts!" he exclaimed aloud, dumping the contents of the tarp and shaking it out in disgust. "I made a commitment to stop serving sin, but how do I stop my thoughts?" But there was no one to answer those questions and he wasn't sure he would have the nerve to ask anyone, had someone appeared.

As Zack vented his exasperation, energetically piling up many broken branches on the tarp, Uncle George's solution came to mind. Up at Bible Camp Uncle George had talked about runaway imaginations, especially imaginations that fantasized about other people. "Harness your thoughts and efforts to do something for God," Uncle George had counselled. "Pray for God's help to edify that person spiritually. Make it your mission to do what you can to help *them* do what is right and grow in faith and service to God. Positively pursue the opposite... "

But I am so weak and she doesn't want to listen! he thought anxiously. *How can I help someone like that? God, please show me what to do!*

Taking a break from his work, Zach bowed his head quietly to pray, begging for God's help and mercy. *Dear Heavenly Father,* he prayed, *I hate my thoughts. I'm being led astray by my own foolish heart and I need Your help. Please, if Melissa is someone that You are calling – please give me wisdom to know how I can help her. If she is only leading me astray please give me strength to overcome. I am so weak."*

The brief moment Zach spent in prayer fortified his mind. He was able to think things through in a more rational way when he was done. He now felt fully convinced that to go to Melissa's house in such a situation, was to embrace temptation. He knew

God's advice is *'to flee'*,[159] not to make 'provision for the flesh, to fulfill its lusts.' [160]

And Hannah and Noah might be coming next weekend, he reminded himself. All of a sudden he stopped and marvelled, *How amazing that Hannah texted me when she did! That text helped so much. Was it providential?* He couldn't be sure, but the message had come at just the right moment. *What if I hadn't met Hannah this summer?* he considered, *or reconnected with my other good friends? What if I hadn't had time to think about where my life was heading and realize that I wanted to turn it around? Where would I be right now? What would I be choosing?* He smiled to himself. *I feel like God sent me to camp – kicking and screaming, because He knew that's where I needed to be.* The thought that God might be watching over him and lending a hand, strengthened his resolve.

The door opened and Aunt Sandra stepped out with a tray.

"You're here!" Zach exclaimed.

"Yes, I'm waiting for your Uncle Peter to come by. He's going to come with us to the hospital."

Aunt Sandra's eyes were full of anxiety when she brought over the iced-lemonade.

"How is Uncle James?" Zach asked.

"Not good at all," Aunt Sandra said with dismay.

"Oh," Zach was disappointed. *But he's been on the drip since Tuesday. Why isn't he getting better? I need to go see him.* He looked around the yard. There were still many broken branches and limbs scattered on the ground.

Aunt Sandra followed his gaze. "Why don't you come with us, Zach," she encouraged. "Don't worry about the clean-up." Suddenly emotional, her face contorted with grief. In a high-pitched voice she added, "It just doesn't matter right now!"

---

[159] 1 Corinthians 6:18; 2 Timothy 2:22
[160] Romans 13:14

Seeing the tears well up in her lovely blue eyes, Zach reached out to give his aunt a hug. He didn't know what to say, but he tried, "He'll be okay, Aunt Sandra. He's going to get better!"

"I hope so, Zach," she sobbed. "I... I couldn't bear to... "

Aunt Sandra could say no more and Zach patted her back awkwardly as she tried to control herself. Finally, she shook her head silently, gave a little wave and fled back to the house.

About five minutes later Uncle Peter arrived in the McKinley's van, with all his family in tow.

"Hey, Zach!" his uncle called out, as he opened the door of the van. "Good to see you! It's been well over a year." Looking around quickly at the mess of broken branches, he added, "Are you doing this all by yourself? You need help!"

Greeting his uncle and aunt with enthusiasm, Zach explained that Hurricane Kennedy had brought disaster all over town. "Almost everyone is helping somewhere today," he shrugged.

When he looked into the back of the van there were three sets of shy little eyes peering at him. Zach held out his arms with a smile. "Hey, who's going to give me a hug?"

Jimmy and Seth were quick to jump out but Susanna hung back timidly, holding tightly to her dad. A year was a long time in her short life; she wasn't so sure about Zach.

"We should get the EdenTree crew out tomorrow afternoon and help the neighbours," Uncle Peter suggested. "There are probably a lot of people who don't have anyone to help them."

"I'm on board for that," Zach agreed, hugging his little cousins. "And I imagine there are others in the meeting who will join us." Winking at Susanna, Zach held out his hand, but there was no way she was coming over!

Uncle Peter picked his daughter up and held her close. Coyly, she turned her little face away and would not look at Zach.

"Susanna takes a while to warm up," Uncle Peter told

Zach, "but when she decides she likes you, she's your friend for life. Isn't that right, Sweetie-Pie?" he asked, tickling her tummy.

There was a giggle and two little arms squeezed her daddy's neck tight. But she kept her face hidden in his shirt.

"She's the most like her mommy," Uncle Peter said quietly, with a wink in Zach's direction.

Aunt Jessica looked over with an amused smile. "You mean… the outgoing part?" she teased.

With a laugh, Uncle Peter pulled his wife close. "Definitely the 'friend for life'!"

Zach carried the two boys in for a quick bite of lunch and then headed off with Grandma, Uncle Peter and Aunt Sandra to the hospital. Aunt Jessica stayed back to look after their children. Everyone was happy to see each other again, but with all the anxiety over Uncle James, the conversation soon centered on what was happening at the hospital.

"Are Thomas and Purity here as well?" Aunt Sandra asked.

"Yes," Uncle Peter nodded, "We were all on the same flight. But they'll visit later on with Kara. They don't want to overwhelm James with too many people at once.

At the hospital, Uncle James was breathing with difficulty when they slipped in to his room. He was still hooked up to the IV drip and a monitor. An oxygen mask lay nearby. When Uncle Peter called out to him he slowly opened his eyes.

"Pete?" he questioned, looking up wearily. He glanced around the room with confusion. "You're here?"

Uncle Peter reached over and clasped his brother's hand. "Jess and I have flown back for a visit, especially to see you! I'm sorry you're so sick, James!"

"I'll get over it," Uncle James said weakly with a half-smile, but then he went into a coughing fit. Aunt Sandra was instantly by his side, trying to help him sit up and get rid of the phlegm. Zach could hardly believe how raspy his uncle's breathing sounded.

When the attack was over, Uncle James rested back against the pillows. He looked so pale and weak. Aunt Sandra settled herself on the edge of the bed and at his request she placed the oxygen mask on his face.

Zach found chairs so they could all sit around the bed.

After his bout of coughing Uncle James didn't try to talk again. He did his best to nod or shake his head as they told him about the various events of the last twenty-four hours, but soon his eyes began to close and he fell back to sleep.

It was disturbing to hear the rattling sound of Uncle James' laboured breathing. As the others talked, Aunt Sandra didn't take her eyes off her husband for more than a minute. She clung tightly to one of his hands and Uncle Peter held onto the other.

They hadn't been in the room long when Zach's dad joined them. It was his second visit that day. "Pete, so good to see you!" he called out cheerfully, but the smile on his face faded when he heard James' troubled breathing.

Pulling up one of the chairs that Zach had brought over, Andrew didn't voice his deep concern for Uncle James' condition. Even though it looked like his brother was sleeping, there was always the chance that he may be listening. It would do no good to cause alarm. They were all troubled. No one knew what to make of it. Surely Uncle James would recover, but it was worrisome how much worse he was getting.

"Jake and Esther didn't come with you?" Uncle Peter remarked disappointedly.

Zach's dad shook his head. "With that wild storm we had, there are trees down everywhere! Jake's helping Brett with his yard today and Esther and Lisa are helping the McKinleys. Everyone will be at Mom's tonight for dinner though."

Uncle Peter nodded. "Mom says Jake's been spending a lot of time with Brett."

"Yeah, I thought it was a good thing at the start – you know, it's better to be playing sports and stay active than hanging out with kids in town that have nothing much to do. But now…" Zach's dad shook his head anxiously, "well, everything just seems to be getting out of balance."

"In what way?" Uncle Peter asked.

"Well," Zach's dad hesitated, glancing quickly in Zach's direction, "in several ways." He sighed, "Like you, Pete, I believe that sports is a great way for kids to learn how to work with others – how to be part of a team. We've always tried to make sure that we do our part to support the team and be on time – but the games never came before God."

Turning to Zach, his dad asked, "Do you remember the year that you and Jake couldn't play because the practices conflicted with Friday night Youth Group activities?"

Zach nodded. "And you never let us play Sunday mornings."

"True, but it's been a struggle lately to keep it all in perspective, hasn't it, Zach?"

"But that's because we have a good chance at winning the Provincials next season," Zach spoke up, defensively. "It's a once-in-a-lifetime chance, Dad!"

His dad looked helplessly at his brother Peter and said no more.

Uncle Peter looked thoughtful. "Tell Jake that I'd like to take him out for lunch sometime next week. Maybe he and I can have a chat." Then Uncle Peter looked over at Zach. "And I'll help you finish the yard work tonight," he promised.

Zach grinned. "Thanks, Uncle Peter."

They stayed in the hospital room for another hour, while Uncle James slept restlessly. When prompted, Uncle Peter told them about the mission work he had been doing in Jamaica. Zach was fascinated. Hearing about his uncle and aunt visiting poor brethren and sisters that lived alone in mountainous places; about them putting on puppet plays to teach Bible stories to eager groups of children: hearing about them driving around rugged, dirt roads to reach remote villages and visit interested friends – it all sounded like an exciting, life-transforming challenge!

Suddenly a new realization hit Zach. *Has it really been Brett I've been unwilling to disappoint?* he thought to himself. *Or have I only been justifying my own desires. Jesus has done far more for me than Brett. Jesus gave up his whole life to save us! His whole life was consumed with living for God. He never spent any time following his own desires. And Jesus asks us to 'follow him'. Maybe,* Zach thought with a heart-wrenching twist, *maybe I could give up my 'super-twelve' year. I could leave basketball behind. I could leave my future in God's hands. A year in Jamaica with Uncle Peter will be a chance to 'positively pursue the opposite' of all that pulls me backwards here! I can spend my time serving others and serving God. And it might even be an adventure that I'd like to have!*

"This sounds really exciting!" Zach said to his uncle. "Maybe I should join you in September."

Both his father and his uncle looked up immediately.

"That would be great!" Uncle Peter said.

"Why do you want to go?" his father questioned skeptically.

Zach was surprised by his father's skepticism. "Shouldn't you be happy that I want to go?"

His father tried to shed his skeptical look. "Sorry, Zach," he apologized. "I'm still adjusting to the new Zach. I shouldn't have looked at you like that. It's great that you want to do missionary work if it's for the right reasons. But you've only just been baptized. It would probably be better for you to grow spiritually and develop here in your own Ecclesia first. There's plenty to do here – lots of young people to encourage and CYC classes to give. It just seems to me that it's best to develop with some solid Bible study and commitment at home before heading off to influence others overseas."

Feeling a little deflated, Zach sat back in his chair.

"You feel he needs mentoring," Uncle Peter clarified.

"Exactly."

"It's not like he will be going there on his own," Uncle Peter reminded his brother.

"True," Zach's father acknowledged. He sighed. "Why do you want to go, Zach?" he asked his son kindly. "Tell me. I want to know your reasons. Is it an adventure you're after, or something more?"

"I can hardly say that an adventure doesn't sound appealing," Zach admitted slowly. The smile on his uncle's face encouraged him to continue. "Dad, I've been thinking things over and I'd like to make some *big* changes in my life – for good. I'd like to take the focus off me – and what I want, and put it on God and what I can give. It's hard to do it here; there's a lot pulling me backwards."

His father nodded slowly. No one spoke for a moment or two. "I guess you will have your uncle and Thomas. And there is an established Ecclesia in Jamaica. "

Having thought about the idea for quite some time, Uncle Peter explained the work he hoped to give Zach. He was sure there would be plenty of Bible study, pastoral care, leadership at the vacation Bible Camps and best of all – involvement with the Youth Conference.

"Having Zach there, and Jake too – if possible," Uncle Peter said, "will encourage the other teens to participate. If they can see our teens excited about studying the Bible and living their life for Christ, it will help to motivate them to be more involved."

Andrew listened carefully to his brother and seemed to warm up to the idea. "I'm not trying to discourage you, Zach," he told his son. "I do believe there's a lot of good you can do right here in Stirling, and plenty of teens that need encouragement! But I understand that helping out in Jamaica could be a really positive experience. I'll support your decision, whichever you choose."

Before anything more could be said, Uncle Thomas and Aunt Purity arrived with Thomas's mother Kara. There were affectionate greetings all around once more, and then the others decided to leave. Uncle James was still sleeping and Aunt Sandra wouldn't be lonely now with all the newcomers.

CHAPTER 30

A Talk with Uncle Peter

The sun was just beginning to set when Zach and Uncle Peter headed outside that evening to finish the cleanup. Aunt Jessica had made a fabulous meal and all the family members that were able to come enjoyed it. Uncle Thomas and Aunt Purity had come to dinner, as well, along with Uncle Thomas' mother, Kara. Now Aunt Jessica was reading her children a story before they went to bed and Zach's dad was driving off with a plateful of food to take to Aunt Sandra. Everyone understood that Aunt Sandra wouldn't be leaving her husband again until he was well on the road to recovery. Surely he would be better soon! Uncle James was in the best place possible and they all felt fairly confident that with prayer and good medicine he'd be home in a few days.

Before the cleanup began, Uncle Peter and Zach walked around the gardens. Uncle Peter gave his nephew tips that would help the plants grow better and pointed out perennials that were getting so big they would need to be divided in September and transplanted.

After they brought out the lawn tractor and trailer to haul away the broken branches, Zach told his uncle that he was serious about missionary work.

"Zach, I would love that!" Uncle Peter exclaimed with delight. "Look, I'll pay your way out if you'll come for the year! There's so much you and Jake could do to help the young people," he encouraged. "There are three teen guys who haven't committed their lives to Christ yet – they're still trying to determine which path to choose. And we're all so keen to run a Youth Conference! There's a large group of young people that live long distances apart. It would do them all so much good to do the study and then get together to talk about the Bible. Since you're attending the Youth Conference this year, you could bring back some ideas for us!"

As they picked up the littered branches and tossed them into the trailer, Zach remembered a conversation he'd had at Bible Camp. "Uncle Peter," he said thoughtfully, "I hope we can talk Jake into coming, too. But if we can't, Noah Vandeburg wants to do missionary work. Could he come along?"

"There's enough for you, Jake *and* Noah to keep busy!" Uncle Peter assured him.

"Really?"

"Of course!"

"Can I text Noah right now?"

"Sure."

Zach took out his phone and eagerly punched in the news. For the first time ever, Noah responded immediately. He was very eager to be involved.

From that point on the conversation between Zach and his uncle became quite animated. While they laboured together cleaning up, they discussed all the possibilities ahead of them. Time went by quickly. Uncle Peter was so enthusiastic about Zach's abilities that Zach dreaded to tell him about the struggles he was having. However, he knew he wanted to talk to someone that he looked up to, and Uncle Peter was right there, ready and available.

After the fourth load of branches was dumped near the garden shed, Zach mustered his courage to talk to his uncle. Filling the trailer with what they hoped would be the last load of broken limbs, Zach asked, "Uncle Peter, did you watch many movies before you were baptized?"

"Too many."

"Bad ones?"

"Unfortunately, yes. I spent ten years of my life running away from God. I have a lot of regrets. "

Zach wasn't sure what to say next, so he didn't say anything. He just kept piling wood.

"Why do you ask, Zach?"

"Well, because… I saw one the other week and I can't get it out of my mind."

Heaving a large branch into the back of the trailer, Uncle Peter turned to face his nephew. "It's not easy, I know," he replied compassionately. "We can so quickly forget the good exhortation we hear on a Sunday, or the Bible readings we did the night before – yet worldly images keep blasting into our minds even when we come to detest them and would love to find a way to delete them permanently."

"You still struggle with them?"

Nodding solemnly, Uncle Peter admitted, "Yes, although not nearly as much as I used to. The last movie I watched like that was while I was still living in Australia and running away from God. But even today, on a Sunday morning I can be sitting happily next to my beautiful wife, fully absorbed in the exhortation I'm listening to, and one of those images will just strike me out of the blue. Before I know it, my mind has been taken some place that I didn't want it to go."

Zach sighed. It was reassuring to know that Uncle Peter, a man he highly respected, and a good example in many ways, understood the problem he was having. "So, what do you do about it?" he asked earnestly.

"Don't feed it," Uncle Peter told him firmly. "That's step number one. This world is corrupt. Try as we might, we can't completely stop ourselves from seeing things that excite our base nature. But when you have a choice, Zach, never choose to feed the flesh. The more you feed the flesh – whether through lustful movies, games, addictive novels, abusing alcohol or drugs, or the vast array of trash found on the internet – the stronger the pull becomes for more. Eventually you'll want to start doing the things you've been seeing and hearing and reading about. Even if you do those things, you still won't be satisfied; the flesh never is.[161] You'll have to keep increasing your level of indulgence to reach the same level of gratification, all the while searing your conscience and making it so much harder to maintain fellowship with God. It's a vicious downward cycle."

"Is there any way to reverse it all?"

Uncle Peter smiled and stretched out his shoulders. They hadn't finished the cleanup and it was getting dark, but the conversation was a higher priority. "It's very difficult while we're in this mortal body," he replied. "Even if we were to go and escape to some remote island with no electrical outlets, or billboards, or any other people, we'd still find our nature capable of inventing wickedness all on its own."

Sawing a few large branches so that they would fit more easily into the trailer, Uncle Peter told him, "Another thing that helps me when my mind is repeatedly going down a path I don't want it to, is to instantly stop and pray for forgiveness and God's help. We can, to a certain extent, change the path our minds take, by putting up mental stop signs and asking God to be involved."

Mental stop signs, Zach considered with a smile. "I'll have to try that," he told his uncle.

As Uncle Peter walked to the far edge of the lawn to get one last branch, a message came through on Zach's cell. Zach stopped to take a look. It was from Melissa:

Just wondering if you are coming over tonight? I found our music :)

I'm so glad I'm here with Uncle Peter, Zach thought, *this is more temptation than I can handle. I need to overcome evil with*

---

[161] Galatians 5:16-21

good… Somehow I've got to let her know I have a new allegiance.
Zach texted back:

Sorry, Melissa, I'm helping my uncle tonight. I've made a decision to be a 'new man in Christ'. If you ever want to know why this has changed me, I'd be happy to tell you.

Zach paused and took a deep breath before pressing 'send'. He was fairly certain Melissa would understand the implications of the message. It could well be the end of her flirtatious advances, which he would miss but found very difficult to handle. Mustering his resolve, he pressed the arrow. The message sent.

"I'll tell you what helps even more," Uncle Peter added as he returned dragging the large branch behind him.

"What's that?"

"Learning to love God."

"Okay... but, I do love God."

"I'm sure you do," Uncle Peter nodded, as Zach helped him wrestle the last branch into the trailer. "But does God feel loved by you?"

Zach looked at his uncle with a quizzical expression. Over and over he had heard how much God loves His creation... but no one had ever asked him if God felt loved by him in return. "Well... I thank God for... for all the love He has shown to us," Zach stuttered. "I'm sure He knows I'm sincere."

Wiping the sweat off his forehead, Uncle Peter took a seat on the garden tractor. "I hope you never experience this, Zach," he said with a grin, "but sometimes people fall in love with 'being loved'. They may enjoy getting all the attention, the gifts and the letters – but never really love *the giver* of that love."

In his mind, Zach imagined himself lavishing gifts and flowers on Melissa. He could see her revelling in the beautiful things she was receiving... but what if she only loved all the flattering attention but never really cared about him as a person?

"That would stink."

"It would. And we can do the same with God and Jesus. We can be thankful and happy for all the love they have shown to us – but never fall in love with *who they are*." [162]

"How can you tell the difference?"

"Well, if we really love someone we will want to find out all about them. We will want to know what pleases them. We will go to great extents to discover what is most important to them and do our best to bring happiness to their lives, right?"

"Right."

"So, we know we are falling in love with God when we *want* to make the effort to get to know Him, when we get excited about His plan and purpose for us and this earth, and are in awe of His morality and His commands."

"And what if we don't feel that excitement?"

Cocking his head to one side, Uncle Peter replied. "Force yourself to find out more about them, and you will fall in love. When you understand who Jesus was, his selfless character, his motivation to give his life for the world – you will want to be like him and his Father."

Zach nodded. He understood. Even the study he was doing every evening on Job's interaction with God was pulling him in the right direction.

"The more we learn to love God and His Son and desire to bring them pleasure," Uncle Peter added, "the more we will stop longing for things that bring them grief." [163]

It made sense to Zach but he knew how close he had been to causing grief only moments before. He moaned, "I'm just not sure I'll ever get there. My thoughts are sometimes totally corrupt!"

---

[162] Nathan Schipper, Sydney Youth Conference 2011:
http://study.sydney2011.com/conference_recordings
[163] 1 John 2:5-6; 15-17; 5:1-5; John 14:15,21,23

It was getting dark. Zach knew his uncle needed to get the last load to the shed so that they could unload the wood. He picked up the saws and rakes, and put them in the trailer.

Pulling the tractor keys out of his pocket, Uncle Peter held them in his hands but he didn't start the engine. "Brett has been a great coach to you and Jake through the years, right? He's fair and considerate?"

Zach agreed.

"So, Brett's not going to kick you off the team for missing ten shots if he sees you're putting in your best effort?"

"No... but he might sub in another player."

"True, he might feel that you need some time out. But that would be for your benefit, right?"

Zach nodded.

"But if you or Jake were to rest on your laurels as the team captains, or feel that you could get by with minimum effort, you might be benched for the game?"

"Of course."

With a smile, Uncle Peter expanded his analogy. "God knows we're going to make mistakes and that we can't be perfect – but He's reading our hearts and minds. He simply asks us to give 'all' that we can. [164] He knows better than any coach if we are really trying or just coasting." Pausing to look over at Zach, Uncle Peter added with a smile, "God is on your side, Zach. He wants you to win, every time. [165] If you ask Him, He'll work in your life to help change your heart."

---

[164] Mark 12:30; 1 Samuel 16:7; 1 Chronicles 28:9; Jeremiah 17:10
[165] Hebrews 12:5-13; John 3:16; Ezekiel 33:11-17; 2 Peter 3:8-9

CHAPTER 31

Job's Covenant

When Zach sat down to do his workbook Sunday evening he felt tired. His whole body ached from the continuous heavy work he'd been doing since the hurricane. He hadn't heard another word from Melissa since he'd reminded her that he was a 'new man in Christ'. That Sunday morning, he and his whole extended family had gathered to remember the sacrifice of Christ, as they faithfully did on the first day of every week. After the service was over, they had a quick lunch and then Uncle Peter organized a large crew of willing volunteers to help clean up their neighbourhood. They went throughout town, offering to help wherever there seemed to be a need. There were many elderly people and single moms that were thankful for the assistance.

Looking up at the calendar in the kitchen, Zach realized it was August fifth. Jayden would be coming back from his mission trip to Uganda the next day. *I wonder how it went?* Zach pondered. *I'll have to give him a call.*

Little did he know that there was less than a week before the return of Jesus Christ to the earth.

A text came through from Noah. They had been texting frequently since Zach had told him about the need for missionaries in Jamaica. Both of them were very excited about heading over with Uncle Peter in September. The text read:

Hannah wants to help me make some David and Goliath puppets to bring to Jamaica. Maybe you and I can put together a little theatre when we get there. I found a good plan on the Internet. Have you convinced Jake yet? He's not answering my emails.

Zach texted back. Still haven't convinced Jake. I'll see if Esther will help make some puppets too.

That would be great! How's your uncle doing?

The same, or worse. He's just not getting any better. Aunt Sandra is there all the time now.

Mom and Dad want to drive out and see him next weekend. We're planning to stay with the Symons for the week. We'll drive back in convoy with you guys to Conference, God Willing! See you then.

Sounds fantastic!

Turning his attention to his workbook, Zach was happy to be on Job chapter thirty-one. He was three-quarters of the way through. To his surprise, the very first verse began with, "I have made a covenant with my eyes; why then should I look upon a young woman?" *Hmm,* thought Zach, *this may be interesting.*

There was a link back to Job chapter one, where Job is described as a man who fears God and shuns evil. *Do I shun evil?* Zach asked himself, *or do I embrace it longingly?* It took only a second for *Hell Rider* images to flash across his mind. The pull was always there to view more. *What does God see when He looks at my heart? Does He feel loved by me?*

A text came in from Jayden:

Just landed in New York. Sitting here at the airport waiting for my next flight home. Our trip was great. Have to tell you all about it. How are things going there?

Zach spent another fifteen minutes texting with Jayden. When he was done, it was difficult to refocus on his study. As happy as he was to have his phone back, he now realized how distracting the continual stream of messages could be. Persevering, he found that the workbook went into great detail about Job's righteous decision to guard his eyes. There were several questions and references to look up, all of which dealt with this insidious issue – so prevalent in today's modern society with its twisted tentacles reaching into every avenue of the media – of pornography and immorality. The notes pointed out that David had said, "I will set nothing wicked before my eyes; I hate the work of those who fall away; it shall not cling to me."[166] Jesus said, "But I say to you that whoever looks at a woman to lust for her has already committed adultery with her in his heart."[167]

Reading the verses, Zach felt conscience-stricken. *Indulging in lustful thoughts is actually like committing the sin!* It was a heart-pounding realization. God wanted him to take his thoughts captive![168]

The passage continued, "If your right eye causes you to sin, pluck it out and cast it from you; for it is more profitable for you that one of your members perish, than for your whole body to be cast into hell."

I'm sure God doesn't want us to really take out our eyes, Zach mused. *But, if that laptop belonged to me, I would certainly delete all the R-rated movies and put on a blocker. It works well for the computer and the Smartphone."*

Another text came in from a school friend, inviting him to play pick-up soccer at the park.

It suddenly occurred to Zach that he had never had such an interrupted Bible study session, and it was all because he had his phone back. *I don't have a laptop,* Zach thought. *But I do have a phone that I need to control.* Picking it up, he took the small black device to his room and left it on his bed-side table.

Returning to his study, Zach read through a section with some straightforward warnings about the dangers and negative long-term effects of pornography. Zach thought it over carefully. *There are very clear reasons God doesn't want us to be involved with this stuff. Looking at pornography would definitely make*

---

[166] Psalms 101:3
[167] Matthew 5:28
[168] 2 Corinthians 10:5

'provision for the flesh' and destroy the new man God is creating in me.

At ten o'clock, Zach headed to his room for the night. Jake was sitting up in bed with headphones in his ears, watching another movie. He looked over for a brief second to acknowledge his brother's presence then quickly turned back to his screen. Zach climbed into bed and fell asleep quickly. He was still exhausted from the week of heavy cleanup work.

Startled in the middle of the night, Zach woke up to see a familiar, flashing, eerie-blue glow in the room. Opening his eyes, he saw that Jake was still sitting up in bed, looking at pictures from files on the hard drive he should have known not to open.

The moment Zach moved, Jake minimized the screen.

Zach sat up in bed. "I know what you were looking at," he said grimly.

Jake shrugged. "It's just pictures."

"What's with you, Jake?" Zach implored. "Its pornography and you know it!"

Zach had still not completely figured out what he wanted to say to his brother, but after his talk with Uncle Peter he knew he had to say something. Between Uncle Peter's words and the warnings he'd read in the workbook he was better equipped. "You're going to destroy yourself with that stuff," he told his brother. "It's going to consume you. It's going to be all you can think about. You might just be looking at pictures now, but if you fill your head with that kind of trash you're going to inflame your lusts so badly that you'll act on it."

"How do you know?" Jake asked, a little unnerved. "Are you judging me? You don't know *my* thoughts."

"I know how I felt after that movie you talked me into watching," Zach told him bitterly. "That was bad enough. Why are you doing this to yourself? You know as well as I do that we're

245

only supposed to think on things that are good.[169] And what about the verse that says we aren't to make provision for the flesh to fulfil its lusts?"[170]

Jake gave his brother a scornful look.

"Jesus says it's as if you're committing adultery if you lust after a woman! It's sinful!"

Everything Zach had been learning came pouring out. "Did you know that when guys look at pornography it makes them discontent with reality? They become obsessed with the photoshop perfection and can't be satisfied with less. You could damage any real relationships you want to have. And you'll hate yourself because you'll feel so guilty and so consumed with lust! You've got to stop, Jake! The sooner, the better."

"Man, you sound just like Dad," Jake said, shaking his head in disgust. "Where did you get all this from?"

"There was a whole section on it in the workbook. There was a personal letter written by someone who had been addicted to pornography and came to realize the harm it caused. Seriously, you can read it yourself if you want."

There was a sullen expression on Jake's face but he remained silent. Although he had been baptized for three years now, his 'new man in Christ' was not growing stronger, it was withering away. But every now and then, when godly sustenance was forced down his throat, the new man revived and stabbed hard with the sword of the spirit.[171] This was one of those moments. Jake suddenly realized the predicament he had gotten into. "Maybe I *should* read that letter," he said.

"I'll get it right now."

But Jake wasn't sure he could handle so much so soon.

---

[169] Philippians 4:8
[170] Romans 13:14
[171] Ephesians 6:10-17

"I'll read it in the morning," he said, shutting the computer down and tucking it under his bed.

They were both quiet for some time, each thinking that the other had gone to sleep, and then Jake whispered. "Zach, are you asleep?"

"No," Zach replied. "Why?"

"I can't... stop myself," Jake replied, almost desperately. "I know it's wrong. I know I shouldn't be watching stuff like that but... I tell myself I'll stop and then before I know it, I'm doing it again. I wish I'd never started looking at it at camp. I wish you'd been there with me, and then we could have been strong together... "

"Jake!" Zach whispered compassionately, moved by his brother's confession. "Is that why you've changed? He sighed deeply. I wish you had gone with me, instead. Then you would have heard all the great Bible talks and been with friends who would have helped you *want* to change your life – like they helped me change mine! Why don't you give back that laptop tomorrow and come to Conference with me? Better yet, join Noah and me in Jamaica. Let's make a break from all this and do something positive for God."

"Maybe I should get rid of this laptop," Jake mumbled.

"You definitely should! If it belonged to you, you could erase all the movies and put a blocker on it – but it's not even yours. Remember, Jesus says if your eye offends you, pluck it out and cast it away.[172] Anyway, it'll be easy enough to find Trevor's last name and get his address. Brett will know it for sure."

"Yeah, you're right," Jake agreed. "I'll give it back. This stuff is killing me."

"And if you want to come to Conference, I'll help you

---

[172] Matthew 5:28-29

through the workbook. We still have time."

"Okay," Jake agreed. "Thanks, Zach. Good night."

"Good night, Jake."

Will he finally give it up? Zach wondered, as he lay in bed trying to get back to sleep. He hoped his brother was truly serious about changing.

Can I give it up? Jake wondered, as he tossed and turned. *It's going to be so hard to do!*

CHAPTER 32

The Battle

As Jake lay awake, thinking about all that Zach had said, he knew his brother was right. He needed to change; he needed to pray. Even though bedtime prayers had been a habit ingrained in him from a child, he hadn't prayed regularly for weeks. Somehow it just hadn't seemed right to pray lately, not after watching R-rated movies, viewing pornographic files and even reading the creepy novel he had started. For so long he'd been telling himself that one day he'd turn things around and ask for forgiveness and everything would be all right again. *It's time*, he told himself. *I've gone far enough. I'm already consumed by this. I don't want to destroy myself. I want to follow Jesus, not my flesh.*

Jake prayed earnestly for God's forgiveness. He confessed everything that he'd been doing wrong and asked for God's help to overcome. A wonderful sense of relief flooded over him when he said, Amen.

I'm forgiven, he thought happily. *I can start all over. I'll go to Youth Conference with Zach and change just like he did. I know it's what I need to do. I'm going to stop pursuing a friendship with Melissa. I'll give the laptop to Brett after work tomorrow and ask him to contact Trevor. I'm sure he won't mind. I'm going to make a fresh start!*

The next morning began with a full day of hard work. Allan pruned and weed-whipped the trees. Jake mowed, and Zach dug up Mrs. Watson's overgrown herb garden. She wanted tulips instead.

As he rode the mower around the yard, Jake had plenty of time to think. The joy and relief he had felt the night before was fading fast. In his rush to get to work that morning he had forgotten to bring the laptop to drop off at Brett's house. It was still at home under the bed. It was still a temptation.

There was a lot that Jake didn't fully understand about God's grace and about sin. He hadn't yet grasped that, while it is true that any sin can be repented of and turned away from and completely forgiven if repentance is genuine – the truth is that sin can be destructive and even permanently damaging. As his dad often said, "Giving in once greatly weakens our defenses against the next onslaught. Sin isn't a toy that can be played with for a few hours and then discarded." The monster raging within him was of Leviathan proportions and difficult to control.[173] He was becoming a slave to sin.[174] He couldn't defeat the inflamed desires with one simple prayer and by sheer will power. Flesh can't overcome flesh. This wasn't going to just go away overnight. Jake needed help – lots of help – Divine help. All day long, as he mowed grass at Mrs. Watson's, the monster inside him kept demanding to be fed, and concocting devious plots to get its way.

Even so, Jake was holding on to the commitment he'd made the night before. He knew he had to give up the laptop. Borrowing Zach's phone on the way home, he sent a text to Brett.

Hey, Brett, he swiped. One of the Black Hawks' players left his laptop at the basketball camp since he was in such a rush to leave. If I bring the laptop to you, can you make contact with his coach? I should have done this sooner – sorry. Jake.

Brett replied a few minutes later:

Sure Jake, no problem.

Handing the phone back to Zach, Jake breathed a sigh of relief.

---

173 Pople, John; The Suffering of a Righteous Man, A Study in Job, Class 5 & 6. Retrieved August 6, 2013 from
http://www.bibletalks4u.com/pople-john.htm
174 Romans 6:11-23

"So, are you doing the workbook with me tonight?" Zach asked. "And I'll get you that letter to read."

"Yeah, sounds good."

"Just one more movie," the monster begged. It threw tantrums when Jake told himself that the Job workbook was now on the menu. His flesh raged against such a substitute. How dare he offer a nutritionally sound meal when Leviathan demanded soda, chips and ice-cream sundaes! The more Jake tried to block out the demands, the worse the demands became. He needed help.

I've already been sinning in just looking at stuff, Jake pondered, *but I'm sure that God has taken me back now that I've prayed and asked Him to. Will it hurt to look at stuff just a bit more tonight? I have to give the laptop back tomorrow… this is my last night… ever. I'll ask for forgiveness again, tomorrow night.*

During their workout before dinner, Zach tried to encourage his brother to stay committed to going to Conference and to begin doing the workbook with him.

"I've thought it over, and I think I'll plan to go next year," Jake told him, as they ran up the hill. "It's too last-minute-ish to try and make it happen now. But I told Brett I'll bring the laptop to him tomorrow."

"Jake," Zach pleaded. "It's not too late. I'll help you. You can do it."

"Youth Conference begins in less than two weeks. I doubt I can get in at this late date. There is probably a waiting list."

Zach was lagging behind, but he called out, "Why don't you phone tonight and see if you can register; see if there's any room?"

At the top of the hill Jake stopped to let his brother catch up. "Are you feeling okay?" he asked, when Zach reached him.

"Yeah. I'm not dizzy today, just a lot slower than you."

"You'll be in shape by November. You've got time."

"My training is over in September," Zach replied, as they

251

turned around at the top of the hill and headed back down.

"What? You can't leave, Zach!"

"I'm committed. I told Uncle Peter I would help him in Jamaica."

"But what about Brett? Don't you feel committed to him? Think of everything you're giving up! How will we win the Provincials without you? How could you let down the team like that? How could you even possibly think of not being there in November?"

Reaching the driveway, Jake grabbed a basketball and took his position to play 'Thirty-Three'. Setting up at the three-point line he sunk the ball angrily. Having battled with the flesh all day, he felt irritable and frustrated. And now he was angry that his brother could even think of leaving the basketball team. They needed everyone to come back for a 'super-twelve' year to even have a chance. And he hated the thought of giving up the laptop. On top of it all, he no longer had a phone; it wasn't so easy to keep in contact with Melissa. All the things that were most important to him seemed to be slipping from his grasp.

"It will be really hard to miss out on basketball," Zach admitted, watching his brother make all his points faster than ever before. "I'm sure it was hard for Moses to turn his back on the good life he led in Egypt. This is a choice that I feel God wants me to make – He's led me to make. I don't mean to be all preachy, but our commitment has to be first and foremost to God, Isn't that right? We've both made the commitment to serve Him first when we were baptized."

Looking in the opposite direction, Jake drove the ball angrily through his legs, bouncing it hard toward his brother. Instinctively, Zach caught it and found his position. But before he attempted the three-point shot, he made an earnest appeal, "Jake, I'm really excited about going to Jamaica now that I've made the decision. Helping Uncle Peter with mission work is something I want to do! Having Noah come along makes it even better. If you came too, it would be perfect! Please think about it."

As they hit their shots and tried to keep score, Zach told Jake about some of the activities he was looking forward to. It took a lot of explaining on Zach's part, before Jake could even begin to appreciate that such a venture was worthy of consideration.

Jake nailed his foul shots. "Thirty-one for me!" he cheered loudly, "Your turn." While he was starting to appreciate that going to Jamaica might be an interesting experience, Jake told himself that it wasn't for him. *There's no way I'd let Brett down like that, even if I decided to change in every other way.* He felt quite self-righteous over his loyalty to Brett. *And who will help Allan and Derrick run EdenTree?* Frustrated, he watched Zach finish his round.

"Only twenty-five for me." said Zach.

"And it took almost three minutes!" added Jake. *That blow to his head did some damage alright,* he thought angrily. *Zach has lost his mind!*

When Zach entered their room much later on that night, Jake was lying in bed with the laptop.

Zach sighed and looked very discouraged. "Did you phone about Conference?" he asked his brother.

"No."

"Why are you watching that thing again? You said… "

Jake lashed out, "You're making such a big deal out of this," he retorted. "I'm only watching movies and pictures. Have I changed my life? Am I getting drunk every weekend, or visiting night-clubs? It's no big deal and I'm giving it back tomorrow!"

"Jake, I'm your twin," Zach reminded him. "I can see what this is doing to you!"

"Give me a break!" Jake retorted, throwing his pillow in his brother's direction. His eyes were angry and almost hateful.

"What's happened?" Zach pleaded in astonishment. "Last

253

night you wanted to change…"

"Shut up!" Jake yelled out.

Zach climbed into bed and turned out the light. *Maybe I need to talk to Dad about this,* he told himself. *If Jake doesn't give that laptop back tomorrow, I will tell Dad.*

Angry tears welled up in Jake's eyes. He was angry and irritable. Every good decision that Zach was making only aggravated his conscience. *He's so self-righteous!* he thought. *Who is this new Zach that thinks he can start telling me what to do?! I liked the old Zach better. We had so much more fun together! This Zach is driving me crazy!*

Turning over to go to sleep, it briefly crossed Jake's mind to pray. *But God didn't help at all today,* he told himself bitterly. *I can't give up this stuff. I'm too weak! What's the use?*

Unfortunately, while Jake had prayed the night before, he had not given any sustenance to the emaciated 'new man in Christ'. While he had confessed the battle that was raging inside him to his brother, he didn't ask to be kept accountable, or appreciate his brother's attempts to do so without being asked! He needed a worthy cause to fill the void that had been dedicated to the monster; without such a goal he was destined to slip back even further than he had been before. Sadly, as usual, he had paid little attention to the Bible readings that his family did every night. He had also passed on the opportunity to study with Zach and read the insightful letter. Weakly, half-heartedly, the pathetic soldier of Christ was struggling in vain to find the 'Sword of the Spirit' – the only weapon that could begin to win back the strongholds of faith.[175]

Had Jake known the countdown to Christ's coming was no longer years, or months, or even weeks – but only a matter of days,

---

[175] 2 Timothy 3:15-17; Hebrews 4:12-16; Ephesians 6:17

perhaps he would have had a stronger desire to overcome the flesh. But he didn't know, and in his obsession to follow his own wayward desires, he was missing all the clues that God was sending his way.

Zach's Smartphone vibrated on the table between them. Looking up, Jake could tell that his brother was asleep. Picking up the phone curiously, Jake saw that it was a message from Melissa. He read it:

Can you please tell Jake I need to talk to him? If I can text him, that would be even better. Melissa

This is Jake, he swiped. What's up, Gorgeous?

I just had the biggest fight with my mom. I really need to talk to you, please!

Do you want me to call?

Please come over. I need someone to hold me.

Jake read the words over a second time. *Melissa needs someone to hold her – and she's asking me? I'm the one she wants?* He didn't think twice.

Where?

My house. I'll be outside.

On my way.

Very pleased to be the first friend Melissa would call when she was upset, Jake quietly pulled his clothes back on and tiptoed over to the window. Zach didn't stir. The window slid open easily and Jake hoisted himself up and swung his leg over the ledge.

"What are you doing?" Zach asked suddenly, stirring sleepily in bed.

"Just heading out for a bit," Jake told him, wishing his brother had stayed asleep! "I'll be back soon."

"Are you going to see… *Melissa?*"

"She's had a big fight with her mom," Jake explained impatiently. "She needs to talk. Go back to sleep and don't worry about it, okay?"

"Did she ask you to come over?" Zach questioned.

"She did. We're good friends. She just needs to talk."

It had been only two days since Melissa had invited Zach to dance and he had turned her down. *Is she using Jake... or me?* Zach wondered. Since the night before when Jake had confessed his desire to change, Zach felt much more compassion toward his brother. He empathized with the powerful struggle his brother was having. He felt his own foolishness, earlier, was somewhat responsible in causing his brother to stumble. He wanted Jake to overcome.

"Hold on," Zach pleaded. "I know you want to change and get your life right with God. Melissa isn't the kind of friend you need. Don't go!"

"But – Melissa needs *me*," Jake said proudly. Undeterred, he swung out the window and dropped to the ground.

"I'm only going to cover for you this one more time," Zach told his twin firmly. "If you keep doing this, I will have to tell Dad about everything... for your own good."

Looking back in the window with a grin, Jake reminded his brother quietly, "Think of all the times I covered for you. You owe me at least twenty more!" Sliding the screen shut, he headed for Melissa's.

As he hurried along the dark road, taking a short cut through the park, the pathetic soldier suddenly found his sword or maybe was given a great deal of Divine assistance. Jake vividly recalled the words of Proverbs seven. He and Zach had once acted out these verses as a Sunday School skit: "For at the window of my house I looked through my lattice, and saw among the simple, I perceived among the youths, a young man devoid of understanding, passing along the street near her corner; and he took the path to her house in the twilight, in the evening, in the black and dark night. And there a woman met him, with the attire of a harlot, and a crafty heart... "

Jake knew well that the Proverb ended with the words,

"Her house is the way to hell, descending to the chambers of death." He and Zach had made very graphic signs for the harlot's house and the chambers of death. They had played the parts with full-fledged dramatic flair.

Come on, Jake argued with himself, *that isn't talking about Melissa. She's my friend… she's upset. I'm only going to her house to comfort her like a good friend.* But regardless of every justification he gave, the new man in Christ, who had been silenced so often lately, refused to withdraw the sword that pricked his heart. While Jake would not acknowledge the promptings of the growling monster within, he was surprised at how clearly he could remember Proverbs chapter seven. Numerous times he had read it with his family and many times they had discussed such matters in Youth Group, but it had never impacted him before, like it was now.

Turning the corner onto Melissa's street, Jake suddenly stopped. The sword of the spirit was still jabbing away and he was feeling the pricks. *What am I doing?* he asked himself nervously. *I should be fleeing temptation not making provision for the flesh. [176]Maybe I should text Melissa and tell her my parents won't let me come, or something like that. I'm being a fool! I'll tell her I can only talk on the phone.*

He looked over at Melissa's house and then he saw her sitting at the end of her driveway. She was wearing a cute little dress and her head was buried in her arms. Under the streetlight her copper-coloured curls shone. Jake could see that she was sobbing quietly. Compassionate by nature, Jake couldn't bear to see someone he loved, so upset. He had to at least hear her out. He longed to provide some comfort.

"Hey, baby, what's wrong?" he asked, coming closer.

---

[176] 2 Timothy 2:22; Romans 13:14; Proverbs 2:10-19

Melissa stood up and reached out her arms.

Jake pulled her close. It felt good, really good to be so close to Melissa.

"Thank you for coming," she whispered earnestly, wiping her eyes with her hand. "I need to talk to you so badly. But let's go to the trailer or my mom might hear me. She thinks I'm locked in my room."

Looking in the direction that Melissa was pointing, Jake saw the large RV parked in the backyard. Melissa's family was well off. The house trailer was luxurious.

"We can get in there?" Jake asked with astonishment, fully expecting such an RV to be locked up tight. *No, don't do it!* the little soldier cried. *Flee! This is more temptation than you can handle. Think of all those great talks you heard on dating last year. Stay in public places, keep it accountable. Never date someone who doesn't love God even more than they love you.*

Are you kidding? This is perfect! the monster laughed.

"I have the keys," she smiled wistfully, pulling him toward the RV. "It's my hang-out place. Come on."

Ignoring the Bible passages [177] that were now racing through his mind, Jake followed. *I'm just helping a friend,* he told the panic-stricken soldier. *Melissa needs me. I have to at least find out why she is so upset. I'll leave if she gets too cuddly...*

But Jake wasn't being true to himself – the devil had entered his heart;[178] the little soldier could not restrain the over-stimulated man of the flesh.

---

[177] Proverbs 5:3-14; 2:11-22;1 Corinthians 6:13-20
[178] John 13:2; Eph. 4:17-27; 6:10-18; 2 Tim. 2:24-26; 3:1-5 (slanderers)

CHAPTER 33

Burned Up?

Jazzy music was coming from somewhere close by.

Sleepily, Jake raised his head and realized Zach's phone was ringing.

Picking it up, he glanced at the time to see it was only six-thirty Tuesday morning. His rendezvous with Melissa had lasted until five. He'd only come home then in order to slip into bed unnoticed. He still didn't fully understand what was so terrible about being told she needed to 'do her part around the house or she would lose her allowance'. Sure she and her mom had called each other some awful names, but nothing that couldn't be forgiven. However, the 'comforting' had been very enjoyable even though it had spiraled out of control. They were now officially a couple. The monster within was happy even if the weak, distraught soldier was completely mortified. Guilt weighed heavily on Jake's mind.

"Hello," he mumbled into the receiver.

"Sorry to disturb your beauty sleep," Allan joked on the other end, "but I just got a call that Derrick is sick. Remember we're going to double-dig Mrs. Watson's new garden area today?"

"Right. That's a huge job," Jake moaned. "It's going to kill our backs."

"Do you know anyone we could ask to help? It's supposed to rain tomorrow. I'd really like to finish it today."

Zach wearily opened his eyes. He could hear the conversation. Allan's voice always came through loudly on the phone. "We could ask Jayden," he mumbled. "He's back now from Uganda."

Even though Jayden was still jet-lagged and feeling rather

dazed with Zach's early morning call, he agreed to help; he needed the money.

Jake and Zach pulled on their clothes, quickly packed some food for both breakfast and lunch, filled a few water bottles each, and then jumped into the car.

As they drove down the road towards Jayden's house, Zach asked how the talk with Melissa had gone.

"Great," Jake replied evasively, worried his brother might probe too deeply. "We're going out."

"You're going out with her? Jake, are you crazy?!"

"I'm not crazy. I'm in love," Jake replied defensively. At least that is what he thought. His eye twitched. His brother's gaze was disconcerting. This was his moment of triumph, so why did he feel like a failure?

"She told me I'm the first guy she's ever really loved."

"Is that right?!" Zach replied with a slightly sarcastic tone, trying not to let the admission bother him. He wanted to help his brother; he was very worried about him. "I thought you were going to change your life?"

"I'm still going to give the laptop back," Jake said loudly, as they pulled up in front of Jayden's house. "Although," he faltered, suddenly realizing he'd forgotten it again that morning, "I guess I forgot it. I'll have to take it to Brett after work."

There was a suspicious look in Zach's eye and it was unnerving his twin. Neither one said another word until Jayden got into the car and then, of course, they wanted to hear all about his mission trip.

The boys met Allan at Mrs. Watson's house and looked over the site. She wanted her front lawn turned into a garden. Living as she did, on a sloping, rocky hill, it had been very difficult to mow the grass. Turning the hill into a garden seemed to be the best solution. It was the first design project EdenTree had embarked on that summer.

Allan was already stripping the sod and turning it upside down in the trenches they had dug the day before. Two large piles of dirt lay on the driveway, having been delivered the night before. The black pile was triple-mix and the other was topsoil. These had to be shovelled into the trenches on top of the turned-over sod.

Jayden's cheerful attitude lightened the work substantially. He had plenty to tell about his trip to Uganda. "Breaking up sod," he told them, "is easy compared to hand-digging *trenches* for building foundations. We even had to mix the concrete by hand!"

As they worked, Jayden told stories of orphan children sleeping on the ground at night with just a few skimpy blankets to share between them. "And yet," Jayden continued, "do you think those kids were complaining? I heard them all singing at night! That's right!" he added, smiling at his friends' astonishment. "They're out there singing the songs they were taught by the kind folks who took them in!"

As they turned over the ground, sorted rocks into piles and carted the good dirt to fill in the holes, the crew peppered Jayden with questions. What was the food like? Did he get sick? Was it too hot? Did he have any fun? Could he talk to the kids in English?

Jayden answered their questions one by one and then said, "I'm going back there, some day. I don't care if all the meals are the same. I felt so happy there. I was helping out. I was doing something good for someone else. I was making a difference. To see those little faces light up when they see they have nice homes to live in – no more lying on the ground at night – it was worth putting up with all the heat, the flies, and lack of showers! Man, I did miss a good shower though!"

It took most of the morning to do half the lawn but Jayden kept them all entertained till lunch. Taking a much needed break, the crew stretched out on the last remaining strip of grass.

"This world is such an awesome place," Jayden said, lying back. "It's kind of sad it'll all be burned up one day."

261

"All burned up?" Zach queried.

"Isn't that what God's going to do? Burn up this earth and make a new one for eternity?"

"I've heard that there will be fire," [179] Zach replied, sitting up and reaching for his lunch bag, "but even in Noah's day when the flood destroyed the world – the earth didn't disappear – it's still here."

"I'm sure it says somewhere that even the 'elements will melt'," Jayden argued, unwrapping his sandwich. "Everything will be destroyed, including the planet. God's going to make a new heaven and earth."

The boys gave thanks for the meal and then continued to debate. The only trouble was that no one really knew the exact wording of the Scripture and they didn't have a Bible handy to turn up any passages.

Allan pulled out his phone. He had several versions of the Bible on it. In a moment he clarified the matter. "You're all talking about Second Peter chapter three," he said, finding the reference. He read verse five to seven, "'For this they willfully forget: that by the word of God the heavens were of old, and the earth standing out of water and in the water, by which the world that then existed perished, being flooded with water. But the heavens and the earth which are now preserved by the same word, are reserved for fire until the day of judgment and perdition of ungodly men.'"

After a moment's contemplation Allan said, "Peter does compare the future purging of the earth by fire to the flood in Noah's time – just like Zach was saying."

Zach reached over and gently punched Jayden in the shoulder with a laugh, "See, told you so!"

"Okay, one point for you," Jayden replied good-naturedly.

Allan continued, still reading the chapter, "Listen to this.

---

[179] Ezekiel 38:19-22; 39:6; Isaiah 66:16

Peter says that, 'the world that then existed *perished*, being flooded with water.'" [180] Tapping his screen, Allan was able to look up the word. "'Perished' means 'to destroy fully'. That's interesting. We have plenty of fossil evidence on this earth that there was once a global flood, but as Zach said – the planet *is still here.*"

"Okay… interesting… does it really matter?" Jayden asked, savouring a chocolate chip cookie he'd picked up. "What's the difference between God creating a whole new planet, or purging the old one?"

"There is a big difference," Allan replied thoughtfully, munching on his own cookie. "It matters because God made promises back in the Old Testament that can only be fulfilled if this earth remains."

"Huh?" said Jayden. "Like what?"

Allan reached for his water bottle and turned to Jake. "What promises do you remember, Jake?" he asked, unscrewing the lid from his bottle. "You're awfully quiet this morning."

Jake had been silent, very silent. All morning he had been thinking about what he had done the night before. He thought that he should feel happier, and wondered why he felt devastated. Inside, he felt a huge sense of loss, even though he kept telling himself that he had made gigantic gains, gains he'd once coveted badly.

Had he talked to his dad or his uncles – the spiritual mentors he needed so badly – they might have told him that the loss he felt was the loss of integrity. He had sinned. He had lost integrity before God, with himself, and with the future wife he hoped to have one day. His dad or uncles might have prayed with Jake to ask for God's forgiveness. They might have encouraged him to form a plan to deflate the monster, reinvigorate the new

---

[180] 2 Peter 3:6

man in Christ and flee temptation.

Feeling like a failure, too weak to overcome, too sinful to seek forgiveness, the apathetic soldier of Christ was no match for King Sin. Turning to Allan with a glazed-over look, Jake asked, "What are we talking about?"

Jayden and Allan laughed but Zach didn't.

"What's with you, Jake?" Allan asked with a puzzled look; unaware of the battle Jake was fighting. "We're talking about the promises that God made concerning the future of this actual, physical earth. Why do we know it won't be completely burned up?"

Jake realized the others were having an important discussion. He wanted to join in. "Well, I guess because God made promises to Abraham that He still hasn't fulfilled," he said slowly. "Wasn't there a time when Abraham was on some high hill, and God told him to look in every direction, and that He would give him all the land he could see?" [181]

"Exactly," Allan replied. "And Abraham never received that land in his lifetime. God even told Abraham to get up and walk in the land. [182] If God is going to burn up *this* planet and make a new one, why would He go through all the trouble of showing a specific piece of land to Abraham and telling him to walk through it? Why not tell Abraham that in the future God would make him a better land to inherit?"

"Didn't God also tell Abraham the exact boundaries of the Promised Land?" Zach added, taking a large red apple from his lunch bag.

"He did." Allan nodded. "God told him it would be from the river of Egypt – the Nile – to the river Euphrates."[183]

"I thought God promised that land to Abraham's

---

[181] Genesis 13:14-17; see also Genesis 15:7-18; 17:8
[182] Genesis 13:17
[183] Genesis 15:18

descendants," Jayden argued. "The Jews lived in that land for many years; they've already enjoyed the promise. Why do you think it has to be given personally to Abraham?"

Allan nodded. "There is a New Testament comment on this promise," Allan told him. "In Acts chapter seven, Stephen speaks to the Jews and reminds them that God never fulfilled His promise to Abraham. In fact, Stephen says that God didn't even give him enough land to set his foot on. [184] Abraham had to *buy* a plot of land to bury his wife."[185]

"Really?" Jayden seemed surprised.

"And doesn't it say in Hebrews," Zach added, "that Abraham lived in the Promised Land like a stranger in a foreign country, waiting for the day when God would make a city with foundations?"[186]

"Well remembered, Zach." Allan praised. "And many other faithful people are mentioned along with Abraham in Hebrews. They're among those descendants that you mention, Jayden. All are waiting for the day when God will make a new earth right here on this old one. [187]

"Let's see that passage," Jayden requested, reaching for the phone. Allan passed it to him.

Scrolling through Hebrews chapter eleven, Jayden exclaimed, "But it says here that everyone is waiting for a *'heavenly* country'!"[188]

"When Jesus is in the land ruling over it,[189] Allan replied, "it will no longer be "earthly" – subject to man's dictates – but "heavenly". Like Jesus said in the Lord's Prayer, 'Your will be

---

[184] Acts 7:2-5
[185] Genesis 23
[186] Hebrews 11:8-10
[187] Hebrews 11:13-16
[188] Hebrews 11:16
[189] Luke 1:31-33; Matt. 5:34-35; John 18:36-37; Isa. 9:6-7; Jer.33:14-16; 2 Samuel 7:8-16; Acts 2:29-30

done on earth as it is in heaven.'"[190]

Jayden looked at the verses closely.

"And there's another amazing aspect to all of this," Allan added with excitement in his voice. "In Galatians chapter three, we are told that Jesus *is the primary descendant* of Abraham. In other words, when the promises were made to Abraham and 'his seed' – that's actually singular – one seed. *Jesus is the seed!* [191]Jesus will also personally inherit the Promised Land of Israel, which is the land that Abraham saw from the high hill. And it all fits together wonderfully because the land of Israel is spoken of, throughout the Bible, as the center of worship in the Kingdom Age, the place from where Christ is to rule!" [192]

Jayden nodded with interest, but he still wasn't convinced the earth wouldn't be burned up. Touching the phone screen, he found the Second Peter passage. He looked at the part Allan had read and then read further to verse ten.

"Hey, listen to verse ten," he exclaimed. "It says, 'But the day of the Lord will come as a thief in the night, in which the heavens will pass away with a great noise, and the elements will melt with fervent heat; both the earth and the works that are in it will be burned up.'"

Having found the exact passage he remembered, Jayden pressed his point, "If you're telling me this earth will only be burned up in the sense that fires will consume what's on the ground, how do you explain the part that says, 'the elements will melt'? That sounds to me like the whole planet will be consumed!"

Allan reached for his phone and when Jayden handed it to him, he checked out a few words in the verse. "This might help," Allan said, "An 'element' is 'something orderly'; it's used of laws,

---

[190] Matthew 6:10
[191] Galatians 3:16,27-29
[192] Jer. 3:17; Mic. 4:8; Zech. 14; Psa. 48; Isa. 2:2-5;62:1-7; Matt. 5:5

rudiments and principles.[193] 'Melt' means 'to dissolve'. The 'elements' that will melt – or be 'dissolved' – refers to the laws, principles and governments being totally replaced by new, righteous laws of God."

"You mean it's talking about laws, not the stuff the earth is made of? I'll have to check that out," Jayden said. He tried to summarize all the new information they had given him. "You're saying the earth can't be burned up because Abraham and Jesus are going to be given *the land* of Israel, which will be the center of worship when Jesus returns?"

""And those who are baptized into Christ will inherit the promise with him,"[194] Zach added. "They are descendants, as well. By being 'in Christ' they are Abraham's seed. So, we can inherit the promise too!"

"What? The promise to Abraham?"

"I'll read what it says in Galatians three, verses twenty-seven to twenty-nine," Allan suggested, "For as many of you as were baptized into Christ have put on Christ… And if you are Christ's, then you are Abraham's seed, and heirs according to the promise."

"Why is everyone being given this one tiny, itty-bitty piece of land?" Jayden questioned, munching on another cookie. "What about the rest of the earth?"

"Eventually the Kingdom of God will encompass the whole earth," Allan clarified, standing up and stretching out his sore back. "It will be something like this: When Jesus comes back he will resurrect the dead – those who have been enlightened by the Word of God and therefore responsible for their actions. Then he will gather all those he considers responsible out of the world, so that they all can be judged together.[195] The faithful are made

---

[193] Galatians 4:3,9; Colossians 2:8,20; Hebrews 5:12
[194] Galatians 3:27-29; Psalm 37:9-11,22,29,34; Matthew 5:5; Rev. 5:10
[195] 1 Thessalonians 4:13-18; Acts 10:42; 17:31; 2 Timothy 4:1

immortal[196] and then Jesus and the immortal saints deliver Israel when all nations come against Jerusalem... " [197]

Something was bothering Jayden. "Hold on a minute," he interrupted. "What exactly do you mean by the *responsible* people?"

"Those who hear and understand the Gospel message are responsible to God for judgement,"[198] Allan explained. "All those whom God feels are responsible for their actions, will be raised from the dead and gathered from the earth to be judged by Jesus Christ."

"And you say the faithful are given immortality," Jayden reiterated, "but what about those who aren't faithful? What happens to them?"

"Well, what we do know for sure," Allan replied, "is that the unfaithful don't receive immortality – because eternal life is a gift.[199] Jesus says that those who are unfaithful will be cast out into darkness – 'weeping and gnashing their teeth'. [200] I suppose that means they feel absolutely hopeless despair and... " [201]

"Okay," Jayden replied. "I'd probably call that Hell, but carry on."

Allan continued, "Well, after Jesus and his faithful deliver Israel from being destroyed, the surviving Jewish people will accept Jesus Christ as their Messiah [202] and the Kingdom of God becomes established in the Promised Land.[203] From there, the

---

[196] John 5:28-29; 1 Corinthians 15:49-53
[197] Zechariah 14:1-9; Ezekiel 38:3-23; Joel 3
[198] Psalm 49:10-20; John 12:46-50; Mark 16:15-16
[199] Romans 6:23; 5:21
[200] Matthew 25:30; Luke 13:28; Daniel 12;1-3; John 5:28-29
[201] For a suggestion, see Thomas, John. Eureka, Chapter 19 "The Lake of Fire" This may be retrieved at:
http://www.antipas.org/books/eureka/eureka_3/eu_chap_19/c19_c11.html
[202] Zechariah 12:8-10; Romans 11:25-27; Ezekiel 36:25-28 & ch. 29
[203] Isaiah 60; Psalm 2; Zechariah 12:3-9

message goes out [204] to the rest of the population [205] who have survived the earthquakes, war, and fires ravaging the world. [206] There will be an appeal to all nations to accept Jesus as their Sovereign King. [207] Some nations will gladly submit to Christ, while others will muster their armies to make war against him, believing him to be an imposter – or the Antichrist." [208] [209]

"Jesus – the Antichrist?" Jayden exclaimed. "This is all new to me!"

"That's a discussion we should have one day," Zach smiled.

"Just maybe not today," Allan replied, "or we'll never get this job finished."

"And what happens after the armies fight against Jesus?" Jayden asked, getting up from the ground and reaching for his shovel.

"They won't have much success against immortals," Allan smiled, bringing over a wheelbarrow of topsoil. "Eventually the whole world will be subdued to Jesus, who will rule with his saints in a kindly but firm way, of course, not like the fallible and often corrupt rulers we have now. [210] And throughout the thousand years of Christ's reign, Jerusalem will always be *the center* of worship and the place where all nations will come to learn God's ways and laws." [211]

"Cool," Jayden said.

"That's a lot of info to pass on without giving you any

---

[204] Revelation 14:6-7
[205] Zechariah 14:16; Revelation 11:15; Micah 4:1-4
[206] Ezekiel 38:16-23 to ch. 39; 2 Thessalonians 1:6-9; 2 Peter 3:7
[207] Psalm 2; Revelation 11:15;
[208] Revelation 16:12-21; 17:12-18; 19:11-21; 2 Thess. 2:3-12
[209] Google *"The Antichrst; Christendom's Final Deception"* by Jason Hensley and *"Who Are You Looking For?" A Novel Exposing the Real Antichrist"* by Anna Tikvah
[210] Daniel 2:35, 44-45; 7:14,27; Luke 19:11-19
[211] Isaiah 2:1-4; Zechariah 8:20-23; Micah 4:1-4; Matthew 5:34-35; Isa. 60

passages in support," Allan admitted. "I have a book on it that I can give you, if you want."

Jayden smiled. "Sure, I've already collected a few from Zach."

Lunch break was over. Everyone returned to their positions, digging up the hard, rocky lawn. The section of ground they had completed before lunch looked fantastic, with loose, dark soil stretching smoothly across the slope. They had more than half-finished the back-breaking work. For the rest of the afternoon they continued to shovel, strip sod and bring in wheelbarrows full of rich soil.

By the end of the day Mrs. Watson's front yard had been turned into a lovely garden bed. There were still no plants, but Derrick planned to put them in the following day.

As the weary boys drove home, Jayden took the opportunity to ask another question. "Does it matter?"

Seeing the blank look on his friend' faces, he added, "Does any of that stuff we discussed today matter? We're all good-living Christians. Who cares whether we end up on this earth or someplace else? We'll be happy wherever God puts us."

Zach was driving the car and he waited for Jake to give an answer. Jake, however, was staring out the window, deep in thought as he had been all day. "Does it matter?" Zach repeated slowly. "Well truth matters… " he replied.

"Yeah, but we both believe in God. We both try our best to live the Christian life," Jayden reasoned. "Is it worth arguing about the details?"

Thinking long and hard as they sped down the highway, Zach finally replied, "I know it says in the Bible that we need to worship God 'in spirit and in truth'. [212] You show the spirit of

---

[212] John 4:21-24

Christ [213] in your life – you're a great example to us, Jayden, – but our beliefs differ considerably. We can't both be right."

"Come on, Zach, there are so many churches all claiming to see things a little differently from the others. People spend too much time arguing about the message and not enough time doing it!"

"That's true," Zach agreed, coming to a stop at a main intersection and waiting for the light to give him an advance green. "But the Bible does warn that we will be accursed from God if we preach a different gospel from the one Christ preached. [214] My dad always says that good fruit is important, but we need to be careful we are preaching what Jesus and the Apostles preached, not the fables of men that God said would corrupt Christianity. "

"'Corrupt'?" Jayden questioned, as Zach turned left. "Where does God say that Christianity would be corrupted?"

"In one of Paul's Epistles… " Zach said lamely, picking up speed again. "Do you know where it is, Jake?"

After the boys had explained their latest discussion to Jake, he did remember a passage from the Epistles to Timothy. He tried his best to paraphrase the verses. If he'd had access to a Bible, Jake would have read, "For the time will come when they will not endure sound doctrine, but according to their own desires, because they have itching ears, they will heap up for themselves teachers, and they will turn their ears away from the truth, and be turned aside to fables." [215]

The trip home seemed too short, as Zach pulled into Jayden's driveway.

"Maybe we have some talking to do," Jayden agreed with a good-natured grin, as he opened the car door. "I need to open *your* eyes to truth!"

---

[213] Romans 8:1-16
[214] Galatians 1:6-9
[215] 2 Timothy 4:3-4. See also 2 Thess. 2:1-12; 1 John 2:18-22; 4:1-3

Zach laughed and the two shook hands before Jayden left. Waving out the window as he drove away, Zach was excited about the possibility of having some meaningful chats with his friend.

Had there been another few weeks left to them, the discussion might well have resurfaced in another place, at another time. But there wasn't even a full week left. There were only... five days. The world was about to change!

CHAPTER 34

When it's All Passing Away

"Would you like an iced cappuccino and a doughnut with your lunch?" Uncle Peter asked, stepping into Tim Hortons with his nephew Jake. It was ten o'clock Friday morning and Jake had been working since seven that morning. He was hungry. The doughnut selection looked enticing but instead he chose the meat wrap and a wholegrain muffin.

"I'm having a large iced-cappuccino," Uncle Peter smiled. "Do you want one too?"

"I'd love one, but I'd better have the berry smoothie," Jake replied. "Brett wants us to eat a healthy diet."

"He's worried about what you're eating *this summer?*"

"He's been preaching a healthy diet for the last couple of years. But it's been good for us. I feel a lot more energetic and I don't get sick as often."

Smiling, Uncle Peter nodded, "Hey, I guess that can relate to our spiritual life as well."

Jake squirmed uneasily. "Yeah, I... guess so."

Uncle Peter paid for their meal and they chose a private outdoor table. Sitting down at the table, Uncle Peter asked Jake to give thanks. Jake looked up at his uncle uncertainly. He didn't feel he was in a good place with God. He'd finally given the laptop to Brett, but he still hadn't made the decision to give up seeing Melissa. She'd just invited him to go to the beach with her on Monday and hang-out again whenever he could slip away unnoticed. However, Uncle Peter had already bowed his head, so Jake did as he was asked, repeating a quick, familiar blessing.

As Uncle Peter handed Jake his wrap and smoothie, and

made sure they both had a straw, Jake gazed at his uncle thoughtfully. Uncle Peter had a lot more grey hairs than Jake remembered and his bifocals were hard to get used to. His weather-beaten face was becoming lined. While his uncle was still a tall, good-looking, broad-shouldered man, he was definitely aging. In a few years Uncle Peter would be turning forty. *I wonder what Uncle Peter was like when he was seventeen?* Jake mused. *Were movies as bad as they are now? Did he ever go out with girls like Melissa? Did he ever struggle with stuff like I am? Did he ever fail like I have?*

However, Jake was hesitant to tell anyone about his struggles, especially his father's brother! What if Uncle Peter told his dad what Jake had been watching? What if his Dad found out he was sneaking out at night to 'hang-out' with Melissa? What if his parents started making harsh rules and grounding him for his behaviour? *No,* he told himself, *if I'm going to make changes to my life, I want to be in control – not have restrictions placed on me!*

"So, does winning the Provincials mean everything to you, Jake?" Uncle Peter asked in a friendly way.

"For sure. It's a big deal!" Jake exclaimed. "If we make it to the Provincials, then there's a good chance I'll get a scholarship out of it. Mom and Dad won't be able to help us with university fees, so a scholarship of any kind would be huge!"

"Hmm, I see what you mean," Uncle Peter nodded thoughtfully. "You're thinking long term and that's important. You've got your future to consider."

"It's been a stressful year all around," Jake admitted. "All my marks count on my transcript. A one percent difference can determine whether a university accepts me or chooses someone else."

They talked for some time. Uncle Peter inquired about the courses Jake was hoping to take for his 'super-twelve victory lap', where the best university was, how long a commitment the various choices were and what the job prospects were like at the end of it all. Jake happily told him. He was thankful to have someone care enough to go over the options with him.

"Now you realize, Jake," Uncle Peter said, as they threw their garbage in the dispenser and headed toward the car, "that all the plans that any of us are making, may be terminated by Jesus Christ's return?"

"Of course," Jake agreed. "But then again, everyone has been saying that since I first started coming out to a Christadelphian Sunday School. It may also be another ten years away, or twenty – and in the meantime I've got to get a higher education so that I can get a good job and support a family."

"Not everyone *has* to go the higher education route."

"But I want to."

Uncle Peter nodded thoughtfully.

Jake stopped to consider the route that his uncle had taken. Unlike his two older brothers, Uncle Peter had never gone to university. He had learned his trade on the job and done quite well financially. *But that is because Uncle Peter is special,* Jake told himself. *Not everyone is as talented as he is.*

Climbing into a hot car that had been sitting in the summer sun, Uncle Peter rolled down the windows, but he didn't start the motor. "I often ask myself," Uncle Peter said slowly, "If Jesus came back tomorrow, how would I feel about my life and the decisions I'm making?"

"Do you really think it could be that soon?" Jake asked nervously.

"Jake," Uncle Peter replied thoughtfully, "none of us can know for certain that we'll make it through today alive. Jesus Christ's return is as near as the day of our death. Every day is a precious gift from God and could be the last one we have before Christ's return. But, yes, I do believe we are on the verge of all things being fulfilled. Israel has found vast stores of gas off her shores. Russia has secured a toe-hold in the Mediterranean through Syria, and has shown great interest in developing the lucrative gas fields. The bait is there to draw the King of the North down with an evil plan, and the King of the South has been pushing in provocative ways. [216] The confederacy of Ezekiel thirty-eight is under Russia's control. The American economy is crumbling. We're on the verge of an economic collapse that could cause the hearts of men to fail for fear all over the earth. Natural disasters are occurring faster and more furiously than ever before. We've seen signs in the sun, moon and stars – both literally and figuratively. [217]Europe has become the beast system of Revelation and is rapidly becoming intertwined with the Roman Catholic Church – as we read in Bible prophecy. [218] Just the other day, I saw a notice that in a recent publicity campaign, Europe is proclaiming that they have risen 'out of the abyss' – using the exact language describing the beast in Revelation seventeen! [219]Jake, it's all in place... the signs abound! Seismologists are even predicting that Israel is due for a massive earthquake just as we read in Zechariah fourteen. When the Mount of Olives splits it will trigger earthquakes that will shake the world. It's time to wake up and realize we may be standing before the Judge of the earth tonight!"

It really is remarkable, Jake shuddered. *Bible prophecy is falling into place just as it should. Why don't I want to wake up*

---

[216] Ezekiel 38:1-13; Daniel 11:40-45
[217] Luke 21:25-27. **http://www.biblemagazine.com/library/wj-jrsm/wj-chapter6.html.** Retrieved August 2013. This may be figurative language as in Isaiah 34:1-4; Ezekiel 32:1-10
[218] Daniel 7; 8:19-26; Revelation 13,17-18. See Ramsden, John, *Europe and the Roman Connection.*
http://www.biblemagazine.com/magazine/vol-18/v18i4mag.pdf , pg. 12. Retrieved August 2013
[219] Revelation 17:8 (ASV/ NIV) See also Jenner, Michael. "Out of The Abyss: The European Beast Rises," *The Christadelphian,* March 2013, P. 123.

and accept the evidence? Why do I keep hoping things will just carry on as they always have? Why am I thinking I have all the time in the world to change? Why am I not excited by the thought that Jesus could come tomorrow?

"I've just got one more intense year of school, Uncle Peter," he said slowly. "After I get my grades up and do my best to win the Provincials, then I intend to make time for God."

"Just be careful about leaving God out of any day or hour," Uncle Peter smiled. "It's good to do our best, but keep in mind that if Jesus returns tonight, will your grades matter? Will the Provincials matter?"

"Well no," Jake muttered. "But I am *already* baptized. I have at least made that step. If Jesus stays away another ten years – my grades *will* matter tremendously and the scholarship could mean the difference between being fifty-thousand dollars in debt or being able to pay back my school fees when I graduate."

"Jake, there's a promise God has made about our day-to-day concerns," Uncle Peter told him, reaching for his Bible.

Even before his uncle read from the Scriptures, Jake knew what he was going to say. "Seek first the kingdom of God, and his righteousness; and all these things shall be added to you."[220]

"If you pray for God's help and seek Him *first*," Uncle Peter assured his nephew, "you will be amazed how often all the other things will work out without anxious worry. Do your best, of course, in everything you're doing, but never to the exclusion of God. If you leave God out, and God *cares* enough to work in your life, you may find out that sickness, or accidents keep you from obtaining your worldly goals – as hard as you're trying to make them happen."[221]

Jake thought of his sprained ankle and Zach's concussions.

---

[220] Matthew 6:33
[221] Haggai 1:5-11; Hebrews 12:5-11

"True," he admitted.

"Just one more passage," Uncle Peter smiled, "and then I'll take you back to work."

"Okay."

His uncle began reading Second Peter, chapter three, verse nine. "The Lord is not slack concerning His promise, as some count slackness, but is longsuffering toward us, not willing that any should perish but that all should come to repentance."

Turning to Jake, Uncle Peter said, "It's through compassion that God has allowed things to go on for as long as they have."

Jake nodded. *And maybe He'll allow it to go on just a bit longer,* he thought. *A few more years would be great.*

"'But the day of the Lord will come as a thief in the night,'" Uncle Peter read, "'in which the heavens will pass away with a great noise, and the elements will melt with fervent heat; both the earth and the works that are in it will be burned up.'"

Jake recalled the discussion with Jayden earlier on in the week. It had been over this very passage.

Uncle Peter went on to read, "'Therefore, since all these things will be dissolved, what manner of persons ought you to be in holy conduct and godliness, looking for and hastening the coming of the day of God, because of which the heavens will be dissolved, being on fire, and the elements will melt with fervent heat? Nevertheless we, according to His promise, look for new heavens and a new earth in which righteousness dwells. Therefore, beloved, looking forward to these things, be diligent to be found by Him in peace, without spot and blameless;'"

"As much as you love and enjoy the things of this world," Uncle Peter told him, "don't forget that they are all about to pass away, to be judged, to be cleansed from this earth. In Noah's day, God destroyed the world with a flood because the imagination of man's heart was only evil continually. [222] Don't have any part of this world's corruption, Jake. When Jesus returns, you know nothing else will matter except being with him! You don't want to be condemned with the world."

The words were sinking in and Jake knew exactly what his uncle meant. He had an uncanny feeling Uncle Peter knew that he had been enjoying the world's corruption. *Did Zach tell on me? Is Dad suspicious?* As they drove back to work, Jake thought things over in his mind. It seemed that every time he turned around lately, there was pressure from someone or another to change his life. It was coming from his parents, from his twin brother and now from his uncle.

Okay, when I get home, he told himself, *I'm going to ask God for forgiveness and make changes. I'd better stop hanging out with Melissa. Uncle Peter is right. I need to put God first.*

"Look, Jake," Uncle Peter said, as they neared Drayton's Engineering firm where the EdenTree crew were maintaining the grounds, "I know you have important plans for next year, but if you can see your way clear to join us in Jamaica, I think it would do you a lot of good. I'd love to have you and Zach help us out. Think it over," he encouraged, as they drove into the parking lot.

Jake didn't commit to anything, but he thanked his uncle. He thought about asking Uncle Peter to pray for him, but he didn't want to sound as though he needed help.

However, Uncle Peter prayed to God before either one of them got out of the car. He asked for God's blessing to be on Jake, to give him direction and strength to make the right decisions.

"Thanks, Uncle Peter," Jake said, as they got out of the car. Uncle Peter clapped him on the back as they both walked to the gardens. He commented on the professional maintenance of the

---

[222] Genesis 6:5-7; Luke 17:26-30; 2 Peter 3:3-7

property. "If time goes on," he added, "you and Zach are always welcome to move up in the landscaping company. You've both got great potential!"

Jake laughed appreciatively. Then he turned and gave his uncle a hug goodbye.

Uncle Peter held him close. "You know you can talk to me anytime, Jake," he said quietly. "You know that, right?"

"Yeah, thanks."

"Even when I'm in Jamaica, I can still Skype!"

As Jake watched his uncle walk to his car, he saw Zach coming toward him.

"Hey, Jake," his brother said, holding out his phone, "Brett wants to talk to you."

CHAPTER 35

The Prize

"Hey, you won't believe this, Jake," Brett said on the phone. "This is *amazing!*"

"What's up?"

"All the kids that attended the basketball camp this summer were entered into a draw. It was part of the registration. And *you've won!*"

"Won what?"

"A trip for two to see the FIBA World Championship basketball game in Boston. It's this weekend! All the best international players will be there, including many who play in the NBA. It's all-inclusive – the airfare, the game, the hotel and restaurant package. It's worth a thousand dollars!"

"Wow!" Jake exclaimed. "Sweet! But it's kind of short-notice... isn't it?"

Brett chuckled. "The envelope came in the mail weeks ago and I just thought it was a copy of the receipt from the camps. I didn't open it. I just set it aside. Today I got a call asking me to confirm the names for the airplane tickets and hotel accommodation!"

"So cool!"

"Sure is. I'd be excited if I were you! So who are you going to take?"

Jake thought for a moment. All the changes he'd been planning to make could wait for one more weekend. This was amazing good luck! Zach was his first choice for company; Jayden was second, but then he remembered something. Brett had paid for their registration.

"What about you?" Jake replied. "If anyone deserves to benefit from the registration – it would be you. Maybe you and Jenna should go."

"I was kind of hoping you might see it that way," Brett laughed. "But Jenna's away in Texas, visiting her family, so I'm on my own here anyway. Why don't the two of us go? We'll fly out tomorrow morning? Could you be ready so soon?"

"I'll have to talk it over with my parents," Jake said excitedly. "I'll get back to you tonight."

As soon as Jake was home from work, he approached his mom in the kitchen, where she was chopping cucumbers for a salad. When Jake asked if he could go, she gently reminded him that Uncle James was *seriously* ill in the hospital!

"Have you even been in to see him yet?" she asked.

"No," Jake admitted uncomfortably. He felt really bad that he hadn't yet gone in to visit his uncle. "But Zach said he was sleeping the whole time anyway. He'll be better soon, won't he, Mom?"

"I don't know, Jake," she said anxiously, shaking her head. "We're all very worried about him!"

"But, Mom," Jake pleaded. "Think of what an amazing experience this will be! Brett was so generous to pay for two of his players to go to camp. Now, he gets something for his generosity. He won't enjoy it nearly as much if I don't go with him."

"Jenna might like to go in your place," she pointed out.

"That's what I suggested, but she's in Texas, visiting her family."

"Whatever," his mom said despairingly, with a shake of her head. "If that's what you want to do, Jake, then you make the decision. But Uncle James is in serious condition! I can't guarantee he'll make it through."

Her last words startled Jake, but he quickly said, "It's only for the weekend, Mom."

"Will you be going somewhere for Sunday meeting?"

"I don't know. I'm sure Brett and I will have a service on our own. Or we could meet with the Ecclesia in Boston. They would probably love to have visitors."

"Whatever you want," she said with a heavy sigh, turning back to making salad. Worried about James and discouraged by her son's poor attitude, Lisa didn't have the heart to argue. While she would normally have discussed the matter with her husband before making a decision, this time she gave in.

Jake smiled. He knew he had her permission in word, if not in heart. Quickly, he phoned Brett, before his dad could interfere.

As he and Brett finalized their plans, Brett added, "And Jake, I'll have to take you to the Boston IMAX. It's far bigger and better than anything you've gone to here in Stirling. You'll be astounded!"

That night, as Jake lay in bed, thinking about his conversation with Uncle Peter and his exciting plans with Brett, he decided to postpone his decision to repent – just for a few more days. *Who knows what Brett and I will end up watching in that IMAX*, he thought. In his heart, Jake secretly hoped that he'd have one last chance to see a really exciting, heart-racing movie. *Just one more before I make all the changes I know I should make. Brett is way more fun to hang out with than anyone in my family! One more, and then I'll stick to family-rated movies for the rest of my life!* he promised himself. *I'll come home, pray for repentance and change my ways for good.*

CHAPTER 36

A Call in the Night

Having finished his Bible study, Zach was getting ready for bed at eleven-thirty, Sunday evening. He had just finished studying Elihu's speech in chapter thirty-seven, full of references to thunder and lightning, clouds and rain. *I'm sure that Elihu was watching the approach of a thunderstorm,* Zach pondered as he brushed his teeth. *Especially since the very next chapter begins with God speaking from a whirlwind.* He was glad he had found the section interesting. He was trying not to think about Brett and Jake watching the World Championships in Boston.

There had been a quote on the page, which Zach had taken to heart. It said, "While the way that God works is far beyond our comprehension, it is not impossible to understand and realize that God has the eternal good of a faithful believer in mind. The supremacy of God's power and wisdom should not lead us to feel frustration over the things we don't understand, but rather a humble recognition of that which we do – that God is working to develop a spiritually responsible character, bringing forth praise and honour unto His name." [223]

Suddenly the family phone rang. Zach rushed to the kitchen to pick it up, since everyone else was asleep in bed. Grandma was on the line.

"Sorry if I'm waking you up," she spoke anxiously, "but your Uncle James is not doing well at all. The nurses aren't sure he'll make it through tonight. We're all at the hospital with

---

[223] A Study on the Book of Job, "When He hath tried me, I shall come forth as gold." Manitoulin Youth Conference 2011, page 70.

Sandra."

Instantly alarmed, Zach could hardly believe his ears. *Uncle James is so young! How can he possibly be dying?* "I'll tell my dad," Zach said, anxiously, suddenly trembling from head to foot. "Thanks for calling, Grandma."

Zach's dad was out of bed in a second when his son relayed the message. "Stay here, Lisa," he told his wife. "I don't want to bring the girls."

Susanna, Uncle Peter's five-year old daughter was staying with them that Sunday night, sleeping over with Esther. Quickly slipping into his clothes, Zach's dad joined him outside the bedroom door.

"I want to come with you, Dad," Zach pleaded.

"Let's go then."

Together they made their way to the hospital in the wee hours of the morning. The moon had an eerie reddish-glow in the dark, night sky. Zach commented on its colour, but his dad was too caught up with concern for his sick brother to take much notice.

"This can't be happening," his dad kept repeating. "Surely with today's modern medicine, they can clear up pneumonia. I can't believe they think he's not going to make it. Why can't they give him stronger antibiotics? What's wrong with those doctors?"

Zach knew he wasn't expected to answer such questions. He just hoped that somehow Uncle James would recover. Silently, he prayed again for a miracle.

Entering the hospital room, Zach's eyes took in the sad sight. Propped up against the pillows, seemingly unconscious in the bed, Uncle James was dreadfully white and thin. His breathing was erratic and laboured. An oxygen mask was on his face. Beside him in a chair, Aunt Sandra was clinging tightly to one of his hands and sobbing against his shoulder. "James, please hang on! James, you can't leave me!"

Uncle Peter and Aunt Jessica were sharing an armchair at

the end of the bed and Grandma was seated on the other side. Uncle Thomas and Aunt Purity were standing nearby, looking just as anxious and concerned as everyone else. As Zach and his father entered the room, Uncle Thomas and Aunt Purity came over to give them hugs.

"We'll stay just outside the room," Uncle Thomas said compassionately, patting Zach on the back. "We don't want to overcrowd things."

"Thanks for being here," Zach's dad said sincerely. "We appreciate your support so much!"

Spotting a chair against the wall, Zach brought it over for his dad. He didn't want to get one for himself; he didn't feel like sitting.

"Why don't we rub his chest again with the ointment?" Grandma was saying, her voice high with emotion. She looked very distressed. "They told me in the health food store that in several cases this ointment cleared pneumonia overnight!"

Aunt Sandra was too distraught to do anything more than hold onto her dying husband's hand. She had always known her happy years with James could come to an abrupt end, but she had never thought it would come so soon. Seven years was not long enough; she had counted on so many more!

Uncle Peter obligingly took the ointment from his mom and began to rub it thickly on his brother. Uncle James choked and sputtered.

"No more, Mom," Uncle Peter said, shaking his head ruefully and handing back the jar. "He's struggling just to breathe. Let him be. The doctors and nurses are doing all that they can."

"Please, Peter, can we pray again, that God won't take him?" Aunt Sandra begged tearfully.

Zach could see that everyone was anxious and discouraged. So many prayers had been offered. So many herbal remedies had been tried. The wonders of modern medicine had

286

failed.

"Let's pray," Uncle Peter said.

They all joined hands and bowed their heads as Uncle Peter pleaded that God would spare James' life and restore him to health. "If this be Your will," Uncle Peter clarified at the end. "We know that in everything You work for good with those who love You, even when we can't see any good at all.[224] Help us to feel You working with us now. Open our eyes we plead. Heavenly Father, we trust Your wisdom and Your loving care. In Jesus Christ's Name. Amen."

Uncle James coughed hard for almost a minute. Everyone sat nervously around, hoping he would clear some of the mucus that was filling his lungs. Aunt Sandra patted his back and Grandma held the oxygen mask so that her son could expel the phlegm he was coughing up. When his coughing fit was over, Uncle James rested back against the pillows and closed his eyes in exhaustion.

Watching carefully, Zach could see that Uncle James was struggling to move his hands. With tragic, wondering eyes, Aunt Sandra let go. Feebly, her husband held up four fingers of one hand against his chest and drew a 'v' with the other. Then his arms rolled limply back to his side.

"He must have heard us pray," Grandma said, thoughtfully.

For a moment, Aunt Sandra looked puzzled and then she sobbed, "*Forever!* He's telling us that he'll be with us forever."

"Really? Are you sure?" Grandma asked.

Choked up with emotion, Aunt Sandra could only nod. Taking Uncle James' limp hand in hers once more she held it up to her cheek. She knew that her husband was reminding her of her

---

[224] Romans 8:28 RSV

own passionate words expressed to him, years before. Her thoughts went back to the memorable evening when they had sat together underneath a starry sky overlooking the ocean. It was in that special place, close by the home she shared now with James, that he had first told her that he loved her and... that he had problems with his health.

"Sandra," he had pleaded quietly. "Is it fair for me to ask you to become involved in my life? Are you going to want to look after a sick man – if it comes to that?"

At that tender moment in time, Sandra had suddenly realized that the promises she had discovered in the Bible changed her whole perspective on suffering and gave her a future hope beyond the 'here and now'.

She remembered turning to him and saying earnestly, "James, if you come to share the hope I've found, then we won't have to be afraid of anything. We'll see each other again and it will be *forever!*"

Squeezing his hand gently, Aunt Sandra felt calmer and reassured. She knew that her husband was conscious even if he looked like he was asleep. "You're right, dearest," she said clearly and tenderly, speaking a message that she wanted him to hear. "It will be *forever!* I will be all right," she sobbed. "I have God and His promises. I have Jesus and I know he's coming soon. I have your kind family. And I'll *always* love you!"

Uncle James breathed deeply; very deeply. There was a terrible rattle in his chest and then... nothing more.

Everyone scrambled to find a pulse; to hear a breath; to find any sign of life, but there was none. Grandma whacked the emergency button.

Nurses came rushing in. A doctor was called. Lowering the bed, the nurse attempted CPR, but her hands kept slipping because of the ointment on Uncle James' chest. Aunt Sandra handed her a cloth and she whisked the special remedy off his skin and tried again. The doctor used a defibrillator. For five minutes there was a great flurry of activity with no response from Uncle James.

Eventually, the doctor turned solemnly to the family. "I'm very, very sorry," he said sadly, "but there's no hope of resuscitating him now – not if he is to have any meaningful quality of life."

Aunt Sandra threw her arm across her husband's chest and buried her face against his shoulder, weeping loudly. Everyone else gazed at the still body on the bed in helpless silence.

"He's gone," Grandma cried. "James has gone."

Zach wasn't sure what to do. He'd never seen anyone die before and this was someone that he loved – someone who had been such a vital part of his life. Tears were running down his face. He felt overwhelmed by sorrow. *Why has God taken Uncle James?* he pondered. *Surely God could have healed him. We were all praying so hard. It doesn't make sense.*

They all stayed in the room, grieving their loss. Uncle Thomas and Aunt Purity joined them. Uncle Peter removed the oxygen mask. Grandma picked up the ointment and tossed it into the garbage bin. It was all so sad. Aunt Sandra and Grandma were going to be all alone in the big house. Aunt Sandra had no other family, aside from the brother she rarely saw.

But we'll look after her, Zach thought to himself fiercely. *She's part of our family now.* He wiped the tears away as he imagined himself going to the Oceanview Lodge. He saw himself standing in front of the rosebushes with pruners in his hand, sadly realizing his uncle would never again come strolling out of the house to help him with the work. *Uncle James, I'm going to miss you so much!* he thought earnestly.

Uncle Peter reached across his brother's still body and held on to Aunt Sandra's arm. He was in tears. Grandma was in tears. Zach and his father came close to comfort the others.

CHAPTER 37

Unbelievable!

"He moved his hand!" Aunt Sandra suddenly cried out, sitting back in anxious astonishment and nearly knocking the others over.

Everyone looked over at her sadly. Sometimes muscles continue to contract after death. They all felt dreadfully sorry for Aunt Sandra. They knew how hard it was going to be for her to accept her husband's death.

Staring forlornly at his uncle, Zach saw him *open his eyes!* In the body of a dead man, two, vibrant, hazel-brown eyes were suddenly sparkling with life!

How could this be happening?

Before all the stunned gazes, Uncle James slowly sat up and looked around in bewilderment. He was breathing perfectly normally again, without any laborious gasps or rattles.

Zach looked in disbelief. *Wasn't Uncle James white and frail, just a minute ago? How could I have thought that? He looks so healthy… almost years younger!*

"What did you rub on my chest?" he asked his mom. "That was some powerful stuff!"

With shaky hands, Grandma picked the bottle out of the bin. Everyone was completely in shock and didn't know how to respond. It was as though they felt they were seeing a vision and were afraid to move in case it vanished away. But Aunt Sandra was the first to rejoice.

"James, you're alive!" she exclaimed. "Oh, thank God!"

Looking over at his wife's tear-stained face, Uncle James

shook his head compassionately. Swinging his long legs out of bed, he pulled her onto his lap and held her tight. "It's okay, Beauts," he assured her. "God heard your prayers. He's not taking me just yet. I'm so sorry you had to go through all that."

Aunt Sandra clung tightly to him but was still at a loss for words.

Uncle Peter picked up the bottle of ointment. With a skeptical frown he examined the list of ingredients through his bifocals. "Maybe this stuff is worth using after all," he mumbled with a strange expression on his face. "You'll have to tell me where you got it, Mom."

Hearing the commotion a nurse popped her head in the door. "Is everything…?" she started to ask. Seeing the dead man sitting up in bed, she gasped. With astonishment, she cried out, "My goodness! How is this possible? It's a miracle!" She ran off to bring in the other nurses.

It was all so strange. As happy as they all were, everyone couldn't stop staring at Uncle James in bewilderment.

"You sure had me fooled," Uncle Thomas laughed, shakily.

"What's the matter with you all?" Uncle James chuckled, stretching his limbs. "I feel like I've finally beaten this cough. Whew! I thought it was going to be the end of me!"

A team of nurses and doctors rushed in and initiated an examination of vital signs. None of them could understand what had happened. Grandma showed them the bottle of ointment she had used and they wrote down its name and the store where it had been purchased.

"I've never – in all my years of practice – seen anything like this!" one doctor exclaimed.

"This is unbelievable – just totally unbelievable!" the other doctor agreed.

The nurses checked Uncle James' blood pressure and vital

signs over and over, and he patiently cooperated. Everything checked out perfectly. Uncle James had not only stopped coughing, he was in perfect health in every way. Finally, they gave Uncle James a clean bill of health and let everyone depart for home.

The sun's early morning rays were just beginning to light up the sky as Zach drove with his dad to Uncle James' house. Uncle James and Aunt Sandra were in the back seat and Uncle James was still raving about how good he felt.

"The strange thing is," he was saying to them all in a perplexed tone, "I actually feel better than I have for years – even before my heart-attack! I feel like I'd love to go for a nice, steady, ten-kilometer run! How could I have been clinically dead? There must have been a mix-up somewhere!"

"The doctors and nurses all confirmed that you were dead," Zach's dad replied. "I just don't understand how someone can be confirmed dead one moment and then antsy to go for a jog three hours later! That ointment mom used might have been powerful stuff, but this… this is more like a miracle!"

"Maybe God answered Uncle Peter's prayer," Zach suggested.

"That's the best explanation yet," his dad answered.

"Could it be… the *resurrection?*" Aunt Sandra asked timidly. "Maybe Jesus has returned."

"That's what I'm wondering," Uncle James said thoughtfully.

With a shiver of expectation, everyone else agreed. How else could such a remarkable recovery be explained?

"Only, we're all still here," Uncle James said. "I would have thought that an angel would have appeared to us by now and told us to come away to judgement."

They walked into the log-home feeling rather unsure what they should do next. It was five-thirty in the morning and no one had slept all night. Uncle Thomas and Aunt Purity arrived shortly after, having gone home first to pick up Thomas' mother from the Symons' house. Aunt Jessica's younger children were upstairs in bed, but she had fallen asleep on the couch. She woke up instantly when everyone else arrived home and was astonished to see Uncle James looking so fit and healthy. Since Uncle James was hungry, Aunt Sandra set about making breakfast.

Pacing back and forth, Uncle James was looking longingly out the large windows. Pale pink clouds stretched across the ocean and Zach knew his uncle wanted to go for a run. The pathway that followed the cliffs along the beach was his favourite trail.

"Don't you *dare* go for a jog!" Aunt Sandra called out with a laugh, as she cut up oranges and set them neatly on a plate. "James, we don't know yet if you're really better or not."

"I am completely cured of everything," Uncle James chuckled. "My heart feels stronger than ever! I bet I could even keep up with Zach out there!"

"I don't know," Zach laughed. "You're looking so good, you might just beat me! In fact," Zach exclaimed, suddenly realizing something, "Uncle James, your hair... it's darker... it's... thicker!"

Running over to the mirror on the wall, Uncle James looked in.

At that moment the phone rang and Aunt Sandra ran to pick it up. "Oh, hi Laurie," Zach heard her say. He listened with interest. Aunt Sandra's brother rarely called. "That's okay. I knew you were in Texas... No, no, don't worry...You won't believe this. We all thought James had died, but... *Yes, it was that serious!* ... Anyway, the doctors confirmed he was dead and we were all *devastated*... and then five minutes later he came back to life! ... Yes, I'm *totally* serious... James is completely better, Laurie! He said he doesn't even feel like he has a heart condition anymore."

At that moment, Uncle Peter and Aunt Jessica entered the

house with Grandma. They had driven home from the hospital in Grandma's car. As Zach's dad was telling them about the new developments in James' astonishing recovery and everyone was talking at once, Zach heard Aunt Sandra saying, "Laurie, I've tried to tell you about this many times... I know, but you never had time to listen... Yes, I do believe it has to be the resurrection... There's no other explanation... James looks twenty years younger!"

The doorbell rang. Thinking it would be his mom arriving with Esther and Susanna, Zach ran across the room to open the door.

A young lady stood on the doorstep when Zach opened the door; someone about his own age. She was a complete stranger. He had never seen her before in his life. In an old-fashioned dress, complete with puffed sleeves, she looked like she had raided a second-hand store.

"Peter?!" she asked hesitantly. Her dark eyes were filled with wonder as she looked at Zach in a bewildered way. To his complete surprise, she reached out tentatively to give him a hug!

"Uh... I'm not Peter," Zach said with confusion, stepping backwards. *What on earth is this stranger doing at the door at six o'clock in the morning? And why does she want Uncle Peter?*

CHAPTER 38

When It All Begins to Matter

The message that Uncle James was dying was unbelievable to Jake. His uncle was too young to be dying. But the call had been urgent and he and Brett were taking it seriously.

He looked over at Brett as they sped down the highway. The green Mustang was averaging at least thirty kilometres an hour above the speed limit as they rushed home from the airport. Jake hoped he would get to see his uncle before he died. He felt bad that he had neglected visiting him in the hospital, but even so, deep down, he wouldn't have traded his time with Brett for anything. *Brett is such a fun guy!* Jake thought. *He's so balanced and knows how to have a good time. What a weekend it's been!* Canada had almost won the championship, until the U.S. sunk a three-pointer in the last two seconds. It had been the most exciting game of his life! To cap it off, he had caught the sweaty headband LeBron James had thrown into the crowd.

With the downturn in the US economy, they had passed by many run-down neighbourhoods and crowds of homeless whenever they were on the streets. Brett had kindly passed out twenty dollars to a couple of children who were begging outside the hotel. Inside, they enjoyed the exercise room, a relaxing soak in the hot tub, and the large flat-screen TV in their room. They had a small memorial service Sunday morning, revisited all the hotel facilities, went out for ribs and steaks at a posh restaurant and ended up at the IMAX. Just as Jake had anticipated, there hadn't been any interesting movie choices among the family-rated ones. While the movie that he and Brett saw was milder than the ones Jake had seen at basketball camp, it was still far beyond anything his parents would allow in their house. It certainly had enough heart-racing scenes to qualify as a *'good'* movie!

Having talked about movies with Brett over the weekend, Jake felt less conscience-stricken than he had before. Sitting back against the comfortable leather bucket seat he relished the best scenes and was hardly moved by the weary little soldier's pin-pricks.

"It's only watching pictures," Brett had explained, when they talked about movies. "And the people are only acting – it's not even real for them! As long as what you're looking at isn't causing you to commit the sin, you can hardly say it's having a bad effect on you."

Brett went on to give evidence he'd heard, that the latest study showed an increase in viewing violent movies or playing violent video games actually decreased the level of crime. "Better to get your fix in the virtual world – can't do any harm there," he chuckled.

Jake agreed. *My family is way too 'conservative',* he told himself. *I don't know what Zach heard at Bible Camp, or stumbled across in that workbook, but he's too keyed up about all this stuff. There are so many teenagers – even Christadelphian teenagers – that have done way worse stuff than me. I haven't stolen anything – well, not exactly... I've given the laptop back – I certainly didn't ever plan to* steal *it! I haven't tried drugs. I don't get drunk every weekend. I don't play video games non-stop...*

But... it has affected me, Jake suddenly thought, with a surprising measure of honesty from the pin-prick of the sword. *Should I tell Brett what I've been doing? He'd keep a secret. I know he has struggled with girls; he would understand. Ah... but he'll probably tell me to break it off with Melissa. I'm sure that's what he'll say... and that will be so hard! Melissa asked me to go to the beach with her tomorrow. She wants to hang-out again with me this week. It will be so-o-o amazing! She's so beautiful! I told*

Melissa I love her… and I do… and Melissa says she's never loved any one as much as me! How can I say we need to break up? I'd be heartless… we haven't even been dating for a week. Besides, I've already failed. I'm a full-blown sinner – what's the point in trying to be perfect? Perhaps, if I'm fully committed to this relationship with Melissa, then it's not so bad. I'm not like all the other guys at school sleeping around with whoever shows up for the weekend! I'll be faithful to Melissa… it's sort of like we're married now. That's how I'll view it. I'm sure God will understand. He made us this way. He knows how weak we are… "

The new man in Christ was defeated. Every weak prick of the conscience was swiftly deflected by endless justifications, foolish comparisons to others, and a lack of focus on Christ. [225] Without any sustenance coming his way, he had no power to undo the shackles or remove the blindfold. As it says, in Romans chapter six, "For to be carnally minded is death, but to be spiritually minded is life and peace. Because the carnal mind is enmity against God; for it is not subject to the law of God, nor indeed can be. So then, those who are in the flesh cannot please God."

Jake had underestimated the power sin had to pull him away from God – to lose sight of God's holiness, and wisdom to discern right from wrong. No longer struggling to overcome, he was choosing to give in and justify his actions. And sadly, for the willful, unrepentant sinner "there no longer remains a sacrifice for sins."[226]

Reclining in the leather seat comfortably, Jake's thoughts wandered between the best scenes of the movie, his concern for Uncle James and the date he hoped to go on the next day with Melissa. The concern he felt barely dampened his delirious expectations. *Things will turn around for Uncle James,* he told

[225] 2 Corinthians 10:3-5,12
[226] Hebrews 10:26

himself. *Surely by the time we get there, they'll have found the right medication.*

"Look at the moon," Brett was saying. "Have you ever seen it that red?"

"It is quite red," Jake agreed.

"I heard there was going to be another lunar eclipse sometime. Maybe that's it."

"Cool – another one!"

Strange signs and disasters had become all too commonplace; they had lost their impact.

"I can't believe this is happening to your uncle," Brett said with a shake of his head.

"Yeah, how can pneumonia kill someone?" Jake asked. "Surely with enough antibiotics Uncle James will get better – won't he?"

Brett's phone croaked; it sounded exactly like a frog when texts came through. He handed it to Jake.

"See who the message is from," Brett said.

Jake picked it up. "It's a message from Melissa."

"It's likely for you, then."

The message read:

Brett, please ask Jake what time he wants me to pick him up tomorrow?

Jake's heart raced.

Hey, there. It's Jake," he replied. "Ten sounds good.

Okay! I'll pack a picnic! ☺

You're amazing!

Thanks! I tried to text Zach's phone first, but he's not answering. Is everything okay?

He's probably in the hospital. My uncle is really sick.

Sorry about your uncle. I hope he gets better! Love u.

Jake smiled as he texted back:

Love u more.

He gave Brett's phone back with a dreamy smile.

Tomorrow he was going to give Melissa the best day of her life. This was his girl now. He was committed. Somehow eventually, he'd find a way to bring her to God and get his life sorted out.

"Generally people recover from pneumonia," Brett was saying. "But I suppose what makes it so critical for your uncle is that he has a weak heart. He nearly died eight years ago or so, right?"

"Yeah, I guess he did," Jake recalled. He'd only been a kid at the time, but he remembered his parents talking about a triple by-pass. "Uncle James just seems so healthy. I don't think of him as weak. He even jogs!"

"Sandra looks after him well. He's a lucky man!"

The phone croaked again. It was another text from Melissa:

Jake, I just got a message from Shane to say that he has changed his plans!!!! He's coming back for another semester. I'm so sorry!!! This makes things really complicated!!!! Maybe we can talk about it at the beach.

"What?" Jake remarked, out loud, in dismay.

Jake was about to text Melissa back when Brett said, "We'd better take this exit and get some fuel."

Veering off the highway, Brett fumbled in his pocket. Suddenly, in alarm, he cried out, "I can't believe it!" He checked the glove compartment of his car. "I've left my wallet somewhere!" he exclaimed with panic. "How could I be such an idiot?"

Jake looked over in astonishment. They were only fifteen minutes from the hospital. It was dark. It was past ten-thirty and the gas gauge was on empty. Pulling out his own wallet, Jake counted the few quarters that he had inside. Gas prices had risen dramatically in the past few months; even just ten-litres to get them home required a lot more than loose change.

"We can use my bank card," he suggested.

Brett pulled over onto the shoulder of the road and stopped. "What am I going to do?" he yelled. "I think I must have left my wallet on that plane. I took it out to buy a sandwich... and that's the last I remember!" He pondered the situation for a moment and then slapped his hand hard against the steering wheel. "Darn it!" he exclaimed in frustration. "Maybe the cleaning crew will find it. I'll have to call the airport."

A bright light captured their attention. Was someone stopping to help?

Rolling down his window, Brett leaned out. The bright light was coming from behind and drawing closer. When the source of that light appeared in the window, Jake's heart suddenly pounded with fear. The young man that looked in the window had a bright, glorious aura, like nothing he had ever seen before!

"The time has come," the young man said solemnly. "Jesus Christ is calling you to him."

Instantly panicking, Jake knew they were speaking to an angel. He didn't stop to think that maybe it was a dream, or someone pulling a prank. Without any doubt, he knew this was it. Everything he had been taught about the End Times, about Jesus' return, about the judgement seat, about being called away – was at that very moment complete reality! Nothing else mattered – not the fabulous weekend they had just enjoyed, or the Provincials, or Melissa, or getting into university. It was all over. Everything he had been giving all his time and energy to achieve was entirely meaningless. All that mattered were the things he'd been putting off. He had neglected his relationship with God. *How long has it been since I last prayed?* he asked himself frantically. *I haven't asked God for forgiveness. I'm not ready! I need more time! This isn't supposed to happen so soon. How can it be?*

Brett seemed to be having the same thoughts. He sat frozen to his seat, astonished and speechless.

The car doors opened as if with invisible hands.

Compelled against their will, Jake and Brett found themselves getting out of the car and coming not just before one angel, but two! The brightness of their white robes and shining faces was such a terrifying sight that they both dropped to their knees and bowed down to the ground.

Reaching out their hands, the angels lifted them to their feet. Jake couldn't bear the sorrow he saw in the angel's eyes. *Have I disappointed this angel?* he asked himself fearfully. *Is this my personal angel, the one who watched over me?*[227] *Is there any hope for mercy? Jesus and God are very merciful and full of compassion. At least Brett and I are baptized. We both followed that command. Will God forgive me?* All Jake's sinful thoughts and deeds seemed so much more sinful than he had ever acknowledged before. *I'll say I'm sorry and plead for mercy,* he told himself. *Surely God will forgive me if I'm humble enough to admit my failings and beg for His compassion.*

"Please…" he began, but the angel stopped him.

"Come with us," the angel said. "It's time for you to appear before the judgement seat of Christ."

---

[227] Hebrews 1:13-14; Psalm 34:7; Matthew 18:10

CHAPTER 39

The Stranger

When the angel brought Verity to Oceanview Lodge, he told her with a smile, "This is the Bryant's home. Tell them that Jesus Christ has returned and is calling for them." And then the angel vanished from sight.

Looking around at the unfamiliar surroundings, Verity was unsure of the location. Before she fell asleep in Christ, the Bryants had lived near her in the quiet town of Grandville, Ontario. She had no idea where she was now or how exactly she had arrived. The angel had taken her hand and in a moment she was standing outside this large log home. It looked very welcoming with all the tall windows glowing brightly in the faint light of dawn, but she knew she had never been here before. To her right, she could see a pink ocean stretching far away toward the eastern horizon. Restless waves were pounding in on the nearby shore. She could taste the salty sea air and the breeze felt warm and balmy. This was certainly not any place in Ontario!

Who will greet me at this door? she wondered, walking up the steps and knocking with great anticipation. *Is this Peter's house? Is Peter a believer? Will my message fill him with dread? Or will he rejoice?* She twisted her hair nervously as footsteps sounded across the floor and the door handle turned.

The face that peered out cautiously had to be Peter's! While his hairstyle had changed, his face was unmistakable. He hadn't aged at all. Perhaps she had been dead for only a short while – maybe a month or a year. Yet... there was no recognition in his eyes – none whatsoever! *Has he forgotten me so quickly?* Verity wondered anxiously. *Do I look different?*

302

"Peter?" she said hesitantly, reaching out her arms to him.

The young man looked perplexed and drew back. "I'm not Peter."

"Oh," Verity said, twisting her long, dark hair again. "You look so much like him!" Her mind leaped to a new possibility. "Are you his... son?"

"No, Peter is my uncle."

"Is he here?"

"Yes."

"Please, may I speak with him? *Please* tell Peter that Verity Lovell is here."

"Sure." With a dazed expression, Zach turned to find his uncle.

Verity trembled from head to toe. *Peter is here! I'll soon know how he feels.*

Zach swallowed hard as he stumbled over to his uncles. *Is this for real? Verity Lovell*, he repeated to himself. He'd only ever heard of one Verity. *This must be the girl that meant so much to Uncle Peter! This must be the girl who died in her teens. Lovell is Uncle Thomas' surname. This is his sister! This news will blow everyone's minds!*

Coming close to his uncle, he put his hand on his arm. "Uncle Peter," he stuttered, "There's... there's a girl at the door. She... she says she's Verity Lovell. "

Everyone froze in absolute astonishment. Finally, Peter broke the silence.

"Who... *who*... did you say is at the door?!" he demanded sharply. Zach had never heard his uncle speak in such a tone.

"He said it's *Verity!*" Thomas repeated in utter astonishment.

Peter and Thomas were the first to dash toward the door. The others followed close behind in a confused, excited state. When Thomas recognized the visitor, he stopped and allowed

Peter to pass by. Turning around, Thomas motioned for everyone else to wait.

Peter didn't stop until he reached the open door. He stared in amazement at the young girl gazing anxiously back at him. "Verity!" Zach heard his uncle whisper, "It *is* you! You've been raised from the dead."

Standing in the open door under the golden glow of the porch light, Verity looked tentatively at the stocky, older man with the tanned, weathered face. *Is this Peter?* The man before her was tall and stocky; Peter had been so lean. This man's hair was thinning and darker; Peter had been blond. The tired, aging lines etched on his face hadn't been there before, nor the bifocals.

Her hesitation was noticeable.

Verity," Peter said gently, "you've been gone *nineteen* years. I know by now I must look rather… ancient; but I'm still me. I'm still Peter Byrant."

"Nineteen years? Really?" Verity exclaimed, processing the new information anxiously. *If that's true, then I've been gone a long time! So much may have changed.*

Peter's eyes were filling with tears. The last twenty-four hours had been an emotional rollercoaster. Looking at the young girl in front of him, he recalled fond, distant memories. "I'm the same guy you walked right smack into at school. Remember how all your books went flying?"

Verity's eyes opened wide in amazement. Only Peter would remember their first encounter, which had always been subject to debate. She looked sideways at him with a smile. "No way! You walked into me!"

Peter grinned. He looked just like… Peter! His grin hadn't changed at all.

He held out his arms and she joyfully flung hers around his neck. He was crying and so was she.

"You're alive again!" he exclaimed to Verity, holding her

close. "God has raised you and healed you completely! Jesus has returned to earth at last. Thank you, Father, for keeping Your promises! Thank you for Your faithfulness."

Verity looked up through her tears with elation. Peter was praising God! She hadn't told him the message but he already knew what it was. The angel had brought her to this house. Surely this could only mean one thing... but she had to ask; it was all that mattered. "Peter, are you a... believer, then? Is that why I've been sent here?"

"I am, Verity!" he exclaimed, wiping his eyes. "Thanks to God's great mercy, I found the hope you shared! I'm sorry I let you down when you were dying. I was so scared! I didn't know..."

"Peter," Verity interrupted compassionately, "it's okay. I understood, even then. It all happened so fast. None of us had time to think it through. If you're going to be a part of the Kingdom to come – I'm perfectly content! It *is* here now, Peter. Jesus has returned. An angel brought me to your house!"

Peter pulled her close again. The cup of joy was overflowing. The new beginning for which they longed had finally come!

Stepping back, Peter pointed to all the others who were waiting in the house behind him. "Verity," he said, "let me introduce you to our family in Christ. There are so many wonderful surprises for you!"

With a grin, he asked, "Do you recognize anyone?"

Looking at all the people in the doorway, Verity noticed a tall, dark-haired man who looked like her father. She whispered excitedly, "Is that my brother?"

"You mean you're not sure about Thomas, either?" Peter teased. "What about your mom?"

Thomas and Kara didn't wait to be recognized. They both ran forward to envelop Verity in their arms.

"Mom! Thomas!" she cried out in surprise. Her mother's

305

hair was completely white! "You're all here in the same house together!" she marvelled. "Does that mean... ?"

"Yes, Verity," her mother smiled tenderly. "We are all waiting for Jesus to return. Everyone in this house has come to know Christ."

With overflowing joy, Verity was content. She held her mother and Thomas close and cried many happy tears. Her prayers had been answered – every one!

When she finally drew back from her family to talk with all the others, Peter introduced her to the members of his family. Verity was thrilled to greet every one of the Bryant clan. Even the young man who looked so much like Peter was now quite willing to give her a hug! *This is unbelievable!* she thought. *I prayed for Peter and my family and look how many answered God's call!*

There were still two others standing in the house. They were waiting quietly with warm smiles of anticipation. Peter was very conscious of both the women who were waiting patiently, but especially the one with whom he had shared many happy memorable years. Catching Jessica's eye, Peter was thankful for the look of understanding that passed between them. He had married a remarkable woman; he had no regrets.

Looking back thoughtfully at Verity, Peter saw that she was wiping tears from her face. The last time he'd seen tears in her eyes they had been tears of pain and sadness, now they were of joy and rejoicing. Peter loved her as much as ever and didn't want to see any sadness return.

"Verity," he said quietly, "Do you remember telling me that the few years of our mortal existence are nothing compared to eternity in God's Kingdom?"

Verity thought long and hard. "Did I say that? That's not a bad line."

"You wrote me a letter when you were dying," Peter reminded her with a smile. "I've read it many times. I probably know it by heart."

Verity remembered writing a letter late one night, when she wasn't sure how long she had left to live. The contents of that letter were vague in her mind. She nodded and replied, "It's true that what has happened in the past doesn't matter now."

"I agree," Peter replied, still speaking in the same quiet tones. "And since you are proof that Jesus has returned, by God's good grace we hope to be made immortal very soon. We will all be one with God and our Lord Jesus Christ for eternity." He motioned toward everyone standing nearby, and said, "All of us – together."[228] Hesitating thoughtfully, he said, "Verity, I want you to meet someone... someone very special."

There was no doubt in Verity's mind that Peter had something important to tell her... and that he was unsure of her response. Following Peter's gaze, she noticed the two women standing in the shadows.

Nineteen years have passed, Verity told herself. *A lot of time has gone by. Things have changed. Did Peter marry one of those ladies?*

Peter stepped forward and drew a tall, blond lady to his side. "Verity, this is my wife, Jessica," he said gently. "Do you remember little Jessica Symons?"

Verity's mouth dropped open in amazement as she looked up. "Jessica?"

Jessica embraced her warmly. "Verity, I'm so happy to see you again!" she exclaimed earnestly. "Peter and I have both looked forward to your resurrection. I was devastated when you died!"

"*Little* Jessica!" Verity reminisced, taking a good look at the tall young woman. "I remember you as the cutest little girl who used to sit on my lap. And now I'm looking way up at you! And

---

[228] John 17:20-24

you married Peter… " she trailed off with a sad smile. Then, a sudden twinkle returned to her eyes, "Well, I wasn't here to straighten him out, so I'm very glad he's had you!"

They both laughed.

"I got straightened out all right," Peter grinned, with a loving look in his wife's direction. "And I needed it too!"

Peter looked over at the last person standing in the doorway. It was hard to see her in the dark interior.

Smiling at Verity, Peter told her, "Jess and I have been in Jamaica doing missionary work with your brother and Purity – his wife."

"Thomas married *Purity?* Not… Purity Henderson?!" Verity exclaimed, with disbelief.

But Peter was nodding.

"My brother married my friend?"

"Yes."

"I am so happy!" Verity cried, holding her arms as Purity stepped forward. "You've hardly changed at all!" Verity exclaimed truthfully, clasping her friend close. "I can't believe I didn't recognize you in there!

Purity laughed and hugged her friend tightly. "I'm so thankful to see you again!" she said. "You must be overwhelmed by all the surprises. Look what God has done!"

Verity looked around. "It is unbelievable!" she agreed, scanning all the happy faces of the Bryants, her own family and now a sister-in-law! Everyone was crying tears of joy.

It was at that very moment that Aunt Lisa drove up to the door with Esther and Susanna. Grandma had called her on the phone and told her to come over immediately.

Little Susanna came rushing up to greet her parents. In the lamplight, her wispy hair was the colour of sunshine, and her big blue eyes were shining with excitement. "Look, Mommy and Daddy," she said, totally unaware that everyone had tears in their eyes. "Look at me. I lost a tooth! Esther helped me pull it out and I have it in this bag."

Peter scooped up his little girl and introduced her to Verity. "This is my daughter, Susanna Verity," he told her.

Uncomfortable around any strangers, no matter how pleasant and friendly they might look, Susanna shyly hid her face. Patting his daughter's back, Peter coaxed, "Come on, Honey, you've got to talk to Aunt Verity. She's the reason you have such a beautiful middle name."

"Susanna Verity?" Verity repeated, looking from Peter to Jessica and back again to Peter. "Thank you for remembering me!" Of course there were more tears. Even Zach found himself wiping his eyes.

Then suddenly, Zach's Grandpa appeared, looking so much younger that only Grandma Bryant recognized him! As everyone celebrated the joyful and emotional reunion, they were joined by a *multitude* of strangers. However, these strangers were dressed in long white robes and their faces glowed in a bright, unnatural way. Little Susanna fearfully hid her face in her father's shoulder and wrapped her arms tightly around his neck. Everyone became instantly sober and bowed down to the ground. They knew without a doubt they were standing in the presence of God's holy angels.

"Do not be afraid," one of the angels said comfortingly, "It is time to come with us. Jesus Christ has returned and he is calling for all of you."

CHAPTER 40

Before the Throne of Judgement

Zach wasn't sure how they got there or how much time had passed in travel. It all seemed to happen in an instant. One moment he was standing with all the others on Uncle James' porch and the next moment he was somewhere unknown; somewhere surreal, strange, and terribly awesome! He knew he must be at the judgement seat of Christ! This was no dream; everything felt very real. It was dark like night, yet in the distance, the man on the throne surpassed even the angels in his dazzling white robes and gleaming golden girdle. His royal robes were such an intense, pure white that Zach's eyes hurt to look in his direction. The golden crown he wore on his head cast rays of light across the crowds.

That must be Jesus![229] Zach thought, with a jolt of anxious joy. *Finally we get to meet him!*

Scattered throughout the great multitude, pressed into the barren wilderness, were other glowing individuals, whom Zach assumed were angels. *Has everyone arrived here with their personal angel?* he wondered. Then he looked around anxiously. *Where's Jake?* he panicked. *Why isn't Jake with me? Is Jake here somewhere?*

The golden throne on which Jesus sat, gleamed brightly in the darkness, casting streaks of brilliant light across the shadowy, jagged mountains behind. Enormous thunderclouds filled the heavens, randomly blazing with erratic bursts of energy. Thunder echoed from cloud to cloud and the earth trembled beneath his feet. Covering his face with his hands, Zach fell to his knees upon

---

[229] Daniel 7:9-14,27; Revelation 1: 13-18

the dry, sandy ground. So did his uncles and aunts, and everyone else in the vast crowd. If Zach had been impressed with his insignificance while looking up at the stars, this was one thousand times more awesome and terrible!

"Do not fear," his angel assured him, reaching out to touch his shoulder. The words were said kindly. The angel's touch was comforting. When Zach looked up, all the surrounding noise and people seemed to fade away. It was as though he and the angel were all alone in the vast wilderness. He was suddenly very aware of all his wrong thoughts, the poor attitudes, many things he could have done for others – and didn't…

"Will God forgive me?" Zach pleaded, still on his knees, tears welling up in his eyes. "There are so many things I should have done, and didn't. I..."

"God has seen that in your heart you have a strong desire to overcome," the angel said gently, sitting beside him on the ground. "This earth has been corrupted by immorality and violence and now the time for God's judgements has come.[230] You've endured the temptations that have come your way and fled sinful situations. God has seen that you love righteousness and hate evil, and that you recognize sin is an offence against your Creator. [231]The task of all those that Jesus Christ has chosen, will be to stamp out the wickedness from this world and to teach everyone to worship God in holiness of mind and spirit.[232] He is pleased that you tried to help your brother and your friends once you found the right path."

"But I could have done so much more! I know I didn't try hard enough to help Jake, and Abi, and Nathan, and… my friends at school."

"You could have tried harder," the angel agreed. "Your

---

[230] Ezekiel 8:7-12; Ephesians 5:3-5,11-12
[231] Psalm 97:10; Amos 5:15; Romans 12:9; John 14:21
[232] Isaiah 30:19-21

example in the past caused your brother to stumble. If you had changed your heart earlier and reached out to those in your youth group, Abi may not have been led astray. If you had preached to your friends at school, Jayden and Isaiah may have been convinced of the truth. But God saw the effort you made when your heart was changed and He is pleased."

These revelations cut Zach to the heart. To know that he could have made a difference in the lives of those he loved, and didn't, was agonizing. How he regretted the years of selfishness!

He looked up sorrowfully.

"But fear not," the angel assured him. "You have chosen to be on the Lord's side, Zach, and Jesus Christ has redeemed you from all your sins. You are fully forgiven! God is going to wipe all the sin and temptation from your mind and make you pure and righteous before him. [233]It is God's good pleasure to grant you the gift of eternal life and give you the Kingdom."

Zach looked up astonished. The joy filling his heart couldn't be contained. "I *will* be in God's Kingdom?!" he questioned, still hardly believing it.

The angel smiled at him radiantly. "Yes, Zach. Jesus sees in you a reflection of himself. You are willing to give your life for others. You hate what he hates and love what he loves.[234] You are on the right hand of the Lord Jesus Christ. You are one of his sheep.[235]"

Suddenly, with intense light blocking out all other sights, Zach found himself face to face with the Lord Jesus Christ! Down on his knees, he looked up to see kind, loving eyes which penetrated his own. Jesus was looking at him earnestly. His face shone with integrity and moral resolve. Compassion and love were mingled with a strong sense of purpose, dignity and righteousness.

---

[233] Luke 12:32; Psalm 103:8-17; Malachi 3:16-18; Titus 2:11-14
[234] Psalm 97:10; Amos 5:15; 2 Chronicles 19:2
[235] Matthew 25:32-46; John 10:27-28

The eyes that gazed into Zach's seemed to reach deep down into his inner being, his thoughts – his heart.

"I have forgiven you, Zach," Jesus said. "You are one of my chosen ones for eternity. For you I died and rose again, that you may live. Well done, good and faithful servant; you were faithful over a few things, I will make you ruler over many things. Enter into the joy of your Lord."[236]

It was only a brief moment in time that Zach was face to face with the Lord Jesus Christ in the dazzling white light. He found himself standing once more among the great multitude of people in the rugged wilderness surroundings. Looking ahead to the gleaming golden throne that Jesus sat upon, he saw in an instant that he *was* on the right hand of Christ. The crowd had been divided and he was forgiven! He was saved! He was an inheritor of the promises to the faithful of old! He was going to be made immortal!

Unexpectedly, seven shrill blasts of a trumpet sounded. The Lord Jesus Christ rose from his glorious throne! In the vast wilderness, as the rolling thunder-clouds continued to blaze with spontaneous light and echo with deep, earth-shuddering rumbles, the voice of Jesus rang out clearly for everyone to hear.

With his hands out-stretched to bless those on his right, Jesus said, "'Come, you blessed of my Father, inherit the kingdom prepared for you from the foundation of the world: for I was hungry and you gave me food; I was thirsty and you gave me drink; I was a stranger and you took me in; I was naked and you clothed me; I was sick and you visited me; I was in prison and you came to me. Inasmuch as you did it to one of the least of these my brethren, you did it to me.'"[237]

I should have done so much more for others! Zach

---

[236] Matthew 25:21
[237] Matthew 25:34-36

pondered anxiously, remembering Abi's parting glance and feeling very apprehensive about his brother. Would Abi be called to judgement? Would Jake be forgiven, having given himself over to his fleshly desires? Zach wasn't sure if he could bear losing his brother, even though he was very thankful that in his mercy, Jesus had accepted him!

Zach looked around to see who else was on the right hand side. He was still clinging to a faint hope that Jake would be somewhere in the crowd. He could see Uncle James and Aunt Sandra hugging each other. He could see Uncle Peter rejoicing with Aunt Jessica, Verity, Uncle Thomas and Kara... but where was Jake? Panic set in. *I have to know what will happen to Jake?* As happy as he was to have eternal life, how could he bear to be separated from his twin brother?! They had always been together. *I should have done so much more to help him! I should have dragged him along to talk to Dad or Uncle Peter. I should have erased everything on that stolen computer. Why did I cover for him?* And then it dawned on him, *I never prayed for Jake! Why didn't I ever ask God to help Jake? And what about Esther and all the other kids in the Youth group that weren't baptized? What will happen to them? Why didn't I try harder? Why did I wait so long to change?*

Zach gazed desperately across the wide gap of separation to the group of people on the other side. He heard Jesus speak to those on his left: "Depart from me, you cursed, into the everlasting fire prepared for the devil and his angels: for I was hungry and you gave me no food; I was thirsty and you gave me no drink; I was a stranger and you did not take me in, naked and you did not clothe me, sick and in prison and you did not visit me."[238]

A divine change was coming over Zach, even as he strained to look for his brother and his friends. A tingling sensation

---

[238] Matthew 25:40-43

swept over his body, rushing through every vein, right down to the tips of his fingers and toes. He felt energized with life in a way he had never experienced before – not even in the most exciting, exhilarating game of basketball; not even in the most strenuous workout when an energy surge would take him past limits he had never exceeded before. This was far greater, far more powerful; it was to feel... supernatural! It was *immortality!* It was to be equal to the angels![239] All the foolish thoughts that he'd struggled to cast out – were gone – every one – completely erased and repulsed! Instead, he felt filled with a sense of steadfast purpose, of integrity, of perseverance, of godliness – pure and upright godliness. Mortality was being swallowed up by life;[240] for "this corruptible must put on incorruption, and this mortal must put on immortality." [241] Zach and all the others around him were being transformed into the image of Christ – "the firstborn of all creation." Jesus Christ, the first mortal man to receive the gift of immortality,[242] was now sharing his victory with his chosen – his sheep – those he called his brothers and sisters![243]

It was at that very moment with increasingly keen eyesight, that Zach saw his brother racked with sorrow and despair on the other side, begging for mercy at the angel's feet.

---

[239] Luke 20:34-36; 1 Corinthians 15:49; 2 Peter 1:4
[240] 2 Corinthians 5:1-4
[241] 1 Corinthians 15:53-55; Philippians 3:21; 1 John 3:2
[242] Colossians 1: 12-18; Revelation 1:5; Romans 8:29
[243] John 15:16-19; 10:27-28; Matthew 12:50

CHAPTER 41

Rejected

Things had not gone well for Jake. The fearful sight of
Jesus Christ enthroned in such glory, filled him with
overwhelming dread, not joy. Looking around at all the people
standing near him in the vast multitude, Jake saw Brett close by
and Abi ahead of him.

Abi isn't baptized, he thought, *but she is still young. Will
she be accountable to God? Will God allow her to live out her
mortal existence?* He could see that she was crying in great
despair. *Has she already been judged unfaithful? Why didn't I help
Abi? Why did I despise her for going out with Brian? And what
about David and Nathan?* It dawned on Jake that while he had
been pursuing his own selfish plans, drowning in apathy, his
friends in the youth group had been slipping away!

Jake felt conscience-stricken. How he wished he had
followed his brother's good lead and immersed himself in God's
Word. If only he had spent the summer cleansing his mind and
allowing it to be transformed by God's Spirit power, [244] perhaps
now, he wouldn't be feeling so distraught. How foolish his
basketball dreams seemed, compared to God's promise of *forever!*
The Provincials would never happen now – all that time spent
training had been for naught. He could have gone to the Bible
Camp and filled his mind with good things, as Zach had done.
Instead, he had spent countless hours cramming for tests and
training for a basketball championship that would never come. It
had all taken him away from being prepared for the return of

---

[244] John 6:63; Romans 12:2; Luke 21:34; 1 Peter 1:23: Ephesians 6:17

Christ. Melissa had been a terrible mistake! Yet, perhaps he could still throw himself on the mercy of Christ. *"I'll take you back,"* came rushing into his mind; it was his favourite song. It gave him hope. *Jesus is a friend of sinners,* he told himself. *He'll take back any who throw themselves upon his mercy.* That was all he could rely on now.

"Please," he begged the angel, when he was called to give an account. "I was wrong. I didn't realize Jesus was coming back so soon! I always wanted to change my life... I'll do anything you say now – please forgive me!"

As the angel recounted his sins – his *unforgiven* sins, that had not been confessed in prayer, or forsaken, Jake felt increasing anguish.

"Jake," the angel said compassionately, "you did well to be baptized and to commit your way to God. You started off on the right path and all the angels rejoiced when you gave your life to God.[245] But you didn't continue. You allowed yourself to slide into apathy and indifference. You knew your heart was slipping away from God and you chose to give it over even more fully to the world. You didn't care for the weak in your ecclesia; you despised them. Your example made it harder for them to come to God. They looked at you for leadership and were led even further astray.

"But all *my* good friends in the Truth abandoned me!" Jake pleaded. "I *needed* a good friend; a strong friend and you took all my friends away. My whole ecclesia was apathetic. The talks were so boring! I wasn't getting the help that *I* needed!"

The angel looked at him soberly.

"Was *your* cross heavier than the one your Lord had to bear?"

"No," Jake answered weakly. Suddenly all his excuses

---

[245] Luke 15:7

seemed pitiful... hardly worth mentioning.

"Jake, God sent trials into your life to make you stronger," [246] the angel told him. "Today *your family* is entering the Kingdom. They endured many of the same trials; they wanted to help you. But even if you had been truly all alone in your Ecclesia, Jesus and I were working with you every day. Had you chosen to seek God's message in His Word, we were right there *longing* to help you grow in faith. There was so little that we could do for you because you weren't begging for God's help. Had you prayed more often; had you given God the time that you spent on excessive exercise, worldly entertainment and immoral living, we could have showed you God's power to answer prayer. Instead," the angel reminded him firmly, "you not only chose to fill your mind with corruption, you tried to fill your brother's with the same!"

"But we were only watching *pictures,*" Jake pleaded.

"Choosing to defile your mind is sinful," [247]the angel told him. "And you know where it led you. God is looking for hearts that *love His ways,*[248] not the ways of the world. He wants immortal beings that will teach this evil world to cast off wickedness and love God's righteous laws. God has seen that in your heart you *love* iniquity – it didn't vex your soul – you indulged in it vicariously and gave yourself over to sin."

"Then why didn't you stop me?" Jake pleaded, thinking of how his brother's concussions had taken him out of action and started him on the path to God. "Why didn't you hit me on the head? Then maybe I would have made other choices like Zach did!"

"Jake, you had already made a commitment to your Heavenly Father. You had already promised, at your baptism, to put the flesh to death and strive to follow Jesus. Your decision to

---

[246] Hebrews 12:10-17
[247] Ezekiel 8:12; Romans 1:21,28-32
[248] Deuteronomy 5:10; Proverbs 8:17; John 14:21-23; 2 Timothy 4:8

sin willfully was offensive to God. [249]Yet, we tried in many ways to turn you around," the angel assured him, earnestly. "You were given a way out of every temptation. Brett offered you a way out, but you chose physical fitness over spiritual growth. Your brother's change of heart should have pricked your conscience, but you became resentful. Even when you recognized how positive the Bible Camp had been for your brother, you chose financial gains over preparing for a week that you knew would help you spiritually. And finally, Jake, in a last attempt to bring you to your senses, we allowed your uncle's health to deteriorate."

For me? Jake shuddered. *Uncle James suffered for me? And I never visited him once!*

"We hoped that through your uncle's sickness you would see the fragility of life and reconsider the path you were following," the angel explained, sadly. "God is looking for people who *willingly* choose to serve him and love His ways. He doesn't force anyone to do right or wrong, but He does test hearts.[250]"

"But I thought that Jesus loves us and wants to save us," Jake pleaded foolishly, feeling his hope for mercy was rapidly slipping away. "Jesus forgave people who have done *much* worse than I have. Why can't he forgive me? I'm so young – I'm hardly even old enough to be responsible to Him. Surely God can see that I'm sorry. Can't I just live out my life as a mortal in the kingdom and have one more chance? I'm so young!"

The angel shook his head firmly. "Jesus has tried you and knows that *you don't love him*, Jake. Your heart is with the world; you love the things of the flesh. You made a promise in baptism that you forsook. The door of opportunity for forgiveness and eternal life was open every day, until now. [251] Your Lord Jesus Christ and I have grieved over the choices you've made, Jake. Try

---

[249] Hebrews 10:26-31; 2 Peter 2:20
[250] Jeremiah 17:10; 1 Chronicles 28:9; Revelation 2:23
[251] Matthew 25:1-13

as we did to reach out to you, you would have none of us. "

"You talked to Jesus about me?" Jake sobbed. "You were working in my life?" *What a fool I've been for turning away!* He thought. *This angel has tried to show me the path of righteousness through my brother and my uncles! I can see it so clearly now.*

"Yes, Jake. Since the day you were born, I've conferred with our Lord about you, many times."

"Wait," Jake cried feebly, knowing he was about to be dismissed from the angel's presence, "are you saying that things don't always turn out as *you* plan?"

"No, they don't," the angel answered. "As servants of God we can't interfere with your freewill. We gave you a way of escape for every test of your heart but you chose the pleasures of this world."

Before Jake was able to argue another word, a dazzling white light blocked everything from view. Trembling, down on his knees, he found himself face to face with Jesus Christ. The look of sadness on his master's face was more than Jake could bear.

"Jake, I loved you," Jesus said to him, earnestly. "You were one of mine. Why did you turn away from me? Why didn't you stay on the path to life?"

Speechless and devastated, Jake couldn't find a reason. All the excuses he had poured out to the angel seemed pitiful and foolish now. *Jesus loved me. I was truly one of his. If only I had known! But of course I should have known! Why didn't I believe?*

Speaking sadly and with much regret, Jesus said, "I know you not. You have forsaken me and now I have forsaken you.[252] Depart from me."

Jake's moment before Christ was over. Devastated and trembling, he turned to the angel and begged, "Please may I at least say goodbye to my family?"

---

[252] 1 Chronicles 28:9; 2 Chronicles 15:2; Matthew 10:33

The angel shook his head. "I'm sorry, Jake. But between you and them, there is a great gulf fixed. Your family is in the bosom of Abraham, inheriting the promises God made to all his descendants by faith. There is no passing from here to there. "[253]

Seven piercing blasts of a trumpet sounded. It was the same trumpet call that Zach heard on the other side. Jesus was about to make a very important announcement. Looking up, Jake saw clearly that the crowd had been separated. He was far away from his brother and his family. He was with the rejected – those who were assigned to eternal destruction! He had no idea what that would entail. All he knew was that all hope was gone; it no longer existed for him. He had begged and pleaded and found that there was no longer any door of forgiveness to enter, or hope of mercy from his Lord. As the terrifying realization began to sink in – Jake was frozen with fear. To be banished from his family and friends for eternity was an unbelievable nightmare! And not only that, but he was forever banished from God!

---

[253] Luke 16:26: Genesis 12:1-3: Galatians 3:27-29

CHAPTER 42

When All Hope is Gone

Looking around desperately for some familiar face; some companionship, Jake was sure he could see David and Jerry in the distance. As he walked in their direction he suddenly saw Abi with her parents, right nearby. They all seemed inconsolable. Jake drew near and reached out to take Abi's hand.

Abi turned away from him in despair. "Don't start caring now!" she sobbed bitterly. "You never cared at all about me. You always thought you were so much better than everyone else. Why didn't you tell me to get baptized? Why didn't you warn me to change my life? You knew this was for real! I would have listened to you, Jake! I would have listened! I looked up to you! And now, we've missed out all that God has promised! I can't bear it! I can't *bear it!*"

Jake couldn't think of anything to say. Abi's rejection hurt; her accusations plunged in like a knife. She was right. After his friends had moved away, he had never really cared about anyone else in the youth group; he had seen the rest as too far gone to be worth saving. And now here he was, cast out with Abi and the others. He had received the same fate. He was no better at all. Tears came rolling down his cheeks.

Everyone on their side of the judgement seat was in mental anguish, weeping and wailing. Brett was no exception. Racked with grief and shaking with fear he looked over painfully at Jake. Stumbling forward, he reached out to draw him close. "Jake, I'm so sorry!" he sobbed, hugging him tightly. "I'm so sorry I led you here. How could I have been so foolish! We should have been on the other side – *both of us* – and instead we've missed out on everything! I'm so sorry."

"Why are you saying sorry to me?" Jake cried, holding onto Brett desperately. "It's not your fault!"

Tears were pouring down Brett's face. "The angel told me," Brett sobbed tragically, "that I led you – one of Jesus' lambs, astray. Forgive me, Jake. Please forgive me!" he pleaded.

"I chose... I chose to follow you," Jake cried. It was true. He had made his own choices. Clinging to Brett like a scared child to his father, Jake gazed tragically at all the miserable people around him. A woman in the distance looked like Jenna. She was racked with grief like everyone else. Had Jenna been rejected as well? There were many people that looked familiar but Jake was too distraught to reach out or care. After all, there were no longer any words of comfort or hope to offer.

Fear intensified within Jake exponentially. If they had missed out on everything, what was going to happen next? Would they all be vaporized and destroyed, or left here to perish in this barren wilderness? He could hear the tremendous cheers of praise and rejoicing on the other side of the Lord. Before his very eyes, old people were becoming young again! Youths were taking on an incredibly healthy, vigorous glow. All the diverse attire – jeans, shirts, tunics and various types of clothing from all cultures throughout the ages, were being transformed into the most glorious white robes! Everyone was leaping and shouting with a joy beyond description. Suddenly the vast multitude on the other side broke into a glorious song. It was unlike any music Jake had ever heard before and they all seemed to know it perfectly! From one end of the crowd to the other, hallelujahs swept through the joyful people, as they waved and praised the great King on the throne. "Salvation belongs to our God who sits on the throne, and to the Lamb!"[254] they sang, in a multi-level harmony.

---

[254] Revelation 7:10

In an instant all the angels were at the front with Jesus, surrounding his throne. With glorious, silvery-rich voices, they responded in song, "Amen! Blessing and glory and wisdom, thanksgiving and honor and power and might, be to our God forever and ever. Amen." [255]It was a triumphant melody. Jake had never heard such a crescendo of expression, with perfect pitch and tone. He wished it would never end. If only he were one of the singers! But there was nothing he could do about it now – *nothing!*

"Zach," he found himself crying out. "Mom, Dad, I love you! I never realized how much you all meant to me! I want to be with you. Please, I want to be with you. Please don't leave me!" he wailed. Never had he yearned so much to be with his family. Falling down to his knees, Jake broke down sobbing. He was in complete and utter despair.

---

[255] Revelation 7:12

CHAPTER 43

Overjoyed!

Zach had always loved music but this was beyond anything he had ever experienced, or dreamed! The richness of sound, the depth of harmony, the glorious voices were far superior to any philharmonic orchestra in the world! His own voice had been enhanced in a remarkable way. Singing with all the other immortals in praise to God, vastly transcended the high school musical and even the campfire sing-alongs! Joy burst from his heart, untainted by any other motivation than pure thankfulness to God for the redemption that He had freely given. Elation was too simple a word to describe how thankful he was for the future that now stretched out *forever*. Singing with the others he poured out the gratitude he felt for God's goodness and mercy. All the promises he had learned about in Sunday School and Youth Group were now to be fulfilled. He had been chosen by God, however undeserving he felt, to have a part. The group of immortals that Zach stood with, was to be the 'bride' of Jesus Christ.[256] They would work closely with Jesus, as his chosen friends, to bring the world to acknowledge that the Son of God, once despised, rejected and crucified, was now to be the King of the world![257] Along with the others, Zach knew he would take part in opposing the invading armies that were to come against Jerusalem. He would tell the world that Jesus was King. He would see the temple of Ezekiel's prophecy[258] built under Divine supervision and functioning as a

---

[256] John 3:29; 2 Corinthians 11:2; Ephesians 5:25-32; Revelation 19:7
[257] Revelation 14:1-7; Psalm 149; Daniel 7:13-27
[258] Ezekiel 40-48

center of worship. Perhaps he would be involved in the construction or landscaping the grounds. He would never die! As Zach rejoiced in the awesome privilege God had extended to him, he gazed around at all the other singing saints. *I'll meet Job,* he thought excitedly, *and David and Jonathan, Paul and Peter. All the Bible characters that I have loved!*

The song of praise ended with a crescendo of hallelujahs. Zach reached every note without effort; he had no shortage of breath. *Heavenly Father,* he prayed silently, *I'm so thankful to be a part of all this. What a blessing it is to be granted this gift of immortality and to take part in the work You have planned for this world!*

When the song finished, Zach realized that everyone on the left hand side had disappeared. Jake was *gone!*

Zach was saddened to lose his brother, but it was nothing like the sadness he had felt before becoming immortal. He felt the loss, but he didn't feel panic, or despair, or inconsolable grief. He didn't have any nagging doubts that God had made the wrong decision. Instead, he felt fully convinced in his heart that Jake had chosen the world and God had rightfully given Jake his true desire.

Looking over at his family, Zach was amazed at the changes that had taken place. Uncle Peter looked so young and very familiar! He hardly recognized his grandparents and even his own mom and dad were dramatically younger looking. Everyone appeared fit and healthy; not one grey hair or wrinkle could be seen. All physical ailments had been healed. Together they celebrated the divine transformation that had taken place.

The instant that Zach wondered where Noah, Brennan and Hannah were, he spotted each one. He realized the mental access he had to an enormous "databank" of information. Effortlessly they came together.

"My forever friends!" Zach cheered with great elation.

"*Forever* friends!" they exclaimed ecstatically, joining

hands and rejoicing together. All of them had changed physically but they were still recognizable. In shining white robes with thick, golden belts they had become like the angels.[259] Zach didn't feel the same stirrings for Hannah as he had felt before. Instead, he felt a warm, solid, loyal friendship that was special in its own way but not one that would provoke jealousy, or sinful desire. Human nature had been dealt a crushing blow! [260]Zach was thankful to be forever free of depravity! There was no longer anything to hide, or any thought to cause shame.

"Thank you for your friendship, Hannah," he said to her earnestly. "You gave me strength to stay on course and choose God's ways."

"I'm so glad that both of us decided to choose God's ways before it was too late," she smiled back. "This is everything I ever wanted! We're here, Zach! God has made us His own, and nothing can ever take us away from Him."

---

[259] Colossians 1:15-18; 1 Corinthians 15:20; Revelation 1:5
[260] 1 Corinthians 15:53-56; Hebrews 2:14-15

CHAPTER 44

A note from Jake

(translated from Italian)

Dear Ella,

I should have told you all this at the beginning. I'm sorry that I'm leaving you just when we've found out that we're expecting twins. I can only hope that maybe you'll understand, after you read this.

You often asked why I came to Europe and I was never able to explain. You often asked why I was so depressed and I told you it was a medical condition. The truth is, it's actually much deeper than that – far deeper!

Now that I have been conscripted into the Europa army, I have to tell you the truth. I should have told you everything years ago, but I know how important your religious convictions are to you. I always worried that if I told you the truth, you or your family would turn me in to the authorities – that is why I have kept silent.

For the last few years, I have lived a lie that has weighed heavily on my mind. Ella, I pretended to be a devout Catholic, just like you, so that you would marry me and I could find work with your family. I'm so sorry for deceiving you all. Your family has been so good to me. Please don't tear this letter up immediately. Please read on. You need to understand what I am about to tell you, even if you never forgive me.

I know that you, like so many people here, think that the new "Jews" that are in Jerusalem are the source of all the world's problems. Ella, many times I wanted to explain what I knew about this, but I've been too afraid. Rumours, unfounded reports, and falsified stories have portrayed the man who claims to be the King of the world, to be a savage, untrustworthy dictator who will bring the end to all human rights and freedom. But – I know this man! I saw him personally when he came back to raise the dead and judge those who were responsible to him, just as the Bible foretold (John 5:26-29; 6:39-44; 2 Thessalonians 1:7-10; 2 Timothy 4:1,8; 1 Corinthians 15:49-55). This man is the very Lord Jesus Christ that you, as a good Christian, profess to follow. Ella, don't be deceived by the media, or any religious authorities. My brother and my whole family are there with Jesus, in Jerusalem. They are now immortal. They will never die. They have God's power. No one can fight against immortal beings and win. The God of all creation is on their side!

Why am I so depressed? Ten years ago, Jesus – the new King in Jerusalem – rejected me. Jesus Christ rejected me as unworthy to take part in his Kingdom, because my heart was with the world, not with him. Jesus is loving and forgiving, but not to those who don't repent of their sins and try to lead others astray – that was me. It's been ten long years of heartbreaking agony and regret for me and my friend Brett. He and I were both rejected by Jesus Christ, and transported in some supernatural way to Europe. We didn't have passports or banking cards, so before we came to your farm, we were in a desperate situation. We almost starved. We were homeless for a long time. We were both terribly homesick and depressed. Everything I had ever hoped for had been taken away from me, both my hopes for this life and the one to come! And it was all because of my own foolishness!

When we first arrived here, we didn't want to tell anyone what had happened to us. We were humiliated and resentful that we had been rejected. Eventually, we were arrested as illegal immigrants. Without passports or identification of any kind, we had no way to provide for ourselves or any rational way to explain how we had come to Europe. Had we been able to contact Brett's family in Canada, we might have been able to get the information we needed, but they never responded to our messages and we never knew why. So we told the authorities the truth but that only made things worse. They thought we were crazy – absolutely crazy! We were locked up in a ward with all the lunatics and treated as such. They were terrible months! We were beaten by the other prisoners and even one of the guards. It was the cruelest place ever! Since then I've never told another soul what I know. I'm terrified of returning to prison!

People didn't believe our story then, just as I know they won't now. I was thankful to be with Brett, even though he, more than anyone, led me down the wrong path. But I chose to be led.

As you know, eventually, our passports and banking information came through from the Canadian authorities. Brett and I were able to sort out our identity and citizenship and make arrangements to fly home to Stirling, Nova Scotia. But two days before our flight was to leave, the worldwide earthquake hit. Our hopes were dashed again. Country dwellers, like your family, fared much better than those in cities. I don't know how Brett and I escaped. Buildings crumbled all around us. Power lines came down. Oil pipes and tanks deep in the ground cracked, leaked and exploded. Fires raged for days. So many people died. Money became worthless and air travel was shut down completely. Since then, Brett and I have had no choice but to remain here in Europe. However, recently I heard that ocean travel is possible once again.

It was around the time of all the destruction, that fear and terror took hold on society. With such frightening events many Christians, like you, believe the "Devil" took over the world. The rumour that the new "Jews" in Jerusalem are the Antichrist and the cause of all the world's woes, took off like wildfire. It's not true, Ella. Brett and I knew that when the earthquakes were triggered all around the world, Jesus Christ and the saints had returned to the Mount of Olives (Zechariah 14:1-5). The

330

judgement that began with believers, like me, was now taking place on the world (1 Peter 4:17-18; 2 Thessalonians 1:7-9).

Being without television and the internet, for so long, I've been able to distance myself from reality. But when we went yesterday to the new media center that just opened in Villa Square, reality hit me hard in many ways. The religious leaders appealed to everyone to join forces against the evil imposter in Jerusalem. They ridiculed "this man who claims to be Jesus Christ the true Messiah" and strongly urged everyone to resist his words, and not be deceived by his miracles. They said this new King is 'The Antichrist'! I longed to tell you and your family that this is wrong and that the King in Jerusalem truly is Jesus Christ! But I have been too afraid. I'm sure your parents would turn against me if I spoke the truth. Maybe you would too.

Ella, I will give you a list of passages at the end of this letter. These are prophecies about what Jesus will do when he sets up God's Kingdom on earth. Read them through and compare with what you have seen and will see happening. Don't be misled by what everyone else is saying, Ella. If you ever have the chance, go to Jerusalem and see for yourself. Talk to the people, you might even meet my twin brother, Zach. Question them, observe them – I'm sure you will see they speak for God. Look at them carefully. They aren't exactly like us – they are immortal! Jesus even has nail holes in his hands. He's not an imposter. He is the Messiah he claims to be. He's the King of Israel and of the whole world.

Ella, you wondered why I was so down after watching the news report. But, you see, my heart is completely broken! You were astonished by the size of the temple that is being built in Jerusalem. You were amazed by the incredible topographical changes that have taken place and the beautiful gardens. But Ella, I should be there helping with the work. Had I appreciated what I had at the time, I would be there now with the rest of my family. Do you remember the two young men you said looked like me – the two that were overseeing the new gardens along the river? I'm sure that was my Uncle Peter and my brother Zach. I know they look younger than me – but understand, Ella, they are immortal – they will never age. I'm sure my Aunt Jess was right there with them in the large group of gardeners. I should have been there too! If you ever see another report on Israel, notice the health and vibrancy of those people. I wish with all my heart that I was one of them! I would give anything to have a second chance! If only I could.

Europa News spins the interviews in such ridiculous ways. Half the time they don't even translate correctly. I know the immortals would never say the things Europa News claims they've said. They create fear in your society by warning that the work that is going on in Jerusalem is a calculated, sinister revolt against democracy and mankind's rights and freedoms. The UN is foolish to call for an immediate halt to the construction and demand that Jerusalem be declared an international city. I know you've been involved in raising funds to rebuild the Dome of the Rock and you feel strongly that the new temple should be demolished since it stands on Arab and Catholic holy ground. But, Ella – in this you are fighting against God. It's God's will that this work be done in Jerusalem. It's prophesied in the Bible. Just read 2 Samuel 7, Luke 1:31-33, Zechariah 6 and Ezekiel 38-48.

I grew up thinking that I could always make up for the wrong I had done. I believed there was always another chance. If I made a mistake I could erase it and do it again. I thought I would always have forgiveness if I confessed and repented. I didn't believe that one day it would be too late to change – one day God would say, "It's enough" and close the door. I can't even begin to describe how it feels to have missed out on a one and only chance of a lifetime. I would fully repent now if I could. I have changed so much! I know now that God couldn't have offered a greater promise than He did – and I feel absolutely sick every time I stop and think that somehow it wasn't enough for me at the time. I could have lived forever – truly forever! I could have been with the Lord Jesus Christ. I could have been involved in his work of cleansing the earth of all wickedness and making it a paradise of righteousness that brings glory to God. I could have been with Zach and all my good friends and my family – forever! I could have been under the powerful protection of God, instead of here in Europe, living a lie as an unwelcome foreigner afraid for my life. We never know when the next earthquake may strike, or tsunami hit, or outbreak of plague may sweep across this city. I can't even call upon God to protect anyone I love, not even our twins that you are bringing into this world. God doesn't know me; I'm not one of His and never can be anymore.

Europe is set to resist Jesus and the saints. Fighting against an army of immortals with God on their side is doomed to failure! How utterly impossible! The outcome of this battle is prophesied in Revelation 17:12-14. Read the whole chapter and chapter 18 as well. There you will see the harlot (unfaithful Christianity) riding the beast of Europe (the 10 kings). It's easy to see that in a short matter of time Europe will bring about its own destruction. I could never fight against Jesus. But – to refuse to fight would bring execution or worse – imprisonment! To be associated with me may prove harmful to you and your family. I have to try to get away tonight. I have a plan, but it is risky and dangerous; this may be the end.

Ella, you're better off without me, here. I'm not going to fight against the Son of God and you won't want to be identified with a 'traitor'. Read the material I've left for you and do your best to get out of this country as soon as you can. I've managed to save up enough money for you to take a ship to North America. Look under our mattress. I've heard that many are accepting Jesus as the true Messiah in distant places. Maybe God will have mercy on you and spare our twins. Maybe you will all live out your lives in the peaceful paradise that will come after the world submits to Christ. Paradise will gradually encompass all of the earth. Jesus will reign for one thousand years! (Isaiah 2:1-4; 11:1-10; Psalm 72; Revelation 5:9-10; 20:1-6).

If my plan succeeds, I will try to return to my hometown in Stirling, Nova Scotia, as soon as I can. I've made such a wreck of my life. Please don't make a wreck of yours. Meet me there if you can.

Please teach the twins to love God and obey Him. What I lost – can still be yours. Please read and understand God's message for you and consider carefully the choices you make in the future. If God is on your side, you need not fear anyone or anything else.

I love you and hope we'll be together again soon.
Jake

What the Bible says Jesus will do when he returns

Jesus will return to deliver Israel when all nations come against Jerusalem
 – *Ezekiel 38-39/Zechariah 14:1-9*

Jesus will promise to bring peace when the world submits to him and lays down their weapons
 – *Psalm 2; Isaiah 2:4; Malachi 4:1-7*

Jesus will first turn the Jews to him and then extend his reign to the rest of the world
 – *Isaiah 60; 62; Ezekiel 39:22-29; Zechariah 12*

Jesus will bring peace to Israel
 – *Isaiah 9:6-7; Ezek. 39:25-29; Zech. 9:10; Mic. 4:1-7*

Jesus will build the new temple in Jerusalem
 – *Zechariah 6:12-15; 2 Samuel 7:12-13; Luke 1:31-33*

Jesus will make a new covenant with the Jews
 – *Romans 11:26-27; Heb. 8:8-11; Jeremiah 31:31-34*

Animal sacrifices will be re-instituted in the new temple
 – *Ezekiel 43:7,18-25;44; 45:13-25;46; Malachi 4:4-6*

Jesus will do miracles – *Isaiah 35:4-10; Joel 2:28-32*

Jesus will proclaim he is Jesus Christ (of course!)
 – *Zechariah 12:10; 13:6; Psalm 2:6-7*

The world will be commanded to worship and submit to him
 – *Psalm 2; Daniel 2:44; Zech. 14:16-19; Phil. 2:10-11*

CHAPTER 45

A Return to Stirling, Nova Scotia

It was distressing to view the disaster scene of his hometown – Stirling, Nova Scotia. Having been with Jesus and the other saints in Israel for over eleven years, this was the first time Zach had been sent back to Canada. He had a message to share with his old friends and neighbors; a message which he hoped they would receive.

Since becoming immortal, Zach had been fully occupied with God's purpose to make the earth full of His glory.[261] This work had begun in Jerusalem. After years of close daily contact with the Lord Jesus Christ, Zach and the other saints now enjoyed an intimate bond of fellowship with the new King of the world. [262] Under the leadership of Jesus Christ, their Lord, Savior and friend, they looked forward to ruling the earth with him for a millennium. [263]

The time spent with the Lord Jesus Christ had been very eventful. Early on, Zach witnessed the awesome power of God unleashed upon a faithless and immoral world. On the mountains of Israel, the Northern Confederacy had been overthrown by wild, catastrophic storms spewing hailstones and fire.[264] The defeat of the Northern Confederacy, after their invasion of Israel, had been a spectacular demonstration that God's natural elements are far more powerful than any sophisticated weaponry mankind can create.

---

[261] Numbers 14:21; Habakkuk 2:14; Isaiah 11:9
[262] Revelation 19:6-10; Matthew 25:1-13
[263] Revelation 5:9-10; Matthew 19:27-28; Revelation 3:21; Daniel 7:18-22; Revelation 20
[264] Ezekiel 38:22-23

Many people – Jews, Palestinians, Russians, Libyans, Ethiopians, and Iranians perished.[265]

When Jesus Christ's feet touched the Mount of Olives, he triggered a massive earthquake, which set off many more along the tectonic plates emanating from the mount. [266] It was at that time that Jesus and the saints revealed themselves to the world.[267] The powerful earthquake also split the Mount of Olives in two, completely altering the topography of the Holy Land and elevating Mount Zion above all the hills round about. [268] Everywhere in the world, buildings, transportation infrastructure, and many other towering human edifices collapsed and were burned up by raging infernos.[269]

After those early days of battle and destruction, Zach and Noah worked joyfully with the whole EdenTree crew and many others, to transform the Land of Promise. With an enormous new temple being constructed on Mount Zion,[270] there was plenty of landscaping to do around the grounds. Uncle Peter had been assigned to oversee the development of the gardens along the river flowing out from the new temple structure. [271] Having no financial or material restraints, with spirit-wisdom to guide their plans, and vigorous, immortal strength that never weakened, working with Uncle Peter was a joyful experience! In the day time, they would work on the gardens. In the evenings and on the Sabbath, they would spend hours teaching many eager Jews and Arabs about the true God of Israel and His righteous ways.[272]

---

[265] Ezekiel 39:5-19; Zechariah 13:8-9;
[266] Zech. 14:3-5; Ezek. 38:19-20; Isa. 2:10-21; Joel 3:16; Rev. 16:17-18
[267] Zechariah 14; Ezekiel 38-39; Joel 3:12-14
[268] Zechariah 14:1-11;
[269] Ezekiel 38:19-20; Revelation 16:8
[270] Ezekiel 40-48 (master plans); Zechariah 6:12-13; Isaiah 11:1-5; Jeremiah 23:5-8; Isaiah 2:2-5
[271] Ezekiel 37; Joel 3:18; Zechariah 14:8; Revelation 22:1-2
[272] Zechariah 12-13; Isaiah 30:19-21; 40:1-3; 52:7; Isaiah 19:4,20-25; 27:13; 60:5-7

All around Mount Zion, the transforming work of the saints created fantastic landscapes, parks and gardens that were now unrivalled in the world. [273] The Promised Land was cleansed, transformed, and astonishingly beautiful. Even the river that flowed from the temple was crystal-clear, refreshing to drink, and full of unique, colourful fish that could be seen clearly from the shore.[274] Zach marvelled at how fast the trees had grown beside the river of life. Those special trees were always in bloom, perpetually bearing one of their twelve different varieties of fruit each month. He had tasted each kind, and was delighted by all! Not only was the fruit delicious to eat, but the leaves provided healing for the mortal population.[275]

While the EdenTree crew had been involved in gardening, Uncle James was assigned the role of a treasurer, keeping record of the tribute generously flowing in from the nations surrounding Israel. He had become close friends with a man named Joseph, a martyr from the 1700's. He had even worked with the Ethiopian Eunuch and Matthew the tax-collector, who were organizing and providing materials to all those constructing the temple. Noah, David, Solomon, Hiram, Bezalel and many thousands of others, had followed the Divine plans to construct the magnificent edifice of God's temple, long foretold in the latter part of Ezekiel's prophecy.

Aunt Sandra, Aunt Jess, Verity, Hannah, and Kara had been very involved with one of the schools for the children whose parents were immortal. Esther had long since graduated and even Aunt Jessica's oldest daughter was now a young adult. In the early years, they had loved seeing their mom *and their aunties* at school every day. Often the children were taken on excursions to help with the landscaping activities, or to go fishing in the sparkling,

---

[273] Isaiah 51:3; 35:1-2; 41:17-20; 43:18-21;
[274] Ezekiel 47:8-10
[275] Revelation 22:1-2

living waters that ran into the former "Dead Sea". It was no longer a *dead* sea; it abounded with life!

During the night, while the mortal population slept, the immortal workers, never weary, would gather together with Jesus the King, and talk over the events of the day. Jesus had a vision for the land which gave all of them direction. It was in those nightly sessions that Zach had truly come to know his Lord as a friend, a 'brother', [276] and the righteous leader that every one of them rejoiced to follow. Never in the history of mankind, had such a wise, kind, righteous and completely incorruptible King, held the reins of power. [277] Jesus Christ was God manifest on earth. For the victory over sin that Jesus accomplished in his life and death, God had given Jesus the "name that is above every name". [278] With great joy in his heart, Zach eagerly looked forward to the day when the whole earth would know and appreciate the new era that was about to be ushered in for one thousand years. [279] The whole earth was going to be filled with God's glory as He had intended from the very beginning![280]

With all the preparatory construction work now complete, the Jewish people converted to Christ, [281] and the Arabians bringing gifts,[282] Jerusalem was ready for the people of the world to come and learn of God's ways.[283] Zach had been sent to Stirling, Nova Scotia with the others in his delegation. They had a mission to accomplish if they could convince the people of Stirling to cooperate. All throughout the world, the saints had been given the commission to proclaim Jesus as King and invite everyone to

---

[276] John 15:14-15; Matthew 12:50
[277] Psalm 72
[278] Philippians 2:9-10; Ephesians 1:20-21; Isaiah 9:6-7
[279] Isaiah 2:2-5; Micah 4:1-5; Revelation 20; 1 Corinthians 15:24-28
[280] Numbers 14:21; Habakkuk 2:14
[281] Romans 11:25-27; Hebrews 8:8; Isaiah 60:1-3; Zechariah 12:8-12; Ezekiel 39:21-29
[282] Isaiah 60:5-7; Psalm 78:8-11
[283] Isaiah 2:2-5

worship him in Jerusalem. [284] With the assistance of the immortal saints, transportation was free and instantaneous from any part of the world. Jesus had sent his messengers to their hometowns if there were survivors in those places that would recognize them. Others were sent to regions where the Gospel had never been preached.

Hovering above Stirling, Nova Scotia, [285] Zach and the others in his delegation viewed the desolate city. The once beautiful harbour-town now lay in blackened ruins. The boardwalk, along which they had often walked, was no longer there. Only seaweed and rubble lined the coast. Massive overpasses had fallen on the roads and buildings below, blocking all transportation through the city. Hospitals and apartment buildings still lay in charred concrete ruins. The high school was only a pile of bricks and twisted metal.

When the earthquakes and terrible fires raged across the earth, the economies of the world had collapsed. Without transportation, money, or electricity, the once "modern" civilized countries quickly reverted to primitive conditions. Only in the last year had some of the bigger cities restored a grid of electrical power and revived some means of transportation. However, fuel deliveries were still impossible in most areas of the world and food shortages continued. Water, for many, was difficult to obtain. Devastating violence had broken out in many places, simply over access to water alone. From what Zach had learned from the Lord Jesus Christ, Nova Scotia was functioning better than many other places of the world. Bodies of fresh water had always been abundantly accessible in the Eastern Canadian provinces. Looking down on the countryside from above, Zach could see that makeshift shelters lined all the freshwater lakes and ponds.

---

[284] Revelation 14:6-7; 19:6-16; Daniel 7:13-14,18,27; Revelation 5:9-10
[285] Luke 20:36 compare with Daniel 9:21

As Zach viewed the ruins of Stirling, he hoped the people in his hometown would choose to accept the Lord Jesus Christ as the new ruler of the world. They would have so much to gain. Their community would be rebuilt with the help of the immortal workers and they would learn the righteous ways of God. If the people of Stirling refused to believe and took sides with the European armies that were now preparing to attack Jerusalem, they could anticipate only further destruction and no rain.[286]

Looking at the various makeshift villages, Zach spotted the shack where his former acquaintances lived. It was to those two friends, first, that he had been sent. Uncle Peter and Aunt Jess were to find the people that they knew. Uncle James and Aunt Sandra, Uncle Thomas and Aunt Purity were also part of the Stirling delegation, as were Zach's parents. His father, Andrew, once the pastor of the largest church in town, knew more survivors than any of the others. All together, they had many to find and encourage.

Zach was not only travelling with his family, but he had made a special request to bring along a friend. During the time he had spent in Jerusalem, Zach had developed strong friendships with many of the 'faithful of old'. Labouring to restore the land of Israel, he often worked and toured with people he'd once read about in the Bible. He met Job and all of his fourteen children, now resurrected and immortal! He met Gideon, Samson and even Jonathan. They showed him their favourite haunts and locations where important battles had been fought. With their assistance he discovered special places where God appeared to his people in the past, and vital decisions had been made. Zach and Hannah had toured Geba with Jonathan and Mephibosheth. Together, they had climbed the cliff where the Philistine outpost had once been. As they climbed, Jonathan described, in dramatic fashion, how it felt

---

[286] Revelation 17:12-14; Psalm 2; Zechariah 14:17-18

to be holding on to the rocky hillside, reaching from one precipitous toehold to another, all the while looking up to see the mocking faces of the Philistine soldiers, and praying *earnestly* for God's deliverance! [287]

When Zach learned that his mission was to go back to Stirling and that two of his old friends from high school were still alive, he knew they would be overjoyed to meet Jonathan and hear his stories of faith firsthand. Jonathan was enthusiastic to call the world to worship Jesus Christ and eagerly agreed to join him.

Before the Bryant family and friends separated to find their various acquaintances, they visited the site of Oceanview Lodge. Examining the vacant lot carefully, Uncle Peter concluded that during the earthquake, the ocean waves had risen above the cliff and washed the foundations of the house away. The beautiful gardens had been eroded, as well. Here and there, a hardy perennial was trying to make a new start, desperately vying for a presence among the overgrown weeds.

"There's much work to be done," Uncle Peter said cheerfully. "This earth will surpass all its former glory, once the inhabitants recognize Jesus Christ as their King."

Separating to fulfil their various missions, Zach and Jonathan set off toward a quiet lakeshore. There were very few people left in the actual city of Stirling. Since the earthquake, cities had become garbage-strewn, rat-infested, concrete wastelands. Survivors were forced to seek refuge in the countryside where they could grow their own food and have reliable sources of water. Zach didn't have to ask any strangers where his friends might be; God was directing his way. With a simple request, he and Jonathan were transported to the very spot.

They found themselves outside a large wooden shelter. It was well-built with salvaged lumber. Fruit trees stood nearby,

---

[287] 1 Samuel 14

pruned and bearing heavily. A stack of firewood was piled next to the house. Cows grazed contentedly in a field, and chickens scratched in the yard. Inside a greenhouse, improvised from old glass windows, tomato plants hung heavy with fruit. Corn grew well in the neat, cultivated gardens. Hoeing weeds in that productive garden was a tall black man and his wife. Sitting in the garden, pulling up weeds by hand, was his crippled brother. A young girl was swinging on a tire that hung in a maple tree next to the house. She was singing an old familiar tune, "Jesus, remember me, when you come into your kingdom."

"Jayden! Isaiah!" Zach called out. "I'm so happy to see you're both alive!"

The tall black man stood up straight and looked over with a quizzical expression. Seeing the two men in white linen robes and dazzling gold belts, he and the rest of his family were instantly fearful. The little girl stopped her happy song and ran to her mother's side.

"Who are you?" Jayden said trembling. "Are you... angels?"

"Don't be afraid," Zach smiled. "I'm your old friend, Zach."

"*Zach Bryant?*" Jayden said, with utter disbelief.

Isaiah looked up with great interest.

"Yes, I am Zach Bryant."

"But you look so young; so much younger than me! And where did you get those clothes, man?"

"Why have you been gone so long?" Isaiah called out sorrowfully. "One day you're there and the next day your whole family just disappears!"

"Some from our church went missing too," Jayden stated with a frown. He cried out, "But why didn't God take us? We've always tried to live right. Why did He leave us here?"

Zach could read his friends' thoughts and understood their

343

deep pain and confusion. Through the spirit of God, he could also answer their questions.

"God called everyone that was responsible to Him, to judgement," Zach said gently. "Some of your church leaders and friends knew they weren't preaching the true Gospel message and failed to act on that knowledge. They were afraid of losing their job or their reputations. They didn't love truth, so they deceived themselves and others with lies.[288] Jesus told them to depart from him. He didn't know them. Regardless of the good works they had done, they weren't careful to follow his commands. [289] They never truly *knew* our Lord." [290]

"Then what about us?" Isaiah asked. "Why are we still here? We didn't get judged; we just got *left!*"

"In His mercy, God saw you have honest hearts," Zach smiled. "God has spared you and is giving you a second chance to believe His truth."

"So God gave *you* eternal life," Jayden pondered, looking at Zach curiously. "What about your brother? Why isn't Jake with you?"

Zach began with his story. He told them about being called away to the judgement seat. Sadly, he admitted that the angel had reproved him for not trying harder to share truth with his friends.

"I'm sorry, Jayden," he apologized earnestly. "I wish we had discussed our beliefs long before we did. The angel told me that if we had, you would have been receptive. I regret all the time I spent running away from God before I changed my life. If only those hours had been spent sharing God's offer of salvation..."

"We were just always too busy with other things," Jayden nodded in dismay. "I'm as much to blame as you." With a look of

---

[288] 2 Thessalonians 2:9-12; 1 Timothy 4:1-3; 2 Timothy 4:3-4
[289] John 15:1-14
[290] James 3:1; John 4:23-24; Matthew 7:21-23

concern, he probed, "But what about Jake? Why isn't Jake with you?"

Looking down sadly, Zach told them his brother's tragic story.

There were tears in Jayden's eyes. "That breaks my heart! I'm going to miss him, terribly!" he moaned. "I should have said more. I knew he was heading somewhere bad... I just thought he was stronger. I always thought he was stronger! "

For a while they stood quietly, as Jayden and Isaiah grieved their friend's loss.

Eventually, Jayden broke the silence, "You've been given life, Zach. You've seen our Lord. Tell us about him."

As Zach described his encounters with the Lord Jesus Christ, his friends were enthralled. "Jesus' righteous character and godly wisdom are beyond reproach," Zach told them. "This is a King who will rule the world with a perfect balance of justice and mercy. No one will sway his judgement with bribes or charm. [291] Never has the world seen such a King. Jesus is the perfect manifestation of God."

While Zach continued on to explain what it is like to be made immortal, to never feel pain, weariness or sorrow, [292] Jayden and Isaiah listened in amazement; they longed to have a part.

"And I've brought someone special with me," Zach told them, putting his hand on Jonathan's shoulder. "You see, Jesus Christ, the King who now sits on David's throne, has raised the dead. All the faithful you've read about in the Bible are now alive again and immortal like me. I've been getting to know many of them and I thought I'd introduce you to someone I know you admire." With a teasing smile, Zach asked, "Can you guess who I've brought with me?"

---

[291] Psalm 72
[292] Revelation 7:14-17; 21:4

"How many guesses do we get?" Jayden asked.

"Hey, this is like 'Twenty Questions'!" Isaiah laughed; his dark face lighting up eagerly. "Are you in the Old Testament?" he asked the stranger.

"I am," Jonathan smiled.

Isaiah guessed correctly after only three questions.

"You brought *Jonathan* to us?!" Jayden marvelled. "You remembered?"

Jayden and Isaiah were eager to talk.

"We read the book you gave us," Isaiah recalled, with a nod in Zach's direction. "We learned so much about your friend, here... Jonathan."

"What do you say for yourself?" Jayden asked Jonathan. "How did you stay unselfish? How did you not feel envy towards David?"

With their questions and promptings, Jonathan began telling his life story. Jayden's family listened, fixated, as Jonathan told of his deep feelings for his father. He described the difficult balance he tried to maintain between loyalty to his father the King, and his love for David his friend. [293] He told them of the hope he always held, that one day he and David would live as immortal saints in *God's* Kingdom.

"This vision of hope," Jonathan said, "allowed me to look beyond what was temporary. My father was all about power and keeping the royal lineage in our family. He failed to remember that it was God who had given him the kingdom in the first place. As for me, what I wanted most was the *future* Kingdom of God. And here I am. I'm now a part of the most glorious Kingdom ever!"

With a broad smile, Jonathan exclaimed. "God's kingdom is now here on the earth. The Lord Jesus Christ is going to usher in a time of peace and prosperity for all of mankind. God has given to

---

[293] 1 Samuel 20; 23:15-18

his Son, Jesus Christ, David's throne in Jerusalem, just as He promised so long ago.[294] If you submit to his rule and worship him, your land will be rebuilt and beautified again."

"Sounds amazing!" Jayden exclaimed. "Please, will you sit for a while and tell us more?"

Zach and Jonathan happily accepted the request.

Throwing down his hoe, Jayden came close to Isaiah so that his crippled brother could climb onto his back. His wife excused herself to bring a little refreshment. Everyone else gladly took seats in the homemade wooden chairs down by the water's edge.

There in the serene setting, with the lake lapping quietly against the shore, the whole family gathered around. Jayden's wife poured glasses of cool, creamy milk for everyone. Their daughter brought around a bowl of fresh strawberries. Everything tasted so good! Zach and Jonathan explained many things about the true Gospel message and the Kingdom Jesus was establishing on the earth. Since Jayden and Isaiah had read through all the books Zach had given them, the whole family was very receptive to the message.

"I always felt that God has been looking after us," Jayden told Zach, "even though I couldn't understand why He left us here. So many people died in the fires, the plagues, and the destruction, but Isaiah and I escaped every time. I always remember you saying there would be cleansing fires, but the planet would survive!" With a chuckle, he added, "And here we are!" Then he added sadly, "Melissa died, you know."

"Yes, I know," Zach said simply. "She had no desire for God in her heart. But God saw something good in you and Isaiah. He *has* watched over you like a Shepherd."

"My wheelchair didn't survive," Isaiah mumbled. "But

---

[294] 2 Samuel 7:8-16; Luke 1:30-33

Jayden has been lugging me about."

Moved with compassion, Zach longed to act. Healing power was there for him to use, but... the time wasn't right... not just yet.

"Are you willing to come with us and proclaim the good news that Jesus Christ is the King?" Zach asked.

Everyone in the family agreed.

Standing up and reaching out their hands, Zach and Jonathan took hold of the others. In an instant, they were all by the shores of Sherbrooke Lake, where many residents on the west side of Stirling had set up shelter.

"That was so fast!" Isaiah marvelled. "It would take us a whole day to walk here!"

"How did that happen?" Jayden asked. His wife and daughter seemed dazed.

"God's power is far beyond anything man has ever dreamt or imagined," Zach told them.

"Do you have power to get me a better wheelchair?" Isaiah begged wistfully.

Zach only smiled. He knew the full extent of God's power and was waiting for the right moment.

For the rest of that day they called out to the people around the lake, to come, bring their Bibles if they had them, and hear about Jesus Christ, the long awaited King of the world. When a crowd had assembled on the banks of the lake, Zach and Jonathan told everyone about the work that had been going on in the land of Israel.

The crowd was fairly attentive until a young man stood up and shouted, "It's the Antichrist who leads the work in Israel. Don't listen to these preachers or you will be deceived! For years our Pastor told us that Antichrist was coming and now he's here! Antichrist is this so-called 'king' in Jerusalem! Jesus Christ isn't here yet – don't listen to these men! Antichrist is doing exactly what our Pastor said he would do in Israel. We're almost to the end of the seven years of tribulation. The real Jesus will return from heaven *soon* to destroy this deceiver. These men are wolves in sheep's clothing!"

Others rallied around the young man.

"It's Antichrist who builds a temple for the Jews!"

"Antichrist will say he's the Messiah, but he's the devil in disguise! These men are wrong. They are liars!"

The crowd became confused and the commotion grew so loud that nothing could be heard above it. Zach and Jonathan stood patiently waiting for an opportunity to proclaim the truth.

It was Jayden who silenced the crowd and convinced the people to give the newcomers a chance to prove their claims from Scripture.

Zach showed them many passages as evidence that everything Jesus was doing in Jerusalem had been prophesied long before in the Bible. There were many questions. Some people didn't believe and some threatened to throw Zach and Jonathan out of town. Patiently, Zach and Jonathan encouraged the audience to examine the message carefully in their own Bibles.

In the midst of the crowd was a pretty, dark-haired young woman with two small babies in her arms. She was thin and constantly nursing one of her babies. The other baby looked very frail and lay listlessly in her arms. Zach could see that the infants were in great need. Every time Zach looked her way, the woman's eyes – her haunted eyes – were transfixed on him.

Why is she looking at me that way? Zach wondered. Yet, access to information about this woman was not forthcoming. Often, to wonder was to know – instantaneously. But not everything was readily accessed. There were still future mysteries that God hadn't yet revealed and perplexing problems that even the immortals had to puzzle through together, to resolve. *There must be a good reason God is keeping this hidden,* Zach thought. *I'll wait a little longer. Perhaps she will come to me after Isaiah is...*

"Show us proof!" an older man challenged. "If you really are *immortal* – if Jesus is the King of the world like you say, then give us some miracles! Show us what you can do."

Zach looked toward his lame friend, slumped on the ground beside his older brother. Both of them were looking at him expectantly. With a smile, Zach stepped forward. It was time for God's power to be revealed.

Isaiah's eyes opened wide as Zach drew near. A hush fell over the crowd and they stepped back to give him room.

"You see this young man here?" Zach called out, pointing to Isaiah. "I've known Isaiah since we were both children. I grew up in Stirling, Nova Scotia, just like many of you. Isaiah has a rare bone disease that left him crippled. All his life he's had to depend on others to help him get around. But I've never heard him complain. There were many times I realized my own poor attitude when I saw Isaiah's positive spirit."

No one said a word in reply.

"God can move mountains with a word," Zach told them. "He has power over the storms, the pestilence, and the sea. God has given His power to His Son – the Lord Jesus Christ, who rules in Jerusalem. Jesus has shared this power with those he raised from the dead. As it is written in Isaiah thirty-five, this is the glorious time when 'the eyes of the blind shall be opened, and the ears of the deaf shall be unstopped… the lame shall leap like a deer, and the tongue of the dumb sing.'"

Turning to his friend, Zach smiled warmly and held out his hand. Isaiah grasped it eagerly. The crowd waited in silent anticipation.

With a heart full of joy, Zach spoke to his friend, "In the Name of God and His Son – the Lord Jesus Christ – the new King of the world, I say to you, Isaiah, rise up and walk."[295]

The crowd pressed forward to see if anything would happen. Isaiah looked up in utter astonishment. His expression changed to awe as he felt his legs grow longer and become filled with strength. Ecstatic, Isaiah leaped up. He was amazed at how tall he'd become and the surge of energy he felt inside muscles that had been weak and useless all his life. Impulsively, he broke into a traditional African dance, with legs that supported him and responded to everything he wanted them to do. The crowd went wild with joy. Jayden and his wife hugged each other and wept tears of gratitude.

"God be praised!" Jayden sobbed, falling down on his knees. "Jesus is King! Jesus Christ is King! Let's worship him. He is the only King we want to serve!"

Isaiah raised his voice with a similar cheering cry. All the people echoed their praise to God. Even Zach and Jonathan joined in.

With a rapt smile, Zach looked up and prayed, *Heavenly Father, I thank you immensely for the privilege of healing my friend. Your mercy is great in sparing their lives through all the judgements that have been unleashed on this earth. May they learn and grow in their knowledge and love for You.*

"My child is blind," a mother called out anxiously. "Can you restore his sight?"

"And I'm dying of cancer," an old man said, coming forward, his face lined with desperation. A large tumour was visible on his neck. "It's been years since anyone of us has had access to hospital care. Can you heal us all?"

Suddenly, there was a rush of requests. Zach and Jonathan healed every one through the power of God. "Nothing is too hard

---

[295] Isaiah 35; Mark 16:17-18

for God," they said.[296]

As the excitement grew, Zach and Jonathan climbed onto a high section of concrete, so they wouldn't be mobbed by the crowd. Zach looked out over the ever-growing mass of people and smiled to see his friend Jayden embracing Isaiah. The brothers now stood shoulder to shoulder, eye to eye!

"I'm looking forward to bringing that family to visit Jerusalem," Jonathan said to Zach with a smile. "Mephibosheth will love to make their acquaintance!"

Zach agreed. "Isaiah and Mephibosheth are kindred spirits. And Jayden and Isaiah will be thrilled to see Jesus Christ and walk through the Promised Land. I know they will encourage everyone here to make the same journey."

Jonathan hushed the crowd and then he spoke. "People of Sherbrooke Lake, if you truly want to worship God in truth and serve His Son, our King, who sits on David's throne, then you must learn His ways. In this new order, Jesus will not tolerate everyone doing what is right in their own eyes. The Kingdom of God's Son will be one of righteousness and holiness. If you are willing, tomorrow Zach and I will tell you about the new King and the way that he wants us to live. In the morning we will have classes for whoever wants to attend. In the afternoon we will begin to clean up the rubble to beautify and restore function to your town.

Even with all the miracles the crowd had seen, there were still doubters in the midst. "How will you clean up the rubble?" one man retorted. "Have you seen the enormous chunks of concrete? Not even a thousand men could move one of them!"

Another fellow echoed the same sentiments. "We haven't used the bulldozers for years! Do you have any idea how much fuel they consume? Can you *make* fuel in some magical way?"

---

[296] Mark 10:27

"We do nothing by magic," Zach admonished the crowd. "What you've seen us do this day is by the power of God alone. But, why would we require fuel or bulldozers?" he smiled calmly. "Who can move mountains into the sea?"

Isaiah was smiling and nodding. "God can!" [297] he proclaimed loudly.

Amid laughing jeers from the mockers, clapping and shouts of support from the others, Jayden silenced the crowd. "Listen to me. We've all seen the power of God today, in ways that yesterday we would not have believed possible. My brother can walk! Sally's son can see! Malcolm has been cured of cancer. These men in white robes are not mortal men like us. These men have the power of God. If they believe they can help clean up our city – then let's have faith and lend them a hand!"

The crowd called out their approval. Isaiah was the loudest of all, leaping into the air. Zach was filled with joy. He knew that most of the people were sincere. Tomorrow they would begin to restore Stirling both spiritually and physically for the Lord. But for now, it was getting dark and the people needed to rest. He and Jonathan would spend the night conferring with the others in the delegation, to make plans for Stirling's recovery.

Zach looked over curiously in the direction of the girl with the troubled eyes. She still had not come to them, but he sensed that her faith was weak. It was easy to see that time was running out for her children. *Father, please allow me to help this woman,* Zach prayed.

The request was granted. Reading her mind, Zach understood that while the young woman had seen the miracles, she was still very confused about Antichrist. The strong words of warning she had heard that day from the young man who had shouted out to the crowd, terrified her. She didn't know who to

---

[297] Matthew 17:20

353

believe. She was alone, without a friend. When she glanced furtively again, in his direction, Zach smiled kindly.

As the people filed off to their makeshift shelters for the night, Zach walked over to the dark-haired girl. In her arms one baby cried unhappily while the other still slept, his limbs dangling weakly from his body. Trembling, as Zach approached, the woman held her children closer and looked down at the ground.

"What can I do for you and your children?" Zach asked in fluent Italian. With God's power, he could speak easily in any language. [298]

Hearing her native dialect was a great comfort to the young woman. "I fled Europe," she told him, very happy to communicate in her own language. "I've run out of money and I have no shelter, or food. My children are starving and I don't speak English very well. No one understands a word I say."

Suddenly, Zach knew exactly who the girl was, even though he had never met her. He reeled with the understanding. Pain was no longer a sensation he felt, but compassion overwhelmed him. This woman had been on a long, agonizing journey. She had travelled by ship to a foreign country, tormented by doubts, with faith as small as a mustard seed, hoping desperately that her husband – *her dead husband* – had spoken the truth.

"My little boy," she said, tears welling up in her dark brown eyes, "he just sleeps all the time. I know he must be hungry but he has no strength to nurse!"

Without a word, Zach reached for the baby boy. The woman gave him over willingly.

Touching the boy's head gently, Zach smoothed back his soft blond hair. The baby slowly opened his eyes. Zach looked down fondly. The little boy's mouth and nose were much like his

---

[298] 1 Corinthians 12:10

mother's, but the eyes – the hazel-brown eyes – were just like his dad's.

"Father, thank You for bringing these children to me," Zach prayed earnestly. "Thank You for Your great mercy and Your power to give and sustain life. Please, Father, I beg that You will heal them. May they both learn of You and Your ways, and live long upon this earth."

With Zach's loving touch, life flowed back into the small, limp body. As his mother watched in astonishment, the baby boy filled out and grew stronger. A ruddy pink glow enlivened his face. With a gurgling laugh he reached up with his tiny hand to touch Zach's chin.

"You healed my baby!" the woman sobbed happily. "Thank you! Thank you so much! You must have the power of God!"

"Yes, Ella," Zach said, looking at her kindly and steadily. "Little Jacob will be fine now. I'm so glad you named him after his father."

"You know... our names?" she questioned in surprise. The surprise gave way to courage. "May I... may I ask you a question?" she begged.

"Please do," Zach smiled.

"My husband," she began hesitantly, "he told me to come to this place. He wasn't... wasn't made immortal like you. He's not with us anymore. They... they killed him when he tried to escape."

"Yes, I know," Zach replied gently, looking back down at the happy child in his arms.

"Did you, by any chance," she continued anxiously in Italian, "did you know him?"

Zach smiled sadly, "Yes," he said, "I knew him well. I loved him dearly. Jake was *my brother – my twin.*"

Ella burst out crying, and in alarm, the baby girl she was

355

holding did the same.

"Don't worry," Zach assured her kindly. "You've come to the right place. You made a good choice, Ella, and God has guided you safely here."

Reaching out, Zach laid his hand upon the baby girl. Immediately, strength and vigour returned to her tiny, wasted body, as well. She smiled up at Zach. It was a smile that touched him deeply.

Holding the baby boy protectively, Zach saw Jayden and Isaiah talking eagerly to Jonathan about making the trip to Jerusalem. Turning back to Ella, Zach took her arm. "I'll personally make sure you're all cared for," he promised, leading her towards his friends. "I know just the family who will gladly take you in."

"Seek ye the LORD while he may be found, call ye upon him while he is near: Let the wicked forsake his way, and the unrighteous man his thoughts: and let him return unto the LORD, and he will have mercy upon him; and to our God, for he will abundantly pardon. For my thoughts are not your thoughts, neither are your ways my ways, saith the LORD. For as the heavens are higher than the earth, so are my ways higher than your ways, and my thoughts than your thoughts."

Isaiah 55:6-9

Acknowledgments

Eleven Weeks is the fourth and last in the *Anna Tikvah* series. Years ago I was asked by young teen – Ethan Anderson – to write another story involving the resurrection and reunion of all the characters in the series. I was hesitant to do this, knowing that such an End Times novel would necessitate a lot of speculation and a careful balancing of God's mercy and judgment. Inadequate as I am, I began to see the need for such a book. Although we are living in the Last Days – bombarded daily with 'signs' from God that His prophetic Word is being fulfilled – apathy, disillusionment and the enticing pull of the world are causing many to fall away. As a fellow, battle-weary soldier, this story is an attempt to encourage myself, my family, and all who believe Jesus will return, to persevere and overcome to the End.

I thank God for the experiences of life, health, and guidance from the Word. I am so thankful for many willing friends who shared their spiritual perspectives, gave crucial balance, and guided me to a better understanding of the English language. Thank you to my husband and children for the guy's perspective, basketball insights, and conversations which crystallized the conclusions of this book. Thanks to my mom, my in-laws, Colin Attridge, and Martin Webster for correcting an abundance of grammatical errors! A special thank you goes to my very dedicated sister-in-law, Greg and Miriam Pullman, Ruth Knowles, Geoff and Jenny Henstock, CSSS, and Michael Owen for balancing key issues. I love the cover – Jason Grant! Thanks so much!

Suggestions, advice and fine-tuning are most welcome and will be very important in any future revisions.

Email me: **annatikvah@yahoo.ca**

Order *Eleven Weeks* at **http://www.createspace.com/4771276**

Other books in the *Anna Tikvah* Series:

In Search of Life begins the series, when Verity Lovell meets Peter Bryant in high school. A strong friendship develops as they attend a Bible reading seminar and put their beliefs to the test with the Bible in hand. But will the answers they find, support them through tragic, heart-breaking pain?

Who Are You Looking For? delves into the life of Peter Bryant. After ten years overseas, Peter returns home, lacking faith and harbouring a deep grudge against God. When his mom hands him a popular Christian novel on "Antichrist" Peter is alarmed by the future scenarios portrayed by the authors. With the help of his good friend Thomas, Peter takes a second look at the evidence, and discovers 25 clues from the Bible which guide him toward a very different conclusion than the one his family has embraced. Tensions rise and family ties are strained, as Peter attempts to share his findings, deal with his pain, and open his heart to love and forgiveness once more.

These may be ordered at www.csss.org.au

An Invitation to Forever commences when Peter Bryant invites his family to attend his upcoming wedding. Sadly, his brother James is unwilling to be involved. A new housekeeper, a 'coincidental meeting', and twenty purple cards, gradually bring fresh perspectives and healing to broken relationships. Well-supported by Scripture, this unique novel follows the thread of the Gospel message from Genesis to Revelation. There's a royal wedding to which all have been invited...*it's an invitation to forever!*

Order at http://www.createspace.com/3961150

 **CBMA**
Christadelphian Bible Mission of the Americas

All proceeds from *Eleven Weeks* will be donated to CBMA. The Christadelphian Bible Mission of the Americas is organized for the purpose of fulfilling the charge of our Lord – Mark 16:15-16: *"Go into all the world and preach the gospel to every creature. He who believes and is baptized will be saved; but he who does not believe will be condemned."*

Their mission, God willing, is to preach the Truth of God's Word in the countries located in North America, Central America, South America and the Caribbean Islands; and to encourage and strengthen brethren and sisters in Christ with pastoral and welfare assistance.

www.cbma.net/

Printed in Great Britain
by Amazon.co.uk, Ltd.,
Marston Gate.